1

SISTER SABLE

THE MAD QUEEN

Book 1

BY T. MOUNTEBANK

Translated by Dökk Og Stormasamt Bókmenntir

English version edited by Chrissy Wolfe, EFC Services, LLC

~~~~~~

To contact the author please email mountebank@null.net

11:00 A.M.

General Berringer remembers the night he could have ended it. He remembers the way thunder shook the planks in the floor of his office and how wind had been passing shrill through a break in the lead panes of a window. He remembers his attention had been drawn away from his desk to the darkened night in anticipation of the next lightning strike.

The rain had not yet arrived, just the bluster and threats, and while the glass was still mirror sharp, he had studied himself, wondering how the troubles would define him. He would not have the wrinkles made from smiles his father had formed. He did not teach with laughter. He had been a colonel that night, as lean and muscled as he was now, but the difficulties had been with them for over a decade and his face had begun to show the strain.

He remembers he had been trying to imitate his father's amusement when the sky finally split. Lightning had jumped the clouds, and in that moment, all his concerns were obliterated with the sharp illumination of a figure crouched low and hiding in the palace gardens four floors below.

The Colonel had moved quickly to grab a rifle with night vision while killing the lights. Weapon strapped over his shoulder, he braced a hand against the frame of the window and quietly pulled it open. With the fluid ease of familiarity, he flipped the rifle to cradle in his arm, against his cheek, and then, eye to the sight, he searched for the prowler again in the green tinted night.

5

Years later, he could still not account for why he had remained silent, alerting no one when he found the person again by the wall, a solid silhouette against an eerie stone barrier. Instead, he watched the figure crouch once more and he waited until the sweeping survey of the eastern rooms brought their search to his window. He remembers the shock, a punch to his heart, as the distance closed and their eyes found him in the dark, looking straight through his scope to return his gaze.

He remembers the anxious pause that held them both motionless until the strange interloper stood, stretching out their arms and lifting their head to give definition to their shape. The mass of fabric caught in the storm, blowing wide, until he imagined he could hear the cloth snapping in the wind. The black robe and headdress revealed the night stalker to be a nun, but her strange actions were unknown to him; they defied the fearless, arrogant dignity of the Cloitare, so the Colonel could not bring himself to lower his gun.

Tense, perplexing moments passed before the storm sent another bolt of white light, and in that moment, the figure pulled back the headdress that had blown across her face. He remembers the dread of recognition. He feels again the mental slump. He can see as clearly as if she were before him now how she appeared bold with defiance before falling back into shadow.

The Bound Bride, he cursed the words. How she had come to be alone in the gardens, he could not imagine; her purpose for being there, he well understood. But he questioned the wisdom of allowing her to escape. She was barely fifteen. That very night she had shown them she had absolutely no experience of the world outside the convent, could not even use a phone that had been handed to her. He doubted she had the skills to find a meal, much less disappear. Here he had an opportunity, and uppermost in his mind was the excited idea: *One shot fired at an intruder and it will all be over tonight.* The King would be free, the obligation to the clergy dead. Yet still he held his hand and did not fire until finally she was forced to bring her face out of obscurity. She offered him an impatient expression, a fearless challenge, prompting him to either shoot or withdraw.

He remembers the night. He remembers he had not lowered his sights, but he had made a gesture, a barely perceptible nod, and then he had watched as she ran away.

Now, more than seven years later, she had been found, and the General regrets the night.

She was pushing into the distance, mind free of body, feeling the ether for anything wrong, for any ripple of peril or the warning that would send her into flight. All was as it had been for years, the greatest threat nearby, but still many hours and obstacles away. It was pushing itself into the distance, searching for her, but she was just out of reach.

She dropped back into the present, the *here and now* of the moment. The young man beside her rubbed his coat sleeve against the misted window of the train, looking not upon the fields being plowed under for winter, but beyond them to the old pine forest. He would make fast money clearing the trees for new fields.

She knew she made him nervous. She knew his boastings about being a crew leader were fabricated. She wanted to tell him he was too clean and new to carry the lie. She wanted to lift up her boot and show him the scuff marks, the mud, the stains, and the tar. The cuffs of her coat were darkened and thin. Her red hair, braided thin and piled on her head, was held with chipped enamel sticks. Her jeans were streaked at the thighs where she had wiped her hands, stained with oil and dirt. All this and she was considered well removed from the real grime of hard labor in these lands.

This, she wanted to say, *is how you should appear when you have been away from the motherland long enough to brag, but by then you won't care.*

For the moment though, he did care, and she made him nervous. He continued to run a whetstone over the sharpened edge of

8

a new hatchet while he told her about topping trees, and she gazed ahead at the man who feigned sleep, as though the train had rocked him into oblivion, but she knew he was hiding lest he be drawn into conversation. They were all about the same young age, but the fake dreamer was marked as a true Alenan by his uniform. Conscripted at eighteen, he had nearly served his four year obligation. In the seat beside him, he had put his bag and old army-issued rifle, ensuring at least one less passenger that might annoy him.

Two hours of travel and he thought it might have been preferable to be merely annoyed. He wished he had sat somewhere else. She made him nervous as well. It was in part her faraway stare, but worse was when she returned and her attention laid on him piercingly direct. Even with his eyes closed, he felt the difference. Her hard scrutiny was off him when he peeked to see her looking down the carriage aisle, pale eyes unfocused but searching, appearing slightly dazed, and then she was back.

Only he heard her swear. "Oh, hell no."

The years of separation were over in an instant. The distance between her and the threat that sought her disappeared when the third carriage snapped the rail and the fourth derailed then started to roll. The carriage behind drove into the wreckage. The force tipped the next three cars over and piled them together while momentum dragged another five off the tracks.

10:15 A.M.

He was always pushing into the distance, always waiting for the drop in concentration, the break in silence that revealed her. In the beginning, he had let her slip forward and bolt ahead. He had known from the start she would run away and he would let her because the act would define her. The rebellion was the very thing that would allow her to do what she must.

But then, in that first year, with her sagging into despair and he just behind, just out of sight, thinking he would end the drama within days, she flashed with insight she should not have remembered and was gone. He moved his mind through the distance but did not see her. He pushed himself further and further into the place she had been but found only lingering images and vibrations of thought. He did not fret at first; she would stumble and he would grab her. He would take possession of her with such strength she would be rooted to the spot, and then he would hold her until he arrived. But that was nearly seven years ago. And now from the silence, he heard sounds, such terrible sounds, and he was filled with dread.

10:20 A.M.

Major Dominic was accustomed to feeling unsettled. He had been charged with overseeing the travel needs of this group of Cloitare for nearly three years, the longest any of the King's men had held the position. And less than a year was the longest any of the men under him had managed to endure. There was no friendship, no camaraderie, and scant laughter to be forged on Mission Retrieve. Dominic found it a struggle to maintain the mental comfort he was not even aware he possessed before this assignment.

The Cloitare were oppressive enough in the stone halls of the palace, but here in this mobile unit without the massive double doors to retire behind, it felt as though they occupied every space. He felt constantly watched and exposed, as though they were in his head, judging his intellect. Everything, from a casual idea at dawn to his secret desires at night, embarrassed him for over a year. He'd become exhausted with the exertion of watching and guarding his thoughts, changing them, silencing them; but then, sometime in the second year, the exercise became routine, his mind was orderly and quiet, and the mission less exacting.

The Cloitare even seemed to view him with less disdain, though this didn't make them any more approachable. Of the six, there was only one Major Dominic could bear to speak with. He was the sole man among the clergy of women, and he was a giant, looking more like one of the dark foreign invaders from five centuries ago than anyone seen in Erria today. For so many reasons, Master Aidan was both the most and the least disturbing of the Cloitare. With barely

11

a glance, he could swap your pounding heart into your constricted throat, but he was so preoccupied with his own mind, he seldom acknowledged the existence of the soldiers, and to Dominic he simply gave orders of where to take them next.

The other five, maybe because they were all nuns, the Cloitare Stare was dramatically worse, especially the ones with light-colored eyes—it was all you saw. Their pupils just didn't seem to exist.

He'd been told they were always looking inward, barely breathing, with heart rates so slow they'd be cool to the touch, but who would dare confirm it? As it was, he could scarcely dash in and out of eye contact with them before those steady, direct, cold-as-hell expressions dropped his attention to his feet.

Presently, Dominic was well beyond unsettled. He did not want to be backing across the tarmac where they had most recently set up. He wanted to stand his ground and take an order, but something had changed. The Cloitare were out of their tents and descending on him with an intensity that terrified him. Staggering behind was Master Aidan, one hand to his head and bent at the waist like an aneurysm had just ripped apart his brain, demanding in staccato, "Pilots. Pilots. Medics. At once. Go," waving indiscriminately at both the helicopters and planes.

Dominic felt their singular attention like a threat. Something primal in his gut sent a siren to his head that told him to flee. It warned him he was prey. He retreated. One step back and then another, he was gaining speed to turn and run, but then, unexpectedly, he backed into a truck and came to a stop.

The Cloitare stopped when they had him within arm's reach and then parted to allow Aidan to continue his disjointed commands: "Pilots. Medics. Go."

But Dominic was not reacting. He could not look away, could not find his shoes, the ground, his radio, or divert his attention to any of the objects that let him avoid the Cloitare, that let him give orders and organize his men and mission; instead, he was round-eyed with fear, struck stupid, and near to gun-pulling hysterics by this unnatural attention locked solely on him.

Aidan was silenced. His face shed the image of pain. It became in a moment a placid refuge from where he said gently, "Dominic, look away." And when Dominic broke their gaze and rediscovered his shoes, Aidan continued, "Major, you are safe and in control. You will ready everyone. We are going north."

10:30 A.M.

At first, Aidan saw sparks. They appeared like a welding arc but longer and stronger. He did not have to push into the distance to find her; she had reached out to him in a moment of blind panic. He heard metal screaming against metal.

It was a sound that could not be mistaken with anything except disaster, and Aidan found her in the middle of it. Like he knew he would when given another chance, he grabbed hold of her, and then, held in one place, he went to her. He saw just seconds of it: the old pines out the window, the brown fields, the boy flying forward with a hatchet and dying. He felt the impact. The pain. The momentum that held her. The release and spin that dropped her back. And he was still with her when she was no longer aware.

Dominic had them in the air in less than ten minutes. The tents and supplies were left standing. The old forests were in the north, running the uppermost borders of Erentrude, Alena, and Sierra. They would fly toward the pines until they learned the location of the rail crash.

10:35 A.M.

Lieutenant Fallon wished he were in the cargo plane. The cargo plane was dark and smelled of grease, rubber, and electronics. It had a wall of ports and docks for all his electronics, and a desk designed to hold them in place. But more than anything else, it rarely carried the Cloitare who were staring a hole through his head.

Before the jet was even off the ground, he was thumbing in the search on his phone: train crash wreck. He set the results to show from the last half hour forward. With the jet angled steeply into the sky, he typed out the same search on a tablet and tucked it beside him, and then did the same on the laptop that was being pushed against his waist by the steep ascent. Under his right boot, he held down another tablet with northern maps already loaded.

Loud blips designed to be heard in the cargo plane sounded in succession from each device.

"OMG just in train wreck."

"FUCK TRAINS," and attached was a picture of a carriage strewn with overhead luggage.

"Dude like our train must have hit a cow."

"TRAAAIN CRAAASH!!!"

The laptop automatically replied to each post the same questions: *Where are you? What train? What's your location?*

"Was I just in a train crash?"

"Seriously hurt here." The picture showed bone piercing the flesh of a man's finger. "My train crashed into a field."

15

"Train wrecked. Going to find body pics."

Lieutenant Fallon forgot about the Cloitare. He was scrolling through the messages, hunting for the one among many that would give pertinent information.

The laptop bleeped out a returned message: *Who the fuck is this?*

And another answered: *dude we in a field.*

Then finally from WickedPie: *Eudokia. We need help.*

Fallon called out to Major Dominic, "Eudokia." He typed back: *Tell me from what city the train left and where it was going.*

WickedPie: *Left Eudokia for Balina.*

Fallon: *How long ago? Do you know your current location?*

WickedPie: *Two hours ago. Are you coming to help? Who are you?*

The lieutenant grabbed the tablet from under his foot and highlighted an area between Eudokia and Balina, then passed it to the waiting major. "There. For now, go there."

11 A.M.

Major Dominic was speaking directly with General Berringer, "We're eight hours from the location. I need clearance to enter Alena's airspace within three and then permission to land at Balina Airport or Eudokia Field. The cargo plane is following, but this time it's too slow to be of use, so we'll need vehicles on the ground when we arrive. We'll keep up with where they're taking survivors from here, but you're in a better position to get someone on the ground to find her."

"She was definitely on the train? Hurt? But alive?"

"Master Aidan says so."

"Ok, Major, we're on it." General Berringer felt Dominic's adrenaline fueled focus to capture and return the nun—it had been his task in Mission Retrieve for three years after all—but Berringer was in no rush to assist.

To the men in the communication center waiting to receive orders, Berringer held up his phone and said, "I'll keep the major on this line. I'm going to find Laudin to get clearance."

Berringer walked with speed and purpose out of the room, but once in the hall, he slowed to give himself time to think. The political secretary, Laudin, he could reach by phone, but the person he really needed to see was two floors below on the second level of the palace.

He shook his head and cursed himself. He had all but forgotten the girl. After a year, the constant fear she would be found had subsided, then the years seemed to prove she was really gone. He had relaxed. His King would not be forced to marry a nun. The obligation to the Cloitare would die and buried beside it would be the insane fabricated Revelations of the Prophets. He found himself remembering the night he could have ended it. He should have killed her. To have made certain, he should have killed her when he had the chance. He set his jaw forward. It was too late for should-haves; he needed to make certain she died now.

11:10 A.M.

The intelligence chief was signing papers. It was a monotonous job others disliked but Catherine Girard quite enjoyed as it allowed her to think. And wait. She was supposed to be having lunch with her deputy chief, but that was cancelled when the Guard Dog made contact from Alena. He was in the neighboring country trailing an Erentrude scientist that planned to pass off secret soil reports to his Alenan handler.

Catherine was not so much waiting to hear that the reports had been wiped from the scientist's portable drive and replaced with another version, as to read the Guard Dog's confirmation that the traitor would not be returning home to the motherland.

It was the sort of task the Guard Dog excelled at. He was her own special agent, one whose existence was known only to herself, the King, Berringer, and Laudin.

The soil report was done by the King of Erentrude's own Ministry of Science and showed that Alena's border contained several rare elements in rich deposits of monazite ore. Neither the King nor Laudin wanted the Alenans to know the extent of the metals. Alena was torn between those wanting to rejoin the mother country for its wealth and opportunities and those who would toil away their lives mired in all the misery poverty could serve merely to call themselves free. Girard hated them both. But, by the King's will, the breakaway nation would be reunited with its motherland, and that would be easier without the Alenans knowing the promise of wealth that lay in their boundaries.

19

The scientist was a defector from Erentrude's Ministry of Science, but far from an idealist, Catherine knew he was instead a disastrous combination of bored, disenchanted, and broke.

And the Guard Dog, she mused, was going to rip his throat out.

Catherine stopped signing papers and opened a document on the widescreen that dominated her desk. She shouldn't have kept the message, but she had, and she read it again: *One day, kitty, I am going to leave you on the floor calling my name. My real name.*

She had a whole folder of them. He was the secret she carried.

Opening another, she had just pulled the band from her blond hair to let it settle over her shoulders when her secretary's voice announced an unexpected visitor. "General Berringer is here. Shall I show him in?"

"Of course."

He had closed the door himself before Girard could exit the provocative folder.

"The Cloitare have found the Bound Bride. She's in a train wreck in Alena, someplace called Eudokia. I'm told she is presently alive but injured."

Girard took the news with the delighted half smile of a proper psychopath. "And I assume you have all your soldiers racing there with great haste?"

"I have a jet with eight soldiers and six Cloitare seeking clearance to enter Alena's airspace and land."

Girard was correct in guessing the General hoped she knew a way to have this request denied.

"Alena?" Catherine nodded. "So, essentially a gesture of courtesy. I assume you have already cleared this with their military and merely require Laudin to call for official handshakes?"

Berringer's focus left Catherine's blue eyes to stray across the carved desk, over the glass doors of the bookcase behind her, and then up to the gold molding near the decorative plastered ceiling. It was a hell of a lot different to his office. "I thought perhaps I would get your advice first."

The smile on Catherine's face widened.

Berringer pointed to the coffee service on the low table in the sitting space before Catherine's desk. "May I?"

Gesturing with an open hand, she exuded glee, "*Please*." The likes of Berringer did not come to Girard for advice—the King did, Laudin did, but staunch self-reliant generals did not. This unusual request had her keenly interested. Girard had so many questions, but to ask would imply direction, such as *Does the King know?* Catherine suspected he did not.

The General couldn't sit. Delicate cup in hand, he stood between the chairs. "This northern territory she's in is quite poor but being developed. It has a larger influx of people than work, which would leave most willing to do anything for money. A very threatening place it would be," Berringer declared.

Girard smiled and inclined her head with agreement.

"If everything goes smoothly, it will be at least eight hours before my team gets the Cloitare on the ground." Before drinking, he looked over the rim of the cup at the King's intelligence chief. "That's a lot of time for something to go wrong."

"Wrong?" Girard's amusement had settled across her face to a manageable level. "You are expecting trouble of some particular description?"

Berringer found no enjoyment in the exchange. His words were measured and careful. "It's a dangerous place. Some of the most unfortunate have been killed for less than food. I thought with your people, *as they are*," he could barely endure her people, "you might have someone on the ground that could find her. To ensure security, as it were."

Girard sat forward and ceased to smile, "Yes." Then pulling back, she was more circumspect, "Perhaps. I will see what precautions I can arrange before your soldiers arrive."

11:30 A.M.

Girard pulled her multi-SIM phone into her lap and looked for contact from the Guard Dog. He was silent. Their communication was secured by an encryption program they shared, but even so, Catherine felt at extreme risk. She paused with a sense of trepidation before typing: *Contact me immediately with news of your success. I need you at the train wreck in Eudokia. You will find an injured woman, her picture is attached. There has never been a greater threat. Do this and I promise you anything you can name. Even me, if you still desire.*

1 HOUR EARLIER

There were seven of them piled into the four-seat compartment. She had dropped with the liar and the conscript across the aisle when the carriage tipped to its side. Near the bottom, under baggage and debris, someone was wheezing, someone else was moaning. A broken arm kinked across her chest, and across her waist, the soldier was struggling back to consciousness.

She lay in the heap aware but not moving. She acknowledged the threat within her, *Master Aidan, deepest respects*, and then recognized the presence of the mothers with a mental bow.

As she had done nearly seven years before, she flashed brilliant obliterating silence, a silence of the mind designed to sever the ties that bind.

But one remained: Master Aidan.

In the silence that should have been void, she was held by one tether. Breath stilled, heart slowed, in the skip between beats, she flashed annihilating silence once again.

When she returned, he remained.

She snapped back to the *here and now* with anger, both annoyed to be impaired and vexed to be found, but more than ever, she was intent on remaining free. Above her, balancing his weight on the sides of two seats, the soldier met her eyes apologetically. She followed his attention to her hip and the skinning knife buried in the flesh and bone.

"Mine," he admitted.

The half curl of her lips spoke forgiveness for the unintended. "Take it," she said.

"Maybe ..."

"Take it," she said with flat force.

She had seen it repeatedly in the kinder more emotive people of the world, when forced to confront something awful, they would go to a place that was hard and remote, very near to the place that made them nervous of the Cloitare. The soldier was steadfast resolved when he yanked out the blade, but then he broke. His hands shook as he pulled off his shirt to press it to her hip.

To console him, she said, "It didn't hurt."

"You're in shock." Then from below, they heard another moan. "Hang on buddy," the soldier encouraged.

Thinking she looked frail and delicate, he gently pulled her small body up to the side of the seats, but beneath her heavy jacket, he felt dense muscles in his grip.

Slumping in a tilt that threatened to pitch her back into the pit, he stopped her fall and then laid her flat while she whispered, "I'll just take a moment here."

He reached into the hollow of the seats to haul the boy with the mortal hatchet wound off the pile, then tossing two duffel bags aside, he shifted the dead woman with the broken arm.

While he dug to the bottom, she took her phone from a pocket and sent a message to the name tagged Enzo: *I'm in the train wreck in*

Alena. Too hurt to help myself and I'm in serious trouble. About to lose my freedom. Please come rescue my ass.

Spinning weak from the effort, she scrolled through her contacts hoping someone else capable was near, but they were all farther than Enzo. She tried to concentrate on a plan of escape, but Master Aidan's steady presence unnerved her. He was calling to her, a soft thrum in her thoughts that held her attention, frustrating every attempt to think clear. She needed to lose him and then put vast space between her and Alena. She would go to Sierra, hide and recover with someone she trusted, but as she focused her mind to act, there was an unexpected mental embrace, an affectionate hug across the distance, and with it came the memory of Aidan's protection.

The years on her own no longer felt free but like one long exhausting trial that seemed too grueling to continue. Aidan was offering deep, placid comfort, showing her a place to sink with ease, to go under into warmth. She was fighting not to yield to it, wanting to collapse with gratitude and rest within the depths. His singular devotion pulled at her. She told herself, *Just for a moment. Just to remember what it was like to be held in safety.* Slipping into careless security, she exhaled, letting the breath tremble through her throat as an appreciative moan.

A firm hand squeezed her arm. "You with me?"

Shock and alarm brought her back. *Mad, stupid, ridiculous,* she rebuked herself. He was the Master of Travel and he was in her mind, influencing her will. She needed to burn him off, to pull up such energy it would explode like a star. She could see the action she

26

wanted to take. She believed she could do it. But her body was slowing. Her arm was tired, shaking to hold the phone; it had become incredibly heavy. She opened three new messages thinking the fates that had always protected her would offer some last reprieve, but there was nothing. Nothing she read gave her the slightest hope. All the while, Aidan was softly beckoning, whispering *Come*, gently tugging with the promise of dark, serene quiet, something close to sleep but deeper, someplace she remembered as home. She thought she would lay her mind softly on the edge near him, but only for a moment, not long at all, just near enough to borrow his strength while she considered what to do.

Enzo replied: *On my way. Are you Ok?*

But she did not answer.

11:30 A.M.

No one dared speak to him. He sat perfectly motionless, eyes closed as if in sleep, thin lines of time tracing out from the closed lids, age that had just begun to drag at his cheeks. The black robes of the order laid across his shoulders, his lap, his legs, completely still across his chest and abdomen, showing no sign that he lived. Master Aidan, Master and Mentor to the Bound Bride, Queen Mother, Mother of All, known only to the Cloitare as Mawan, Destroyer of Time.

He had once himself possessed a string of magnificent titles, but that was all long ago, and now he was merely master and mentor to something altogether more deviant, willful, and destructive than he intended.

He was forgotten but he was still the Creator, the Architect, the One. He would bring his life's work into line.

When she surfaced, he was there, the same unwavering authority she had once grabbed to keep from falling. He was the only Master of the Mind the Cloitare knew, her mentor, the guide she had trusted to save her when the darkness threatened to overwhelm, but she had been too long gone so that when he reached for her, she recoiled. He gently called her back, pulling her into an embrace like when she was a child. He felt her slacken and rest, then shock and mayhem, she fought to be released, but he hushed her still again, and then again and again.

And then he held her, remembering back to the second beginning.

28

He was the Master and Mentor, a specter who had materialized from the Revelations of the Prophets, elaborately decorated parchments that were revered but it seemed not strictly believed. Edited versions of the manuscript were common throughout the Errian continent, found in the homes of the faithful and zealously pressed on the skeptical. Few, if any, had not known to expect him.

His arrival had been promised for four centuries, exalted as the harbinger of providence, but standing in the palace outside the Cloitare's double doors, he found himself unwelcome by the nuns. They felt he was many centuries too early. They suspected he was a fraud. But he had known how to open the doors, and once admitted into the convent, he had proved himself with devastating effect. The Cloitare had fallen cowed—angry, resentful, and suspicious as well— but eventually subservient to the destiny they preached.

His recognition as the awaited Master and Mentor was an exciting and glorious thing for the young of the Cloitare, but he had upset the aspirations of the mothers. The most revered among them found themselves subordinate to the Mentor and Mawan. It rankled, until they saw the continent of Erria respond.

The Master and Mentor went before the people and told them what they wanted to hear. "My presence before you means the Mother of All is among you."

From the balcony of the Cloitare Basilica, he had addressed the plaza, "The time has come for the King of the Clementyne Dynasty to unite with the Cloitare and accept the Bound Bride as his queen."

29

It mattered not the least that the Cloitare doctrines forbid electricity; he was heard without assistance to the very corners of the square. "A new era begins when the Queen Mother gathers her children and unites her family, and you, her sons and daughters, are destined to be the most favored of all people."

"*Hear me.*" His voice demanded reverence and commanded with dread. It held the congregants transfixed. "Hear me and know what you hear is the truth. Whatever else may come to pass in the time which starts again now, one thing above all others will remain true: the Queen Mother will be the mother of heroes. The Mother of All will bring lasting peace."

Looking over the assembled faithful, he knew his final words would chill. "The Cloitare are from the people, and the future queen is a babe against the breast in your midst. I call upon the mothers to find her."

All over Erria, people were spontaneously hushed as mothers in black robes parted the crowds, gliding the sidewalks, their close scrutiny of infants creating fear among parents, their conversation with toddlers bringing people to tears. A great many children were stalked home and their families persuaded to give to the Cloitare and the future.

Through the heart of each city and into its slums, the nuns pursued the Mawan, the Destroyer, the Dark Mother of Time. She would be devouring and deadly in her solicitous protection, but the nuns held her secret. The Revelations of the Prophets as the world knew it did not mention her by name. To the public she was strictly the Bound Bride, Queen Mother, Mother of All.

18 YEARS EARLIER

The time to start again, to correct the excesses grown from the past, to raze the ground for the future had become obvious, but Master Aidan had set it himself and for little more reason than he found the present king suitable, the world abhorrent, and himself dangerously indifferent. He did not believe an infant was born that heralded his coming. He was seeking a vessel he could fill. He was the Creator, the first to be prophesied, he did not need a genuine destroyer: he would make one. The mothers need simply find him a suitable child.

Years passed.

King Remius left his teens and entered his early twenties. Nevertheless, every child brought before Aidan failed to stir within him the slightest interest. He was torn. He knew he would make the Mawan, but he also desired some engagement, some hint of significance to be in the child's eyes. He began to despair that disappointment would attend his every creation. It was unreasonable, yet he longed to be surprised.

Aidan sincerely did not believe it was possible, so he viewed the two quarrelling mothers with skepticism.

"She is near the old railroad houses," Mother Isabelle told him. "I am certain of it, but I cannot find her."

"Because there is nothing to find." Mother Vesna bit each patronizing word.

"Yes, exactly." Isabelle was curt, and then with respect to Aidan, "It is nothing that I find."

Vesna threw the first insult, "Your sight lacks the power to penetrate."

And Isabelle returned, "You are blinded by the dark."

Aidan impassively watched the pupils in each of the mother's eyes flare wide. If they had been a decade older than thirty, it might not have happened, but they still held the passion of youth. He expected a rush of blood to color their cheeks, but before their skin could warm, both regained control.

They were in the windowless rooms of the convent's ground floor where the oil lamps gave scant light, but even so, the mothers' eyes were constricted as if in full sun.

Isabelle turned solid orbs of blue on Aidan, saying, "I beg you to go and see for yourself," while Vesna spoke over her, insisting, "This is a matter for the mothers to resolve."

But Isabelle carried on, "The shade begins just beyond the downtown business district, near the boarded up ruins of the inner city. Look for the shadow that shifts like smoke. You will notice it has settled darkest among the rotting houses by the old rails."

"It is the cloud of anodyne, a concentration of addicts," Vesna informed them both.

"It is not the dreams of the somnolent," Isabelle stated. "It is a void, and within it is black silence."

The words shivered down Aidan's spine. It had been so very long since he had been moved, he did nothing to conceal the effect. Instead, he silently repeated Isabelle's words to feel the sensation again.

Vesna studied him for understanding, but she had not yet fully accepted his eyes would tell her nothing. His pupils constricted and dilated according to the light, and his breath changed when he willed it, and, unlike the mothers, the two functions were not dependent on the other. From his arrival, his expression barely rose above apathy. Even before the crowds of the Basilica, he seldom displayed more than cool tolerance, but now the muscles in his face tightened to show interest.

Isabelle stepped back from the unfamiliar smile.

But Vesna was more concerned to see his attention fade into the distance. Her deference was forced and her offer circumspect, "Lest the future Queen Mother's parentage be assumed, we cannot ask you to attend this matter. I will take it upon myself to look again into this darkness." And then when he remained silent, she added, "It is certainly the result of a new street drug."

Aidan's voice was low and remote, "It has been many years since I last walked in the night, and I prefer to walk alone."

~~~~~~~

In the places Aidan cast his mental sights, darkness receded. The shadows evident to the mothers were hidden to him, but Isabelle had also spoken of a void of black silence, and it was this he sought. He entered the slums after midnight, walking the buckled sidewalks before the rail houses, listening to the chaotic turmoil of untamed thoughts clamoring in the ether. It sounded much the same in the wealthiest districts, but the uncontrolled chattering of the repetitive mind was denser here and it stayed awake later.

In some locations it was more frantic, hurtling along under artificial speed, until the breeze brought to him the sweet chemical burn of narcotics, and then the pace slackened, becoming almost quiet, almost comfortable. He passed one dilapidated structure after another, searching for the promised void, undeceived by the sleepers and the dreamers, the stupefied and the stoned.

What he had come for was silence, and the stillness from one house pulled against the edges of the others. He found the neighbors taking shelter at the furthest sides of their homes, unaware of what caused their discomfort, except their walls were too near the place that felt haunted.

It did not lack for light though. Of all the houses on the street, this one was unnaturally bright. In every window, bare bulbs could be seen through the thin sheets used as curtains, but beneath the electric glow was a darkness he could not see within.

Aidan stood before the strip of lawn lost to the weeds and stared into the void with painful wonder. He was the Creator, the Architect, the One, and somehow he had been given a gift, something unexpected. More than anything, he wanted to test his mastery. He wanted to be taxed, to feel the stress of potential defeat, to be engaged and enthralled, to be challenged and matched, and ahead was a darkness his mind could not penetrate.

The emptiness pulled him forward until he was standing on the paint-peeled porch, filled with hope and expectation.

He wanted to draw the whole of the night into himself, to be aware of every detail. The moisture in the air, the smell of decayed wood, the faint scent of perfume, he needed to breathe in everything while taking in the surrounding sounds. He heard dogs barking and a chain link fence rattle as someone bolted over it, and then farther away came to him the steady beat of bass from a parked car.

He gazed over the ruined neighborhood without judgment. It was what it was, and for the moment, it was marvelous.

Turning back to the house, he found the door closed, the lock weak in rotten wood. He listened to music from inside and broke through the resistance when it was at its loudest.

From the open door, he saw the child sleeping on the couch, undisturbed by the blaring symphony, the glare of three electric bulbs, and the noise he had made. He stood attentive at the threshold, smelling the heavy use of someone smoking speed, and then, from an adjoining room, he heard the synthesized beat of techno trance being turned low while someone listened for another disturbance.

Mind free of body, he pushed through the house and found only the girl and her mother.

With the flick of a lighter, he heard the pull of air sucked through a pipe and then the volume was returned to deafening.

The mother did not hear him walking down the short hall or moving through her bedroom door. Her head was bent over the dresser, crushing an anodyne tablet into dust, when Aidan dropped one hand over her head forcing it into her chest and wrapped the other around both her arms to swing her away from the mirror. With the perfect pitch of influence, he commanded her *"Down,"* and she slumped to the floor. Then he rumbled, *"Sleep,"* and released her.

Rolling her onto her back, he examined her.

Just a teenager but with deep gaunt cheeks and red swollen eyes. Her frame was small and delicate, appearing frail from years of use. Her hair was a dull black over anemic skin. Aidan cast his eyes over the room. Stockings, garters, and bras were kicked across the floor. Long links of packaged condoms hung over the bedside drawers. She was likely a prostitute, the child's father irrelevant if even known. It didn't matter; he had seen worse.

Back in the living room, he sat on the edge of the coffee table and studied the child. She was barely five years if not malnourished. Her mother's black hair shone in loose curls against pale skin. Her head rested lightly on the arm of the couch making her image soft with the same innocence seen in all sleeping children. Aidan leaned closer as though something might reveal itself, but there was nothing about the child's appearance that suggested she was responsible for the darkness.

He touched her lightly on the foot so that her eyes opened and she sat upright to meet his gaze.

And there was the blackness. He stared at the blue eyes lost to pupils far too large for the bare bulbs above, feeling a powerful force rip at the edges of his mind, tearing apart the light that defined him.

Marveling at the sensation, he stared full into the destruction and silently recited, *From the Void the Creator is made and to the Void will he return.*

37

The merest hint of a smile pulled her lips upward, an expression that made her seem warmly familiar. With an unhurried curiosity, she examined him. She explored his face, lingering on the scar that split his dark brow in two, and squinted to find the nearly invisible line that once marred his broad cheek bone. Reaching for his hand, she ran her fingers under the heavy sleeves of his robe to trace the hidden scars on his wrists, and with the same certainty, she sat forward to pull the collar from his neck and expose the mark the rope had left there as well. She winced with pain and anger.

Taking his hand again, she flipped it from the light color of his palm to the darker skin on the back, neither as light as an Errian nor as dark as the foreigners who had swept fast and fleeting across the continent five centuries before. Tall, broad, and strong, he was foreign, but his features were sharply defined like a native. She took in the whole of him and then returned her focus to his eyes. She was trying to read something there, or tell him something, or—Aidan felt her push—connect.

If he opened to her, she would stumble headlong and panic. He left her searching.

With great sadness, she said, "It begins."

And after a time, he replied, "So it does."

~~~~~~

"My mother?"

"Sleeping."

She studied him with doubt before exhaling a warning that he would be sorry if she found the facts different. She pushed off the couch and disappeared into her mother's room. He heard the girl pulling pillows and a blanket off the bed to arrange her mother's comfort.

When she came back to the couch, her appearance was somber.

Aidan held her attention firm and said, "I will never lie to you."

"You mean you will never lie to me if I am who you think I am."

"I will only ever say what I mean."

"I have not agreed to be the person you seek."

"You believe yourself to have a choice?"

"That is the one question that troubles me more than any."

"If you are not who I have come to find, then who are you?"

"*There* is the problem," she admitted. Crawling back onto the couch, she held her hand up for him to wait. She was thinking how to tell him. What to tell him.

He watched as she repeatedly formulated then refused explanations. She would draw in a breath, meet his eyes, then frown, shake her head, hold her hand up for more time and start again. Finally, irritated with herself, she blurted out, "I remember. I remember *everything*."

Her whole demeanor sagged as though the confession had been too much.

Intent on hearing the truth, he spoke with his true voice, the voice of influence, the voice of the Architect. He asked, "Do you know who I am?"

She gawked at him in open shock and then laughed. Rocking forward, eyes open wide, she held herself and laughed in hysterics. It bordered on derisive.

Aidan was fascinated. He let the fury of her outburst peak and then settle. As quickly as she entered the mania, she emerged gravely ominous to answer, "You are everything. You are my maker and my undoing. You are my savior and my death. You are the one that has been with me since the beginning and you will be with me ever after. You are the only one that can save me and you are the one who is going to make me forget. More than know you, I *remember* you."

A chill rose on his neck and shivered down his spine, making his muscles tremble to release the effect. He'd been moved. He'd been asleep for longer than he knew, but now he was fully in possession of his consciousness. She did not balk when he brought it to bear on her either.

"What do you remember?"

40

"Everything."

Again he felt the chill. Mind free of body, he moved through the distance looking for her. Going back, into the past, he searched for her memory. He found scraps like dreams of a forming mind, but little to explain the foreboding in her words. She held his gaze unafraid. He pushed deeper.

Back, back through the confusion, through the mind that tried to grab hold of memories that laid disjointed and grotesque over the present: the child that struck out with the practiced blade of repetition, the toddler that fell to her knees but remembered a kick that broke bone, the infant that screamed for retribution.

The mind was in warfare, railing against past grievances too old for the body to conceive.

Aidan pushed through the distress, further into the past, into the black until thunder rent the darkness and then he was himself. Order over chaos. He was himself but undeceived, bitter, wishing he had done different. At the end of his life, he—the Creator, the Architect, the One—had sat down to make one last perfect thing for himself. He had gone into the black to forge, giving everything to be free of himself. In his death, she was made.

He groaned at the monstrosity of his deed. She would remember everything from the first moment he became aware.

She said, "You must make me forget."

It had taken years, but she had forgotten. He had held her in the present, whispering *here and now*, until she lost her way to the past. Now he held her in the distance, remembering her as a child, holding her safe for the long hours it would take to reach her.

He had asked her that night so long ago, "What is your name?"

And she had replied, "What would you like?"

He had known from the beginning what he would rename her.

12:30 P.M.

Sable needed to die. The opportunity to free the kingdom, without obvious culpability, from the obligation that had threatened it for generations was plunging fast into history. Girard's Guard Dog was silent. She did not control him, and it was too frequent he reminded her of this detail in their arrangement. He would neither meet her nor reveal himself. He would no longer work any job he considered too trivial for his skills. He would accept, decline, or change her instructions at will. He could not be shadowed, filmed, or photographed, and he would not tolerate fallback agents ready to step in should he fail.

Early into their unconventional relationship, she had tried to trap him with the offer of an unattainable mission. She pulled it off the top of her head, a wish, if one could be granted, for the impossible.

She wanted access to the internal communications of Alena's Intelligence Department. It would mean getting into the cellar of the Helena headquarters and direct wiring a relay box. It was absurdly farcical.

He had written back: *You doubt my skills, kitty? I will bring you cream.*

If he was sincerely foolish enough to try, she would take him down before he was captured by the Alenans. Commencing at the sewers and closing on the roof, she had agents in the area armed with the full gambit. From bullets to tranquilizers, thermal cameras to biometric readers, there would not be a creature of any significance that would enter the Alenan Intelligence Department without being marked. Her agents would either capture or kill him. After two years of ambiguity, she was past caring which.

She would harass him with single demands, "Update?" or "Well?", but he remained silent for weeks. She wondered whether he would vanish entirely. Then, in the sixth week, she received the message on her phone: *Open the attachment and install the program.*

The folder was named Bitten, and once started, it began blasting documents across her screen.

He wrote: *Now, because I can't trust you, I take it away.*

And he had. The connection to the source was lost.

Then: *Do not bother to ask for it again.*

Months of curt denials later, he resumed communication: *You may come to me with legitimate threats that affect the King. You may not test our agreement again, or I will kill you for the impertinence.*

One of the agreements was not to organize replacement agents to fulfill his accepted contracts. Girard had never been so agitated. She could not waste more than an hour waiting for him to signal his assent. She watched the minutes vanish.

She typed to the team already in route: *Go.*

As yet, the runaway bride had not even been located.

12:30 P.M.

King Remius Clement had taken the news without remark. He stood in the salt flats where the General found him, his attention fixed to the tablet in his hand, scanning the lithium report with the same serious face he presented to almost every occasion.

Berringer suspected, but he could never be sure with the man, that Remy was not actually reading. He believed Remy was instead searching for an appropriate reaction. Berringer understood those responses were limited. He knew Remy to have essentially two: seriously angry and benevolently serious, at all other times he was simply serious. His attempts to be jocular were so disastrous only Berringer could genuinely laugh, and then Remy would smile at the failure, but such occasions were rare.

The two had been friends since they were sixteen, when Remy was a prince and they had served together in the King's Army. Even then he had held himself in reserve, too dignified to run for cover—at least that was the young soldier's assessment at the time—so that Berringer felt forced to tackle him into a trench. Just slightly smaller than Berringer, and without the same training, Remy had gone down easily and rolled over blinking dirt out of his eyes. With a mouth set firm in sharp features, he looked ready to be severe but was surprisingly indulgent, saying only, "Never cared much for long dialogue either."

As the young Remy seemed determined to treat artillery in a casual manner, and every other soldier was too apprehensive to throw the future king in the mud, Berringer had been tasked with keeping him alive. Over the years, the scale of things had become significantly larger, but he'd essentially been doing much the same job ever since.

No one knew the King better, but Berringer could not guess what Remy was thinking. He waved away the approaching workers and stood silently waiting for a reply.

And Remy stared at the lithium report, struggling not to allow a particular emotion to gain enough strength to surface. It had been twenty-two years since the appearance of the Master and Mentor, and Remy had spent most of them learning what it was to truly hate another. In the first year of Aidan's arrival, the Cloitare had forced his father to abdicate, driving his family out of the capital and into the country. Not yet satisfied showing their dominance over the Clementyne Dynasty, the clergy had then scattered his father's advisors into retirement abroad.

He had been twenty when he was crowned King of Erentrude. In his first years, he saw nearly every government on the world's third largest continent, the emerging warring Erria, ripped apart as the fervent rioted against the skeptics, the atheists, and the heretics. To keep his head, he had been forced to his knees in the Cloitare Basilica and made to accept the title of the Chosen King, agreeing to pay the dynasty's debt to the nuns.

The first years had been the worst. He remembers holding a blade to his own throat, taking himself hostage, to prevent the Cloitare from forcing on him their Ministry of Clergy and the laws they had written to be sanctioned in his name. At the time, virtually unknown to the people and untried with the military, his life was the only thing of value he had to bargain with.

He had made his own small council, each of them known to him from when he'd served in his father's army. All of them faithless. The Ministry of Clergy had refused at first to recognize them. In retrospect, Remy was certain it was their blind, youthful optimism and ignorance of the impossible task before them that swayed public, diplomatic, and military opinion. And of course money. The last century of Clements had a tenacious hold on property and industry, particularly the refinement of lithium to store the world's power. He and his three advisors had agreed to gamble large and play with the highest stakes to gain enough influence to rule without constant Cloitare interference. They had been reckless with the newly minted coin, but a simple observation made by Berringer had set their path. When first they gathered, the future general had said, "We will win nothing if we allow ourselves to be led about by the enemy."

And by a tight leash, the nuns had yanked him around those first years. When the Cloitare presented the newly discovered Queen Mother, his Bound Bride, to the masses that filled the capital, he had no choice but to go down on his knees before them too while his advisors looked on in unified rage, not yet strong enough in their positions to defy the Cloitare. In the eighteen years since, they had all become masters of their designated crafts, but Remy had also witnessed the clergy twist the people into an aggressive fanaticism, praying for his marriage to a girl he suspected, against the emphatic opposition of his advisors, was not in collusion with the nuns.

~~~~~~~

Remy had summoned the memory constantly in the months after he learned of her disappearance. It had happened during the weekly meal Sable shared with him and his table. When the mother that accompanied Sable had her attention drawn away, Sable had tapped his foot with hers and then given him such a look of desperate warning, he had continued to stare at her openly even after the mother had spotted the insurrection.

He had held her back after the meal, had demanded the mother leave, threatening with escalating anger until he had frightened the mother and everyone else from the room.

Once alone, Sable must have thought he could not hold the mother off for long because she asked quickly and directly, "How was your grandfather killed?"

It was so quintessentially Cloitare, so utterly without tact, Remy should not have been surprised, yet he was. Dispelling the fury required to force the mother to depart, his answer was blunt, "He was slain by his confidant and guard."

"Why?"

"The man obviously went mad."

Sable considered it. Without guile or judgment, she asked, "Do you believe this?"

The infamous act had happened when his father was thirteen. Callias Clement's master strategist, guard, and dearest friend had cut him down in his private rooms. The reason was never clear. Two Cloitare mothers and a sister had watched it happen, but such was the speed and skill of Orson Feridon, they could do nothing to prevent it. Alerted by the hysterical screaming of the sister, the guards had charged the room. Still clasping the knife used to kill the king, the guards found Feridon heaving sick on the floor and two mothers shielding the eyes of the terrified sister, whispering words to settle her distress. None of this could be disputed.

Feridon had not fought apprehension, but because of his mastery in combat, he was taken into custody with an electronic compliance shackle on his wrist. If he fought, the guards could drop him to the floor in writhing agony, rendering him harmless.

Feridon had been taken to the city prison while word of the king's death spread rapidly around the capital. Then, when the mob descended to tear the traitor apart, he escaped.

Orson Feridon had never been caught. His motive remained unknown. But the prison surveillance video of his frenzied self-mutilation to free himself of the shackle went some ways to verifying his madness.

The mothers swore he had turned without warning, and such was the violence of the attack, the witnessing sister had gone out of her head. Remy did not doubt that either. He had seen footage of the nun wailing loud and inconsolable before the King's Council. She was never able to answer a single question, possibly never understood anything that was asked, and then weeks later, she too was dead. The Cloitare said it was grief.

Erria was rife with conspiracy theories when the Ministry of Clergy stepped in as the Council of Regents, functioning as the governing body until his father reached an acceptable age to take power. Remy never thought his father had completely thrown off their influence. There was a subdued, compliant manner about his father toward the Cloitare that Remy despised and had sworn never to emulate.

At question was whether Remy believed the story of the master strategist's sudden madness. Ultimately, Remy was undecided. He had never been given a credible reason not to believe. And while Berringer voiced nonspecific suspicions about the role of the clergy in Callias's death, Remy accepted very little without evidence.

How, Remy always asked his master strategist to imagine, *could three nuns kill him with Berringer in the room?* The question would make Remy smile and his friend dismiss the idea. Now, Sister Sable, dressed in the Cloitare robes, was questioning him in much the same way.

He said to her, "I will accept what the facts offer." And then questioned, "Why are you asking?"

"I ask because the facts are ..."

He could not imagine why she paused. Her eyes were pale orbs of cold blue, showing neither emotion nor motive nor pupils. The Cloitare Stare was unsettling enough on its own, but the topic made her positively morbid. He expected the long pause to lead to a

50

revelation, but instead, she simply confirmed, "... the facts are Feridon killed him. But why?"

Remy stopped himself from saying the word that came to mind and stared at her with controlled impatience.

"You were going to answer madness again. Do you know the cause of it?"

Sable waited for an answer until Remy warned, "I will not be baited. Continue."

"Was he always mad? I've read he was a respected military strategist. I've also read he was loved by the army. And I've heard soldiers don't love mad generals."

Remy realized this was the most he had ever heard her say, and it was thoroughly patronizing.

She looked to the floor. "I do not mean to be condescending. There are satisfactory answers to all questions, but to find these, I need help."

He had a dozen questions, but first, "Why are you looking?"

She met his gaze to tell him, "I believe the order means you harm."

Blessed hell. Such extreme words, yet the cold Stare of the Cloitare denied any concern. Remy could not conceal his dismay.

Misinterpreting, she responded, "I have no proof to offer. The mothers have become distrustful and prevent me from learning."

He did nothing to mask his growing confusion. "What are you trying to learn?"

"It is important that I know what the prophets first called me. The realm should hold its own handwritten copy of the revelations. I must ask you to find for me the dates each of my titles appeared in writing and tell me what was written."

Taking her by the arm, he tried to bring the conversation under control by guiding her into a chair. "Tell me what has happened."

But she stiffened against the intended direction. "It has become obvious to me the Cloitare are evil. By extension, their designs are evil."

The declaration from the face of someone so young made her appear harsh, and had he believed in anything preternatural, he would think her colorless eyes demonic. He studied her, searching for any signs of empathy or emotion.

Possibly realizing the image she presented, she drew in a breath and softened her features. Raising her heart rate to expand her pupils, her face flushed warm. As if none of this had been presented to him before, she moderated her voice to explain, "They thirst for this union with such desperation neither you nor I are relevant. They have their own unknown objective in sight and their ambition does not include you. It scarcely has room for me." The impenetrable facade practiced by the Cloitare was gone, replaced with fear. "Can you refuse to wed me?"

He had not meant to laugh, but he *had* meant his reply to sound light. "I could, if you'd like the walls painted in my blood."

She had not considered it before, but she saw it plainly and was horrified.

52

Regretting the attempt at levity, he tried to mitigate his words. He took her hand, surprised by how cold it was, but patted it regardless. "This has all been expected. You have nothing to worry about."

Stepping away from him, she shook her head in unhappy frustration. In an instant, her pupils constricted and she disappeared behind the order's blank face. Before leaving, she made the demand, "Have for me the titles."

But the following week when she next joined them, she was numb and senseless with fatigue. When he spoke to her, she mumbled incomprehensible answers to the family pin in his jacket, as though the red-jeweled eyes of the bull could understand.

After the meal, he tried to hold her back again. He started to shout away the mother, but then Sable's face filled with such distress, he feared for what might happen behind the double doors and stopped.

The next meal was the same.

Then, at the third meal, still dazed, she tapped him on the foot and nodded. He held her back with all the drama and more that accompanied the first night. The attending mother was joined by three more that had been waiting in the corridor. It had taken him, punctuated by the sharp orders of Berringer, many minutes to force them out. Girard had pulled the girl to the far end of the room, promising her, "It's a small confrontation. Do not be concerned, there is nothing to fear."

When Remy turned, Sable was warning the spy chief, "For all that is about to befall me for this treachery, let it not be for such lies."

The implication of abuse made them all solemn. Girard and Berringer turned to the King to start.

"Sit," he told them. "We will not be rushed."

~~~~~~

It was gratifying to hear doubts harassed her relentlessly. Her thoughts were exact and unforgiving of sentiment. She questioned the veracity of free will, divinity, and destiny. She could not make the three fit cohesively and the mothers would not answer her questions with the candid realism she required.

"But you are a theist?" Catherine pressed.

"There exists a god, if god is the name you wish to give it, but it is ignorant," she told them. "As real as light, it is energy, but not intelligent. It can be manipulated, but it cannot be reasoned with."

"So the prayers people offer?" Catherine had hoped to hear her say prayers were useless.

But Sable's blank face creased with confusion. Catherine could read her lips as she sounded out the puzzle, turning it for clarity, "Prayers people offer. *Offer*." Her eyes tightened on the word. "Offer. Offered prayers. Offering prayers." The word ceased to have meaning. She asked aloud, "What do they offer?"

And when Catherine looked stumped to know, Sable answered, "I am unfamiliar with this practice."

Catherine leaned in on the girl. "But you do pray?"

"I have." It did not sound common.

"To God?"

"Obviously not. I have explained it as ignorant."

"Then to whom do you pray?"

"To the One."

The three glanced at each other. "The One is God, is it not?"

"The One embodies god."

Catherine sat back. Religious ambiguity annoyed her unlike anything else, and she could not discern in the pale singular shade of Sable's eyes if it were deliberate. She shifted away from the abstract, asking, "The Revelations of the Prophets, what did you want to know?"

"I want to know the titles as the prophets predicted on the day it was written."

"Why though?"

Whatever invention Sable was creating in the silence, Catherine was eager to judge the nun's ability to deceive.

Sable said, "Perhaps a title has been misrepresented. Perhaps the prophets never wrote of a Cloitare bride."

"It matters very little whether we could prove that at this point." Catherine shut it down to see where Sable would go next.

"Such a disclosure, or one like it, could stop the union of clergy and realm."

Girard did not expect to laugh.

And Berringer could not prevent his disbelief from sounding harsh. "Do you have any idea of what is happening in the world?"

With the relentless gaze of the Cloitare, Sable studied him for understanding. When he looked away, she said, "I have never been in the world."

"Have you never connected to the network?" The Cloitare shunned any technology invented after its inception, but still it seemed unreal that a teenager would have absolutely no exposure. Catherine knew at the private girl's school she attended all manner of banned material found its way into the dorms. Pulling out her phone, Catherine lit up the screen and handed it to Sable.

Sable took the phone and, with her full attention focused on it, waited for it to do something. When the screen darkened again, she handed it back, saying, "I am unfamiliar with it."

Berringer threw himself back in amazement.

Girard laughed again, saying, "It is terribly overrated. You're not missing a thing."

Sable's posture stiffened with caution. "We agreed to speak the truth."

The spymaster acted with charming guilt. "So we did. You are missing a great deal. It boggles the mind, really." She turned to the King. "If you'll permit, I will answer her question."

"Explain to her what she wants to know."

Girard exhaled and tried to hold Sable's eyes steady. "Succinctly, the clergy secured a very bloody throne for the Clementyne Dynasty four centuries ago with the understanding a future king would wed a nun. So, as to your concern that a Cloitare bride was not foreseen, allow me to dispel that notion. The title of the Bound Bride was likely conceived the day the Clementyne Dynasty went to the clergy for help, or near enough to it. Not to offend, but what was portrayed as divine revelations had already been agreed as business behind closed doors, written with all the pomposity and flourish the public knows today."

Sable quietly considered it before asking, "By what names am I known? Tell them to me as they were written on that day."

Knowing the titles were the issue that troubled the nun, Girard began to answer slowly, giving first, "The Bound Bride," and after a long pause, "Queen Mother," and as though she could hardly remember, "Mother of All," waiting to gauge Sable's reaction.

"Nothing else?"

It was not what Girard had expected, but it was telling. She would get the final title from the girl, but before Catherine could answer, Berringer shut the door with, "Should there be?"

Sable ignored the question to ask the Colonel another. "When did the Master and Mentor appear in writing?"

"Same time."

"What else can you tell me?"

57

Berringer regretted getting involved. He looked to Catherine for help, and Girard turned away, smirking at the absurdity of it before she could think to answer. Pressing in on the girl incredulously, Catherine stressed, "With over three hundred million adherents, the Cloitare are the predominant religion in Erria, and after six centuries of growth, they are vying to be the third largest religion in the world. The Cloitare have two *walking, talking* god-like prophets alive at the moment, making the Revelations of the Prophets one of the most searched titles in the world. You are, I assure you, more than I can explain in one night."

Berringer did not intend to mock. "You've just been living at home with mom and god, haven't you?"

"Enough," Remy censured them both. To Sable he asked, "What were you expecting?"

"Something different." But when the three looked expectant to hear what it was, she so substantially shifted the subject, it remained lost. "Kings can be killed. Orson Feridon is proof that no one can ultimately be trusted." She shook her head and held up her hand for patience. This was not the way she wanted this to go. She started again. "The convent here in the palace has a vast library recording everything from the beginning of the order. As the—" she stopped short before offering, "the Bound Bride," but it was obviously distasteful, "I should have full access to the collection. There is a vault which is meant to be locked." The unaffected mask of the Cloitare was showing anger while she searched for how to proceed.

Catherine suggested, "You read something you shouldn't?"

"Yes," that was it exactly. Then she leveled them with, "They know the location of Feridon." The reactions around her were pronounced: every back straightened with a sudden intake of breath. Sable corrected, "Well, they did know, perhaps they still do, but I doubt I will ever get the chance to return to the vault. My trespass has made the mothers distrustful."

"Where was he?" Girard asked. Remy leaned forward in expectation while the Colonel held his breath.

Sable's demeanor no longer resembled a nun's, and the traitor's whereabouts were not what concerned her. She dismissed it as inconsequential, saying instead, "Perhaps because they were ruling as a regent council, the mothers did not share this information with anyone outside the highest clergy. It does beg the question why. Why would they protect him in such a way?" Sable laid all her attention on Remy. "It is written they sent two mothers to his location and it is written that he killed them. Yet still they kept their silence." Sable expression was severe. "Do you begin to comprehend what I say?"

Remy was deep in angry thought that this could be true. "It raises a number of serious questions."

"There is only one answer of importance." Sable waited until his focus was solely on her. "The Cloitare are evil."

Remy would not defend the order, but he wanted to know, "What makes you think so?"

She parted her lips and nearly told him before a terrible memory escaped her mouth as a strangled denial. All at once human, she dropped her head. "Please forgive me. My loyalty is not so much divided as dividing. This is every bit a betrayal I am committing, but I have been told repeatedly I must protect you. Yet I would ask you to tell me, any of you, what is more dangerous than the Cloitare? What could the King possibly need protection from if not the order? You see where I lead?" She addressed Berringer, "If he does not marry me, there is nothing to protect him from."

Girard questioned what she heard. "This protection of the King is not part of the revelation preached to the public."

"No?" This visibly troubled her.

"What exactly was said? Who told you to protect the King?"

Sable looked away.

Girard sighed. A practiced interrogator, she empathized, "Dividing loyalties, it's a hard business. Imagine what form the threat will take. What are you defending against?"

Sable's eyes went further away. "You are not going to understand this, there is so much you cannot understand, but there is something out there." They could not have guessed she was looking at it. "It is so great I cannot predict the distance, but I see it. It is …" she tried to find the words to describe it and startled them with, "it is all blood and guts and Cloitare. It would rip through here and obliterate everything if it were not being held in place by my resolve." She came back to the company in the room, her expression once again inscrutable Cloitare. "My resolve is not to marry the King." She stood to leave, telling Remy, "It is the only way I know to protect you."

He had not tried to make her stay. Regret gnawed at him when she failed to show for dinner the next week. The Cloitare sent

60

apologies, explaining Sister Sable was ill. The next week more apologies, Sable had been sent to another convent for meditations. That night, Berringer was ordered to seal off the Cloitare's western wing, to surround the windowless ground floor and guard against communication through the stone lattice vents of the upper levels. He was to block passage through the double doors, refusing all clergy entrance or exit until the Bound Bride was produced. The King would hear absolutely no council on the wisdom of his order.

Berringer was still a colonel at the time, and it was only their friendship that excused his omission. "Remy," he bowed with deep regret, "my King, forgive me, I watched the Bride run away."

~~~~~~

The King of Erentrude stood in the salt flats where Berringer had found him, his head bent to the lithium report in his hand, bracing himself for the return of the Cloitare's attention. While the public believed the Bound Bride was away in meditation, the years had been calm, as near to normal as anything he knew. On occasion, violent expectations had set the streets ablaze when any one of the conspiracies that thrived in the imagination of the faithful took special root, but then Master Aidan would emerge and call for peace. The Master and Mentor alone, he would remind them with his voice full of terrible authority, had been appointed by divinity to pick the timing of the union between the King and Queen Mother.

Remy would mourn the tranquility. He gazed over the blinding white lithium field with desire. It ran wide and flat until it abutted the barely visible mountains that encircled it. He knew every facet of it, had spent years on it, breathing its scent deep into his lungs, savoring it, listening to the low whirl of pumps that sucked the brine from just below the surface, filtering it, refining it, and sending it out to power the world. It calmed him and he would miss it.

The King turned to the General and signaled they were leaving.

1:30 P.M.

The King's intelligence chief had already begun to work furiously against his general. The General's jet would be directed to the smaller airport. There would be livestock—god knows how she would arrange it—but there would be animals on the runway forcing them to circle. The vehicles Berringer arranged to meet the Cloitare would not arrive, and mechanics were already preparing the substitute transport to break down. When they found another way to travel, she would have them directed to the wrong hospital, even if she had to build one from smoke.

Girard did not have time now to talk to the King, but she had been summoned.

~~~~~~

They assembled as they often did in the King's private sitting room.

"What do we know?"

Berringer had been in sporadic contact with Major Dominic on the return ride to the palace with the King and had passed along information as it came. The military jet with the Cloitare had entered Alena's airspace two hours previous, and they were three hours from landing at Eudokia Field.

The political secretary, Laudin, could contribute little to the search for the nun. "The Alenan government has given me assurances they are at our service in the search for your young cousin, Francis, who was believed to be traveling disguised on the train."

The King frowned at Girard with familiar disbelief.

She opened her hands in appeasement. "It was the best explanation for our involvement I could imagine with no time to conceive it."

Remy waved it away. "What else are you doing?" He knew of all the people gathered, she would make herself the busiest.

"The station chief in Alena has sent people to the wreck to locate and confirm it is her. I don't want the Cloitare slipping us a new bride under the bright lights of this sideshow. The Prime Minister's doctor is one of mine. He's traveling to the hospital in Eudokia to represent the government. He's ready to step in and do whatever is required when she's found."

Remy sliced his hand through the air and cut her off angrily. "All that will be required of him is to keep her alive. Do you understand?"

"Of course," she deferred. "The place is remote. Utterly inconsequential. My people will only be arriving now." She glanced at the door.

He would not be hurried. "Catherine, I will be very clear: No one is to hurt her."

Again Girard bowed her head and appeared to agree.

"When you have time, I want to hear all the scenarios we are facing. What to expect if she's dead, if she's alive, crippled, returned tomorrow, next year. I want you back here as soon as you feel comfortable leaving your people running their operations alone."

2 P.M.

"What in fuck's name is she doing out here?" Nika wanted to know.

Enzo checked his messages again. Still nothing. "It's not like she's going to tell us when we get there."

The small plane had left Erentrude's border hours ago. It had flown outside Alena's capital city, Helena, following at times the train tracks to Balina and then out again toward Eudokia. It floated near silent over perfect, square fields with the battery at a quarter charge. Enzo had thrown in half a dozen more in case the situation saw them fleeing across the border into Sierra. And because it was Marlow that had asked for help, he threw in pepper spray, gas masks, rubber bullets, hollow points, armor piercing, and if he'd had grenades, he'd have taken those too. "Hell only knows what she's done."

"It's Radimir." Nika hated the weapons dealer with every black-dyed hair on her otherwise blond head. "I told her not to fuck with him. He's got a sick fetish." The plane's throttle could not be pushed any farther, so Nika kept her heavy boots on the pedals, adjusting to use the tailwind for speed. Hours before, she'd explained it to Enzo, "Marlow was on her way to meet him yesterday when she got a text and dropped everything to deal with it. She said Radimir could wait. And you know he can't. She said she'd persuade him to forgive her later. Fuck knows how that was supposed to happen."

Now Enzo reread Marlow's message while Nika laid the blame on him. "I don't know how you thought introducing the two of them wasn't going to end in anything except bullets and mayhem."

66

"It's not Radimir." Enzo closed the phone. "She was worried about losing her freedom, not her life." He looked out the window at endless farms. Born in Erentrude's capital, the scene could not be more unfamiliar, the grueling work completely incomprehensible to him. Why they didn't all flee over the border to the motherland left him confounded. He could not imagine life without delivered food, and he laughed to picture any of them over a stove. The place they lived didn't even have a kitchen. But beneath them, he was certain those people cooked, eating things they had dug from the soil. The image of someone taking a shovel to the dirt to make a meal made him uncomfortable. It was all too far removed from what he understood to feel secure. "I don't get what she's doing on a train anyway. I gave her new batteries two days ago. Why didn't she fly? What in terrifying hell is out here?"

Nika shared the stress. Marlow didn't ask for help; Marlow gave help. Marlow asked for information. She asked for all your contacts and your cousin's contacts too. She asked for drugs and she asked for weapons and she was not above stealing your tech, but she had never asked for help.

3 P.M.

Aidan held her in his mind. He held her asleep and he searched the distance. It was in the distance he saw the three men. He would not get to her before they did. He held her and he waited.

4 P.M.

The airport's manager had been called by the sheriff and asked to attend the airfield as a very important jet was coming in. The manager said, "Well, it better be a damn small jet, we're only five hundred meters long."

The three men Aidan found in the distance would have landed at Eudokia Field twenty minutes before Major Dominic's pilots, but there was livestock everywhere. Hands shielding their eyes to the sun, they just made out cattle and geese dotting from one end of the tarmac to the other.

As the three passed over the airstrip, they saw a man flapping his arms at the animals, herding them back toward an overturned trailer that had crashed through the fence.

They climbed back into the sky and returned to the fields and the road on the outside of town. Their plane was light enough to carry only a single battery and a spare, allowing them to set down nearly anywhere straight and flat.

Aidan was with them, a silent presence that bothered their thoughts.

The pilot, normally so sure of himself, could not pick a place to land. He worried the fields were too wet, that the weight of the passengers would dig the wheels into the mud and flip the plane. "I need to find a stretch of straight highway," he said.

The two men with him kept insisting it was below them. "There, for god's sake, what is wrong with that?"

"It's not long enough."

"Fuck's sake, Carl, it runs from here to your mother's cunt. Put this bitch down."

"Seriously, dude, just turn around and land on that stretch behind us."

"The wind is wrong," Carl explained.

"Fucking wind, is it? The only wind is coming out of your mouth. Turn the fuck around and land."

"Dude. Seriously. Turn around and land."

"There. I'll set us down there."

"And what? We fucking walk to town? Do you see a car out here? We gonna putter this bitch into town for all to see? Like a fucking parade? Is that it?"

"Seriously, you've got to turn around and land us back there."

Without further warning, the passenger slugged the pilot in the arm. "Turn the fuck around." And then, to ensure compliance, he twisted Carl's ear.

"Alright, alright." Flinching away from the aggression, the pilot began the turn. "Have it your way. If we die, you can blame yourself." He couldn't place it, but he had a feeling something was terribly wrong. He checked and doubled checked the ailerons, the rudder, the stabilizer. Anxiety welled in his chest, quickening his breath. It was the landing gear, but no, the wheels came down and locked. Squinting into the sun to see the road, altitude dropping, the pilot set the flaps to full to give them lift.

Aidan was there, waiting for his moment.

With the asphalt rising fast beneath them, Carl began to pull back on the yoke.

The Master and Mentor dropped his hold on Sable and punched hard into the pilot.

Carl knew flaming pain from the sun as his pupils dilated wide and the road undulated, flashing back ripples of light. His terror was heard by the passengers as a horrific realization, "It's a river."

Panicking without thought, he gave full throttle and pulled sharply up, lifting the nose over the sun and into the cloudless sky. Seized with an absolute conviction he was about to drown, the pilot pulled further back on the yoke. Arms locked with adrenaline wanting to surface from the depths of limitless water, he tilted the plane near vertical until they felt the first sickening pull back to ground as the plane stalled. Carl mistook it for sinking and would not release the yoke. He was still pulling up when wind caught in the flaps and flipped the single-battery plane end over front, collapsing it on its back on the asphalt. Then it was quiet.

Carl's eyes adjusted. Beside him one man rolled to his knees, but behind him, the other had a plastic rod running through his chest. The unfortunate passenger was shaking his head at the pilot in disgust. "Seriously, dude, you suck."

Now they were two.

4:10 P.M.

Sable opened her eyes to rows of old fluorescent fittings hardwired to homemade mercury bulbs. She followed the crude design down the long hall. She lay on the floor in a row of bodies, some curled in pain, others still. The arm of her coat had been purposefully cut to expose the vein from which a needle was taped. Bags of saline and blood had been clothes-lined down the hall on rope.

She had enough time to take it in before Aidan was back, pulling her under. She rolled to push herself up but gasped as the flesh split at her hip. In the shock, Aidan brought her back to the floor, but she was struggling against it, mumbling curses that brought an old man with a nurse's top to her side.

"Baby girl, ain't no need for pain, not when I got the anodyne."

It raced up the vein, searing like fire at her throat and then rushed into her brain, knocking her firmly down and making her swear, "*Motherfucker*."

"Now, I'm going to forgive you for calling me that," he chided. "I ain't never thought of my mother that way. Those doctors will get to you soon. You be a good girl and I'll keep you in anodyne's sunny shine for hours."

4:15 P.M.

The two left the plane on the road and stole the first car that was forced to stop.

"Fucking fresh shit this is."

The pilot sat in the passenger seat feeling angst wrap tight around his heart. Palms wet with sweat, he wanted to rock himself like a mental patient but didn't dare. "I told you we couldn't land with that wind."

"Wind again? You gonna stick with that wind bullshit?" The driver kept one eye on the road, one hand on the wheel, and flipped through pages on his phone. "They're taking everyone to the hospital. Place is called Hospital. Fucking Alenans."

4:20 P.M.

Major Dominic was telling Berringer, "There are no vehicles here."

The General spoke on two lines, "The sheriff says his men are sitting at the airport but don't see you."

"No, sir. There are no vehicles here. Eudokia Field?"

Berringer asked the sheriff, "Eudokia Field?" and then answered Dominic, "Sheriff says they are at Eudokia Field."

Major Dominic signaled his men to circle the airfield on foot again.

"Got a lot of cows here," one told Dominic, "but there are no running vehicles. The manager can't even get his started."

Dominic told Berringer, "They are not here."

Berringer now knew beyond doubt he was fighting Girard. She had not backed down at the King's command.

The sheriff came on smooth, "Well, General, you're just going to hang me, but those boys aren't at Eudokia Field after all. They drove all the way out to Balina. Don't you worry though, I got all the boys' wives coming out there to get you now."

Berringer was of two minds: one was loyal to Remy, one to the King. He paced three quick steps one way and two back. "Dominic, the sheriff is sending the deputies' wives with transport. You do *not* get in those cars with those women. Under no circumstances or misconceptions do you allow anyone in those cars. Have you got traffic on the road in front of you?"

74

"Yes, sir."

"Jack them."

4:30 P.M.

There was no hospital. The driver circled the grocery store the map indicated as Hospital.

"Fucking hell." He glared at the pilot. "Where is the fucking hospital?"

Carl rose above his distress to remember he'd been told where to go. "I was supposed to be driving."

The driver rolled his tongue across his teeth and leaned his head sideways to the idiot at his side. "Did we forget something?"

"West, go west."

4:40 P.M.

It appeared like a wedding reception. Huge white tents with bunting sewn into the hems were spread across the lawn of the hospital. On the tips of the support poles, flags had been permanently attached which waved merrily in the breeze. "Wind," the pilot pointed out.

Through clinched teeth, the driver chewed the warning, "One more fucking word about wind …"

Old gas generators chugged in the parking lot with lines snaking off into the building and tents. The improvised shelters glowed radiant with light, casting dark images of the grim activity within.

The hospital's two ambulances rested with the doors open and victims on the stretchers. Most of the survivors had been loaded into cars that had been traveling on the highway. Occupants of the passing vehicles had crawled through the wreckage, pulling out the living, packing them into transport in the order they appeared. The largest among them had turned their cars over to strangers while they grappled with twisted metal. "Drive, just drive," they'd been told.

The anarchic conveyance of the wounded complete, the parking lot laid full, but still.

"Everyone that's coming to this party is here," the driver said.

"No, not quite." They both knew they had to move fast, to finish it before someone else arrived, but they didn't know who.

The driver flexed back his shoulders to shake off the ghost that had climbed his spine. "If you think you can do your fucking job, search the tents. I'll be in the building."

Aidan released her.

~~~~~~

Those crazy mad ceiling lights appeared and made her smile. She felt warm, too warm for a jacket. She nuzzled into the fleece collar and decided she could not be bothered with removing it. She knew this feeling, this sultry weight that embraced and assured everything was good, so very fine, *no worries in this sunshine*. She wondered just briefly whose place had these ridiculous bulbs. This was not the ceiling of anyone she had ever gotten this ludicrously whacked with. She looked lazily to the side.

Curled in a tight ball, a woman hugged her knees.

Sable rose up to take in the full length of the hall. Looking over the succession of bodies, she noted the presence of family members kneeling among the injured, reassuring with words and touch they were not alone. She watched as a gurney was wheeled out of sight and heard the hall groan in commiseration at the sound of a bone saw.

Putting her back to the wall for support, she was searching her pockets when the old nurse told her, "They took all them weapons off you."

"My phone," she said.

"Don't know if you came in here with a phone, but you and half these other lunatics came in strapped up like you was conscripts from the war a hundred years ago. Don't know what you need all those guns and knives for." He had come to kneel beside her. "Who you need me to call?"

Through the hazy pleasure, Sable reached into the distance. Mind free of body, she followed the connection, a well-traveled path to Enzo.

The nurse tried to catch her eyes. "You zone out, baby girl. Ain't feeling no pain, not you."

Enzo, filled with agitation, was near, but he was lost.

She had to place Aidan. She needed to know which way to run. When she looked, he was there. He drew her near but would not reveal himself; instead, he showed her the man coming down the hall.

Instantly, Sable dropped her head into her hands and cried.

"Now don't you go to crying, or you'll make this old man cry too." As he spoke, Sable wrapped her arm around the nurse and buried her face in his neck.

~~~~~~

The man walking the corridor was just another tired laborer searching for a loved one caught in the disaster. It was likely a sister or girlfriend, as he only paused before young women, lingering once on the bruised and swollen face of a blonde with bleached hair.

It would be easier if the girl still had black hair and pale skin, but he was hunting for the eyes that stared from the picture like dead pools. He saw crying against an old man a redhead with a worker's tan and long thin braids adorned with beads, piled in loops on her head and held with black sticks. The stretch of injured spanned before him leading him away.

~~~~~~

Sable began to whisper. The old nurse could feel her breath hot against his neck, his jaw, his ear. Her voice vibrated in his muscles and across the bones of his face. It was like she was insisting on getting under his skin to possess his frame, but rather than feel alarm, he felt quite suddenly like he had dipped into the narcotics.

"The sunshine is good, isn't it?" she asked.

"*Mmm*, sure is."

"You did this to me." The playful accusation made him laugh. She held the nurse in her anodyne-addled influence to ask, "Did helicopters come in?"

"There was a few."

"Are they still out there?"

"Never heard them leave."

"On the roof?"

80

He laughed again, "Baby child, look around. We don't have no working elevator. They land in the field out back."

Sable's jeans had been cut at the waist to place a compression pack over the wound at her hip. She told the nurse, "I need your belt." She wound it through the loops, assuring him, "I am fine. You are fine. Everything is fine. It's a little trick of sunshine, yes? Good, now help me to my feet."

She clung upright to the nurse and laughed as well, though not from delight, but at how outrageous was the pain, how absurd to think she could walk on this bouncy floor with these rubber legs. It would pass. It would settle. The anodyne would mask the stab in her ribs and, as she brought her weight down on her leg, maybe even her hip. She leaned against the nurse thinking that with just a little time, she might even convince herself she had not been thrown at great speed into the side of a train.

She rested her head on the nurse's chest and whispered, "Hold me," and went again into the distance.

Aidan was everywhere. She saw through him like water that flowed over stones, rippling around objects, tugging at the resistance, but clear. She was searching for the man who blended so perfectly, but Aidan guided her to another. Together the men held a single purpose, a violent image of her and of death. She pursued the first down the hall, but Aidan warned of danger, turned the current, and pulled her back toward the other, toward the tents and the crowd and the street.

The nurse felt her emerge. Slinging braids out of her face like they were wet, she pointed her attention toward the helicopters she'd been told were outside.

4:50 P.M.

He was coming out of the cafeteria where the families had gathered when he saw the redhead sliding down the hall, one shoulder against the wall, her right leg bloody from the hip. She had that great mop of braids shoved on top of her head, but the hair sticks didn't hold it all, probably hadn't held it even before the wreck. She was all fucked up, but she was fucked up sexy.

This is no time to be banging crazy, he told himself as they passed.

From his earpiece, he heard the pilot, "She is not out here."

He said into his phone, "Well, she's not in here either."

Behind him he heard crazy rattling the push bar to the back exit.

He corrected himself, "Maybe she is."

He told her, "There are bolts. Let me get them for you."

She turned, eyes all crinkled in a smile. "God, thank you." Stepping back, she gave him access to the door. "They won't let a girl smoke."

No, he thought, *that's not her*. He turned his back on her to flip down the top bolt and then, as he was kneeling, she ran her hand across his shoulder and cupped the side of his neck. She was whispering some mad shit. *Aw hell, going to get a little crazy*. He reached down to the bottom bolt and those enamel sticks plunged into his temple and were so fast gone, he felt them puncture his jugular before he fell.

83

Enzo's phone rang. He didn't know the caller and wouldn't have answered it but there was Marlow to consider. "Yeah?"

"Where are you?" He heard the clang of metal doors opening.

"Eudokia, trying to find the hospital. The map's all wrong. You're out of breath. Are you Ok? Where are you?"

"Hospital. But I am *fucked up*. Lovely nurse has me rolling in anodyne like sunshine."

"Not all bad then."

"I'm heading for the helicopters. Nika always said I couldn't fly one to save my life." She was dryly amused. "I hope to prove her wrong, but I suspect I am about to make a spectacle of myself."

Then Enzo heard her breath shudder. He heard the hopeless growl of denial, "Oh, no, no," fear as he had never heard her utter. He heard her foot slide on the pavement as she turned to run and the phone clatter across the surface.

~~~~~~

She had not been the subject of their scrutiny in years, now three of them in their forbidding black robes with their cold, relentless stares focused on her. She had come down the back steps and could see the dark outline of two helicopters beyond the pavement in the grass. She had smiled at her fortune. Then the nuns rounded the corner of the hospital. *The Cloitare*. Her heart slammed blood through her veins. She did not know it could beat so fast; the sensation was foreign and overwhelming. In all the years she was gone, she had never been this close to them, and now, muddled on drugs, bent with injuries, she reeled to think she would have to fight them.

The anodyne could not convince her everything was fine. Panic carried her above the narcotic. "Oh, no, no," she refused to believe she was about to be caught. She spun to avoid the group, but the landscape tipped with trauma and sedatives, and her body resolved to thwart the reckless action. She fell, hands to the ground, disoriented but recovering, ready to flee when she felt him. *Aidan*.

Suppressing a scream into a strangled cry, she closed her eyes and knew with a sense of crashing finality it was over. Everything in her sunk: all emotion, all fear, all hope. It was the state of the condemned. She became perfectly still and heard his soft approach over the gravel-strewn pavement. She knew precisely where he stopped. Already down, she folded further.

Head bent in respect, she addressed him, "Master," and then, "Mentor."

Aidan took in the sight of her: the dyed hair, the braids, the jeans, the dirty boots, and the blood. None of it mattered. Before him was his life's work. He said, "I find your honor lacking."

She bowed deeper.

Two more nuns had followed, and now all five came to encircle the two. Picking up the phone, Mother Vesna gently closed it before throwing it into the grass. Sable heard the approach of men too loud to be of the Cloitare. She recognized the metallic clink in their uniforms of gear and guns shifting against the other. Standing at the perimeter to shield the order from scrutiny, they were an issue but not a threat—nothing they carried would be used against her. Sable considered her condition, the space between her and the helicopters, the drugs and the number of nuns. It could all possibly be overcome, but then there was Aidan. That she might be captured was always a possibility. She had been told what to do. She had agreed to do it. Braced for the hardest part, she smothered her pride and made herself humble.

"Much time has passed."

"It has," she agreed.

"I have missed you, anawa."

The affectionate term for a favorite disciple made Sable sink lower. Her voice shook with the truth, "I, as well, have missed you."

"And now, anawa, what will you do now?"

Sitting back on her feet, she lifted her face to him. It had been so many years for her—most of her teens and now into her twenties— she was not the same, but he was, still disconcertingly perfect despite the scars, faultless in form and expression, the face the Cloitare tried to imitate but had turned callously inanimate.

There had been a plan and she had agreed to do it, but the hurt and guilt as she prepared to betray was intense. She did not think she could go through with it, not until she thought of the future, and then she discovered her integrity could still sink lower. "Forgive me,

86

Master Aidan." She dropped her eyes. "I did not know how to end it. I have longed to return."

He was silent.

And she was the wide-open water, void of thought and intention for him to inspect.

He said at last, "I have never lied to you, anawa."

A stone of shame rippled the surface. She stilled it.

He asked, "You would return with me of your own will?"

She met his eyes with flawless conviction. "It is my greatest desire to redeem myself."

Subtle shifts in the black fabric surrounding them showed the nuns relaxing, but then, from over her shoulder, a compliance shackle was being pushed on Aidan by Mother Vesna. In an instant, she was outraged and alarmed. "Those are illegal," growled from her throat an unexpected rebuff.

"Of your will you would come with me. This should make no difference."

"It is electronic. It violates Cloitare doctrine."

"For you, they make an exception. For you, they always make exceptions."

"It is not necessary," she insisted.

"I have never lied to you, anawa. I see plainly you intend to submit to me while you are weak and defy me when you heal."

The wall of mothers stiffened.

Aidan accepted the bracelet from Vesna.

She pleaded for sense, "You can drop me at will. You don't need it."

"The mothers insist." He reached for her hand.

The years had seen her give respect to another master of a different art. Sable grabbed Aidan's hand and started to twist his wrist. With her feet tucked under, she already suffered the greatest disadvantage, but her rise to stop him was met with the strength of the mothers pushing her down. She rolled with the force of their direction, down and over, accepting the pain it brought, flipping to come up on her feet with Aidan at her back. Still low in a crouch, she started the spin around Aidan's leg that would leave them behind, but she was pulled up by his hand on her neck, his voice in her ear, commanding, "*Quiet*."

The sound of appeasement choked in her throat. Her body fell slack into delirium as the mind gave into the voice that controlled, the anodyne, and the warmth. A plea for mercy was about to drop from her mouth, but instead, the sound of surrender brought her back to the moment. She knocked aside her compliance to recover. Grabbing his arm, she threw herself forward, curling to the side, trying to come around and hook her leg around his to knock him down, but habit picked the wrong leg, the wrong move, and then it was too late to correct it.

He followed her momentum in the circle, dropping his arms to trap her hands, circling her leg with his, stretching the cut at her hip but not intending to make her scream.

Balanced on one foot, she tried to shift him, but he remained motionless. She wrestled her hands for freedom, but her wrists were tiny in his grasp. Desperate now, she dropped the whole of her weight, hoping to pull him forward so she could flip in his hold, but her weight was nothing compared to his size and he remained unmoved. She knew panic and horror, started thrashing to gain any measure of freedom that would let her slip through his grasp. Then wailing denial that this was happening, she rattled the nerves of the soldiers.

Finally, she knew she was defeated and he felt her settle then yield. She begged just once, "Please," but he rolled his voice, commanding with persuasion, "*Be still.*"

There was a last sob of fight before he felt the shake of exhaustion tremble across her body. He coaxed again, "*Still,*" his voice slowing, dragging out the order to a rumbling murmur, "*Quiet like the night.*"

She wanted to resist but the direction was compelling.

Sinking already, he pulled her under with the demand, "*Return to the dark.*"

He supported her body while Vesna took the bracelet from the ground and clasped it around her wrist.

Mind held passive, Sable felt the cuff whir to life, heat, then expand pliable to tighten flush against the skin. She had given respect to another master, his hand crippled from the wrist, the bones crushed to the thumb with an improvised club. It had been a less painful

89

option than staying in the shackle, he had said, a frenzied assault on his self for freedom he could not regret.

AFTER

Enzo and Nika returned to the airplane hangar that was home in disbelief. Searching for an explanation as to what had happened, they made Max break into the carrier plane Marlow called the Pigeon. It was a tech freak's fantasy chamber. When Enzo had first met Marlow, she had just come from some technophobic religious boarding school and could barely operate a phone. He had struggled not to throttle her. But eager for knowledge, she had pulled from him everything he knew before eating up Nika and then finally devouring Max. Only Max understood what all laid in the hold.

"She learned well from the master," he acknowledged, "but she can't beat a master." He pulled the memory drive from her onboard computer and prepared to break the security.

His workspace was filled with new equipment, hundreds of memristor cores stacked and connected, all dedicated to finding her encryption key. It left no room for him to work on the old hardware recently stolen from the hospital, so the hospital hard drive sat on the floor and Max sat before it, his legs crossed with a tablet in his lap.

Every time he looked up to roll the tension from his neck, he was confronted by the Pigeon. No one except Marlow had ever cared for the ugly cargo plane, but now that it loomed outside the rolling doors like an angry bird, squawking of her disappearance, everyone found themselves placating it.

"Ok, big birdie, nearly got your mamma." Max played the unsuccessfully erased files from the single emergency room surveillance camera. He frowned and called across the hanger, "I got it, but no one's going to like it."

Enzo came to kneel on one side of Max, and Nika leaned into the images from the other. Max played the video again. They watched Marlow slumping down the hospital hall, her shoulder into the wall for support. Enzo exhaled frustration, "There she goes."

"And now…" Max waited for the moment, "she is out of the picture. Last seen going in the direction of the dead man with those nasty little puncture marks of hers."

The three stared at the screen, lost for an explanation of what had happened next.

Nika walked away to press Max's padded headphones hard over her ears. She'd saved Marlow's final words to her phone, and over the past month, she'd played it repeatedly. The sound of the plastic case skidding across the pavement was followed by Marlow's barely audible voice. Even with the audio cleaned, Nika had to strain for the words. "If I didn't know better, I could swear she said master."

"Not Marlow. I couldn't even get to her to call me a master hack. I bet she'd even kick the shit out of her strategic trainer if he'd asked it." Max laughed.

"No, she'd die before she'd bow to anyone," Enzo agreed.

Nika tried sounding it out again. "Two words, the first starting with *mmm*."

In unison, Enzo and Max offered, "Motherfucker."

"What I want answered, more than what she said, is what in holy terrifying hell the army and the Cloitare were doing palled up there." Enzo had demanded it before. "Sure the army went there to get the King's cousin—"

"That diamond-clad high-heeled bitch was not on a coal train." Nika dropped the headphones to rest around her neck.

"I can't see it—she'd be one hell of a freak I'd like to meet if she were—but fuck it, sure, she was on the train. It at least makes some sort of sense." Enzo's voice dropped to quiet disbelief, "Until you throw in all those nuns."

It had all been said before and Nika didn't want to repeat it again. She turned away to watch the flat screen on the wall as the Bound Bride, just returned from years of meditation, was presented to the King. The nun led a wide procession of Cloitare across the open courtyard before the palace, taking the whole black mass up to the waiting king.

Nika imagined when the show was over and the media started dissecting the footage, the straight backed king was going to be shown with an angry face for the humiliation he was about to suffer. But then, unexpected, the Bound Bride, having stopped just close enough to touch him, dropped seamlessly to her knees. The company behind her shifted. The Master and Mentor went down behind her almost immediately, but the black sea at their back wavered and rolled before falling in uncertain increments before the King.

"This shit right here is why the rest of the world calls us fucking knee benders." Enzo was scornful of the display.

93

"Well, isn't that something." Max watched the screen. "I thought His Royal Remy was supposed to keel over before her."

"Fuck them. Fuck them both. And the cousin. They took Marlow. She did something awful and they took her." Nika glared at the image of the Cloitare laid low before the King.

"We don't know that."

"If they didn't take her, where is she?"

Max was skeptical of anything that stepped too close to conspiracy. The network was full of the wildest explanations. "What could the army, much less the fucking clergy, possibly want with Marlow?"

Enzo tapped her still encrypted drive. "You need to speed this up and tell us."

~~~~~~

It was almost a pity the live presentation in the courtyard had proceeded as it had. The three advisors were anticipating the confrontation of power as the King refused to bow to the Cloitare. It was going to be their defining moment, a reversal of previous deference, a defiant demonstration to all of Erria that the King was on equal footing with the Cloitare and would concede no further. But then Sable had sunk to her knees and remained stubbornly low until the whole of the assembled clergy were forced to follow or appear in conflict.

It left Girard with an unfocused aggression in her chest for a battle denied. Assembled in the King's private rooms, she could not wait to speak. "Quite a convincing act of loyalty. I expect you want something for it."

Sable pulled the corner of her lips slowly up. "Perhaps." She lingered on the spymaster with vicious humor, turning the exchange into a psychotic contest until Girard looked away. "Surely seeing all those black robes shake in outrage is worth at least a thank you." Then her demeanor became solemn and she turned to the King. "But it was not an act."

Remy had once again expelled all but one Cloitare from the room. He stood in front of his desk, facing the lone nun. His face silently challenged her statement.

"Would you like me to kneel again to prove myself?"

He remained speechless. When she went down, he was both shocked and annoyed. "I did not expect you to. Get up."

She rose, saying, "I have always been loyal to you."

Girard's voice was filled with false sweetness. "Loyalties still dividing? Or have they split?"

Sable directed her answer to the King. "I have never betrayed you."

Remy was aware she did not turn Cloitare eyes on him. She allowed him to hold her gaze and study her. "Where have you been?"

"Within your lands and out. Among your people and mine: the royalists, the rebels, the pious, the fanatical, and the indifferent. I have been many places. Too many to name."

Laudin asked from behind, "Did anyone recognize you?"

"No. Never."

The King rested back on his desk and motioned for the three advisors to sit. Sable he kept before him. He leaned forward and took her hand, pulling her toward him as he pushed back the sleeve of her robe to reveal the shackle. Anger and disbelief played across his features. "I had been told, but seeing it …" She seemed calm though. "Have they hurt you?"

Comfort showed in her smile. "There was never a need. Only Master Aidan has the control and he is not cruel." Flipping her hand to hold his, she said, "I must ask you to help me. Help me escape."

Behind her, the three advisors sat rigid with hopeful expectation, but Remy frowned.

She did not wait for him to refuse. "You are safe as long as I hold my resolve not to wed, but anyone can be broken." She glanced back to Berringer. "Can they not?"

His head dipped in brusque agreement.

"My King, the Cloitare will harm you if we marry; the people will destroy you if you refuse. As long as you present a willing face to unite but the mothers do not present me, you are safe. The clergy will be held responsible for the failure. But they will break me. I will agree for reasons my mind will invent to save itself. And then you will die. I am certain of it. With me as queen, they will kill you and your lands will be ruled by a council of regents from the Cloitare."

The conviction of her words stifled the room.

"This is the time to help me. Give me what I require to hack this unfair bangle off my wrist. I cannot fight them with it on." She took his other hand. "Please agree."

Remy's expression was harsh. "It is a foul thing I would not have on you. Regardless of why you want it off, I want it off." With a gesture, he gave Berringer and Girard permission to assist.

Sable did not spare them her brutal face. "I need—" and without courtesy, she reached into Girard's jacket pocket to pull out her phone. Setting it to record, she began a detailed list of equipment.

Only Remy still recognized the girl that had feared for him so many years ago, feared for him enough to run away and change herself.

~~~~~~

Lieutenant Fallon thought he had put the Cloitare behind him when Mission Retrieve was closed. He thought the transfer into General Berringer's information security team would keep him well clear of the modernity eschewing clergy, but on entering the private hall, he encountered the nuns in force, dozens of them, crowded outside the King's rooms. They turned on him, a great swath of hissing fabric, and saw clearly his intent. They knew him for what he was and what he carried, and they hated him.

He clamped onto both shoulder bags and buried his head. *Keep your head down, walk fast, head down, walk fast.*

The hall throbbed with focused intimidation. William Fallon heard his heart pounding in his head. He knew he wasn't breathing, just running the gauntlet, head down, walking fast.

When he got to the door, he fumbled with the knob and the weight of the bags. The nuns stepped forward in perfect unison, darkening his periphery. He pawed at the wood trying to knock, and again, hands wet with terror, unresponsive with adrenaline, he pulled and pushed at the door. The nuns moved closer, forcing the sound of wordless terror from his burning lungs.

When the door opened from inside, the Lieutenant tripped forward, gasping for the air he had denied himself. He dropped the bags just steps inside and then hurried across the rug until he heard the door close. Thinking himself safe, he bent at the waist, hands on his knees, and heaved the fear from his lungs; then he saw the black hem of a nun swirl across his shoes and convulsed.

"*Shhhh.*" Her hand laid on his shoulder. "They are such a ghastly lot, are they not?"

It seemed to him that her mirthful empathy gave them a bond, and then it was all quite funny. "I hate when they do that," he chuckled.

He rose to Berringer's disapproval, but Sable would have none of it. She linked her hand in his arm and walked him back to the bags. "I hope you packed to impress."

Within minutes, she ceased to be even distantly regal. She became instead one of the tech heads that gather at conventions and exude wonder over what they've seen, what they've made, and what they're going to do with what they've learned. Across an ornately carved table, Sable and William became engrossed and ignored the room.

Fallon pulled out a portable programmer, circuit boards, and encoders. Sable dug through the second bag, setting aside a variety of rare DC plugs and brittle cables cracked with age. "Nice, nice."

"Now this," she thrust her hand with the shackle at him, and then turned it to expose a small opening, "has to be an old DC port, right? What else could it be?"

Fallon turned her wrist over to inspect it. "That's the only opening. How long have you had it on?"

"A month."

"Have they tried to recharge it through the port? Or would they even know how?"

"No one's touched it."

"Think it's been updated?"

"I imagine it was pulled out of a vault. Why take time to update anything more than the battery?"

"Where does it get its signal to, uh, you know …" Fallon grimaced, "… activate?"

"Remote. It's a slide ball that can be carried discreetly in a pocket, but I don't know the range. Other than to mold itself flush, the thing has been idle. We're looking at fifty-year-old tech. They'd have to update to a modern battery, making the port superfluous. A modern bat would never need recharging, or god save the person who wore it. But, unless you can correct me, considering the age, the port should still give us access to—"

"—the memory," they both finished in agreement.

While she'd been speaking, Fallon had been trying to get a wireless signal from it, but it was lifeless, transmitting nothing. "We'll try to get the site code with my friend here, little Miss MayMay," he patted a circuit board and resistor, "microcontroller for the malicious."

Sable picked it up and put it down with derision. "Wi Fry, unless you've got some jack-happy skills I've never heard of, that thing couldn't open a hotel safe."

He covered the ears of Miss MayMay in mock offense, and then taunted Sable with dry confidence, "Catch up, analog."

Sable laughed.

The four watching the interaction were uncomfortable with the familiarity passing at the table, but neither of the hackers was aware.

"Expect it to be encrypted."

"I've got software for that." He patted a laptop.

100

"How long do you think? Minutes? Hours? Can we find an old algorithm for it?"

Lieutenant Fallon sat back. "I'm searching for old codes now." He tapped the laptop once more. "Considering its age, I'm thinking minutes, but I really can't say until we see what it is." He was already worried, so he spoke his greater concern. "What if it's protected?"

She looked at him confused.

He frowned. "Of all the technologies for them to embrace." He opened his hands to the shackle as if he couldn't bring himself to say it. "I mean, it has a purpose. What if we set it off?"

Sable sat upright and became a nun again. "Well then, I will scream and you will read the code." She ignored the straightening of Remy's back. To the General, she said, "Cover my mouth so the mothers do not hear."

"Stop." The last part of the exchange had struck Remy sober. He came off the edge of the desk where he'd been watching. The room was paralyzed, waiting. To Sable he said, "I will not have this."

"We are only speaking of possibilities," she spoke breezily to dispel concern.

To Lieutenant Fallon, the King asked, "Is this risk likely?"

Fallon was formal. "With respect, it must be considered. I apologize for my ignorance, but this is the first time I have seen a compliance shackle. No one from either of our generations," his gesture circled the room, "would have any experience with one."

Thinking she was about to be denied, Sable became harsh. "People scream, die, and cry for you every day. This is nothing by comparison, and nothing to what happens if we don't get it off." Then she saw the tone of her abrupt dismissal was an insult to his apprehensions. She quickly remembered where she was. "Please, Remy," she softened her voice, "Lieutenant Fallon is right. It does have a purpose, so far better to let me hurt myself than allow someone else." And then to further dispel the offense she had caused, she bowed her head, "Please, my King, permit me this liberty."

He did not appear satisfied, but he opened his hand to signal they could continue. To Berringer, he said, "You will not muzzle her," and then severely to Lieutenant Fallon, "You will stop at the first sign of distress."

Sable grabbed William's hand and shook the strain out of him, smiling, encouraging, "This will be sunshine, Wi Fry, pure easy sunshine."

~~~~~~

Lieutenant Fallon didn't know at first what was happening. He had only just put the barrel connector into the DC port when she went wide-eyed, pulled her manacled fist to her chest, and fell as a tight heap of black fabric to the floor.

Berringer was the first to start shouting, "*Off*. Turn it off, Lieutenant."

The King's voice roared over the General's, "End it. *Now*."
102

He had already turned off the programmer when she added her own voice to the pandemonium, a muffled wail suppressed by her robes and posture. Fallon ripped the converter cable from the programmer, cracking its brittle insulation with the force, but it silenced no one. The King and General were still bellowing for him to stop. He reached into the ball she had made of herself and tried to get at the connector in the port, but she was locked into herself.

Berringer forced his hands through her arms and brought her up, freeing her to shake the room with a full-throated, mind-rending scream she unleashed from the lungs. Fallon and the King winced low under the piercing gale to grapple with her hand for the plug. When Fallon touched the broken connector, he was sent backward yelping. He shook the current from his hand, smothered the flame in his shoulder, and coughed embers from his guts. Remy held on longer, twisting before her in a howling spasm before the flow of fire forced him to release. Fallon tried snapping it out by the cable, with her all the while shrieking, loud and hysterical, but the cable was disintegrating, crumbling apart with age, leaving shorter and shorter lengths.

Then Aidan was among them, pushing between the three, a great black mass in robes, freeing the connector with a growl. There was shocking silence, abrupt but fleeting.

The King exploded with unrestrained fury. "Remove it at once!" Reaching up, he pulled the Master and Mentor around by the shoulder.

The General dropped the nun and stepped between the two, prepared to take Aidan down if he responded to Remy's aggression.

Forcing through, the King shoved at the wide chest of the Mentor, demanding again, "Take it off, or, by your gods, I will destroy you."

Girard, who had not come to her feet for the whole of the screaming debacle, backed her king now. "Devil be warned, you will do as he says."

The Master and Mentor took the abuse, allowed it to turn him around, knock him back, insult him. He said simply, "It is not my decision," and looked to the open door where Mother Vesna had entered.

Remy did not hear or did not care. He pushed past Berringer once more to order a third time, "At once, take it off."

Aidan stepped back and bowed. "Again, it is not my decision."

"You were not invited," Laudin informed the Cloitare pushing into the room.

Frustrated by the lowered head of Aidan, Remy sought another.

Mother Vesna stood in the fore, her attention sweeping over the details of the room: the nun on the floor, her mentor humbled, the King out of control. She judged the scene in the room poorly. Her arrogance focused the King.

"You, woman," he pointed at Vesna, "you have been the bane of my life and will be no longer. You will take the abomination from the hand of that girl or you will see the end of this elaborate fiction today."

Of all the things, Laudin did not want this exchange to escalate. He pushed at the group, yelling, "Every one of you out." His voiced cracked in desperation. "Catherine, help me."

Girard flew at the mothers. "All of you," and she ate the word whores, "start moving."

But Vesna would not be shifted. "If the King wishes to end our centuries of alliance in dishonor, then that is the will of the King and for the people to judge. Your future is your own, but will you so readily martyr your bride?"

The King felt slapped. His voice lowered to a growl, "We will witness your death before hers."

Girard broke through the gathered nuns' resistance, and together, she and Laudin pushed them out, cursing them like cattle, loud and crass to drown out anything Remy could threaten or Vesna return.

On the floor, unaware of the fray, Sable crawled toward Lieutenant Fallon. "Wi Fry," she rasped, "we gotta ground that motherfucker."

Aidan pulled her up. "Not today, anawa. Today we return to the convent."

POLITICS

The political secretary could not shake the feeling that the whole palace had become cursed since the return of the Bound Bride. The place had never been particularly vibrant, as though something in the old stone walls, with their ancient display of weapons and deep colored tapestries, forbid levity, but of late it seemed a malign entity ruled the halls. Places that had been quiet heaved with grief. Laudin had gone to the billiard room to change his own bleak scenery and found the staid housekeeper sobbing into the back of a chair. Tears he heard behind many closed doors. The rooms of Berringer, normally so lively with his wife's tempestuous need to ensure her husband's passion, sounded dull and boring. Baleful images harassed his dreams, shadowed his days, and then hounded him to sleep again. He knew from the wan faces around him, he was not alone.

He did not want to be working in his rooms, but conflict on the border with Alena had erupted when the genuine mineral report surfaced showing rich deposits of monazite. Laudin had tried to distance the King from the Ministry of Science's original publication that no ores containing rare elements had been found at the border town, Ulphia, but the Alenans had responded by violently purging Ulphia of royalists.

After the third night of public hangings, on the King's order, a combined arms brigade of infantry and armor rolled across the border. They sealed the town off at the highways to prevent further influx of extremists and set a curfew after dark, transporting away to Erentrude those thought responsible for the worst violence. The Alenan government silently bore it, telling its public the support had been requested, was welcome and temporary, but no one believed it. One hundred years past, when Erentrude and Sierra nearly went to war, the territory had taken advantage to split away from the realm. Reunification had been every king's ambition since.

Laudin assured the world it was strictly a police action, but Sierra, on Alena's eastern border, threatened to call it an invasion. Sierra had been a member of the World Security League for centuries, and with powerful old allegiances, the country was respected, but Erentrude was a dangerous emerging nation full of wealth and vital resources. If Erentrude could not buy the outcome it wanted, the kingdom simply threatened to withhold lithium from the world market.

The Errian continent was always bristling with threats of war, so not only did Sierra not want Erentrude as a neighbor, the world's most powerful countries wanted space between them as well. Laudin had spent many days with Sierran President Pavlović assuring him they shared the same desire for an independent Alena. Only now—with the promise of trade in rare elements and the King's tanks still sitting on the minerals—Pavlović had begun to suggest to Alena a possible alliance.

Laudin would have gladly thanked the Bound Bride for the show of loyalty in the courtyard that had seen the script flipped, the King standing and her bowed in service. For the first time, Laudin was grateful to have the Bride; President Pavlović had his own fanatics to deal with: the religious who decried involvement in the conflict as an affront to the future Queen Mother.

Adding to the turmoil was the rise of the charismatic Felix Magnus, voice of the Libertines, calling for civil disobedience from the significant number of skeptics, anarchists, and all other manner of revolutionary types that defined the nihilist nature of Alena. The armor battalion in Ulphia faced roads blocked with many hundreds of protesters sitting with arms linked. The infantry was splattered in paint, either thrown at them or dropped from roofs in balloons. When they didn't have a thousand red laser pointers blinding their movements, they faced the incessant rhythmic chant of a lyrical question: "Freedom be dumb?"

Laudin had watched video as Felix Magnus told the crowds, "Our own Prime Minister tells us we are playing a dumb game of politics."

And the crowds chanted back the question, "Freedom be dumb?"

"Freedom, dumb? No. Our freedom is specific. Demand absolute freedom."

They returned, "Absolute freedom!"

"King Remius says our idea of freedom denies moral structure, but his morality is false. Show him we will not feel shame." And the crowd followed Felix, lifting high in their hands pills, glass vials, pipes, bongs, and oversized syringes filled with paint. "Eat the dogma!" And the crowd went cheering, roaring mad then briefly still as lighters flicked, illuminating the mass of dissidents. Across the

108

video, Laudin could hear the sound of sucking through pipes, the gurgling of bongs, water bottles tipped to swallow pills, and again the roar as smoke exhaled over their heads.

"How are we to use our freedom? The libertine answers: We will do what we want."

And the crowd affirmed, "We will do what we want!"

Making Felix Magnus seem practically welcome was the emerging armed resistance which intelligence said was equipped with old technology left over from the Sierra-Erentrude standoff of last century, and everyone knew the weapons weren't coming out of Erentrude.

"A train wreck." Laudin shook his head. "The whole thing is one long train wreck."

"You should have put that dog down years ago," Berringer blamed Girard.

Girard understood that, as things go, the report would have eventually been leaked, but they had been expecting many more years, even a decade, to formalize a protectorate over the lost territory.

Nevertheless, Berringer was right. She had relied too singularly on the Guard Dog, had indulged his many idiosyncrasies in exchange for his successes, none of which amounted to anything now. And still the Dog was silent. The scientist had passed off the report and escaped to Sierra, but before the Sierrans buried him in seclusion, Girard had seen one last photo of him with a broken arm. She

109

suspected the scientist had somehow gotten the better of the Guard Dog and killed him. A sad, disappointing end.

The days had been full of sad spectacles. Girard didn't want to, but she liked Sable. The nun had returned with a confident amusement which Catherine recognized. Catherine imagined if she had ever suffered a maternal blunder, she would have had a daughter much like Sable, a surprising, demented replica of herself. But the creature the mothers put before the King was not to be envied.

Berringer said it was sleep deprivation, but what Girard saw was a body uninhabited. The Cloitare brought the blinking, breathing thing to the King's rooms with the optimistic promise it had agreed to wed, but Girard suspected they were merely testing the strength of the nun's conditioning.

On the intricate rug before the King's desk, she stood in the center of four mothers and barely managed to keep her mouth from falling open. Master Aidan stood apart, observing the demonstration from just inside the door. Girard kept expecting him to wave away any association with the group and back into the hall.

Mother Vesna was trying to prompt Sable to do something, but the nun gave no indication she was aware. Putting her hands on Sable's shoulders, Vesna walked her two steps closer to the King, whispering to make her react, but she remained vacuous.

Sickened, Remy had approached and tried to get Sable to see him, but the vacant form showed no sign of intelligence.

"Well done, Mother Vesna, you've created a corpse bride. No one should take any notice." Girard could not stand to look.

110

"This is but her first acceptance. She will be made suitable."

The King left the room without speaking to the Cloitare. He had come to hope Sable was correct, that they would break her. She would marry him and he would protect her.

The inevitability of it made the three advisors uneasy.

BUSINESS

Marlow would have loved the insurrection. It was the only thing that took the joy out of it for Enzo.

He was in a newly acquired hangar outside Ulphia waiting for Nika to deliver a stock of batteries from their supplier in Erentrude. She was flying in a wide circle of avoidance around Salt Mountain to evade security at the border.

Over the last month, Enzo had procured a number of odd buildings besides the hangar. On the outskirts of Ulphia, just beyond the army perimeter to the south, he had a house, and on the perimeter to the east, he had a garage, both were dedicated to selling King Remius's Ministry of Energy's counterfeit batteries. Mostly he sold to locals who could prove residence in the city and move through the army barricade, and the locals would then smuggle the batteries to the radicals that had gathered inside the city before the army arrived. The last peculiar structure he had obtained was in the heart of the city: a three-table cafe that traded drugs to the soldiers.

Enzo had moved his whole schismatic army of loners and freaks to the border town to take advantage of the uprising. Those not in the buildings were dealing out of their pockets wherever they dared. And every one of them was so thoroughly incapable of conforming to anything approximating a social norm, even the illusory one set forth in Alena, Enzo had been obligated to bring Max as well. The army had allowed the police in Ulphia to stand, but they pressed the police for more arrests and greater enforcement of laws long ignored.

112

Back in Erentrude, Enzo's crew had dealt smartly in drugs and counterfeits, but they would bang all night at the technos, rolling in the warm sunshine of anodyne and synthetics, then snort, inject, or drink themselves precariously close to oblivion. At all hours, you could find them steering recklessly close to the precipice with god only knew what in their possession, but they were loyal. They hated anything that passed as authority so spitefully they would scramble their own brains before talking; though, when Enzo was truly honest with himself, he recognized he had never really tested their resolve. They knew if Max couldn't free them, Enzo would send Marlow. She had a consummate loathing for confinement—whether it was a jail or a pair of handcuffs—and an equal disdain for the people who confined, despising police, prosecutors, and judges with such hostility, she was particularly useful to Enzo and easy to motivate.

She would bribe, persuade, haggle, threaten, or kill to prevent any of his people from being sent to prison.

He had learned of her particular flair for persuasion way back at the beginning while acquainting her with the possibility of synthesized music. He still rolled his eyes to think of it. "Did your parents have you locked in the basement? It was for your own good, wasn't it?"

She'd only ever stare at him when he asked.

She'd heard Max raging frantic about having only just been informed of a dealer's arrest and having no time to get into the prosecutor's database to change the charge of possession of illegal substances with intent to supply to a more pleasant public intoxication when she asked in her original, refined, and genteel accent, "Would it not be less difficult to simply convince the judge against incarceration?"

"Where the fuck did you find this kid?" Max had not formed an opinion of her until then.

"Sure it would," Enzo had insisted. "But neither of us can be seen in the courthouse. I'm going to have to ask you to do it." In the beginning—thank the satirical gods—she had little concept of irony either.

He always wondered if her first, last, and only explanation of success had been deliberately menacing. "I suggested imprisonment would be … *unhealthy*."

He had never really learned to tell if she was laughing behind those moments of chilling sincerity.

This new operation spreading through Ulphia could be treacherous without her, but Alena had developed an exceptional tolerance for a person's right to pursue happiness down nearly any path imaginable, so much that Enzo felt they were safer in the conflict than at home. *Mind your own business and keep your hands to yourself* was the unwritten law of Alena.

So far, the police in Ulphia were more concerned with the chaos six battalions of young soldiers could inflict on a civilian population than who was cranking the soldiers up high or dropping them low, and the local authorities were never going to care who was supplying the dissidents with batteries to circumvent the curfews and blackouts or to power up the night rallies. Enzo had the army to fear, but they were half his profit. And he knew the army wasn't going anywhere, which made him think their move to Alena might be permanent as well.

REPRISALS

Berringer would later wonder if any of them should have predicted, not so much what, as none of the advisors could have guessed that, but instead that a dramatic turn was unavoidable after the next failed presentation of the Bound Bride to the King. It seemed more obvious in hindsight that someone, perhaps all of them, would break, but it would have been hard to determine who first. He would spend his life wondering if the worst of it could have been prevented.

It had been so swift to result in such devastating retaliation. Four mothers, including the Mothers Vesna and Isabelle along with Master Aidan, had brought Sable to the King's rooms. Master Aidan stood with his head bowed just inside the door. Berringer was certain in his reflections that the man's posture was designed to separate himself from the scene.

The four mothers centered Sable among them on the carpet again. Berringer and Girard were on one couch facing them while Laudin was across the carpet on another, and Remy stood before his desk.

Sable had much the same vacant mannerism, only this time she would agree to anything asked of her. Mother Vesna was close at her side making her perform these tricks, saying, "The King would like assurances you have accepted your position and have agreed to wed."

Appropriately, Sable responded, "I have."

"You will accept your duties as the Bound Bride?"

116

"I will." Her focus floated just beyond them but on nothing.

"Do you accept your role revealed by the prophets as the Queen Mother, Mother of All?"

"I do."

"You will marry the King?"

"I will."

Mother Vesna, who had never shown pleasure, allowed a satisfied relaxation to demonstrate her triumph. She addressed the King, "The Bound Bride will complete her training with us shortly and will be free to wed. We will speak soon of our requirements."

The group shifted to leave, but unexpected to all, and even himself, Remy snatched Sable from their midst. Vesna looked shocked then irate and tried to pull her back, but at the first rash step forward by Remy, Berringer had come to his feet and now blocked Vesna's attempt. The mothers surged forward, denying the King had the right. Then Girard and Laudin were before the group. Only Aidan stood uninvolved at the back.

Disturbed by the display, Remy had pulled her across the carpet, asking, "Sable, will you please just trust me and end this opposition?"

So courteously, she answered, "I will."

Girard turned to see the glimmer of hope in Remy's face and, perhaps disgusted that only she could see the obvious, tersely demonstrated the startling, "Sable, would you like to drink poison?"

And Sable replied pleasantly, "I would."

117

Remy closed his eyes to the lesson. While he steadied his breath, Sable began to focus on the family pin in his jacket. She reached out to touch the crest, tracing the curve of the bull's spine.

To the Cloitare, Remy ordered, "End this quickly and give her to me."

With her finger, Sable circled the emblem. Down its tail and back to the red-eyed head, she followed the horns up to Remy's face and then smiled as though she had not expected to see him. She said simply, "Remy."

Then, with a sharp breath of awareness, she appeared in full.

She snapped, "*No.*" But afraid she had already agreed to something permanent, she grabbed her wrist, dug at the shackle, and exhaled with relief to find it there, certain they would not wed her with it on.

She gave Remy a brief smile of reassurance before she switched to her tormentor. Berringer saw the smile grow hungry and the eyes tighten on Vesna. Her approach on the mother was deliberate, bestial, designed for violence. From where Berringer stood, he could hear her every exhale, exaggerated, predatory, and intended to alarm.

She'd gone deliriously savage.

Locked on Vesna, she issued cruel, measured threats. "You are not strong enough to break me. I will return again and again to smite you. All your plans will fall to my resolve. I will turn all you see black, then in the darkness, I will hunt you. In the night, I will devour you."

118

All the while Vesna was pushing back into the group, waving Aidan forward, insisting, "Stop her, stop her."

"You will know the darkest fear and you will know me as—"

"*Anawa*." The word split the air.

Sable stopped, the sneer settled, but still she held Vesna in her focus to declare, "I will destroy you."

Then, in defiance of all their expectations, she moved to go back to the convent, calling them harshly to follow, "We are far from finished."

~~~~~~

Berringer thought nothing of it; the Master and Mentor had been marked leaving the palace at sunrise. Before Sable disappeared, he had done this twice a year, and every time he'd leave Girard's people spinning in circles, hunting for him within the hour. He'd return in three days. The news was nothing more than the resumption of routine.

Then, the following night, as he and Remy shared a drink, he got the call, "It's the Bride, sir. You'll want to come. We're outside the Cloitare doors."

He rose to leave, responding, "Tell me."

"C. I. U." Conscious. Injured. Unresponsive.

The General stopped as he was about to close the door. "Secured for the King?"

119

"Yes, sir."

Later, Berringer would show Remy what the cameras had recorded. The wide corridor was empty all the way to the double doors that dominated the wall. Both doors opened full into the hall. Behind, unseen, the second set would have been opened into the cloister. Blackness rolled forward, filling the antechamber, and then a single dark form was ejected with force. The nun staggered on her own for several steps before stalling and dropping. The darkness withdrew and the doors closed.

The video showed the guards who were stationed under the cameras step tentatively into view, moving cautiously toward the unexpected scene. They bent to study the form and then the area erupted with activity.

She lay now with her eyes taped shut to save her vision from the Cloitare Stare that would not end.

The King's physician had cooled saline in wine buckets and poured it over her wrist, rinsing the burnt skin that caught under the shackle. At a loss, he had bandaged the whole horrible thing. Dr. Branson could trace the places across her body where hands had grabbed her and he could guess the force required to hold her while someone had cut an X across each palm. He washed away the salt that was packed deep in the wounds and stitched tiny knots into the flesh before wrapping them as well. She all the while had not even blinked.

Remy held her bloody robe in dismay. "What have they done, Lucas?"

120

Berringer sat beside his friend who watched the unmoving figure in the bed of the medical room. He didn't know what to say. Remy wanted to know what the Cloitare had done to Sable, but Berringer wanted to know what the Cloitare had just done to them all.

~~~~~~~

The King recognized the resolute posture that sent Berringer speeding past his door. Too often of late, he had seen the soldier square his shoulders, set his jaw, and glare the hatred he reserved for the clergy. Berringer walked quickly, purposefully for the medical center with Remy right behind. His fast step was explained shortly as "Aidan is back."

Guards had been installed outside the clinic on the King's instruction that no Cloitare would have contact with Sable again. The General heard Aidan growl, swiping his hands in front of him as though he were clearing a cobweb. Even with Berringer shouting from behind for the guards to stop him, they appeared too dazed to see. The General did not understand why, and there was no time to demand answers.

Black robes in disarray, he went directly for the room where Sable lay immobile. The two men following saw Aidan sink low, press his head to hers and disintegrate with an agonized plea. "Forgive me, forgive me, I did not see it. I would never have left. I would tear down the heavens to change it."

121

Berringer had been staggered by it, but he regained his purpose and went to evict the Mentor. Remy held him back.

"I will suffer the black. I will find you. Hear me, anawa," he continued to call for her to emerge.

Dark shadows dressed in habits soon pressed at the door. The great imperturbable calm Master Aidan possessed could not be estimated until it was lost. The room saw before them a revenant rise; roaring grievance pulled him up. The howl for vengeance found the Mother Vesna.

Berringer threw his arm across Remy's chest and reflexively stepped them back from harm.

The mask of the three mothers who had come to inform the Master and Mentor his selection was wrong, the imposter exposed and expelled, cracked to realize their mistake. Terror sunk their faces. They thought to retreat, but Aidan was already among them.

He grabbed Vesna by the throat and pulled her to his face. "You would dare?" Her feet left the ground. "Are you so bold as to challenge me?"

"She is mine." He shook Vesna to accentuate the possession. "*Mine*." Throwing her into the wall, he grabbed the next.

"You would usurp me?" He pitched this mother down the hall and captured the last that had spun to escape. Pulling her back against his chest, he finished, "This treachery will be paid." She collapsed but he dragged her behind. He seized the Mother Vesna as she fled past, choked her to the floor as he walked, and then launched her into the retreating back of the mother farthest away. Bellowing outrage

122

clenched his stomach, arched his back, and dropped them both to the floor. He bowled the mother in his hands into them. From the pile, he picked Vesna and threw her again, and he would have delivered them such through the palace to the double doors had they not gained their feet and run.

~~~~~~

When Aidan returned, Remy was waiting. The King had sat down to wait in silence, wanting to feel the stretch in time that kept the Mentor away, imagining in his absence the fury that rained down in the convent as the minutes passed.

Berringer sat across the room struggling to answer if what he had witnessed might be called right, or merely justified, or would the man who had trained him in the strategy of war denounce the attack against the women. Had the Cloitare done half as much to his wife, his mother, or Remy, Berringer would have killed the lot; nevertheless, the violence he saw disturbed him, and he knew he could not leave the King alone with its maker.

Doctor Branson had come to wait too. When he saw Aidan enter, he began to unwind the bandage from Sable's wrist.

Remy's expression angrily accused the Mentor. He pointed to the shackle, "I said before to take it off."

Aidan took her hand and then, dropping his head again to hers, he begged her to accept his guilt. He rolled his thumb over the ball as he took the controller from his pocket, all the while pleading to reach her. The bracelet hesitated then whirred to life, retracted its pressure and released. Aidan expected it to drop, but it was mired with blood and fluid, stuck with skin burnt and blistered. Remorse rumbled in his throat.

The doctor pushed through with saline and a bucket to catch it.

Aidan could not remember when last he had explained himself. He sat beside the King, both men staring ahead, and said, "The mothers brought it to me. They insisted on it. I did not consider there might be another controller. I did not see their deception. The fault is mine. I would give my soul to change it."

The King said it for himself, not Aidan, "She has been hurt; she will recover."

"No," it was a profound sigh of denial. "No, much more than that has occurred. She would not have liked it, but she would have gathered herself and while the blood dropped to the floor, she would have laughed at their archaic attempt to shame her. She would have dared the mothers to do better. They dared." He looked at her eyes sealed shut. "They did dare to do worse."

"I told you to take it off. They were banned for good reason," the King's voice rose with authority. "Yet the Cloitare will not accept the law of this or any other land. Arrogance robed in sanctimony."

Aidan sat in silent agreement. "The shackle is only a part of it," he said. "What happened in the cloister could not have transpired had I not permitted it through neglect, but neither the blade that cut her nor the shackle alone brought her to this. This," he took Sable's

124

bandaged hand, "this was a punishment as old as the order. It is called the shattering. There is not a nun alive who does not fear it."

Remy's anger prevented him from saying more than, "Explain."

"The stillness you see before you is of no concern. She alone I taught to escape into the void, to protect her most valuable mind in the dark. She is merely waiting to return when it is safe, but she is far away in the night, unaware of the time that passes."

"And when she awakes?"

"If she can speak, she can be saved. If she screams, she is shattered."

Remy felt punched by the memory of her shrieking on the floor of his room when she had pleaded to free herself of the shackle, to be the one, if anyone must, to hurt herself. He never wanted to hear her voice raised in grief again. Livid it was a possibility, the question growled through his teeth, "What did they do to her?"

"They expelled her from the Cloitare. But the Cloitare have many secrets and they cannot banish a member without securing that knowledge. To do that, they must take away the voice that can betray and shatter the mind so no contact can be made. On the scale of damage," Aidan shifted his hands to show it would not balance. "Because of my errors, she will not have escaped it without sacrifice. The shackle would not allow her mind to escape. They brought her back again and again to break her apart. You must accept that you cannot understand in full what has happened; it is a matter of the mind, the mind of the Cloitare, which can act as one. They turned

125

their mind against her, or the part of itself that was her." Aidan knew it held little meaning for the uninitiated. He explained more simply, "Religion requires rituals to unite and intimidate. In the shattering, they would have assembled the convent, and on the altar they would have cut the signs that deny a nun to give or receive. Had she been penitent, she would have offered her hands for each member to place salt in the wounds. This was not symbolic, but very real. Her condition tells me what any of us could have guessed: she was not bowed with remorse. They forced her to hold it. Had she been humbled by the ritual, they would not have united their minds and driven her out, shattering her and the ties that bind, taking from her the voice that makes her dangerous and the eye that makes her divine."

The King had come to his feet and was pressing his temples against what he was hearing. "Of all the bloody things to pass in war," outrage shook his voice, "such a vulgar act has not been seen."

"Perhaps not," Aidan conceded, "but then the realm and clergy do not acquire territory in the same manner."

~~~~~~

The General watched her turning toward the two men's voices and motioned to the doctor that she was waking up. Branson had just removed the tape from her eyes when she grabbed his hand, twisted it near flat to his arm and drove him in the direction he was leaning to escape the pressure, pressing him down onto the mattress as she pushed herself up.

Aidan was on her before the General could cross the room. At the sound of his voice pacifying, "Anawa," she forgot the doctor, letting him slide sideways to the floor, while Aidan took her by the shoulders. She sat on the edge of the bed, swaying slightly, drunk with confusion.

Helping the doctor to his feet, Berringer kept his focus on her face.

Her brow was pulled together, searching to understand the scene before her. She found Aidan and then grabbed a hand full of her black hair, but this only further confused her. Spotting Remy, she squinted her eyes as though she might be able to see events more clearly, but then gave up to stare at her hands. She looked like she might speak, but instead, she dug frantically at her wrist, drawing it up to her mouth to chew on the bandage, clawing and biting to get it off. Blood soaked through the white mesh before Aidan could wrestle it behind her.

Her expression, so painfully bewildered, slackened when she left the room to search her mind; then the nightmare split from her mouth. She wailed from the ruins. It robbed hope from all who heard it. Pulling her head against his shoulder, Aidan's voice rose over hers, a horrible disparaging lament that nearly drowned out the sound of her terror.

Feeling dread spread from his chest, the General backed away from it. He understood it was over. She was gone. The people were going to climb the walls and burn the whole place, Cloitare and kingdom, to the ground. He started to calculate how much time he had to get the city reinforced, to pull the brigade out of Alena, and call home the peace patrols. He did not have time to fantasize about getting the King to leave; Laudin would have to argue that futile case, showing Remy the countries that had agreed to accept them. Berringer wondered how long he had to prepare before Erria learned the great promise of a united future had been tortured into madness.

~~~~~~

Girard went to see for herself. Before that night, she'd never had a problem sleeping. She could put her head against a concrete barrier and doze through flying bullets in a springtime war, but tonight she'd been battling with her sheets for hours. She'd irritably thrown on clothes to get it over with, convinced the insomnia was caused by the accusation she leveled at herself: coward.

The Clementyne Dynasty would be next to face the public's riotous ire, and she was not going to twist all sentimental over the loss of a mind. She wanted to slap herself, and there was no better way.

It was well past midnight and Sable had a fist full of Aidan's robe with one hand, and with the other, she was marking her mental slide down some unseen slope as she told him, "Slipping." Her finger followed a thought as it sunk and she told him again, "Slipping," then showed him the slide, "Slipping," again the hand slide, "Slipping,"

128

hand slide, "Slipping," and she seemed prepared to go on indefinitely. Girard sat down to confirm the insanity was lasting.

Sable's timing was perfect, repetitive, meditative, like signing papers. Catherine went over her strategy.

She would start by dropping everything into the PIT, her online Propaganda and Information Team. They wouldn't even have to manufacture a story this time; the truth would be clear when she gave them the recording of the nuns casting Sable from the double doors. The PIT needed to emphasize the King's fast response to aid the Bride. Remy wasn't going to like it, but his grief beside her needed to be played over and over until he was unassailable. Catherine needed pictures of Sable's hands while the cuts were still fresh and horrifying. The hands, but not the wrist, that raised too many questions. Evidence of the shackle would come out—these things always did—but by the time the public learned Sable was wearing the shackle because she refused to wed the King, the public would have spent its energy tearing down the Cloitare. The Ministry of Intelligence would ensure the public had everything it needed too. And here Girard sunk deep, spreading her thoughts over the territory, thinking of the people she would call upon, the networks to reinforce, the propaganda to be boosted. She would call home from Alena and Sierra her legion of agitators and instigators. And bombs, she decided, to finish the clergy, they were going to need bombs.

Behind all the furious scheming, Sable kept slipping. The intelligence chief rose to leave, feeling braced for the fight.

Aidan let Sable rant, but he called to Girard, "Hold off on your plans, Catherine."

The hour, the lack of sleep, uneaten meals, she had stood too fast. The blood had rushed from her head and toppled her back into the chair. She had heard him though.

"The Cloitare will beat you. This time you would give the public the truth, but your history is filled with fabrications, monsters of smoke, and acts so vile even you might quail to revisit them. The mothers are not passive. They are aware. They will fight you with everything they know, and they will not stop there. They will show you such inventions as you would think impossible, lies born of flesh your best cannot battle. If you strike them, they will destroy you and your king. Politics does not have the authority of religion."

Sable sat on the edge of the medical bed clutching the front of Aidan's robe, and he stood before her, unmoved since she awoke. His devotion would not allow him to turn, so the whole lesson, threat, and warning had been punctuated by the random appearance of Sable's hand slipping beyond his arm.

Over the continuous repetition of Sable slipping, Girard spoke to Aidan's back. "The clergy has this funny way of not admitting anyone is in charge, something about all mothers being the mother of all, but if I had to guess, I would say you are as high as it gets." Despite the uncertainty he had instilled, she was smirking. "And now, if I understand, you offer me advice, concerned perhaps I might scuff up my shoes when I kick down your doors."

"You need not trust me, you have no reason, but set your mind, master of deception, to how you would foil your own plans. What happens when the Cloitare denies your every accusation?"

"Your anawa is mad."

"This? The clergy might call this a divine trance. Temporary."

Catherine scoffed. "And the cuts?"

"What would you say?"

She had already searched and knew there was no accessible information on the ritualistic slicing of an X into the hands of nuns. Free of evidence, Catherine would portray it as an honor to receive the marks.

"The mothers often express regret for not finding you as a child."

The compliment chilled Catherine's blood. There was no need to confront him with the video; the recording did not clearly show it was Sable. The prophet before her, set to deny Sable had been cast from the Cloitare, could easily counter her every move. The battle would not be a decisive victory for the realm.

Aidan's voice had been patient, seemingly without opinion of Catherine's actions or attachment to their outcome. Now he was brutally dismissive. "You have no weapon to go to war with the Cloitare. *Hear me*," the throaty roll of the command held her attention. "All the paths you consider will lead to defeat."

Multiple images of the King's destruction played fast through her mind. With a desire to know his intention, she asked, "The path that does not?"

"Patience," he said while Sable slipped around his words. "You do not yet possess the weapon for the battle you seek."

~~~~~

Girard did not sleep. She accompanied Remy and Berringer with Dr. Branson in the morning to find Sable continuing her mad descent down the slope, still telling Aidan her mind was slipping.

With Remy leaving, Sable told herself, "Stop."

The fist full of robe she had not released, she drew closer, pulling Aidan to eyes that only he might recognize as cognizant. "Go save them."

"Who, anawa?"

It seemed to Remy she was blind, that she was trying to get Aidan's attention but could not see she already had it. She said, "Find them."

"Show me."

She struggled to keep her focus on Aidan, body swaying, eyes swimming. Now agitated, she pushed at him, telling him, "Go."

He waited.

"Go save them."

"Who, anawa?"

She stopped searching his face to ransack her mind. "Sister … sister." She could not find a name. "She would not obey." Pulling Aidan closer, her voice lower, "The salt, she dropped it." She fought for the memory. "One, then four, more, but four would not give it. Four," both hands gripped his robes, "they refused." Then she pushed at him to act, "Go save them."

For the first time, Aidan pulled his attention away from her, telling Branson, "Quickly, put her out. I cannot leave her conscious."

"Leave her? Where are you going? Explain," Remy demanded.

"There were four sisters who would not take part in the ritual. She is right to fear for them."

MAX

The magnetic Felix Magnus, voice of the Libertines, had managed to spam Max with a message. He'd been calling for civil disorder. Max thought the only way the world would know it was not just another domestic street brawl was the bands of yellow the protesters had tied around their arms to appear united. Working class Alenans were all in the same gang for the moment.

The conflict was outshining the furor of the religious who were, Max thought, entirely too fucking loud and well represented for their small numbers in Alena. The royalist minority couldn't put enough of their considerable wealth behind the sectarian lunacy to pull the public's growing infatuation away from the uprising. Traditional news speculated about wedding gowns, but people swapped pictures of soldiers painted yellow. And the government, just desperate to hold onto power and align with the winning side, was saying nothing intelligent, but doing nothing stupid.

Max wasn't really needed in Ulphia. Enzo's kids weren't being arrested, and he wasn't going to get his head cracked open while locking arms in the street. He didn't chant slogans or throw paint, so instead he worked on getting into Marlow's data. It was taking time because he'd found a second drive, and she'd done some crazy shit to lock up the hardware. Max didn't want to destroy the thing falling for the traps she'd set.

"Master hack, huh?" Enzo laughed.

"Hell, yes. I saw 'em, right?"

"And how long now?"

Max didn't know. "The whole unit's in a wet tank until I figure out how to keep it from blowing up. I never should have turned those screws."

SALT MOUNTAIN

Nika was glad she wasn't one of the moles in the mountain. Those poor devils hacking away for ore were a desperate lot. When the empire eventually exhausted the lithium brine in the great bowl of the mountain and looked to the elevations for more, they were going to find quite a few of the peaks run through with tunnels.

Nika was not very far away from their folly though. She was in the sky with a hold full of counterfeits stamped with the King's perfect seal. The batteries had half the life of the King's but sold for a third of the price and, making sales even brisker, none of them had exploded in the last five years. The old Jenevuede Pulp Mill, outside the capital with its clandestine refinery, had improved production after burning down its original home in the disused oil refinery.

Erentrude, with hardly any pollution, was still foreign air to Nika. It held the plane lighter, smelled different, and required the darkest sunglasses. Without them, the sun would come down unimpeded and blast through your retinas to scorch the back of your skull. It played havoc on the circular bowl of Salt Mountain, creating such wild drafts not even the dumbest of fools would fly there, which made security incredibly light.

Nika was in their peaks flying for Enzo's new hangar when her eyes began to itch. Smoke. Definitely smoke.

Simultaneously, she scanned the horizon and the panel but saw nothing to account for it. Before she could turn in her seat to look behind, the cause made itself known.

The explosion was a shock in the quiet above the clouds. She flinched and ducked as though a gun had been fired at her back. It had been loud, decisive, and over in the flash that created it. Next would come the flames.

She knew the sound intimately. In the angrier moments of her delinquent youth, she had deliberately overcharged the batteries she'd stolen just to hear them pop. The blaze that followed was mesmerizing. Shock and then long burning beauty.

She still had power in the motor, but the spare light flashed empty. Behind, in the hold, she heard creaks, hissing, and the snap of a buckle ripped from the harness. The batteries sitting over the auxiliary compartment had warmed with the overheating spare. With it now on fire, the cargo was getting hotter, swelling, pushing against the constraint of space. The first hint of smoke would signal quick death. If any of the batteries flared, it would all be over before she could land. She would end as a bang in the sky and a rain of stunning color.

Mountains and more mountains save for the flat in the center. "Sweet sister Sable," Nika swore. The option was insane. Not daring to reduce the throttle, she dropped nose to the ground and dove down the side, aiming for the King's own runway of salt.

~~~~~~

Enzo thought he was back in the same nightmare, only this time he didn't have the innocence to think he could wake them.

137

He had tried to sound calm, "Just put her down and run. Put her down wherever you have to. We know where you are; we will get you out."

Nika kept her phone on through the descent, the hard landing, the sliding stop. Enzo heard her running from the plane, screaming for the soldiers who were speeding to the impromptu landing to turn the vehicle around. "Back! Back! Run the fuck away." But they skidded to a stop beside her and threw her face first on the salt.

Enzo knew they felt the heat of the explosion.

It cracked on and on. The first blast burst into another while the ground was smacked with flaming debris. Enzo heard shouts to run. He heard their first steps crunching over the salt before the tantrum of destruction really kicked off. A flare-up in the center split the plane in half. He heard a flat panel ripped from the ribs flapping free through the air, but he never heard it land as pack after pack detonated in staccato. It was a warehouse full of fireworks set off with a machine gun. The ground splintered open, swallowing what remained of the plane, sinking it in a sizzling hiss of brine, but still the batteries erupted, sending geysers of water splashing across the salt flat and into Enzo's earpiece.

Enzo wondered how far they had gotten. He listened for the worst.

He heard a harsh breath expelled as someone was brought down, and then commands to "Roll, roll, roll," while another was screaming, "I'm on fucking fire!"

His taut muscles weakened to tremors when he finally heard Nika's first words of denial: "God damn liquor, man. Who knew booze could do that?"

RECOVERY

For a week, every time Sable surfaced, she told him, "Go save them."

And Aidan would promise, "They are safe."

Then she found some sort of footing, a little island with space to gather memories, and she asked, "Where are they?"

"In the convent."

"Then they are not safe."

"They are under my protection," he assured.

It was not meant as an accusation, "I was under your protection."

She would never find the memory, and he would never lose it, of the first days when she held him fast by the robes afraid of drowning in an unfamiliar sea of broken ice and battering whirlpools. Sleep only came when the doctor put needle to vein and forced her there, but on waking, she would latch hold again.

Aidan was waiting, hoping that enough of her would gather to recognize she was gone.

Hands wound in his robes, frantic not to drift away and be lost, she had pulled them both to the floor. With rare clarity, she saw the madness of it. Sable spoke through with a frustrated plea, "Help me."

It was what he had hoped against expectation to hear.

Releasing his fear, Aidan submerged himself in the violent current to become the anchor in time, constantly reminding *here and now*.

Here and now, like when she was a child and needed to forget.

Here and now would bring her to the present, above the slipping fragments that gave no support.

She was with him and then she was gone, losing her balance on concepts that could not carry weight, sliding under, coming up, and every time Aidan called her back with *here and now*.

~~~~~~

The king of Erentrude had been schooled in politics, economics, languages, as well as the basics from mathematics to biology, and he took a particular interest in chemistry, but he had never been taught the fundamentals of mental management. To be in the present seemed meaningless in practice when the present was merely the place in which to plan for the future or review the past.

"Few are the numbers that possess the present," Aidan had told him. But it was there he needed to be if he would see Sable.

Aidan had warned, "She is not fit to travel," to the future or the past. The Master and Mentor made the established sound fantastic. Like magic, they all moved through time.

In the beginning, Remy would arrive to find her serene, but within minutes of speaking, he would have managed to turn her blind and frantic. He had tried once to console her, saying, "You will be better soon," but this made things worse, sending her forward and back. Better how? And why was she worse? She went looking for answers while he watched her slip under.

The search would always draw her features together in angst, squinting to see through the confusion. Wherever she went, Remy recognized, it was entirely too bright and the landscape harsh and perplexing.

So Remy learned to stay in the moment, never to mention what laid ahead or behind. He learned it was quiet in the present. And then he learned it was calm. He would visit with chocolates and fruit, intending to be brief, but then, transfixed by her simple smile, he would settle. He began to arrive knowing he would stay, bringing with him a tablet to silently read while she watched.

She stared excessively long, but he did not mind. The expression, so open and defenseless, was too earnest to cause distress. He considered it was her dress. He had never seen her in anything except the austere robes of the order, but here in the medical rooms, she wore pastel-colored cottons that changed the shade of her pale eyes. She looked soft and harmless, her face too vulnerable to be Cloitare.

He watched her slowly chewing on the gifts he brought, returning his gaze with warmth, completely unlike the nun who had run away and without a trace of the guile when she returned. He knew whatever she had been through, she had not come out the same.

~~~~~

"Look, fucker." Max pointed at the screen. "I know where she is. I just don't know how to get her out."

It wasn't what Enzo wanted to hear. He stalked away from the live video of Nika sitting bored on the edge of the stone shelf of a bed.

"I've found her detainment report." Max tapped open a file where he'd saved it. She'd given her name as Ellis Dee. "But this shit is not the same as civilian release. These cunts don't have some hundred arraignments an hour I can lose her in. They don't set bail. The soldiers who arrested her aren't handing it over to a cheap-suited prosecutor to file the charges. All the gaps I use to free our dealers don't exist in their world. She's a single entity being held without charge in a near-empty military prison. Look at it: it's running on a skeleton crew while their buddies are off in Alena hosing down our customers in the detention camps. Every soldier in that prison knows she's there. And making her disappear is not any easier with her good looks or that goddamn wheels-on-fire arrival she did. Some bullshit electronic message by a general to release her is going to be hard checked, then they'll know I'm in their system and someone is trying to get her out. You need to sit the fuck down and give me time to find something to exploit."

Max had slept very little in past six months. He'd spent the first five months obsessed with Marlow's memory drives, but since Nika went down, he'd been snorting lines of amphetamines and eating anodyne to take the edge off.

143

While he waited for some change in Nika's status, he'd been scrolling through military reports all the way back to the day Marlow had vanished. He didn't think the army had her. It was a strange coincidence the King's cousin was on the same train when Marlow went missing. But if they did have her, fuck knows what name she had given them either, so he searched for Alenan landings and missions, but those results referred to a file called Retrieve that was off the shared lines. The file was on a private network and Max couldn't access it unless he was in-house. Unable to make progress there, he searched through the financial accounts for Alenan and Eudokian expenses, but there was nothing of interest. When he searched for the Cloitare, he was directed again to the in-house server and the file Retrieve.

While he cursed the closed network, the screen with Nika filled with soldiers. She rose in alarm and retreated to the wall while slapping them back. One soldier locked her arms and another went for her shirt.

Enzo grabbed Max's shoulder. Neither could speak for fear of what they might see. But the soldiers went for her arm. Her friends saw her head loll as the needle was pulled from her vein.

As she was hauled from the cell for questioning, Max kicked back from the desk and dropped his head flat to his knees. "We need fucking Marlow."

Enzo knew this too, but said, "I suspect Marlow needs Marlow."

~~~~~

Remy was there when the doctor said the bandage on her wrist should stay off. Branson had told her, "When it is properly healed, we can discuss ways to reduce the scars."

But she had dismissed the idea with finality. "It will not be necessary." She had mastered the present and moved to a fatalistic future Remy found foreboding.

The King spoke to Aidan in the hall outside the room where she slept. "She is not going back to the Cloitare."

"She is the Mother of All. She *is* the Cloitare."

"She will not pass its doors again."

"She must. She is the Mother of All and she is obliged to unite her family." Aidan stopped Remy from proceeding in the futile argument. "She *will* gain control of her house. In destroying her, they have transcended her myth. She is more powerful than you can imagine. The old mothers assured the young that if she were truly the mother the prophets revealed then the mind could not harm her. She returns from a place no shattered life has. They do not know why. They do not know where I taught her to hide. It is impossible for them that she should return, and yet she does. Her title is incontestable, as it must be to protect you."

Remy was infuriated with the obscure. "Protect me from what my own people can't?"

"The future." Then Aidan inclined his head with deference to the memory. "And the past."

145

~~~~~~~

When the scar on Sable's wrist became a thick band of red and her palms began to scar white, Aidan sought out the King.

Remy was alone in his rooms sitting in the large circle of couches and chairs that seldom held anyone except his three advisors. He was looking again through pictures of the plane that had unexpectedly landed and then exploded on the salt flat. Images of the wreckage were followed by remnants of the batteries that had been recovered with the Ministry of Energy's royal seal. Had the salt not cracked under the repeated blasts and dropped the plane into the brine, nothing would have remained.

The pilot was being held by the army. Berringer had told Remy she was claiming to have no knowledge of what she was carrying, but this contradicted her running from the plane warning it was about to explode. After some nights awake, she admitted she had picked up the load on a disused airfield some eight hours away, but when a team went to inspect it, they found it had washed out in heavy rains months previous. If she was unaware of the rains and the erosion, it was likely her plane had been loaded at a strip closer to the mine. She told them to believe what they wanted but held to her story, telling the interrogator, "Did your boys tell you how I came smoking down the mountain? I am a bitch of a pilot. I don't need an airstrip. So what if it washed out? I can put any plane down on any runway no matter its condition. I picked up where I said I picked up." They had shot her full of hypnotics, but the most she would tell them was, "I've had better." Even when they showed her pictures of the mucked up strip with the cavernous hole in the center, after she cracked with spontaneous laughter at the ridiculousness of her assertion, she still insisted she'd done it. "Damn bumpy it was. But like I said, I'm a bitch of a pilot."

"Anyone can be broken," Berringer repeated Sable's words.

When Remy did not want to hear what his advisors had to say, he would retreat behind the desk that overlooked the sitting space. "No," he said after some thought. "Just hold her and wait. She's a pilot. She'll want her freedom soon enough."

Remy moved behind the desk again to receive Master Aidan. The man always dominated a room, but he seemed larger this time, threatening not with authority but zeal. He was a mass of vitality focused on Remy, and Remy was alarmed.

"I will speak to you this once with my true voice, King of the Clementyne Dynasty, may you not be the last. Hear me and know what you hear is the truth."

Remy felt embraced. He felt like he was quite small, someone's pet, and he'd been scooped up into the hand to be cradled there for his own good. He felt the boom of Aidan's speech resonate in his chest and head, vibrating his mouth and nose, terrifying his heart.

"The time has come to fulfill the bargain made for your crown. The Mother of All is among us and you are the son that needs her. And I, in whose name it was written, will grant you both a choice: you may save the other or not of your own will. May neither

147

of you falter or all this within and all that beyond is lost. Your rule will end and the blackest night will begin."

The master put the small animal down. The reverberation would settle gradually while Remy regained possession of his self.

"I will take the Bound Bride into the convent. She will know nothing of the preparations that occur beyond its doors. If you would save her, have your witnesses ready for when we emerge. I will give you one month. Stand at the altar ready to receive her. I will then give to her the same option. She will accept you or she will be the death of us all."

The sensation over Remy vanished leaving him in a hard reality with sharp edges. He considered for the very first time that the prophet promised by scripture before him was something more than a man. But through the fear of such unknowns, the threats and ultimatums of Aidan's words began to solidify in Remy's mind. He knocked away the touch of something ethereal. His royal prerogative had just been invasively assaulted and provoked to rage. "I refuse every part of it this very minute."

"Know what you do: to ensure the prophesy lives, the mothers will kill her and your people will tear clergy and empire to the ground in her blood."

Remy's temper gained strength. "I will never allow the Cloitare, which includes you, near her again."

"The nuns will call her an imposter."

"Then she will be free."

"I will not allow it."

Remy lost what remained of his poise. "*Mothers in hell*," he shouted, "all to protect me?"

But Aidan was impassive. "I do not care specifically about you. You are acceptable for your role, exemplary if I must, perhaps even fated. I am attached to what happens if you fail. I am conscious of what occurs should this dynasty fall. You will marry her, or she will die."

~~~~~

The Master and Mentor had bowed deeply when told he was forbidden to see Sable again. "Such is the King's will." But Remy knew it would not end at that.

As he left his rooms for the medical rooms, he vowed Sable would never learn of the threats he had heard. He did not as yet know what he would do with her, where he would put her to keep her safe, or how Girard might fix this with the public. All he knew definitely was he was tired and wanted to go back to the crystal white calm of the lithium field.

When he entered her room, he was brought to a stop. She was once again in the robes of the Cloitare, awaiting her mentor's return.

"Master Aidan has returned to the cloister and you will be moved tomorrow to secure quarters." His voice still held annoyance from his exchange with Aidan.

"Remy," she smiled to console him, "the time for that is long past. There is only one way to end this that does not result in your ruin."

His irritation with them both could be felt. "You will not be permitted to return to the convent."

Her serenity deepened to meet his frustration. "It must be concluded with the Cloitare."

"I am told they will kill you, but I suspect you know this. I assume you intend to push them to this end. You will be held under my guard until a suitable conclusion is agreed between us."

Before he could leave, she took his hand, and then opening the fist, she drew it up to her mouth to press her lips into his palm. She said, "There will come a time when you will doubt yourself. You will think you could have done more, or you could have done different, but you will be wrong. You must remember, this was all decided by fate, or accident, it matters not which. All it was ever going to take was one break in the tracks for everyone's plans to be pulled off the rails. Everything after that was set, just waiting to happen. Remember, when you think back, remember there was nothing you could do to stop what happens."

~~~~~~

Retrospective vision, Berringer cursed its clarity. Why, he rapped his thoughtless head, why had he not done more than increase

150

the guards? He should have barred all the windows and bolted the doors. Guards weren't enough.

A rough stone-sharpened butter knife and a pile of glass stacked at the base of the centuries-old window explained her escape. When Berringer reviewed the video, he knew where to look. She was the specter that hung at the top of the arch, carefully chiseling at the lead for hours. She had removed the black robe to climb the room's stones in nothing but the tight under suit, a cat burglar breaking out. The outside cameras showed the windows, curtained at the bottom, bare but dark above the transom, with a shadow prying loose panes before vanishing to set them aside. Over and over, she put her bare feet to the rocks and materialized at the top until she had cleared a space wide enough to escape.

The guard below leaned against the wall, spoke into his radio, and later talked with another guard on patrol, but he heard nothing to draw his attention to the dismantling above.

He didn't hear her slink from the hole or pull herself slowly barefoot, robe tied around her waist, along the rock face, stealth stepping down the line of cameras until she could drop. She donned her robe and appeared as a nun walking the grounds. She entered the palace and then disappeared behind the double doors.

Remy covered his eyes but did not hide his angry mouth. "Send someone to the doors. Tell Aidan I wish to speak."

~~~~~

Girard made Berringer watch while she played the wall creeping segment again, and then once more while she laughed with apprehension and respect. "I don't know which of us to feel sorrier for if he marries her."

Laudin joined them in the King's rooms. "Then it's settled. I will arrange for as few dignitaries as possible to attend, but what excuse am I going to give for the wide-ranging insults?" He looked to Catherine.

"Invite them to the reception. If she turns and runs at the altar, then we can at least hope no one sees Berringer tackle her in the grass."

"Find an excuse," Remy waved it at Girard, "to hold it in the small chapel." He felt slow and numb with fatigue. "Bring in my parents, my sisters, a cousin or uncle, that will fill the pews."

"And if she runs?" Berringer had no desire to tackle a nun.

"Let her."

Remy wanted to return to the tranquility of the wide-open salt flat with the comforting chug of pumps, the salt you could smell, the burn of the sun in summer and the bite of the wind in winter. He wanted to drop his black shades to this mayhem and be blinded by white.

He imagined in time Aidan's admission would fade. "She is not entirely sane. You have seen the expression; you will know when she goes under."

"How insane are we talking?" Girard had asked. "I know we can't hope she's just talking-to-dolls crazy. So what do you mean?"

"Who knows what form her madness will take? It is yet unformed."

The great apparition who rose from the dust of Cloitare scriptures, who had entered their lives over two decades previous, pulled Remy close so that only he could hear. "After this, I leave her with you, to find from you what she will. Know what I have done for you. I have made you a weapon, a shield, and a refuge. She will return to you in multitude what you give her. Give her the whole of yourself and she will make you a legend. Give her nothing and, I promise you, she will drop you into the abyss and show you the void. Understand what you have: she could make me a god, yet I give her to you."

ACCEPTANCE

Every time she moved into the distance, she was overwhelmed by Aidan. She had not pressed to go further. He was the mentor and her mind was fractured. Once, she had been the unfathomable water the Cloitare could not disturb, but they had found a way to freeze her then shatter her. She stepped across the floes looking for land. She tipped less frequently, but the waters were perilous.

The distance seemed preferable, but Aidan's infinite presence said no.

They walked outside the cloister that day. It was the first time since her return she had walked in the open in daylight. It should have been to the sound of the grounds under care, but nothing she heard fit with her memory. It was silent of life. There were no gardeners, no visitors, no one crunching across the gravel in a hurry to see the King or his advisors. She pushed into the distance again but found only Aidan.

They had stepped through the palace's silent halls to exit the back that spread over the garden. Bordered by shrubs, they walked the grass to the boundary where the old chapel sat square and squat. The walk had been unhurried. As they climbed the chapel steps, Sable felt a mental embrace, as though Aidan were holding her dear. The steps were few and as they reached the top, Sable felt his affection turn to loss, such terrible sorrow she turned to Aidan to question his pain. He held her firmly before himself and then leaned her to the side, to see beyond him to the palace, the upper windows filled with cameras and recorders.

154

She exhaled the betrayal and closed her eyes to the trap. She knew before the spin what waited behind. Pushed without effort to the open doors, she hid behind the Cloitare Stare.

To those in the chapel, it appeared like a teacher imparting final words on a pupil. Aidan held her shoulders in the open arch and leaned down to tell her, "It is now your choice what happens to the King, his empire, the future, your people. I will not stop you from leaving. I have never lied to you, anawa. I tell you, if you turn your back on him, the King will die this year."

Aidan pushed her forward so she wouldn't fall back, and then he was gone. Behind her, the people recorded her judgment. If she turned away, the King's people would turn with her. The Cloitare would disown her. She would not have the influence to talk down the crowds.

She scanned the chapel for one of the King's advisors, any of them, to see if they supported this action, but the chapel was filled with faces she did not recognize.

The King stepped the distance between the chapel's two pews and held out his hand.

She had told him there was nothing he could do and here he had done it. She felt the train wreck. She felt breaking acceptance.

~~~~~

The General had Girard in his ear. "Keep the family back and the way clear. You have to trust me."

Keeping Remy's family held livid in the chapel had not been the plan. Berringer was watching the King and Bride return across the garden to the palace. He radioed back, "She looks fine to me."

"She isn't. She's a woman that's just been tricked into submission and she'll barely be keeping her head together."

It was not the grand wedding the public expected. It was quiet and grim with the King in muted regalia and the Bride as a nun. They walked alone and silent from a crypt of a chapel through the palace and into the King's private quarters.

Sable was still looking from dead eyes when she entered. She swept them over the valets waiting in the corner where Girard had pushed them and then to Girard holding open the door that led to final privacy. Catherine was closing it behind Remy when Sable started tearing at the headdress and robe.

Remy removed the short sword from his hip and the sash from his chest in preparation for the mental collapse. Sable ripped her headdress and hair free in one violent move, then shrugged off the robe like it were on fire and stamped it out.

He approached her, hands out to pacify, but she backed away shaking her head. He expected her to accuse, but she came out pleading, "I am so sorry."

"Come here. Everything is fine."

156

But she continued to step back around the room. "I didn't know what to do. I didn't know. So many people were watching."

He lunged for her, grabbed her, saying, "No, hush," and pulled her close.

She rested a mere moment against him. She said, "I've killed you."

He was going to tell her she was wrong, she would see, but they heard a voice, the tone high in arrogance, demanding to see Sable, Vesna was insisting.

In the next instant, Remy felt himself turned and released. He saw Sable flash silver against black and open the door. The scabbard fell in the arch, the blade was free, and Remy was racing to catch her.

Girard said, "Whoa, sister," but Sable spun Girard in a circle and drove her into the King.

Giving her his best smile, Laudin raised his hands and started to say, "There's no need for—" but before he could finish, Sable ducked past him.

Both hands on the hilt, she was swinging down with speed for the mother's neck when Berringer ran into her. It should have been simple. He had one hand on Sable's wrist, another coming under her arm, and knew he would disarm her in a second, but before he had control, she cartwheeled away, tossing herself over his arm to land in a crouch. She meant to get past him, but he grabbed once more for her wrist and also her head, pushing her sideways and down, but again she flipped with him.

It took him back. He remembered his first loss on the mats when he thought none could defeat him. He remembered the mirthful lesson, *You can't hold the wind.*

What have you done, old man? he asked the voice from the past.

The General reconsidered his stance and the Bride did as well.

He was the fortress that held against the storm. She couldn't move him, wanted to be no place near him, but still she wanted what lay at his back. He circled with her attention keeping the mother behind.

Remy commanded, "Sable, that is enough," and came forward to control her, but Berringer knew she was not in her head. He told the King to stand clear, but no one was listening.

With the General's attention dividing, Sable stepped back in the room, the blade held before her, angling toward the King to separate the General from what she was after.

Berringer ordered, "Vesna get out."

The astonishment that held her was broken and the mother moved for her life.

Sable's eyes went left for the King. She feinted with the point and then flipped to the right.

The General fell for her bluff. He reached out thinking he'd find her before Remy, then had to race for the door.

Sable was swinging up from a roll with the blade in one hand. She had Vesna in line with the edge when Berringer stepped into her arm and was at last able to force her around. They danced down the wall, both fighting to lead.

Go where the wind blows until you find yourself shelter.

Turning to the outside, to the wall, and again out, he stopped the next spin against a substantial carved cabinet. Squared in its corner, Sable couldn't circle or turn, and the sword that was not meant for him became her undoing. Locking his hand over hers on the grip, he began to pull up. The sharpened edge of the blade followed her leg.

The General didn't want to hurt her—he didn't want to be hurt either—but the idea Sable might slip him and he'd have to chase her again made him firmly determined. Still pulling up on the grip, he drew the blade away from her leg, but she pushed forward to follow, knowing he wouldn't cut her, hoping to drive him away, to give her space from the wall; but he slammed her back, knee into thigh, hand twisting the scarred wrist that was forced to drop steel, while with his other, he fought for control until he restrained her completely.

He watched her try to shift and saw her expression turn to complete disbelief. Then, in the next instant, as realization conquered confusion, there flashed in her face recognition. It reminded him of the night she had first run away. She had spotted him from the gardens and against the stone barrier, she had pulled back her headdress. Now, against another wall, they recognized each other once more, she with a slight rise of the lip, half a smirk, surprised it was him. This time, she inclined her head, but she offered respect not collusion.

159

Then Vesna's voice, rising with indignation, set the wind raging again. Berringer saw the sanity in Sable's eyes go out. She'd cast them through the wall, down the hall, and fixed them for blood.

He thought, *She's gone. Utterly gone and not coming back.*

The General shouted out the door, "Get that goddamn mother out of here."

~~~~~~

When Sable had returned enough to her senses for Berringer to release her, no one doubted her when she warned, "If I see any one of those black-clad bitches, I will tear off their heads and roll them through the halls."

She had retreated to Remy's bedroom to prepare for the reception. "You're not considering it?" Berringer had asked.

But Remy was adamant, "Keep the Cloitare behind their doors. It was a moment of madness. It has passed. The tension is gone. She will behave." Then less resolute, "Nevertheless, stay near."

To observe her now, no one would imagine that hours before Berringer had felt the need to clear the King's chambers of everything sharp. She had stepped from his room in a gold-colored dress of silk, lace, and beads. Hiding her scarred wrist was a wide jeweled cuff that Remy had made especially for her. She would prove herself expert at keeping her hands clasped, her palms down, always in mind to conceal the ritualized X cut into her flesh.

160

But she didn't fully transform until they left the private quarters behind. Her posture relaxed, shifted to ease, and she put on a smile. In the next breath, she made it appear perfectly sincere.

Throughout the long reception, she held the right tension in her eyes and her mouth so that everyone she met was riveting beyond measure and incredibly dear. And not once did she falter.

Remy had assumed, but he couldn't confirm, not until they stepped back into the private halls, that she was not genuinely enthralled. But once alone, her face relaxed, her body hardened, and Sable as he knew her reemerged.

He showed her to the door that would be her rooms and made to leave, but she held him back, saying, "I will join you."

He took her hand and said kindly, "In time. We have time."

But she shook her head to deny it. "Until this is …" she shrank from saying the word *consummated*, so said instead, "… *finished*, I'm still a nun. My place is in the convent."

He looked on her with compassion. "They will never know."

"Yes, they will, and they do, and they are waiting."

He smiled with indulgence, "How do you think this is possible?"

"Within the mind, the Cloitare are one."

Remy was flummoxed, but he was more concerned to see the fear in Sable's face, a fear turned to begging, "Please, Remy. I need the division. Please don't deny me."

Wrapping an arm around her waist, he assured, "Sable, I would never deny you. If this is what will give you peace, then yes, you will join me."

DOUBLE DOORS

At 3:00 a.m., Berringer was woken by the call. "You're going to want to see this." It was a soldier near the Cloitare doors.

"Send it to me."

"You won't want copies of this traveling. You'll want to see the video here."

At the guard station, Berringer watched the screen and felt the sickness spread.

He went to wake the King himself. "It's your Bride. She's taken an axe and entered the convent."

They passed the place she'd taken it off the wall.

"Was it sharp?"

"What she took wouldn't need to be." Berringer knew what horrendous injuries even a dull axe could inflict. He hoped she was just hacking through a lock, maybe breaking into the library vault she had spoken of years before.

In his robe, Remy stood before the double doors. "Bang on them again," he told the guard.

When she'd been behind the doors for close to an hour, Remy told the General, "Get explosives. I want them down."

"Remy ... Sir ... *Sire* ... " Berringer was prepared to plead for restraint.

"Down, Lucas. I want them open or down."

Walking away, Berringer told a guard, "Get Laudin and Girard."

~~~~~

In the manner he found most conducive to changing a person's mood, Laudin was speaking leisurely. "I suspect she has merely gone in with the thing for effect, to grab their attention." He sounded unconcerned. "I am sure they don't know we're here. The doors are thick and no one has heard us at this hour. We risk coming across as rather over-reactive."

Remy didn't look at Laudin. "The doors opened for her, and she did not knock. They are aware I am here."

"Ah, yes, though they were likely expecting her." Laudin shifted. "She is quite capable. Obviously trained. I am sure she is in no danger."

When that failed, he tried, "It is clearly a ritual. She has gone to symbolically sever ties. The clergy are quite active at sunrise. I imagine she will walk through these doors with the first rays of light. We could go have some drinks while we wait."

"General, where are my demolitions?"

Laudin knew when the man could not be talked down, but he tried regardless. "Remy, can we consider for a moment the consequences of this action?"

164

Around the corner, blind to the King's distress and deaf to the discussion, Berringer had amassed soldiers and a medical team, and running toward him with bags over their shoulders were Lieutenant Fallon and company to see if there was a less violent way to open the doors. To the men with explosives, Berringer had told them to pick and then check and recheck their munitions with meticulous, exhaustive care. He told Remy, "Soon," and then the doors began to open.

In the moment they parted enough to allow passage, one then two more nuns in robes without shape, torn and untied, stumbled forward supporting a fourth. Beyond the vestibule, still in the large first chamber of the cloister, Sable followed with the axe dripping at her side. Berringer could see her dress was a devastating color, streaked dark over gold, and her mouth was scarlet.

It all happened at once. As Remy pulled the injured nuns past, he called for Sable, but behind her, a group of mothers entered the chamber and one snapped her name with damning censure, "*Sister Sable.*"

The tone made Sable tighten her eyes. She hefted the axe into both hands and with booming authority, instructed, "Close the doors."

The inner doors sealed before anyone could get near them.

~~~~~~

~~~~~~

"Did she do this to you?" Remy asked.

The nuns that could walk had the Stare. One said, "No."

"The four," said Girard. "These are the four she sent Aidan after."

While medics assessed the nuns and removed them, Lieutenant Fallon dropped his bag at the inner door and prepared his gear. He was searching for an electric or magnetic signature, a wireless signal, something to account for how the nuns knew when someone was on the other side without them knocking, without peep holes, or obvious cameras. When he had given up hope of finding an explanation, the doors were pulled opened again.

The nuns in the chamber were on their knees, faces to the floor, and Sable walked from them trailing a hem soaked in gore. She was, from cruel face to bare feet, splashed in red.

Remy advanced, shedding his robe, and Berringer stalked beside him to grab the axe from Sable's hand. When the General called his troops to assist, the mothers rose and refused, denying anyone not of the order the right to enter, and pushed forward to remove them.

Evicted from the convent, they walked without speaking away from both sets of closing doors, a procession of silence that moved through the halls leaving savage foot-prints that ended in the King's rooms.

Remy retreated behind his desk to put something between them, to get distance from the monstrosity. He had never before had

166

his right of command so blatantly, so violently disregarded. It was not a question he ever had to ask. He was furious. "Why? Explain this. Why?"

She was detached, appearing remote with her own certainty. "The four sisters are in the condition you saw for their loyalty to me. I went to get them out."

"I could have gotten them out! With dialogue! You took an axe."

"There was no time for discussion. You saw them. One is close to death."

"You had no right without asking me."

Her expression was too removed to know how this struck her. After considering it for several quiet moments, she must have decided she would have been denied because she demanded suddenly of Berringer, "Would you leave soldiers behind?"

She was reaching out to him for an approval he could not give.

Remy exclaimed, "No one left them. You never gave anyone a chance to leave them." He looked her up and down. "Whose blood? Whose blood is that?"

She glanced at herself then went far away, gazing blankly ahead.

"Did you kill Vesna?"

"Yes."

Remy did, and yet did not, expect the answer. He certainly did not expect it to be so casually admitted. He steadied himself and then,

167

showing a false calm, a cool to reflect hers, asked, "How many people did you hurt?"

"Hurt?" She repeated the word slowly like it was foreign and her mouth had never formed it.

Berringer took in the whole of it. He knew her dress was not red. The long skirt that escaped the King's night jacket was staining the wool carpet. Through the lace on her chest, he saw the flesh still wet beneath. In places where the fabric was saturated, it sponged color through the robe meant to conceal it. You didn't get covered like that unless you had gotten up close, had really gotten stuck into it. It covered her hands, her neck, and colored her mouth like she had kissed them dying and then wiped it away. The axe had been wet straight down to the grip of the handle. She had not hurt anyone. Berringer made the correction for Remy: "How many did you kill?"

Now it was clear, but she wasn't going to say. She looked recalcitrant; she looked away.

Slamming the desk, Remy demanded, "How many?"

"Eight."

The King dropped into his chair. Laudin heaved air from his stomach and Girard hit a short, hysterical note of astonishment. But Sable's posture defied criticism.

Remy shook his head and stared at her. "Eight." The number had no meaning. "Eight," he said it again. "You killed eight people tonight." Then near defeated, "What are they going to do? What have you done?"

"They will do *nothing*," she bit the word with contempt. Her hate for the clergy animated her. "They will do as they have always done and maintain the illusion. They will remain silent and unquestionable."

"You left them eight bodies. You went in and slaughtered them. Even if we could … just how can any of us avoid questions with eight bodies?"

"They will hide them, they will burn them, they will enshrine them in oak, deify them in gold, or dig up the flagstones to bury them, and if all else fails, they can damn well eat them, but you need not worry as the Cloitare do not betray their own."

"The scars on your hands say otherwise."

Sable flinched. The defiance was gone and the color of her cheeks began to match her dress.

"So," Remy observed, "you are capable of shame, but for all the wrong reasons." He swept his hand across her blood-stained appearance, "You have been trained. Who taught you?"

She met the question with a face full of shock and then dropped her focus to the floor. Berringer watched her breath deepen.

Remy waited before angrily asking again, "Who trained you?"

She closed her eyes to say it. "I cannot tell you."

Silence as Remy absorbed what she said. Chewing anger, he asked, "And why not?"

"I gave my word before training." Her attention stayed low. "I swore not to say."

169

Remy looked at Berringer with fury. "Now I have two of you? Is this common? Do all masters of strategy demand such anonymity? Is she trained in the same way as you?"

Berringer answered the last question. "Our ways are very different."

Remy considered her: the bowed head, the flesh and dress stained. He spoke harshly to dismiss her, "You require sleep."

She made herself humble. "I would go to the sister that is near death." Then in concession to the long night of impertinences, she offered without irony, "If you will permit."

Remy pointed at her clothes.

"I will, of course, change."

He nodded with a numb, unreadable face. "Of course you will."

~~~~~~

"Mass murderer, who would have guessed?" Girard walked with Berringer outside the King's rooms. "Well, now that we know in what manner her madness will manifest, *wow*, did your job not just get more exciting? What are you going to do with her? Do you have enough men for her? You'll want to remind the ones you've put on her that she climbs walls." Catherine laughed gaily. "I've never seen you stepping barefoot across the side of the palace. Never seen you backflip either. What do you call this thing she does?"

170

Berringer mumbled, "Whirling Wind."

"Whirling Wind." Catherine played with the words, "Whirling, whirling. Imagine the look on Laudin's face if she lays waste to a delegation of Sierrans. Whirls us all into a frothy mix of blood and war."

The General grumbled, unamused.

"Strange, isn't it, that you both have secret masters? If only you were trained in the same art." Catherine was watching him for a reaction. "Brings to mind the little whispers I hear of acrobatic killers, trained by some elusive old man. This master and his school are so mysteriously hidden, it's become practically mystical in the telling. Every teenage kid with a sword wants to say he's been trained by the Laughing Master. Have you heard of him?"

"No."

"Pity. Try as I do, I can't seem to find him."

"Excuse me, Catherine." Berringer pulled away to follow Sable to the medical rooms

Catherine's interest was too intense, and even if she were not trying to interrogate him, he would hardly joke about it. The whole night was disturbing enough on its own, but Berringer knew, and he suspected Catherine did as well, it was not in the least common to swear confidence before training. He knew of only one master that asked it.

Sable had looked to him for support in her actions because she knew who he was. As she whirled around the room trying to kill Vesna, he recognized her as one of his father's trained pets, little devils designed to torment the son. They were the scourge of Berringer's youth, those "flipping little monkeys."

His father had dug up the lost Way of the Wind in a search through his own master's collection of writings detailing the methods of ancient schools. Bored and unchallenged, the master strategist revived the art and discovered a deficiency in his prodigy and heir. At the time Berringer left his father's school to enter the military as an officer, his father had resurrected from the air just two who could successfully harass his son into swearing.

The Laughing Master thought they were funny as hell. They wouldn't engage. Their strategy was evasion. You'd step in to block or control, but rather than make contact, they'd just wheel away, spinning you in circles until they could land a knife in your back. There were so many reasons Berringer didn't like them. There was nothing honorable about them; they were strictly assassins. The forgotten school had called them the Whirling Wind, but ever since Berringer had cursed one a flipping monkey, his father had been training the clever little beasts to ruin his life.

The secret strategist would have known whom he trained, but he would not have predicted the skills would be held by one that would go feral. Berringer respected his father with great devotion, but he believed the man's mischievous humor could very well be the undoing of them both.

THE TIES THAT BIND

Enzo watched her wrap her arms around her knees and rock. He wanted to yell at Max to stop waiting and do something.

Nika was bored past screaming. She couldn't do this shit. This was some shit Marlow could do, sit in a white cell for days on never-ending days turned to weeks into months with the lights hysterically on and only the T-shirt and shorts she was wearing for amusement. She knew the exact number of stitches in all the hems and how the numbers varied as the clothes were changed.

Marlow had once tried to teach her to attend her thoughts, had told her to observe them and be aware. Nika had done it for a few days with Marlow right beside her, tapping her hand every time her attention strayed. But following her thoughts only served to convince Nika she was completely insane. She'd been repeating the same words and ideas, had conceived nothing original, and all of it was nonsense.

"It is the understanding that leads to silence," Marlow had said.

"Fuck that, bitch." Nika had swallowed a handful of sedatives and passed out. She woke up declaring, "I never want to play that game again. I do not have the skills for it."

They were barely sixteen and Nika had not considered it since. She had said at the time, "We'd have more fun if I taught you to fly."

The two had met on a faraway coast while Nika was standing before the flaming hull of a ship. In the first dark of night, she

173

realized she was not alone. It was more a sensation than any noise that made Nika look. And there was a redhead creepily standing beside her, silently studying Nika's work.

She was about to tell her to fuck off for the scare, but the girl's face was so reverent and serene, it reminded Nika of a statue in the children's cemetery. Nika turned back to the boat and asked a question. When she received no reply—which had been happening a lot since the war—she asked it again in the Sierran language. "It's gorgeous, isn't it?"

Marlow returned in Sierran, "It puts off a lovely heat."

"It's alive."

The unexpected visitor pondered the notion. "There is energy, but it is not alive in any sense I recognize."

The accent was from Erentrude, and the pronunciations were genteel society. Nika looked the girl up and down. She was dressed for the slums. Nika switched languages again, this time to Erentrude. "You've seen too many highbrow movies."

"Yes," she agreed in her native tongue. "It is quite irritating, is it not?"

Nika thought she was spectacularly weird. She pointed at the fire and asked, "You want to see it breathe?"

The stranger held Nika's expression sincerely. "Yes, I very much would."

"Eat a few of these."

The redhead took the bag of mushrooms and handed it back empty. Nika had laughed. "Yeah, you're gonna see shit breathe alright. You let me know when, and I'll start another fire."

Hours of walking later, Marlow stopped before a Cloitare temple built of wood. She said, "Show me it lives."

However weird she was, weirder than Nika, Nika knew right then that she loved her.

When the flames broke the windows and licked up the walls, Marlow agreed, "It is beautiful, and it is alive."

"Let me show you more. It gets so much better when shit explodes."

What Nika wouldn't give right now, in the white walls of prison, for a lighter. She rocked and tried not to follow her thoughts.

When she heard the bolt being released in the door, she fought down her excitement. To have a conversation, even just to deny information, would be freedom.

Enzo watched her walk from the cell. Minutes later, she was returned. She fought at the door but was shoved in regardless, and then Enzo heard her scream a question at the guards before they withdrew.

~~~~~~

Berringer read and then reread the transcript. What interested him was not part of the interview when the prisoner suggested yet again they should all "go snort a line of your daddy's cum," it was just something she yelled from her cell: "What were you fuckers doing in Eudokia?"

Berringer left the report but kept coming back to the question. Something about it stuck. It was the accusation of someone who knew better, of someone who had been there. He wondered what had been on the train that was of interest to her. There was no record the train had been shifting counterfeit batteries, which didn't mean they weren't there, the damn sheriff could have been selling them, but the woman was a pilot. Why would she care?

Puzzling over it, he called the prison, "Keep her awake."

Enzo and Max took turns monitoring the screen. The soldiers repeatedly gripped her shoulder to give her a light shake. They kept her moving, walking the short steps of the cell, standing then sitting then pulling her up again when she tried to rest her head against the wall. Deep into the third day, the young soldiers left.

Enzo slapped Max on the thigh. "The muscles are gone."

They watched a trim figure walk in with a chair and motion for Nika to sit on the stone bed. Enzo noted, "That's gonna be a hard son of a bitch."

"Is that …?"

"General Bear?"

176

"Aw fuck."

"Corporal?" the General barked out the door. "Why hasn't she got a mattress? Get one in here now." He looked Nika over and commented, "You look like you could use a coffee." Again, he turned his voice out the door, "Bring her a coffee."

From the corridor, Nika could just make out someone cautioning the prisoner might throw it at him, but he stared at her and said firmly, "No, she won't do that," then asked, "Black, cream, sugar?"

"Anything," she said. When the coffee arrived, he let her drink and then hold the warmth of the cup to her head.

With his hands clasped between his open knees, the General sat forward and said, "You've got yourself into a bit of trouble."

He was waiting, but as much as she wanted to hug him for the drink, she wasn't talking.

"That was a great plane you had. Blue Hawk 599. I used to fly one back in my youth. Couldn't have made it come down the mountain like you did, but it was a hell of a plane."

She hid her smile in the coffee.

"Have you eaten? I'll make sure they bring you something after we talk so you can get some decent sleep." He sat back. "I remember nearly killing myself in that bird." He laughed at the memory. "You know how the altimeter freezes if it's rained?"

She drank to keep from laughing.

"I was so low I could have read a gravestone on that mountain. But then I was never much of a pilot. Where'd you learn to fly like that?

"My father."

"Started you young, did he?"

"*Mmm,*" she nodded.

"Best way really. All the real geniuses start young. What'd you start in?"

"A Redbird."

Berringer laughed so genuinely she laughed with him.

"They're shit, aren't they?"

"I'm surprised you're alive. No wonder you're good." He smiled on her. "Kid, I like you. I don't want to hold you here. Youth wasn't made for walls. What was on the train?"

"No one you'd know," she said it before she knew she was thinking it.

"Don't worry about it." He waved away the look of self-censure. "We already knew you were at the hospital." He was fishing and trying to pull something in. "You'll fly across all of hell to save someone you love." He cast again, "It's a pity what happened to them."

"*Fuck you.*" She let loose with the screaming accusation again. "Fuck you for it. What did you—? Oh, fuck you."

He let the tired defeat of her last words settle her shoulders low before offering, "Just ask me and I'll fix it."

She considered him so earnestly, Berringer thought she might accept his offer and reveal her interest, but then she abruptly shook the idea off, finished the drink, and said, "No, I'm done. You're good and I'm stupid, but I'm done."

"Alright, kid. I'll make sure they treat you right, and when you want my help, you just ask."

~~~~~~

Berringer questioned Major Dominic, "Did anything happen in Eudokia you failed to share?"

"Sir?"

"Did your men hurt any civilians?"

"No, sir, none at all."

Berringer didn't like the direction his mind kept going. There'd been someone on the train the pilot held his uniform responsible for affecting. Berringer watched Sable from the second floor window. She was staring with Cloitare eyes at the stammering housekeeper who hoped to affirm all was to Sable's wishes.

Poor nervous woman, Berringer thought, *there was not a single wish of Sable's she could fulfill.*

Berringer could see Sable was dismal and wasted. She'd been caught ten months ago and had returned to drop before the King a well-shaped beauty which not even the bulk of robes could conceal. Her face had been pleasantly colored by the sun, and despite having

179

spent a month in a military hospital, she was radiant with life. Even six weeks past, when she had pulled an axe from the wall, she still maintained just enough vitality to wield it, but now the General saw her ghostly white in the sun, hollow and haunted. She hadn't looked this bad during all the days and nights she spent next to the injured nun's bed. The four nuns had been moved into a domestic room weeks ago, and even Amele, who no one dreamed would live, now seemed vigorous compared to Sable.

Berringer knew the reason: the King would not speak with her. Remy wanted her to say she was sorry, but Sable would only bow her head and respond, "I will not lie to you." In the first week after the massacre, Berringer had heard her begging forgiveness, but Remy said she wanted absolution without guilt and denied it. Sable did not think she had done wrong. When Remy asked her if she would do it again the same, she pleaded for him not to make her answer.

They presented pleasant faces at meals, but when the door to the private hall closed, she would go someplace distant and frozen. Every day she went farther, someplace colder.

Berringer knew he couldn't directly ask her about the pilot and then hope to guess her feelings. He needed her to ask him. He wanted to see her feign disinterest but have to ask nonetheless. If she were anyone else, he would call her to his office and let her see a picture of the pilot on his desk, but he could not think of a reason Sable would need to come. He felt awkward doing it, but he could imagine no other way. He walked with the still amiable couple back through the main halls to the King's quarters. Keeping Sable between them, he passed a tablet with the young woman's picture on it to the King, and said, "Ellis Dee, the pilot with the counterfeit batteries, she's about to break."

Sable had no reaction. Berringer wondered what made him think she would. Remy closed the screen to black and said nothing. It had been so clumsy and for nothing, except now the King thought he'd lost all sense of discretion. He walked with them into the private hall and felt the chill as the doors closed. Sable wordlessly dropped from their company as they passed her rooms, and he followed Remy to the end.

Remy was faring far better than her, but he looked oppressed. He told Berringer, "I'm going back to the salt flats tomorrow."

~~~~~~~

Well, I've done it now, Berringer thought and called Lieutenant Fallon to his office.

"Lieutenant, you are here because I think I can trust you, but if I can't, you better get the hell out of my sight before I figure it out. And I move fast, son, I move real fast."

Too alarmed by the threat to respond, Fallon could only nod.

"This goes no further, Lieutenant. You and I are the only two people who will know of this conversation."

"Yes, sir, I understand." *I am too slow to outrun you.*

181

"You had a fairly technical conversation with Sister Sable when you tried to get the shackle off her wrist. From your exchange, do you think she has the ability to gain access to our secure network if she wanted?"

Berringer watched him search his skull for answers. "Possibly, sir. It's hard to know. We weren't discussing that."

"If I told you she might try to do this tonight, or in the next few days, could you catch her?"

His eyes went big and sought a place to settle. They finally rested back inside his head where they jumped from one idea to the next. "Can you tell me where in the network she might be going? What is she after? And from where you expect her to gain access?"

~~~~~~

For the second time in one night, Sable moved her mind through the distance into the corridor. When she found it still empty, she exited the King's rooms, leaving his computer clean of her trespass. She moved down the private hall, back to her chambers, and then she returned to the distance.

Moments later, security cameras recorded the progression of the four sisters from their shared room as they walked down the stairs and through the passageways that led to the guards outside the King's private hall. Sable held the door open.

182

Just before the sun rose, three sisters left. They moved back under the scrutiny of the cameras straight to the garage where video showed one of them could drive.

Under the trees and well beyond the palace's gate, Sable was untying and shrugging out of the robe while she steadied the wheel with her knee. The sister beside her pulled at the great swath of material beneath her and passed it back.

"Don't let them wrinkle, Amele," Sable told the woman in the mirror. Beside Amele was a pile of black cloth that had been draped to fill the seat.

"Lieutenant Fallon first," Sable told them. "Then we arrange things at the airport." She pulled cash out of her pocket and handed it to Ava. "For travel. I have to be back before anyone expects me to leave my rooms, so it's just the two of you on the ground after that."

Leaving the King's woods to enter the city, Sable glanced at her companions dressed for public in her clothes, looking almost like civilians, almost but not quite. She remarked on the obvious, "You two need shades."

~~~~~

With the sun just above the horizon, Lieutenant Fallon came back to Berringer. He was so roused by what he had discovered he did not appear sleepless. "The whole prison system needs to be firebombed. It's past saving. It's completely unsecure. I wouldn't let my grandmother search for recipes on it. It needs upgrades. Parts of it

183

have been ignored for a decade. It's a real whore's cunt of the scariest shit. Sorry, sir, I am completely geeked out."

The General watched him with steadfast composure. "Take a breath, Fallon, then tell me."

William wanted to rant about the architecture, the microcode, the kernel, and a particularly insidious rootkit, but instead he put his hands in front of him to illustrate a large circle. "There are rings of security. The outer rings, say ring three, if it's breached, it will gather information, and ring one will give access to hardware, like cameras. Well the prison had someone in the kernel, the core, right in the center of it with access to the whole thing and everything in the network the prison had access to. The place needs to go offline right now."

"Who was in the core?"

"Well, it wasn't the Queen, but all the same, I'd say they were after the pilot. They took control three days after she landed."

"What can you tell me about them?"

"Not a thing. There are layers of encryption and a chain of relays. We can tear apart the virus they came in with and hope they left a signature, but that's so unlikely, I shouldn't have mentioned it."

"Is it secure now?"

"No. No, it's a mess. I have them out for the moment, but they can come right back in the same way until we completely change the software, and more than half the hardware can't support the new software. That's not all. You have to assume they did a memory dump of everything they had access to, and I don't know where all they went." Fallon didn't think Berringer fully understood. "It's a
184

catastrophic failure. If they did the dump, and I don't know why they wouldn't, they have copies of everything we have to read, release, or blackmail at leisure."

"Ok, Lieutenant, take it offline. Get the people you need and see that the whole thing is cleaned up. There will be no mention of the Queen or the prisoner to anyone. I want you, Fallon, to make sure there is nothing on any of the networks that remain active that will give information about the pilot. Not a goddamn trace that she's there."

If Sable was going to go for the pilot, she'd either have to find another axe or she'd have to play an old game. Berringer remembered the stack of glass panes under the window and knew he was moving into territory his troops had been lost in.

~~~~~

The woods were still in his mirrors when the plain sedan entered traffic behind him. Lieutenant Fallon had been on his phone since walking out of the General's office. He was the asshole waking everyone up. He needed to eat but had little time, so he pulled into the first drive-thru he passed. He did not see the sedan follow.

He had just paid and then he heard at his window, "*Wi Fry.*" He remembered her hand on his shoulder, the words she had spoken, the empathy she offered; he remembered the bond. "*Let me in, Wi,*" her voice was low, full of breath, and rumbled from her throat.

He unlocked the doors and she sat beside him. She sounded as though she were absently murmuring a poem, and she only broke to tell him, "You want to park there." He went where she directed while she returned to the slow, indistinct cadence of a lyrical verse.

"Are you praying?" he asked.

"Just talking aloud."

"It's pretty."

"I know." Her voice became softer, just a whisper, and he strained to hear. He needed to hear. He leaned across the seat, his face angled to her, and she pulled him closer, her mouth to his ear. *"I am the blackness, all embracing, all sound, all forms vanish in me. I am the blackness, the witness, all time bends to me. I am the blackness that holds you, binds you, your will. What I place within will remain to inhabit the dark. I am your mother, your destroyer, the blackness that sustains."*

~~~~~~

Before the sun was high, a single sister returned with the car. She walked with her mind in the distance through the King's halls, murmuring as she approached the guards who allowed passage without question.

Within the hour, Sable reemerged. Her manner had become so barren of life, she knew she appeared no more distant than normal, yet her movements were from memory. For all that she saw before her, she could easily trip over an object rearranged, or a person in her path, but her presence was so forbidding, people fell back to avoid her.

From one end of the great hall to the other, Sable made a slow circuit of the overhead cameras to show she was still present in the palace. While her body wandered, her mind lingered in the distance with Amele and Ava. Ready to join as one, Sable was energy for the sisters to draw upon; she would make them powerful.

Eyes pale and lifeless to the palace, she waited in her sisters' thoughts.

~~~~~

Flicking through the screens on her desk, Girard watched Sable move smoothly across the great hall and disappear back into the private quarters. How she hoped Sable would do something exciting. Berringer should have come to her before he made that poor play with the pilot's photograph on the tablet. Of course Sable would not react, and if she had, Catherine did not trust Berringer to have caught it. He'd given Sable the whole of the night and most of the morning to do what she would, and now Catherine was forced to play catch-up.

Earlier, Girard had watched the recorded video of the four nuns going to their sovereign protector, because that's exactly what she was. In one glorious night, Sable had created a little cadre of devout agents who had already shown they would risk death for her, and she'd rewarded them by laying waste to their enemies. It was too beautiful to have been conceived with intent. Catherine mixed envy with conjecture, knowing two of them were still on the loose.

"Ah, Lucas," she sighed, "you let them get away."

Before anything else could slip by, she pressed Berringer for a chance with the pilot. "I'll take her wide awake or half asleep, I don't care, just let me speak with her."

"Tomorrow," Berringer promised. "After Fallon gets the prison secure again."

~~~~~~

The only thing about the uniform Amele liked was the hat. The third time she aligned the shirt to appear straight, she decided buttons were infernal, and neither of them could get the laces on Ava's boot retied as Sable had shown them. In the end, they slip knotted it like the belt on a robe. They stood in Lieutenant Fallon's uniforms watching the prison and saw William leave the front gate to retrieve software he had forgotten in his car.

~~~~~~

It wasn't like Fallon to be unorganized. The major in charge of the prison stood outside the secure box of a room attached to his office and rebuked him. "Lieutenant, you understand no one enters or

188

leaves until you have us back up? So you damn well better have everything you need."

The prison's server was protected by single access granted only by the Major to pass behind his desk. In the small area, Fallon and his assistant shared control of a single terminal. Lieutenant Parker told him he needed sleep. "Man, you look like no one's at the wheel."

"While we erase the drive, I'll take an hour on the floor and then we'll load the software and finish."

As the prison system's drive prepared for new software, the cameras stopped recording. The Major paced in and out of his office while Fallon laid his head against the wall and Parker concentrated over a handheld game player.

~~~~~

At the prison gate, the corporal returned his attention to the road to find two soldiers before him. Ava whispered of generals and Amele pushed her hand through the bars to wrap it around his throat, saying, "*Let us enter.*"

Inside the doors before the long stretch of corridor, they both seemed absurd. The soldier in the security booth stood and told them to stop.

Amele commanded, "*Let us enter,*" and Ava rumbled the air with control.

He balked at whatever they were trying. Seeing how small they were, the way the uniforms had been folded and tucked and yet still did not fit, he decided it was some sort of joke being played on him by the corporal at the gate. He opened the door to meet them in the hall and heard Ava humming. When Amele reached for his chest, he thought it was seductive, that maybe they were strippers, and now he was open to whatever they had in mind. Amele whispered, "*Quietly you fall,*" and he did. One hand on his neck, one over his eyes, she said, "*In the darkness you forget,*" while Ava murmured of being lost in the night.

They followed Fallon's instructions to the cells, Ava melodiously conjuring shadows and Amele reaching out to command the guard on watch with her hand, "*Into the darkness.*"

The air filled with frightening shapes the soldier knocked away.

Amele pulled herself up, rolled her jaw, and swallowed blood. Firmer now, both hands against his jugular, she demanded, "*Down into the dark,*" and dropped him to the floor to take his keys.

The cell door opened onto Nika squinting into the gloom as Amele said, "*You are in the black and cannot see. You are in the void; the only sound is me.*"

~~~~~~

Remy collected Sable from her rooms as was his custom before dinner. He had made it a point from the beginning to look in her eyes and take whatever was there without shrinking. He had felt the breach expand as the weeks passed, aware she retreated to view him from ever greater distances. He knew the hollow that lie between them widened and deepened with every day, but standing before her that night, he heard the wind blow.

For the first time, he could not bear to look.

He remembered Aidan's warning, "She will return to you in multitude what you give her. Give her nothing and, I promise you, she will drop you into the abyss and show you the void."

She had been right in declaring the clergy would say nothing about what she'd done, and with the same certainty, she believed she was right to have done it. Remy didn't know what was more infuriating, that she had done it, or that she was incapable of remorse.

Venturing into the intimate territory only once, Laudin had said, "She has been through a great deal in the last year. I am not excusing the incident, but I have too often seen educated minds get stuck in a pedantic defense of meaning. She has asked forgiveness but cannot be sorry, and you would have her regret the action over the outcome. She certainly regrets losing your favor."

Remy had said flatly, "She killed eight people. She has no right to be particular with her remorse."

She was baffling in her inability to recognize what was wrong, and he knew it was wrong, no arguable defense could change that, but

191

the killings disturbed him far less than he wished. His affection for her should have expired the moment he saw her ready the axe and turn from him to continue her violence, demanding the doors be shut while she rampaged. But what overrode his abhorrence of the carnage was the desire that caught his breath when the memory came unbidden of her body under his. He wanted to feel her cling to him again, to hear the sound of yielding that came from her throat, to leave her looking dazed so that her eyes met his searching.

Something had happened. It had not been expected. He had made her bury her face in his neck to keep from crying out and she had given more than she intended. He felt it in his chest: power, a tremendous flush of energy. He felt indomitable. He'd made a beastly sound and she looked at him with guilt, like she'd betrayed something horrible about herself and he had rebuked her. But he was not angry, he had wanted more.

It was this that wound around his heart and yanked him still every day. He could not concentrate for pulling the memory in with his breath, filling his lungs in a feeble attempt to recreate it, and nothing he could do with himself would abate the need she had created. He wanted what Sable could do without caring what she'd done, but his intellect damned him with ethics.

Before he had removed her dress, he had asked for the sake of courtesy but completely without caring, "They tell me you are a virgin." He assumed it was a mere artifice of the Cloitare, but she had replied yes, as though it were obvious and somehow meaningless. He had been astounded, asking, "But why?"

192

And then she was just as mystified. "Because I was bound to you." She had studied him, trying to understand why or how he had missed something so important in her title. Then, with comprehension, she closed her eyes on her own ignorance. "You do not see it. To you it is merely a word." Smiling with what appeared to be sympathy, "I will let you discover the meaning for yourself."

He had bent to kiss her as a skeptic, silently amused by her belief, by the suggestion of something esoteric. Drawing her near, he kissed her lips, but his passion for her was still undecided. He had a fondness for her, an affection that had never been sexual. To raise his desire, he needed to overlook her and focus on the body. Dropping his mouth to her neck, hand trailing the outside of her breast, across her side to the hip, he felt her respond.

Hours earlier, they had danced and she tried to lead. Tight with control, she would not relinquish self-possession, making him compensate with strength to direct her. But in his room, under his touch, she yielded, and with it came just a hint of what she offered. Her every murmur of acquiescence surged through him like a current, bringing him to life, creating a need to hear her louder, make her surrender weaker, building a craving in him for what was in his hands.

Gone were all reservations that Sable was not what he wanted. Like madness, he was in the moment, possessing the present, his attention centered on making Sable give more until she gave everything in a rush that filled him to frenzy.

It had been overwhelming. If they were really bound, he had felt it. Wide awake, feeling invincible, his whole being charged electric, he had laughed to himself that she could have looked on him with sadness if this is what it meant.

Then unable to accept her defiant sense of justice, her indefensible violence, he tried to sever ties with her only to be consumed. She responded by withdrawing, slowing her heart cold until he could feel the chill when he walked at her side. Now, behind her dead eyes, she was traversing a landscape of ice, determined to drag him with her through the most barren of waste, tugging at the bond, forcing him to follow, and he finally understood her expression of pity.

He had met her stone cold at her rooms, unable to hold her gaze, and he'd delivered her to his guests the same. He had expected she would emerge from her frozen remains to charm again, but this night she had no sentiments to share, no interest in appeasing. She held a drink but did not consume, met no one's eyes, and could not be engaged. At the long table for dinner, she sat to his right, her Cloitare face staring relentlessly ahead, unnerving Remy's visiting cousins until they began to stutter. Catherine was at her wittiest to rescue them, but three dropped utensils and one spilled wine glass later, the cousins gave up all pretenses of enjoyment and started throwing back spirits at an alarming rate, and Sable cared not the least for their discomfort or anyone else's. She was blind to it all, content in her isolation to turn the meal into the most arduous event any of them had ever endured.

194

Feeling responsible for it all, it seemed clear to Remy that Sable had decided to demonstrate she could take not just him, but everyone, into hell.

<p style="text-align:center">~~~~~~</p>

Amele sat Nika in the plane and Ava stopped humming.

Sable returned. Back from the distance, she found herself in the hall with Remy, the door to her room opening to admit her. She dropped from Remy's side as was routine. She waved away the lady's maid as she did every night, saying, "Leave me, please."

Hearing the door close, she fell into a chair, face in her hands, bent to her knees, exhaling the day, and again the days, then muffling the heaving turned to crying, she covered her head against the whole cursed stretch of days in the palace. She started to tremble.

"I had no idea you were so miserable."

His voice seared through her, leaving abrupt terrified silence. She instantly made herself still and rearranged her features. She came up blank, staring at the wall, heart beating too fast for proper defenses.

Slow, slow, she told herself, *slow*. She had been startled and she no longer reacted well when alarmed.

Pulse measured, pupils gone, she turned slowly to put her cold focus on the King. She knew he was hoping for something in her expression, but she had nothing he wanted. She had bleeding sorrow

195

wrapped around her neck always threatening to choke her senseless, but she would spare them both that scene again.

Remy faced her Cloitare Stare with determination. "I am going to the salt flat tomorrow and would like you to join me."

She wrestled sorrow's grip off her throat to speak. "Yes, of course."

He watched her. He wondered if she would give anything, any softening of her features to help him, but she returned his gaze unmoved, too far away to see he was trying. He nearly said something earnest, an offer to start over, but the desolation was vast and her eyes dared him to hold them. He said instead, "Well then, tomorrow."

~~~~~~

"Are you telling me it was magic, Lieutenant Fallon? Because that's what I'm hearing."

"She was there. We installed new software, brought the hardware back online, and she was gone."

"And not a goddamn thing caught on camera." Berringer stalked around the prison's security booth. "Nobody leaves." He swept the whole stone building into his gesture. "And nobody sleeps. You corporal," he pointed at the soldier who had been in the booth, "I am starting with you."

~~~~~~

"Fallon, you kill stealing motherfucker," were the last intelligible words spoken by Max since being permanently kicked from the military network. He knew the name of his nemesis from a program he'd written to find any new mention of Mission Retrieve, and there in the military record sent to the major in charge of the prison was Lieutenant William Fallon, information security specialist, cleared to inspect the prison network, and formerly assigned to Mission Retrieve.

Max had already been awake four nights when Fallon shut him down. He'd been dropping his head every six hours to pull powder up his nose, and it had been at least a month since he'd reacted to the burn.

Half a day later, Enzo dragged him across most of the hangar to get the bag of amphetamines from his hand, snarling his exasperation, "You are going the fuck to sleep."

In protest, Max grabbed a pair of Marlow's hair sticks he'd been keeping on his desk and tried to stab him, but Max was in no condition to fight.

Enzo forced him to the ground and laid on top of him until he thought Max might heave into tears.

Thinking he could trick him to sleep, Enzo had chopped sedatives into his drink and then watched it go untouched for hours. Now he wasn't fucking around. He'd only let Max up from the floor enough not to drown him and then, bottle to mouth, forced him to swallow.

An hour later, Enzo was sitting on the concrete floor with Max sleeping on the couch at his back. He was absently staring at the flat screen as video from last night's rally showed Felix Magnus working the yellow-banded Libertines into a frenzy. The square in the border town had never been designed with ten thousand in mind. Residents of Ulphia had pushed in from the side streets when Felix spammed their phones with the time and place for assembly. The King's Army had just started to push through from the outside when a massive paper effigy of the King being ridden with bit and saddle by a nun was set ablaze. The fire rapidly spread to a tree in the first changes of autumn then to a banner strung from the windows in the occupied courthouse. By accident or assistance, the fire lit the curtains and gathered fuel as it spread so that to a backdrop of burning authority Felix called for "freedom from coercion" while the crowd shouted, "Freedom be dumb," until it sounded like a meaningless drum beat.

Nika should have been there.

It had been a long time since it was only Enzo and Max. He had only just taught Marlow how to use a phone when she declared she was off to see the war on Sierra's most southern border. Max had said, "Well, that's the last of her." But she had returned a month later with Nika. Nika had taught her to swear.

They were such a strange pair. Marlow always looked somehow dusty but cultured in denim and boots, and Nika kicked around in shiny black leather with T-shirts so obscene mothers in Erentrude would pull their children into their skirts. Enzo had not been sure about Nika—she kept burning shit down. But Marlow had shrugged and said, "You steal power and he hacks grids. Her vice is her art. I would be damned to tell you, or any other, not to do what you will."

Something in the way she said it made Max stop as abruptly as Enzo's argument. Head lifted from his keyboard in consternation, Max ordered, "You're fucking sixteen. I'm half a decade wiser than you, so shut the fuck up." But it had stuck. Like a mantra, it played in their heads, *do what you will*. Enzo had let them and fast saw the potential.

Nika's skill in a plane changed everything. It opened to Enzo contacts and possibilities beyond local theft. Her willingness to fly perilous became Enzo's business. She'd land a plane on a warehouse roof for night security to load and then come home bragging it had been too easy. By the end of the year, Enzo had rented their first permanent hangar, and to Nika he'd given a platinum lighter to burn whatever the hell she wanted to the ground.

Now Nika was hugging her knees in a cell and Marlow had vanished. The combined absence destroyed. Enzo couldn't sleep without pills. Max couldn't function without powder.

Enzo was too awake and waiting for a delivery. He'd ground the last of his sedatives into Max's drink. Through the open doors, he felt the morning drop dew in the building. He saw the unfamiliar plane coming in but thought nothing of it. They would go to the main building, but once on the ground, the plane cut its rudder and rolled with the wind to his hangar.

She dropped from the cockpit, just feet on the tarmac, then ducked under the wing to smile at Enzo.

He tried to get up but his legs wouldn't work. His muscles went weak and then everything stopped as inertia took over.

He pulled his face off the floor to Nika's bare toes.

She sunk to his level and, despite the tremble in her voice, tried to sound light, "Some weird ass shit just happened."

SALT MOUNTAIN

She is the Ice Queen, Remy thought when he saw her. If he had not witnessed her collapse the previous night, he would not have suspected there was anything inside her alive. He remembered the months he spent with her in the medical room, before she remembered how to defend against emotions, when she was still soft and vulnerable, so unlike the trained Cloitare he faced now. But since he'd seen where she went when she thought she was alone, he knew beneath the ice she was not dead, not even permanently frozen, just terribly broken.

Before leaving the private hall, Remy stopped and turned her rigidly to face him. He searched her face, hoping again she would give just a little, and when she didn't, he leaned down to kiss the top of her head, placing his lips above the enamel sticks in her hair. He took her wrist and examined the wide bracelet with sadness. "If you had wanted it, I would have torn down the doors for you. If you had asked it of me, I would have given it. When you have a problem, Sable, come to me."

He only knew he reached her because her face briefly flamed from white to color.

For all he hoped to achieve in a day, Remy thought it preferable to be driven the hours to the salt flat. In the line of armored vehicles, Berringer was in the fifth transport with the uniformed soldiers, asleep in his seat.

From the backseat of the car, Remy was offering details about the area, pointing out how the flora and fauna rapidly changed with

201

the elevation, describing the geology and formation of the salt flat not yet in view.

He had taken Sable's hand, determined to hold it no matter how awkward she planned to make it. He held it until his blood warmed the cold from her fingers, and he held it even when the heat made them both uncomfortable, though neither would show it.

He was coming near to an end of what he could present without boring himself any more witless. Never before had he attempted trivial banter, and now he was down in the dregs speaking about the weather. "As we descend into the bowl, the mountain becomes more and more barren until it turns to desert. In the spring, the clouds manage to make it over the peaks and the rains make the area quite stunning. I think you would enjoy seeing it then too."

Through it all, she gave only as much as she'd been forced to once before. Proper agreement, her focus straight ahead, nothing more than a lesson she recalled from the nuns.

He said, "The summer was long this year, so we will see very little life, but there is a beauty not seen anywhere else."

And she agreed but saw nothing.

With his free hand, he pressed his temples, and then in a moment, once again composed, he said, "Sable."

"Yes."

"Sable," he called her attention sharply.

Slowly, she turned and put him under the glare.

"Let it remain in the past."

She was still staring but she rose from the depths, the frost clearing from her sight. She was considering what he said, and she considered it for a very long time, all the while coolly testing his strength, searching him for stability, seeing if he could take what she gave, then for the first time since she froze deep, she dropped her eyes from the fight. He watched her shift so that she settled with her body inclined ever so slightly toward his, and he felt the thaw when she declared, "The most desolate places have the potential to create powerful life."

~~~~~~~

They had come on a day when the clouds streaked white through the sky and smudged the horizon so it was impossible to tell where the flats ended. Remy loved it no matter how it appeared. He loved the crisp blue on white of the winter, the white on white as it was now at the end of summer, and in the spring, when it was all blue from the rain as the water mirrored the sky, he loved it just the same.

Sable had only seen it in pictures. Remy knew it would have to affect her.

Berringer woke to the change. He heard Sable laughing. The flats were so smooth they had ridden far into the center, and Berringer, who had spent the night grilling soldiers over the missing pilot, had slept through it. He emerged from the car to see Remy watching Sable with pleasure. She had her lips parted in awe beside him.

Stretching in every direction crystal white, the flats were a genuine wonder, and Sable was drawn in by the scale of it. She left Remy to walk alone in the immaculate light, marveling at it, pulling in the scent of salt warmed by the sun. Meters beneath the crust was the lithium brine that powered the world.

It was practically unfair that one country should have such easy access to eighty percent of the planet's known supply. The idea made Sable glance back at Remy with concern. Beside him was the General, surveying the vigilant formation of soldiers, marking the ones that had jogged well ahead of her, pointing his attention into the elevation as a signal they should be scanning the peaks for possible threats. Even with all this, neither of them seemed troubled by the risk under their feet.

Sable turned and kept walking for silence, into the stretch of white, mesmerized by the illumination of the clouds stretched thin over the salt, refusing to shield her eyes against the glare that blinded. White underfoot and white above, it did not devour like the night, but obliterated all form with brilliance. It was pure and it was clean. In the quiet, Sable pulled it in and then laid her mind out on it.

Remy saw her fall to her knees. He understood. This was his temple. His god. His salvation.

~~~~~~

The General wouldn't say it, but he watched her kneeling, unmoved for hours, and was thinking, *She is crazy as hell*.

She had asked Remy to stay until night. When Berringer learned of the request, he had looked around at the empty landscape and scowled, "Why?"

"It is something she needs to witness," Remy explained.

"What is there to witness?"

"The darkness over light is what she told me."

It rattled the General. After hours of pushing the soldiers, each would admit, though they knew it made them sound insane, a memory of shadows, a fear of the dark and the night.

"Like fucking wraiths or something, there was something in here. There were shadows under the lights." Then, like a memory just surfaced, "It was Fallon. He turned off the lights."

Fallon denied ever touching the lights, and Lieutenant Parker, who'd been beside him, said it never happened. They'd been in the computer room beside the Major's office and hadn't seen a thing. The Major had supervised them the whole time and knew nothing about the escape until the cameras were brought back online, and it wasn't until the General arrived, that he heard any mention of wraiths or shadows.

The guard on the gate kept saying it was too dark to see if anyone had been observing the prison and could hardly be convinced it had happened in the moments before sunset. Berringer sent the whole lot to the medical center to be tested and then changed their posts permanently. Only Lieutenant Fallon had been spared transfer.

"So where has she gone?" Remy asked.

"Into the night." Berringer swept his hand across the sky in disbelief. "That's what they said when I asked. Where did she go? And they all shrugged and told me, '*Into the night*.'" Berringer laid his focus on Sable with suspicion.

Misunderstanding his expression, Remy said, "She is going to be fine. You did not need to come. The next time, trust us to be in excellent order with your men."

Berringer chewed a sound of denial. He looked across the flat at the soldiers in uniform on the perimeter, scanning the elevations with binoculars for movement, then closer at the suited security team that stayed near the King. "If she decides to kill someone, I don't know which of my men could stop her. She's been trained in—damn, I hate to give it such a dignified name—but that was the Whirling Wind. None of my people have been trained to counter it. None of them have seen one, and I'm not doing backflips for them. If it was anyone else, I'd tell them to just shoot the flipping monkey before it did any harm."

"Aside from the blade," Remy's sideways glance was nearly apologetic, "it did not appear she gave you much trouble."

Berringer wished it were so. "She's good, Remy. Not the best of a small lot, but then she was motivated by madness and didn't follow the tenets of her craft to disengage when she struck me. Had she, I never would have caught her."

206

"Her training is unique?"

The General grunted agreement. "It went out of fashion over three centuries ago. The Way of the Wind trained killers for hire, but the method died soon after the pistol. The gun was the world's great equalizer. In their day, the school's disciples were some the best for a very specific role. They can defend themselves adequately if backed against a wall, but they didn't study for combat. They emerge to strike quick death. They're taught to abandon a fight and kill later if challenged too strongly. It's the only reason I pinned her: she didn't relent. But their craft has little use today. Flip all they want, they can't dodge a well-placed bullet or a machine gun."

Remy stared ahead at Sable kneeling on the salt. "Then finding the person that taught her should be easy."

Berringer thought of his father. He wasn't the Laughing Master when infamy found him. He didn't gain that title until after the birth of his son to his young wife. Lucas knew him only as fair and magnanimous, dependable and honorable. There was no one he trusted more. Sable had complained once of divided loyalties, but Berringer had never felt its corruption before. "As you know, I swore my own oath of secrecy to train, you knew that when we met. I would be loath to try and break another's. If you'll permit, I will respectfully bow out of that obligation."

Remy looked into the setting sun without speaking. He knew that if Lucas had not known from the start who trained the assassin before them, he would not give a toss about breaking Sable's promise and would not have left the two of them alone for an instant. Remy

207

knew his wife and his chief of defense shared the same strategist, but Girard had not yet found the location of the infamous traitor.

~~~~~~

Nika had a tremor she didn't have before. It was in her voice and in the hand that tried to drink the water Max pressed on her. "I should have never flown it here." She knew it was true. "I should have dumped it and got another, but I am so seriously fucked in the head right now." She put the water down before she dropped it. "I had enough trouble keeping my shit together to get here. You guys have to go deal with it. I don't even want to burn it."

Enzo was burning more than a plane in his mind. All their identities would have to go too. And they needed to get out of this hangar with their gear immediately. They needed space from whoever Nika had just led back to them. To hurry it all along, Enzo had cut out lines from Max's stash of amphetamines and let everyone at it.

He was furiously ripping cables out of Max's computers when Max called him to the plane.

Enzo thought it had to be the speed mixed with too many sedatives because Max seemed entirely too complacent, even pleased with the situation. "Nika wakes up in the plane and the transponder has already been ripped out. Ripped full the fuck out and left dead in her lap so she can't for a second think there is anything obvious in the plane to track her. Who would have prepared it like that?"

Enzo was too busy mentally packing to care or guess.

"Look." Max tried to press on Enzo his goggles and black light. He was pointing deep into the empty pit hacked out of the dash. "Know whose half-wiped fingerprint's in there?"

"I don't need to look at it, Max. It's a fingerprint, and I don't read fingerprint."

Max put his handheld scanner under Enzo's face with the match on the screen. "It's fucking Marlow's."

Enzo stopped the pack and burn. The whole airport went in and out of focus and he swayed with it. He was again not very sure on his feet.

They both turned to study Nika. She was pacing around the plane Enzo told her she was going to have to fly them out in, patting the fuselage like it were a beast to be tamed, telling both it and herself, "We got this. We can do this. It's no big deal."

"This plane is safe." Max was certain. "There's not going to be any tag on it leading the King's men back to us."

"Keep checking it. We're still moving, but we might have time for Nika to sit down."

She had ditched the cotton prison garb for a shirt that told the world to "eat shit." She hadn't said much more than someone, probably General Bear, had arranged her release and she knew it was so she could be followed back to her contacts, but she was going on four months in solitary with so little sleep it seemed more like a year, and the split between what she knew needed to happen and what she was capable no longer existed. Neither Enzo nor Max cared. They'd burn it all to the ground and go under, but Enzo wondered if it was necessary.

Enzo hated to ask it of her, but he had to know, "Do you think Marlow had anything to do with getting you out?"

Nika pulled back with disgust. "Hell, no. Marlow wouldn't dose me. That was a big, black scary acid trip. Those fuckers drugged me." Her memory squinted into the dark. "Everything was as fucked up as it ever was and then shadows seeped into the cell, like some kind of dark living smoke, but," she shook her head at Enzo knowing he wouldn't understand, "it was feminine. I know that sounds mad, but after four months in a prison with mostly men, you can't mistake the presence of ..." she struggled to describe it, "the darkness was female." Then she wiped it all away with her hands. "It was hallucinations. It was acid, a really heavy dose, but they've tweaked it. It didn't come on like acid. It was just suddenly a full on, out of your head, bad trip. And then it was over. *Bam.* Cold sober, I am sitting in that plane with a bashed up transponder in my lap and a key in the ignition. I can't remember details because I didn't recognize a damn thing as it was happening, but I knew I was on the scariest ride through dark hell. There was nothing about that shit that said Marlow." After a moment, she conceded, "Well, that's not exactly true." Eyes watering at the edge, she looked up to the high-domed ceiling to keep tears from falling and told Enzo, "The whole time I thought I heard her telling me everything was about to be sunshine."

Queen Mother

Inside a tank overlooking the front of the burned out courthouse where Felix Magnus spoke, a crew commander passed a second paper packet of sunshine to his gunner. Holding one nostril closed, he noisily pulled powder from the first packet deeper until he felt it burn his throat and tasted the bitter effects. He shuddered and allowed his arms to fall to his sides while his eyes blurred into nothing.

The King's Army was present on the side streets leading into the square where the protesters gathered. It had been a strategic risk to lift the curfews and give Ulphia the right to assemble, but the loosening of restrictions had seen the fury of the working class reduced. Just two weeks after thousands had cheered as the courthouse burned, the protest was down to just a few dozen dedicated radicals. The soldiers had been warned Sierran agitators would try to provoke a deadly reaction, but, unless their lives were threatened, the soldiers had been ordered to take it. The policy was working. The dissidents were becoming bored. Felix Magnus spoke to a dwindling crowd.

"What I wouldn't give to fire a round straight through his face." The commander readjusted his helmet to settle the crawl of his scalp.

At this range, the gunner didn't need to use the tracking system, but to provide some amusing relief to the monotony, he locked Felix as his target. "Pretentious prick." The gunner snorted from the packet and lifted his voice mockingly high, "They won't let

211

me do what I want." Shoulders bent and heaving, the gunner sobbed, "Daddy told me no and made me cry." Trying to maintain the tantrum over the advancing stupor, he ended slowly, "I'm gonna do whatever I want."

In one of his screens, the commander saw men from infantry ducking behind the tank as paint splattered the street and the tank's side armor. "What the hell are they on at the checkpoints not to catch paint balloons?"

"General needs to send more pressure washers. We're gonna spend all night cleaning this bitch." The gunner pressed his eyes into the sight and ran his thumb in circles over the fire switch. He felt the tension in the button like erotic pleasure. "We could show them the ultimate libertine act."

Drifting in careless inertia, the commander's voice held no concern, "Gunner, I say do whatever you want."

~~~~~~

It was not uncommon for someone to be rapping lightly on Catherine's office door in the late evening, but Sable had never appeared after the summons to enter. Sable acknowledged the peculiarity of it by lifting her features with ironic enthusiasm.

"I hoped you had time to speak."

"Always," was Catherine's reply.

The two sat facing each other in chairs before Catherine's desk. The sound of the night rally playing live from Ulphia was soft in the background. Sable looked to the side to watch it play large on the wall. The number of protesters had diminished measurably and each night they assembled smaller. They held the blackened courthouse and its lawn with Felix calling for disorder from the top of the stairs.

"Their singular desire does in many ways reflect my own." Both hands in her lap, Sable thought of a way to begin this most vulnerable of conversations. She considered the events that had brought her to seek out the intelligence chief and then, distressed by the memories, she held the wide bracelet on her wrist. "You know what they did and you know how I returned it."

Catherine was seldom unsure of what was transpiring. She could think of few conversations in the last decade she had not expected, and all the surprises had somehow involved Sable. The strangeness of the occasion made her response serious, "I know what you've admitted."

"That is enough to begin." She covered the jeweled reminder by relaxing her hand. "Despite what happened, I receive a request every day from the Cloitare to return and accept the ritual that would shed one title for the next. They are becoming more insistent, stalking me through the halls of late. They wish to continue the progression from Bound Bride to Queen Mother to Mother of All t—"

Girard nearly heard her say to, to another title, but she stopped short.

213

"The Libertines," Sable pointed at the screen, "they have my sympathies. Had a train not wrecked, I would be there among them. I am an anarchist at heart." A sense of futility allowed her only part of a smile. "But I am a realistic nihilist. I know it can never work. There will always be insatiable egotists who need to dominate and control, and there cannot be anarchy if no one follows the rules." At the joke, she caught a bitter laugh in her throat. "To have the free world Felix imagines, people must be willing to take away another's freedom or their life to ensure it, and there are not enough servile psychopaths to police that sort of libertine paradise."

Girard absorbed the admissions. With perfect clarity, she saw the impetus that had consistently set Sable in motion, a calamitous revolt against authority. Yet she was erratically humble and deferential to some: Master Aidan, the King, and, of late, Girard had watched her give a wary respect to the General. "That is a dangerous position to hold when you would be queen of a kingdom."

"I will only be queen to a king."

"Ah." Catherine understood. "Loyal only to the individual."

"I have no desire to lead, and no desire to follow. Though, to my secret shame, I serve rather well when I respect the instructor." It was impossible to tell if her smile was meant to flatter or dare Catherine to try. "I have always resided more in the moment. I do not possess your grand vision of," she made a circle of all that was before them, "the scheme of things. And since this," she flicked her wrist, "my actions tend to be visceral without regard for consequence." Sable relaxed her whole demeanor to appear casual, "There are outcomes I desire but do not know how to achieve. I need your instructions."

The spymaster barely dared to hope she heard correctly. Girard believed she had just been offered control of the ultimate agent. She believed the Mother of All, with her self-professed nihilist axe-wielding rage, had just asked to be brought to focus under her directive.

The offer would not be refused, Sable knew, but the negotiations had yet to begin. Sable wanted to give Catherine time to accept what had been extended, so she moved her eyes to the screen as Felix Magnus told the crowd, "We will do what we want and accept no other law." Not as loud as she had heard it weeks before, the crowd chanted back, "We will do what we want."

Felix raised his hands into the air to declare, "Do what you will shall be the whole of the law."

The place Felix Magnus occupied erupted in white smoke and dust. A low thundering explosion made the crowd stoop in a wave that broke into panic.

Girard saw Sable come to her feet and call out with dread, "*Catherine.*" When Catherine looked at the screen, Sable said, "That was the sound of a tank."

The white cloud was dispersing with the breeze, revealing rubble and a gaping hole in the wall of the courthouse.

Sable said with terrible dismay, "We've killed Felix Magnus."

~~~~~~

Ulphia's radicals returned in force with renewed vigor and malice. The square, with its burnt and blasted courthouse, could not contain them. They surged into the neighboring streets, pressing toward the mobile command of the King's battalion. No one believed the assassination of Felix Magnus was a mechanical error.

In under a week, Ulphia had stopped throwing paint and now threw anything that burned or exploded. The well-armed country of conscripts had an instant rebel army, but their hundred-year-old rifles couldn't penetrate the modern army's armor, and their snipers were, for the moment, untrained and inaccurate shots.

Civilian casualties filled both the city and military hospitals as the army fought to suppress them.

A second uprising was happening in the capital, Helena, as many thousands more pushed against the Prime Minister's administrative house, demanding he order King Remius out of the border.

"Let them tear down the government," Remy had said. "We will move into the absence to restore peace." A second battalion and the airborne division were readied.

Girard and Laudin both confirmed Sierra's President Pavlović was secretly offering alliance if Alena would declare war.

"We have to remove Sierra from the equation," Catherine told Sable. Girard had come to her rooms in the morning without the King's knowledge. Sable had been gracious at first, sitting them in couches across a low table like they were friends, but once

216

Catherine's purpose for being there became clear, the more openly Sable regretted her hospitality.

The intelligence chief had spent the first days trying to pin Sable down on what exact outcome she desired but did not know how to achieve without Catherine's assistance, but Sable had refused to speak further, saying, "We will return to it when this catastrophe is over," as though she knew from the moment Felix was obliterated, it would lead to war. A war with Alena the kingdom could handle, but the world did not want to see Erentrude go to war with Sierra. It would be devastating, and Girard thought Sable could stop it.

"You told me the nuns want you to accept the title of Queen Mother," Girard repeated to Sable's menacing stare. It had become her silent refusal. "With Cloitare confirmation, you can call upon Sierra's religious to force President Pavlović to withdraw support for the uprising. We need him to disassociate his administration from Alena."

Sable gave the impression she might climb over the table that separated them, and in her expression was the same unhinged mania that had sent her after Mother Vesna. When she moved her body forward, Catherine concentrated on the objective. "If you were to make an appearance as Queen Mother, you could rouse the faithful into action."

Sable's eyes tightened, but Catherine wasn't done. Days ago, Sable had shown her weakness and Catherine was determined to soften the edge. "Will you not do it for Remy?"

Then, exactly as it appeared, but still Catherine did not expect it, Sable came across the divider. The speed of her movement made Catherine push back into the couch with a shriek of alarm.

Sable now sat on the edge of the table, pressing Catherine's knees together with hers. Grabbing Catherine's wrist and the back of her neck, Sable pulled her close to the murderous question, "You would send me back in there?"

"I would send you to hell to save Remy."

The honesty stopped her, but the insanity persisted. Sable laughed. "You already tried that, kitty." She pulled Catherine to her lips and pressed a hard kiss against her mouth, then released the spymaster to confusion.

Rising from the table, Sable walked away to give a long overdue report. "The scientist was traveling by train. He was in the last cars and I near the front. I had hours to switch the report, but then there was a break in the rails. I believe you know the rest."

Catherine did. It was crashing into place. Never mind exchanging lascivious comments with a nun, she had sent the Guard Dog a picture of Sable with the instructions to kill. She'd sent it after the wreck and had no idea if it had ever been read. Catherine did not want the fear hanging over her the rest of her life. She asked the question she most needed answered. "Did you receive the new assignment?"

"I did." Sable watched Catherine close her eyes to the treasonous act. Imagining how Sable would use it, the King's most-clever advisor resembled a hostage with no options for escape. Sable

218

was offended. "Catherine, you forget with whom you deal. If I were so aggrieved by the attempt, I would have killed you. I do not deliver prisoners. I do not blackmail. I was your assassin, but I never helped you enslave." Then turning the contempt on herself, "If I were braver, or as loyal to Remy as I want to claim, I would have let your men kill me. But I wanted to live. I thought I could evade capture. I have killed far weaker risks to Remy than myself, so do not insult the shreds of my sanity with your guilt, or more properly your fear of exposure." Sable's madness was diminishing to calculated reason. "I have been in a unique position to know you have no boundaries when it comes to protecting the King, which makes you entirely too important for me to risk. That final assignment will *never* be mentioned again."

Catherine didn't like it. Secrets held by people living in such close proximity tended to reveal themselves. Revelations were always worse than admissions, especially where the King was concerned. "The last mission aside, it would be better to tell Remy now you were the Guard Dog than for him to learn it later."

Sable scowled.

And after Remy stopped fuming, this would also allow Catherine to shift blame for the whole disastrous outcome of the Guard Dog's failing. If Sable had swapped the report, Catherine would not be asking her to go back into the convent.

Catherine was about to speak when Sable shouted her down, "Do *not* tell me I am responsible for all that is happening." She turned her back to accept responsibility, "I am well aware."

The spy chief appealed to the agent she knew, "It may already be impossible to turn Sierra aside."

Sable was familiar with the game and glared over her shoulder.

Catherine threw aside tactics to say bluntly, "You know my directive is correct."

With some semblance of control, Sable sat again before Catherine. "I know you are right, but I don't want to do it." She struggled to keep her attention on Catherine and not let it fall to her wrist. She did not want to submit to any ritual the Cloitare could devise.

The two women looked at each other: Sable waiting for Catherine to develop another plan and Catherine waiting for Sable to fold.

Neither moved, and the minutes stretched until Sable furrowed her brows. If she agreed, she would have to put on a robe and go to the double doors. She dropped her head into her hand at thought. She imagined she would spend most of the ritual kneeling, and this made her groan. She would swear vows she didn't mean to accept a title she loathed, and all this again at the altar where they had been once before, but this time, if they touched her …

Catherine watched her raise her head and could tell by her eyes she was leaning into violence.

"We may all come to regret this," Sable announced, "but, as you said, it will be done for Remy."

~~~~~

The King was stalking the length of carpet when Berringer and Laudin entered. Before him, sitting by each other's side, Sable and Catherine had their attentions fixed steadily in their laps. Berringer didn't know which between the two could drive a man faster to destroy all four of his senses in a bid to survive, but by appearances, they had joined forces so that Remy was certain to suffer.

Remy stopped before Catherine and flung his arm out at the new arrivals. "Tell them."

"It seems Sable was the Guard Dog."

Berringer stopped where he stood, but Laudin had to find a chair.

Remy waved it away. "Tell them what you would have her do."

Sable spoke over Catherine. "It is my decision. I will accept the title of Queen Mother to speak to the people and destabilize Sierra."

Laudin was shaking his head yes with vigor but was still wild-eyed from what he had heard upon entering.

Berringer looked at Remy who indicated *This*, hand open to Sable, was the source of his frustration. "Well?" he demanded of Lucas.

It was too much to take at once. Berringer knew how Catherine used the Guard Dog. He reconstructed his image of Sable

221

once again from the beginning and then answered Remy's waiting temper, "As a friend, I would caution against it, but as your general, I have to beg yes."

Laudin spoke with great conviction. "It would neutralize our biggest problem."

Indicating Sable, Berringer asked Remy, "May I?"

Assuming his hand gesture meant proceed, Berringer asked her, "Do you think you can go into the convent without killing anyone?" It was a possibility no one had wanted to acknowledge. Only Sable and the General did not appear shocked by the question.

Sable's long consideration prevented Remy from stopping her answer. After a time, her short decision was "Yes."

It sounded harsh when the General responded, "I don't believe you."

Sable seemed to agree. "I doubt myself as well. But if we can assume the Cloitare have moved beyond wanting to hurt me, and I enter with a peaceful objective, then surely no situation should arise to spark conflict. I will presume if their ritual does not involve my blood, I won't complicate it with theirs."

"You presume," the General repeated with scorn.

"Remy, wait," Sable stopped him from interjecting. She spoke to Berringer with candor, "I wish you could have judged me before the Cloitare sent me under. You would have no more liked me than you do now, but you would never have doubted me. Do not imagine I welcome this obscurity. Presumptions are the best I can offer from where they have left me." Sable glanced briefly at Girard. "For years I strived to protect Remy's interests, so I am hardly pleased that I am the undoing of all that was achieved. Before you damn me, remember that I could not stop this." She offered her wrist to the General.

It was a punch to his gut, but before he could show sympathy, she hinted at words he had heard before. "The fire does not have to burn down the house."

He knew the lines of his father's master by heart: *I gave you fire, but when it blistered your fingers, you tried to hide and it burned down the house. So I gave you the wind, but when it unsettled, you built a wall for it to knock over. Then I gave you water, which you tried to contain and now all your children are drowned. Finally, I give you the soil and hope you have learned how to grow.*

Sable said, "The most destructive forces can be focused if you don't fight against their nature." To Remy, she said, "I may be insane and unstable and everything the General will tell you, but I am powerful. If you try to contain me in this house, I will destroy it, so you'd do better to set me loose in another. Let me go to the Cloitare."

~~~~~~~~

In the end, Sable stopped asking. She gave no further opposition to the King's objections, so for that, she appeared to assent, but within an hour of leaving Remy's rooms in unspoken compliance, she went to the room of her sisters, and then shortly after, one nun left for the double doors.

When Remy could not find Sable for dinner, Amele was found waiting outside the private halls with an answer.

The three advisors were called back. Laudin was the first to enter and see the pile of black fabric at Remy's feet. To Catherine, who entered next, he pointed at Amele with contempt. "It is this that most offends. They give the impression of being respectful, but that is only in posture." To the General, who could think of only one thing that would account for the scene of fury before him, Remy said, "They are all quite capable of assuming an attitude of obedience, but then they do whatever the hell they please."

Neither the three advisors nor Sister Amele could tell Remy how long Sable might be gone. Sister Amele, with her perfect blank face, could not describe the ritual Sable would encounter as there had never before been a Queen Mother, and as she was only a sister, she could not shed any light on the ritual for becoming a mother. When Remy told her to go into the cloister and return with Sable, she said, "I, like my other three sisters, promised ..." and here she formed silent words until she found, "*Sister Sable* that we would never enter the convent without her knowledge. She insisted when she left that we must not follow."

Catherine knew Amele struggled to find an appropriate title to use for her protector, referring to her eventually as Sister Sable, but this was not genuine. It was not what they called her. Remy only heard her refusal. The night ended in outrage that nothing had been answered.

The next morning, the clergy told their public spokesperson that the Queen Mother would speak at the Basilica the following afternoon. As the Master and Mentor had done, she would address her adherents from the balcony overlooking the plaza.

Lieutenant Fallon pushed his phone with the message into the General's view, and pressed behind that, he offered a tablet showing it was breaking headline news.

"Cursing hell." The General started organizing security while Remy told him to come.

When Berringer arrived, the King had his elbows on the desk and both hands pressed hard against his forehead. The General had never seen Remy's hands shake before.

"She said she would be the death of me, but I do not think she appreciates how."

Berringer hated to see it. "This is going to be a hard one to turn around."

"Send a message to the Cloitare that if Sable is not returned to me by sunset, I will not permit her to speak." The King lifted his head and grimly told Berringer, "You will ensure this is enforced."

~~~~~

As the sun began to set, Laudin was on the phone with their ambassador in Sierra. The diplomat had spent hours making all shades of promises to President Pavlović's administration that the emerging

Queen Mother would say nothing to provoke turmoil. Laudin was told it was not possible to see the street for the crowds that were gathering outside the embassy, and the ambassador believed they were of two minds: one religious and the other supporting President Pavlović, as though it had already been decided the two could not coexist.

The Basilica in Erentrude's capital where the Queen Mother was expected to speak had barred the doors, accepting only the clergy and Berringer's team of security and sound engineers, but the plaza was already completely impassable, so few of the mothers could get through.

In Helena, protesters began to fire weapons in the air. And in Ulphia, the King's Army cut the power.

Berringer was waiting with the guards at the end of the long corridor looking at the double doors when they opened. Sable emerged alone.

Before he met her half way, he recognized the Stare. Her pale eyes were empty and haunting, the pupils invisible, making Berringer wonder how she could see. Her face was cold white and emotionless, and the robes seemed to emanate a chill, like she had come from a freezer. Through the Cloitare's passage and into the main hall, he walked at her side, but he could not guess her state until she set her course away from the private quarters. He thought to guide her correctly back to Remy, but she cringed at the expected touch and hurried her steps, though to where he could not yet imagine.

"Sable, please," he tried again to direct her, but she flinched away, still firmly determined to pass unimpeded through seldom-used corridors.

When he saw they were clearly going to the medical area, he asked, "Are you hurt?"

But she said nothing, just kept her frozen focus straight ahead. There was something very wrong with her, so he did not stop her going through the first door into the clinic or the second into the treatment room, but when she punched her fist through a glass cabinet to grab the largest bottle of anodyne, he stepped in to take it away.

She ducked and spun to avoid him, and circled for the drawer with syringes but then reconsidered, knowing she couldn't shake him. Backing away with the wall coming close, she ripped the lid off with her teeth and poured the anodyne down her throat.

"Mothers in hell, Sable," Berringer cursed, and then called the doctor to come.

~~~~~~

Having done what she intended, Sable dropped to the tiles. She was sitting in the first obscuring mist of the drug when Branson entered. He knelt before her while opening a bottle of emetic and said with firm insistence, "Sable, I need you to drink this." When she did not respond, he reached to brace her head and put the liquid to her mouth.

227

Grabbing his wrist, she laid her vacant eyes on him. She was still waiting to be completely lost in the fog, so she was able to speak with piercing clarity, "We are going to see your blood if you don't get out of my face."

The doctor felt himself grabbed by the collar and slid backward across the floor. He'd balanced the container upright without spilling, but still, he was intensely annoyed. "General, that was completely uncalled for."

Helping him to his feet, Berringer prevented the unsuspecting doctor from moving forward again. "Is it going to kill her?"

"It was probably not enough to be fatal."

Berringer said, "I don't accept probably. I can make her drink it."

"You and where's your army?" Sable sounded bold, but she'd come up standing on the hem of the robe and stumbled where she stood.

"It's a good precaution, but may not be necessary." Branson stepped beside the General to ask Sable, "Have you done this previously?"

Bent at the waist, she pulled at the headdress while the Stare clouded over. "You know, my mother was a fiend."

The doctor watched her fumble with the fabric to free her hair. "The risk would be a reaction, but I think if she came straight here looking for it, she's done it before."

"And with far less trouble," she assured. "Apologies for the mess." Still struggling with the length of the robe under her feet, she let Berringer steady her by the arm.

She was trying to stand to her full height when Remy appeared at the door. In the same moment, Berringer felt her weaken and had to grab her from falling. She was warm. The frozen rigidity was now a fever he could feel radiating through the robes, but she was shivering, or maybe trembling.

"I'm so sorry," she pleaded near hysterical to Remy. "You were right. Please, please don't shun me. I swear I will never do it again."

Remy sighed and came forward to take her. He had no idea what she was never going to do again, and there were so many things he could hope for, and though he had walked the halls to the medical rooms with exasperation tightening his jaw, he was so relieved to see her, his only thought was to hold her. He knew he would do whatever was required to make it right again, forgive the defiance, correct whatever damage she had wrought, and he imagined spend the rest of his life trying to conceal her instability from the world.

~~~~~~

The same night Remy had first taken Sable to the salt flats, he had pulled her back into his bed. He felt again the swelling of power in his chest when she gave herself over to his touch, but he could not convince himself it was real. It was a trick of his mind created by his desire to have her. When the memory of it caught his breath, he would seek her out, trying to prove it was illusion, but all perspective was lost when sound broke from her throat. It was the only time he was certain he controlled her. She would abandon self-possession to follow his lead, trusting his direction like at no other time, and every time he took her over, made her cry out or shudder relief, he felt it the same: with her exhale, fierce intensity would surge into him. It would send him feral, raging in all directions, chaos unfocused until he gave it a purpose, fixed it as his own. The need to conquer and triumph over the material would surface. He would feel invincible and she, as though glad to be rid of it, would fall into sleep.

It was only then he would see the X on her hands, vivid scars turned white that Aidan told him meant she could neither give nor receive, an ancient ritual that marked her at fault. She was adept at hiding them while she was awake, but when she slept, she returned to the terrible ceremony that marred her. Every time he saw them it was the same: she would make one final exhale before guarding her wrist under her body and then falling asleep. If he didn't free her hand before she started to dream, she would wake up screaming with the memory of people holding her down. Even freed of the weight, she struggled through the night fighting the past, waking him with rumbling growls of hate or pleading denials. Every hour found him murmuring, "Hush, Sable. You are safe. You're with me," hoping it was enough to keep her asleep.

He should have faced each day weary, but instead he was filled with passion to take back what had been lost, and then to take more.

230

He thought of Alena, all her city names were from the saints, just the same as in Erentrude. They were one realm and should never have been separated, but a hundred years past, when Erentrude and Sierra were close to war, Alena had split away. They were long accustomed to voting in a democracy, so they would not come back easily, but when Remy lay with Sable, he knew it could be done; and even more, beside Alena was Sierra. Sable breathed out power and he wanted to expand.

But tonight everything was different. He'd gone to the medical rooms when he learned she had broken into the narcotics and arrived to find her begging forgiveness. Moving forward, he had taken her from Berringer, and then gasped to feel her latch hold. He never understood how she had brought down Aidan. In his mind was the memory of her lost in madness, dragging the Master and Mentor by his robes to the ground. It seemed unreal, a concession made by a man three times her size, but Remy knew it was not feigned in the moment she dropped him.

He knew nothing about anodyne, narcotics, or drugs. He didn't recognize the heat or the embrace of delirium when she grabbed him. He heard her pleading, "I was wrong, please forgive me," while pulling him into a space too hot and confined for them both.

At her touch, he exhaled, but he could not draw another breath in. She wasn't giving, she was taking, and she took until she brought him to his knees.

And he willingly went under into darkness, sinking to a pulse drumming in the night, pounding in his heart, beating frenzy.

He fought the hand that tried to pull him up, cursing the separation, telling Lucas, "Let me go back into the night."

Berringer had already seen a prisoner vanish into the night, and the phrase didn't settle well with what he was seeing. When Remy tried a second time to take possession of Sable only to fade unconscious, Berringer stood between them while Branson checked Remy's pulse. Once the King caught his breath, he came up waving them both away.

"This is ridiculous," he said to Berringer.

The General knew something was happening, but he could not imagine what. To his mind, there had been far too much activity since Sable was returned, and last night, Remy spent the hours pacing through the palace hoping she might re-emerge. It was exhaustion, Berringer decided. Simple exhaustion.

Thinking to spare his friend further discomfort, the General lifted Sable by the arm to deliver her where Remy could not.

She came up easily and at first staggered beside him, but once they entered the main hall, she regained just enough of her senses to try and shrug off Berringer's support. Rather than fall away, he gripped her stronger, and when she moved to spin from him, he blocked her then simply walked her on.

"Listen, motherfucker, take your hands off me or we're gonna brawl."

Remy was taken aback, certain what he heard was not Sable's voice. But Berringer laughed like his father and replied, "You, little mother, just drank a bottle of anodyne, so I don't think you'll be too much trouble."

The laugh had fooled her. She relaxed thinking she was walking with someone else. She told him, "It was a very bad idea."

"The action does invite criticism."

"Not the anodyne," she corrected, "but to think I could deceive the Cloitare. Such an awful mistake."

~~~~~

"You accepted the rights of a mother," Isabelle was telling her the next morning. "As you now understand, it comes with obligations. Your first is to affirm your new title."

Sable was still in the robe from the previous night and had done nothing more than sit upright on the couch in Remy's front room to receive her.

"I am willing to speak at the Basilica, but it is not my decision to make," she gestured again, referring Isabelle to Remy.

Sable knew Remy was not aware of what Isabelle really meant. Sable had accepted, Isabelle might have ended it there. That was the worst of it. She had accepted when she should have refused. To receive the title of Queen Mother and the clergy's support, she had accepted to connect far more deeply with the Cloitare than she expected. Her head was crowded. She was not alone. She wanted to go back and obliterate them with drugs, better drugs than anodyne, something ruthlessly synthetic that would shock the Cloitare mind senseless.

Already, the connected mind wanted her to be passive, to stop the raucous emotions that shook the foundations. She was an unsteady addition tacked onto the house, a depraved all-night drug den where she had hidden last night in the smoke.

Isabelle would not give her attention to the King. Her admonishing words were for Sable. "Your adherents slept in the plaza. The world is waiting to hear you speak." She stood and gave a curt bow to Sable before leaving.

When they were alone, Sable met Remy's eyes. She had spent much of the night too oblivious for coherent speech and the rest of it sleeping. "You have no reason to trust me," she told him with all the new connections blazing fresh in her head. She could have tried to shut them down, but then she would turn on Remy a lifeless stare. Instead, she spoke to him with a heavy Cloitare presence in her mind. "I have finally learned and I am sincerely repentant. I promise I won't do it again."

"Sable, there are many things I would like to think you would extend to me the courtesy of not doing again. You will have to tell me which of the many you speak."

It would take the whole day for her to reflect on everything she had done over the years that would offend him. "If we were counting, this would be the third time I went covertly into the cloister

234

against your will only to make things worse for us all. I am promising not to ..." the word that came to mind was sneak, *I promise not to sneak around behind you*, but that was too awful, so instead she said, "act in opposition to you."

Remy sat for many moments wondering if he could believe it. In the end, he did not think she was capable, but he inclined his head to show appreciation. He asked, "What did they do to you?"

Sable felt the Cloitare flare with warning. She looked away.

"You oppose me when you do not answer."

She closed her eyes and agreed. "They moved through my mind." She shook her head, "You cannot understand that." It was too subtle. "They froze a path through my mind to travel." But she doubted this either would make sense to the uninitiated. While the Cloitare screamed for silence, she pushed forward to explain, "Much like all the cities in your kingdom are connected by roads, so too are all Cloitare. Some are seldom used one-lane affairs leading to a small town, like the path to an initiate, and others are superhighways leading to Jenevuede which is comparable to the mothers. My city was laid to ruin, the roads destroyed, the waters tainted. I was an inaccessible blight on the landscape, but the mothers fixed that last night by flash freezing roads through the waste. They brought me back into the one mind. They made me travelworthy."

Remy was no longer certain what was real. He remembered being pulled into darkness, but to accuse her would make him sound insane, and any admission she might speak would make them both sound crazier.

She reached out to help. "You are the king of land with conquests laid upon soil. Your kingdom is solid not ethereal. Do not be concerned by these troubles that blow in the wind for they are mine to defeat. I wish I had not, but I have created for you a very real problem which gathers outside the Basilica today. I told you I would not act in opposition to you, so tell me what you would have me do."

"It would be disastrous to keep you from speaking." He sighed and looked at her. "You do not even know what you have done. When the clergy announced you would speak to the public, riots broke out in front of the Sierran embassy between Cloitare adherents and supporters of President Pavlović. We had to ask Sierra to control the violence, and when they couldn't, or wouldn't, we were forced to fly out our staff to keep them alive."

Sable was grim. "Was anyone killed?"

"We've not yet confirmed any deaths, but we're receiving photos of many religious who were beaten beyond recognition. Girard shows me the signs that Pavlović's supporters were organized by the government."

"The embassy?"

"In possession of the rioters. They have demanded President Pavlović support the Alenans, who in turn have their Prime Minister's house surrounded. They want me out of Ulphia."

Sable was quiet and thoughtful. When she spoke, she stated a fact, "And you want Alena."

The simplicity shocked him. He felt it asked him to defend his intention, which pushed him to anger.

236

But she was without judgment. "I am your most powerful weapon. Use me. I can turn the people to fight for you."

It was not how he wanted to take back the breakaway territory, but she was right, and his three advisors could not stop reminding him of it. He wanted to keep a stark divide between her and the battle, but regardless of what was said, the Cloitare had made certain she was going to make an appearance. He felt like he was yielding under pressure, but he agreed, "Ready yourself to speak and I will see that the correct words are prepared."

~~~~~~

It had taken the cars over two hours to move through the crowds to get Sable to the Basilica. It had taken just as long to convince Remy he shouldn't come. Having to arrange both security and sound with a day's warning in an already full plaza had been a trying ordeal for the General and every other person involved. It was secure, but the military presence was hardly subtle. To minimize the tension the armed uniforms created, both he and Girard pressed street-clothed agents into the plaza. It was all so unexpected, neither of them expected any organized action against the realm, but if the General had his way, they would reschedule and do it right from the start.

The General was happy the one thing he did not have to contend with was Sable's contentious behavior. She had spent the morning deferring every decision to Remy or making concessions when pressed to choose.

Though it was asked, no one really expected her to wear a Cloitare robe, but in deference to the clergy, she agreed to wear black. She pulled her hair up with sticks and let others pick the simple dress and jewels. She let Remy refuse the invitation to prepare in the convent, though she permitted the mothers to come inside her rooms with Remy present. She interceded and asked Remy to consider what the mothers wanted her to say, and she accepted what Laudin and Girard had written without opinion. She wanted the four sisters to accompany her, but when Berringer maintained it would upset his preparations, she assented to leave them. It was the most docile any of them had seen her.

Berringer was at her side as she entered the Basilica. He and a dozen soldiers filled the rear vestibule with Sable at their center. Outside, the plaza was surrounded in rapturous appreciation, scattered applause, and voices raised high in praise at her arrival. It clamored through the door, but the stones began to absorb more of the tumult as he walked her to the open arch of the side aisles.

The vaulted arcade afforded them room, but she pushed closer to his side. At first he gave her space to take the lead, prepared to walk behind, but then it became clear she was using him as a shield, guiding him forward to remain half hidden at his back. Watching the black mass of robes move down the center nave to accept her, he felt her hand clinch at his jacket to stop.

The Basilica resounded dully with the teeming outside, but inside was sparse, revealing only a few nuns who had managed to transverse the crush of people. Sable scanned the side aisles and overhead to the balcony. She glanced right to the altar from where ten mothers were approaching, and then left where another twelve were filing into the nave. She retreated, pulling the General with her.

"My teams have been here since yesterday. You are perfectly safe," he assured her.

But she surveyed the assembling mothers and told him, "I'd be safer with the crowd."

The group of mothers stopped in front of him and laid upon him their collective Stare. He knew only half by appearance and few by name. They wanted him to stand aside, but Sable's grip told him to remain at guard.

"Queen Mother, if you would," and one of the mothers reached past him to take Sable's arm.

Sable slid smoothly aside to hide entirely behind the General, making his voice thunder with the command for the mothers to "Move away."

He called two soldiers in front of him and then stepped Sable back among many more. "Sable, tell me what is happening." What he saw before him was a creature trapped, searching for a path of escape.

Her attention lingered on the arch that led to the exit. She looked from the mothers to the exit then returned to him with a decision. "I need to be alone."

He moved to usher her down the side aisle, but she denied it was required. Before she dropped her head, he noticed it took but an instant for her pupils to disappear. She was going someplace cold and remote, where she was untouchable, and then barely breathing, she went further. Berringer recognized it as she had been there with the King.

When she turned her attention back to the mothers, she met their cool expressions with the deep freeze of barren ice. She pressed through the two guarding soldiers and lifted her face higher to be acknowledged.

The nuns bowed their heads and said in unison, "Queen Mother."

From among them, Sable addressed just one, "Mother Maisa, I will make my own way to the balcony."

Maisa though had other plans. "Queen Mother, if you would, first come with me," and signaled they would walk.

"There is nothing to discuss." Sable's frigid refusal pitted her against the mothers in a bitter contest of wills. The stones of the Basilica could not account for the concentrated chill as they stood each other off.

The mothers shifted. Berringer thought they were conferring amongst themselves, whispering words too vague to hear, while Maisa spoke with care, "You will find there is much for us to agree, *now come with me.*"

It was quickly over, but Berringer saw Sable flinch. He knew from her increased breath her frozen mask was broken, and then he saw defeat bow her head as she followed the turn of the older mother, walking with her toward the altar.

Berringer walked uncertainly behind while the other mothers followed and the soldiers spread into the aisles.

240

"As you have allowed, I will prepare you for what you will say."

Sable wavered going forward, but Maisa walked on snapping, *"Come."*

Sable remained slow, but passive, until the altar was before her. While Maisa waited on the elevated platform for the new Queen Mother to join her, Sable turned with the same silent, deliberate, and obstinate step which Berringer was already familiar, walking quickly for the alcove in the side aisle that led to the stairs, the upper floor, and the balcony.

Mother Maisa gathered her robe and raced to push past the General and catch Sable as she began to climb.

"There is much we need to agree, so I will ask you to *stop* and come away." Maisa's words were mostly pleasant, but with one hand on the balustrade, Sable bent gasping with pain.

Berringer was beside her when she pulled her hand from her head and drew herself upright. "Perfectly fine," she told him and proceeded as though nothing had happened, starting again for the higher level.

"We will go back to the pews," Maisa enunciated each word.

Every sound uttered by the mother slowed Sable, even swayed her, but she was not stopping. On the second floor, the entire procession walked the arcade.

Falling back against the wall to let them pass, audio technicians stood against batteries the clergy had never before permitted. Lieutenant Fallon raised his head from the sound system,

241

thinking Sable appeared intoxicated, as Mother Maisa adamantly suggested, *"You want to come with me."*

Sable breathed against it, but she stopped when the mother took her arm.

Maisa was pressed against her whispering when Berringer came around to look Sable in the face. He didn't like it. Her expression was blank, completely void of all living expressions.

"Excuse me, Mother Maisa." The General forced himself between. Turning Sable with him to the side, he heard Maisa's mumblings rattle through his bones and had to physically shrug off the desire to fade into a daze.

"Help me to the balcony." Sable's voice could hardly be heard.

He walked her forward, more to get distance from Maisa and the nuns than bring her to the open doors that showed the plaza in part shadow. The Basilica's high pinnacle blocked the sun as it began to leave the sky, and with the light radiating around the stone work, no one could see into the darkness that laid beyond the terrace.

"I'm going to have you sit down," the General said.

On the edge of obscurity, Sable pulled against the General's direction to gaze out on the crowd. She was a silhouette that was not a nun, which made the silence roll. The sound of people hushing set Maisa into action.

"I am here to give you guidance," but Maisa's tone did not agree.

Sable turned with righteous anger, thrusting the palms she always kept hidden in the mother's face. "You can give me *nothing*." Her bitter hatred made Maisa look away.

Then, from all the mothers, came murmuring vibrations that grabbed Sable's attention.

They were on holy ground, but the General no longer cared. To his troops, he pointed at the mothers and commanded, "Move them out."

While his attention was diverted, Maisa seized Sable's outstretched hand. She was already insisting, *"You will receive my instructions."*

But the instant Maisa touched her, Sable pulled the hair sticks from her head and was snarling, "Neither to give nor receive," as she plunged them at Maisa's heart.

"Damn it and hell," and more cursing in the General's head because he had moved too late to stop her.

Sable had the Mother wrapped in her left arm, pulled close with an expression much like she would kiss, in her right she held the sticks inside Maisa's chest and threatened to twist. "Tell me what you would have me say." Sable seemed insanely interested, but Mother Maisa could utter nothing but silent protests.

When Sable thought Berringer would stop her, she moved them into the light. She stepped out of her shoes as an act of habit before a fight.

The crowd saw Sable's back, that she was holding something black, and at her side was the outline of a man.

She looked completely savage, from the disheveled hair to the blood-covered hand and now bare feet. Berringer had to stop her from turning around.

While Sable's focus was on the offending mother, the General signaled for the soldiers to shut the doors, but Sable made Maisa squeak by turning the sticks, telling her, "If they close them, you will die." She pulled the mother tightly to her chest, dripping poison in her ear, "Now you may use your influence on them instead of me."

Berringer stopped the soldiers. He sounded calm, "Sable, you are burning down the house."

The simple statement struck her still. It came from someplace far beyond the Basilica, from someplace safe.

While he had her attention, the General asked the question that could most easily diffuse: "Tell me what you want so we can end this."

Sable met his eyes sincerely, nearly begging, "I want them out of my head."

She was turning her focus again to Maisa, but Berringer called her back. "Done. It's done, Sable. They are out of your head." He tried to make it sound like magic.

She regarded him as though he were mad. "No, they are not. They are definitely still here." Her eyes went accusingly to the group of murmuring mothers the soldiers were forcing toward the stairs.

"Give me a minute and they'll be gone."

She shook her head; he didn't understand.

"Sable, we can fix this," he was thinking of the present, but she was answering for the past, "I can't see how."

"Just give me your hand and nothing will have happened." Confused about his meaning, she squinted now to see him. It was the same expression he had seen when she had been too lost for words, searching for meaning in the shattered place the Cloitare had left her. When she found him, she appeared baffled to see him, so the General said again, "Just let go with your hand." She was drifting to see what he meant, so again, he demanded her attention, "Sable, *no*, give me your hand."

And she thought she might, but when she relaxed her grip, Maisa pushed for freedom.

Reflexively, Sable yanked her close. Then looking the nun over, she saw the scene for what she'd done. She shut her eyes and silently denied it had happened, but tight in her embrace, Maisa was spilling the truth across her hand. Releasing the mother, Sable told the General, "I have to make him forgive me," and turned into the light.

~~~~~~

Across Erria's screens, Sable appeared gloriously unkempt. Hair tumbled down, eyes manic, and behind the balcony's iron bars, the public could see the Queen did not wear shoes. But the worst of it was her red hand, which she smeared dry on her hip and thigh.

Catherine's face fell. She turned to the King and watched him sink into his chair with dismay. Catherine called the General.

245

Sable took the microphone from the podium, clipped it to her dress, and stepped close to the railing to gaze over the people with rapt adoration. "Hello, my children."

The plaza was stilled. "It feels as though I have been away from you for a very long time." She breathed deep to pull them in, "But it has only been a year since I saw you last."

Sable was completely off script when the General answered his phone.

"I will never lie to you," Sable said. The air in the plaza rippled with meaning. She let the words settle before confessing, "My meditations were not in a convent. I was among you all the time."

"General, the King wants to know what is happening." Girard heard him organizing movement. Behind Sable in the shadows, a line of his men could be discerned blocking access to the balcony.

Berringer had more immediate concerns than discussing what had brought them to this. "Ask the King if he wants me to cut power."

Remy watched Sable control the plaza. "I was with you to know you. I know you as a mother knows her child, and I love you as only a mother can. I give to you a mother's love."

An unexpected emotion choked the crowd.

"I am your Queen Mother." She held them in a tense mental embrace and then smiled. The release broke through the crowd as relief turned into joyous spoken affirmation.

"Let her go," but Remy knew it was perilous.

"I was seven years with you in Erentrude, Alena, and Sierra," Sable said each name slowly, distinctly. "You accepted me as your sister. You sheltered me. You fed me. You taught me and protected me. I return as your mother to provide the same." She wiped her hand again on her hip, making her look like she'd been baking in the kitchen.

"It saddens me to see there is conflict. Our time together is to be prosperous and happy. We are meant to create and unite. But our family is troubled. There is separation. You are all my children. You are all welcome at my table. You are all expected to come." Sable was the benevolent provider that had called them to dinner.

"But understand a mother's love is blind. She sees only her children." The threat changed her face.

Remy sat forward with tension.

"If you cry, I will cry with you. If someone threatens you, I will defend you. If they dare to hurt you, they will know my wrath. If you are lost, I will tear down the forests to find you. I will not allow you to suffer. You are under the protection of your mother."

Her words forced some to tears, but for others it ran as a shiver of warning.

"And your mother is under the protection of King Remius." She let the warning unsettle before pulling them back into her embrace. "You give me your love and your loyalty, and I take it to defend it. I give it all and myself to the King. Hear me, my children, I am your Queen Mother and I am calling you home."

~~~~~~

247

~~~~~~~

In the King's rooms, Girard saw Laudin's pale face turn queasy. "Well, that just undid every promise I made."

The King nodded. "It was an escalation." He considered the threat of Sierra and the loss of the embassy. "But now was not the time for subtleties."

Laudin had a hint of hysteria in his voice, "She just laid claim to three countries and called the religious into action."

Remy smiled. "She did indeed, and in my name."

Catherine smiled with him. Things were going to get interesting. She didn't want to tell Remy what Sable had done, why she had appeared unannounced and untamed before the public with soldiers at her back. By the end, Sable had them so enthralled it was hardly noticeable, but it was going to be questioned all over Erria, highlighted by Sable's critics, and parodied by the skeptics. The clergy and the army were working together to keep Mother Maisa alive and deliver her to a military hospital, the hair sticks still lodged in her chest, stabbing her heart with every angry beat.

"We will of course shield her," Maisa had frankly dismissed the General's vaguely spoken suggestions for discretion. "We have never betrayed one of our own."

Catherine need only think of a good reason why Sable was speaking with blood on her hand, and she might very well turn that over to her Propaganda and Information Team as well. Known as the PIT, they had the world abuzz today with conspiracies showing President Pavlović's administration had organized the beating of the

248

religious that had gathered outside the Erentrude Embassy. Catherine would never have let her agents get caught out by something so obvious and simple. She stressed the details. Her agents and agitators would blend all the way down to the litter in their pockets, or their station chiefs would be entering data in a cubicle for the rest of their lives. Had fifty of her agents shown up with matching black boots, cudgels, and haircuts, she'd have killed them all herself. It was going to be the undoing of Pavlović that she could prove ten of them were retired military and three of them worked for government contract security; and if she could prove the three today, she'd have all fifty within the week.

But the crew of the PIT didn't have to prove a thing. They could say whatever unfounded, outrageous thing they liked. They turned the whole of their considerable focus to the issue. They bantered in live chats, forums, games, and even dating sites about the heinous, underhanded act of President Pavlović. If someone tried to defend the administration, the PIT would swarm and burn the defender to the ground with scorn, irony, and abuse. When the landscape was blackened, a reasonable voice would emerge to extinguish the smoldering remains with a rational conclusion, designed to align judgment with the realm. Their presence online was intended to dominate, and to set public opinion was played like a game.

Catherine was thinking they would not yet address Sable's bloody hand. She would let the PIT start the rumor it was a secret Cloitare ritual—*blood of the mother* or some such occult-sounding nonsense—and Sable certainly had the scars for it. The goriness of it would further undermine the accessibility of the Cloitare, and Catherine would use it, and anything else she could manipulate, to make a deep division between the public and the clergy.

~~~~~~

"I am a god," Max announced. He kicked back from the desk with his hands over his head to accept the adulation of his invisible devotees.

"You glorious son of a bitch." Enzo knew exactly what it meant. He left Nika watching the televised presentation of the Queen Mother to come behind Max and see the folders he'd recovered from Marlow's second memory drive.

"Alright, Marlow, what were you up to?" The first document they opened was from Erentrude's Ministry of Science and was filled with technical descriptions, percentages, and graphs that neither of them understood. They skipped to the end to read the conclusion clearly stating Ulphia did not have enough concentrated minerals of value to justify mining.

Max frowned at Enzo. "Yeah, that's what you think it is."

The data was destroyed in another folder, but two images remained. Max drew close to the screen to study a schematic, reading within the cross work of connecting lines the details of sensors, switches, speakers, heat sinks, and master alarm. "Security blueprint," he confirmed. He opened the next image revealing the street view of a townhouse they both recognized as being in Sierra. For a week, you couldn't see past the online conspiracies that said it was a Sierran safe house. The theorists claimed an Erentrude intelligence defector had been killed there and showed photos of the man with the King's flag knotted around his neck and his mouth stuffed with Sierran money. It had come across as so extravagantly sinister, it had to be faked. Most people laughed to think anyone would believe it was real, especially with both countries denying it. Erentrude did not have defectors and Sierra would not lose one if they did.

Max yanked an imaginary knot around his neck. "You think Marlow?"

Enzo did. "She was gone that whole month."

In a second folder, Marlow's phone had dumped messages. They read Enzo's message back to Marlow, "On my way. Are you Ok?"

"I sent that right after she asked for help."

Of the other messages, only one was important: *I need you at the train wreck in Eudokia. You will find an injured woman; her picture is attached.*

"Oh, fuck no," Enzo said when the photo of the Bound Bride opened next. "Fucking fuck no." He spun around in a fit of frustration and then looked again. "That explains the army and the clergy at the hospital."

"Yeah, it does, but it raises more questions than it answers."

Enzo was having trouble making it all fit too. "Assuming those are contracts to kill, Marlow was already on the train with the Bound Bride when that job was sent. She asked for help because she

251

was afraid of arrest, but then half a year later, her prints link her to Nika's escape." Enzo glanced over the desk to Nika, staring at the screen. "We think Marlow was trying to kill the Bound Bride."

"She's the Queen Mother now." Nika could not take her eyes off the screen. "Says she's been living with the people the last seven years. She sounds like …" Nika could not place it, but there was something familiar in the genteel accent. "She sounds …" the voice took her back, and also the face, "She looks …"

"A bit too zealous," Max said when he glanced at the screen.

"Fuck her," Enzo said. "We need to find Marlow."

~~~~~~

Roused into righteous action by the Queen Mother's call to come home, and outraged by the violence inflicted on the family of her followers by President Pavlović's supporters, the religious took back the Erentrude Embassy in Sierra by midnight. The ceremonial spilling of blood within the Basilica had set the mood, and the Queen Mother's bloody hand became the symbol for revenge with her followers dyeing their right hands red to surround Pavlović's home with menacing intentions. The military fired tear gas to disperse them, but when evidence proved the embassy attackers were employed by a security firm with government contracts, the protesters regrouped in larger, more determined numbers. Within days, they forced Pavlović to openly condemn the protests in Alena, and to further distance himself from the scandal, he came just short of supporting King

Remius's presence in Ulphia, saying for their mutual benefit, "For the preservation of peace and order, great leaders call upon the military with a heavy heart."

Sable had delivered, but the King had also handed Berringer his ass for letting her go heart-stabbing crazy. The General had argued only once through the whole damning tirade, demanding, "Are you making me responsible for her actions?"

And when Remy said he was, Berringer was insolent with the presumption, "Then you will allow me free reign to ensure it doesn't happen again?"

The issue found the two men standing in silent confrontation. The King felt challenged, knowing whatever Lucas was suggesting would oppose royal rights and would ultimately find Sable at fault. It had taken Remy great effort to be fair while the General refused to back down, but such a conflict between them was so unheard of, he braced himself to be wrong and reluctantly agreed.

The General went directly to Sable's rooms to search for weapons. There were several things Remy might consider vague, but not among them were multiple sets of sharpened hair sticks. He found a long, stylish chain belt she had filed at one end to a cutting edge—and could no doubt swing with deadly effect—and finally, beside a sharpening stone was a combat knife. The General offered it all wordlessly to the King.

Remy flicked his thumb over the cutting edges. He considered the most deliberate alterations for a lengthy time before evenly telling Lucas, "Ensure she does not kill again."

On the ride back to the palace, Sable had apologized to the General for the attack in the Basilica, but she looked more humbled to find the table arrangements changed to seat the General to her right at dinner. It was only because Berringer thought it would be pushing Remy too far that he didn't have all the knives removed from the settings.

When she tried to leave the private halls, she was respectfully stopped by guards and asked to wait for General Berringer. It quickly became obvious that wherever she went, he intended to walk by her side, but neither would openly acknowledge it. She made only one attempt to end it, telling him when he arrived, "I am just going to the sisters' room," and he had responded simply, "Then I will escort you." Understanding the change was permanent, she had backed away in abashed horror and made no further attempts to leave her rooms, calling instead for the four sisters to join her.

Because he was going to be responsible for her for the rest of his castrated life, Berringer started training six of his soldiers to counter her flipping monkey moves, but with none of them able to bend backward to play the role of the wind, it wasn't going well. Lucas knew he needed to talk to his father and have another of his pets sent to teach them, but he constantly worried about revealing his father's location, and the arrival of a new cartwheeling assassin would overly excite Catherine.

But he worried most for Remy, though Remy would not hear it spoken, saying with angry finality, "She will not hurt me." If Berringer even hinted at the concern, the King would silence him with

254

a look, and once with his fist bashing down on the desk. The topic could not be broached.

Until the General solved the problem of how to train a replacement, he was on call to be Sable's restraining escort. Each night he would walk ostensibly with Remy, but with Sable between them, to dinner and then back to the private halls.

Every night for the first two weeks of the new arrangement, Sable arrived at the table with a slightly different expression. At turns she was amused, confused, or mentally slow, and once she fell into a dazed stupor.

Remy knew from the start she was sending Amele out to buy her every style of drug, but he didn't ask the General to stop it. Remy had taken the news with tired patience, willing to grudgingly allow one impropriety to avoid something worse. He wanted to know what she was taking and had silently, reproachfully confiscated from Amele syringes before she could enter Sable's rooms. Worried she might inadvertently, or perhaps even intentionally, kill herself, Remy had Dr. Branson incessantly pestering her for mindless reasons. Every hour the General was running up and down flights of stairs, from one end of the palace to the other, as he didn't trust Sable not to show Branson his own blood if he annoyed her.

Once Sable's drug consumption became an unspoken concession of her obliging confinement, Amele made no further attempts to lose Girard's people. The sister led them nearly every night to someplace a little stranger than the last. Dressed in clothes that denied she was ever a nun, she would take them to nightclubs, afterhours clubs, and private parties. Her last stop had been unusually quiet, a little commune of artists and students with a lab. Across the entrance was scrawled in ink, "Leave your ego at the door."

Sable had already swallowed the pill when Girard learned what it was.

"It's called chapel hazardous, or *hazard* to help those who don't already know to avoid it," Catherine explained to Remy. "It's synthetic. Taken to the extreme from a popular psychotropic, it's a chemical dead end. The changes made a hallucinogen most people find too harsh to be desirable. It's a hell of a powerful entheogen, certainly not something you would take socially. The hospitals saw a lot of people on bad trips when it first hit the street."

In the first two weeks, Sable had consumed a systematic list of known chemicals. From animal tranquilizers to shamanic roots, she was searching for something. When she fell into chapel hazardous, she sent Amele back for more. It was the first time she made a second purchase, and the quantity she wanted saw the commune cooking through the night.

Weeks passed while Sable was not seen at dinner, and during that time, not a single mother passed through the double doors.

WINTER

The first month of winter was upon them, but it did not stop the Alenans from gathering in front of the Prime Minister's administrative house. Down the length of the wrought iron fence, a similar group formed repeatedly. Two were students, one worked chopping trees, there was a grandmother who urged caution, and a doctor with his wife made assembling seem respectable. They were all agents of Girard's and they were making friends among the protesters. The teams were scattered through the crowd: two students, one laborer, married conservative, and always the grandmother holding those around her back, warning *Careful. Be careful.*

It was four weeks since the Queen Mother had spoken, and Girard's agents felt the wave was breaking. They wanted the order to go.

But Remy was losing focus. When he reached for Sable, he heard tragic misfortune darken her voice. She returned to him something dreadful, bleak visions of failure that caused him to doubt. He would come to hold her, but she lifted to him eyes of devouring blackness that made her unbearable to touch. Throughout the days and into the night, she ate the pills from the artist commune, hiding behind closed curtains in an unlit room, staring purposefully ahead with blind concentration. When he could get close enough to ask her to stop and come back to him, she would tell him, "Soon. Soon it will be over."

In the slow hours of the afternoon, Berringer was called by the guards posted outside the private halls. There were two mothers who wanted to see Sable.

"Mother Maisa, you are looking well," the General told her. Her month of recovery gave no indication of what had transpired.

"You have no right to stop us." She was penetrating Cloitare.

Berringer smiled at Mother Isabelle and then asked of Sister Amele, "Sable has agreed to see them?"

The three had matching faces, but Amele lowered hers to agree.

The General knew there was very little to consider. He laughed at Maisa. "You, absolutely not."

Outraged to be so derisively refused, Maisa tried to make clear their relative positions. "The *Queen Mother* has consented to see me."

"I am a soldier that doesn't care." He opened the door to Isabelle and Amele, but blocked the path of Maisa. "What happened before is never going to happen again."

When the General entered Sable's rooms behind Amele, Sable was peering through a curtain to gaze over the gardens. He assumed she was aware of the guards who constantly watched her windows.

She dropped the fabric to banish any brightness so that only indistinct outlines of contrast gave shape to the objects in the room.

"Sable," the General spoke from routine, "you know I am going to have to see better than this."

When he turned on a light, he was pleased to see she did not shrink to shield her eyes. It was the first time in weeks her pupils were sober. She set them on Mother Isabelle. "I assume you are here to bargain for peace."

258

Isabelle crossed the room to speak discretely but was annoyed to find the General proceeding her movement. Every step she took to Sable brought the General with her until they were standing in a conference. She expressed her rigid disapproval, but he simply waited without interest.

Isabelle spoke tersely. "You agreed to accept."

Sable shrugged and smiled. "You can travel freely." From her hand, she threw a single pill in the air and caught it. "The territory is hazardous, but I have not stopped you from entering."

Berringer watched the closed face of the Cloitare meet the grinning dare of Sable and wondered who this time would give in first. Sable gathered energy, pulling at something malign until her teeth began to show.

Isabelle looked down. She wanted to do things differently. "You should send your guard away."

Sable laughed. She tossed her voice airily and motioned to the door, "Yes, General, you may leave," and then laughed again with scorn. "I am not the one who controls him."

"If you do not, then I will."

Sable stopped smiling. Berringer knew the posture of her body, the relaxation that came before a move, the centering of intentions that meant she was preparing to strike. He was immediately between them. He asked Sable severely, "Are we about to have a problem?"

Her answer was a warning to Isabelle. "No, a problem would be most disagreeable."

259

Without taking his eyes from Sable, the General said, "It's time for you to leave, Mother Isabelle."

Sable dropped the drug into her mouth and then offered her hands to Berringer as a gesture she would be easy to catch. She leaned to see past him, speaking to Isabelle around the pill, "We should settle this quickly." Berringer could not break his attention from Sable to see Isabelle's reaction, but he watched Sable become malevolent, promising, "I know these dark roads well and I can keep us on them forever. I have only one demand."

Isabelle's voice was no more pleasant, "Speak your treason clearly."

"I won't ride the freeways screaming, but no one travels through my mind." Sable held the treacherous hallucinogen in her teeth, waiting for an answer.

The soft shifting of fabric meant Isabelle had either inclined her head in agreement or denial, but she was certainly turning to leave.

When Sable spit out the pill, the General knew he had just witnessed her win large against the Cloitare. He understood what had been implied, and for all the ferocity and dedication Sable had given it, he was beginning to think it might be possible.

~~~~~~

The King was sitting across from the political secretary in the sunny front room of his quarters. He did not hear her, but he was certain he felt Sable coming down the hall and was not surprised to see her open the door without invitation. She gave no indication she saw Laudin. She stopped before Remy, eyes never having left him, and exhaled softly so that her body relaxed.

The King motioned for Laudin to leave.

When he was gone, she pulled her skirt up and dropped to straddle Remy's lap, running her hands through his hair, pulling his head to her chest, whispering, "I am back, take what you need."

The sun was beginning to set when the King called Girard and told her to start the revolution.

~~~~~~

The crowd in front of the Prime Minister's administrative house was agitated. In pockets, it was being focused, united.

The students started it, rallying those around them, "Message everyone you know. Tell them to meet here tonight."

The laborers agreed. "Enough." They drove their fists into their hands. "We have given the Prime Minister more than enough time. We end this tonight."

"I'll be right here beside you," the doctors told their wives.

When their numbers had swelled, the grandmothers, who had always advised restraint, threw caution to the wind and called for decimating havoc, pointing the way forward. "We go over the fence."

It was a work of devastating beauty. Catherine watched the wave of violence on her screen and gave the next order to go.

Alena's cities were pitched into powerless darkness.

~~~~~~

"Seriously, this place is getting too depressing." Nika watched smoke fill the northern sky and could find in it nothing attractive. Rebels, foreign agents, provocateurs, or whatever they were being called at the moment, would have taken out another warehouse of food, or fuel, sending Alena further from recovery and ensuring the country's continued dependence on Erentrude aid.

The decline started the night the protesters had climbed the iron fence to seize the Prime Minister's administrative house. A turbine in one of the country's coal power plants had shut itself off. The pull for power on the grid had been redirected, but it overloaded the next circuit, shutting it down as well. In a system always running close to critical, it quickly turned into a cascading cycle of failure until the whole country went dark.

Batteries and generators at the cellular masts had lasted a week, but the blackout had upturned the financial district. With no one being paid, the fuel stopped moving.

Enzo and Nika had studied the landline phone for what seemed an absurd amount of time, pressing random buttons to make it send the number they were calling before figuring out how to use it. "So *that* is a dial tone." Nika wondered who had decided to use such a horrible noise.

They were calling home to Erentrude to arrange a pickup of batteries. "We've gone primitive," Enzo told them. "No easy contact from us for the foreseeable future."

The last time Nika had been to the pulp mill to collect counterfeits, she had read about the virus taking out the power plants in Alena. The generators had shut down to protect themselves, but when they were brought back online, attack codes took control of the turbines. The operators' screens showed the turbines accelerating slowly, but the code spun them wildly fast, gaining speed until the blades ripped free and broke through the casings, destroying the entire thing

Of the eleven plants in Alena, eight had been destroyed and three sat dormant while technicians tore apart the software looking for the cause of the sabotage.

For the freedom fighters, it was a grudging recognition. "If it weren't for King Remius' army at the airports dispensing food, the country would be starving." But winter was only starting and Alena had not converted to run their households on battery power. Old chimneys were opened in houses to burn wood, and in several places, fires had taken the house and the neighborhood back to their foundations. After one month of total blackout, trash was burning in the streets where it piled and sewerage ran untreated into the rivers.

Nika was flying out of the mess in Marlow's ugly Pigeon, using it to replace the cargo plane she'd been forced to sacrifice to the King's lithium brine. The first time back in the air had seen her at the controls talking to herself, "Nothing to worry about. Done it thousands of times. Nothing's going to happen." Her concern for the plane was a fear of being caught, of going back to the cell, the isolation, and then the dark living smoke that came to free her. After three months in the air, she only felt it at night when the moon was gone and the instrument panel was the sole source of light. She feared what was behind her, what she could not see, afraid to look for seeing tendrils floating in the cabin. She would end up talking to herself to keep from panicking, imagining she might throw down her headset and pitch herself out a side door, damn the altitude and lack of parachute.

And the Pigeon seemed worse than any other plane. Its surfaces reflected memories of who was missing and Nika didn't want to touch them for fear of displacing more of Marlow's prints, as though each lost trace of her removed another chance she might return. Enzo felt it too. He thought Nika's resistance to use the Pigeon was an unnecessary respect for property Marlow had never observed, but today he flew with Nika and felt the absence fresh. He was shaken every day that Marlow had called him for help and the last words he heard from her were fear-drenched denials for what she saw was about to befall her.

"We've been going about this the wrong way." As they entered the clean air of Erentrude, Enzo saw the shape of things clearly. "Max can only go so far electronically. We need to play this like Marlow. We need to grab somebody by the fucking throat and rip the answers out of them."

"I like it, but whose jugular are we going after?"

"I'm thinking General Bear."

Nika could hardly speak for laughing. "Oh damn, and I thought I was the one who went insane. You're thinking a bit too big for yourself."

"I don't have to be anywhere near him to bitch-slap him. Every relevant search Max did inside the prison for what might have happened that day in Eudokia referred him to a private network and a file named Retrieve. Then, right before Max was kicked from the system, he gets a hit for Mission Retrieve in the military record of the tech sent to secure the prison software. Fallon, Lieutenant Fallon, we're going poke that fucker with a battery-powered ass-kicking stick to get the Bear's attention."

Enzo was glad to see it all plainly now, but he hadn't come to Erentrude to think; he'd come with Nika to get their money to the Count. The hedonistic accountant had been buying every flavor of anodyne to nurture his habit from a client's teenage son for years and he barely recognized his dealer as an adult when Enzo came to him complaining of "suitcases shitting cash." Trading drugs for his services, the accountant had begun his criminal life lightly, nothing more than making hard currency respectable by getting it into the system, but then Enzo just kept referring more people to him and from them he had stepped heavily into economic fraud. Every new contact seemed to bring another until he also found himself with the problem of too much money. In the inspirational cloud of smoke provided by Enzo, it made beautiful sense to become the financial proxy for Erria's most corrupt, transferring electronic funds covertly to serve criminals of every title. With the clients the Count managed of late, if Enzo were not the friend that had originally named him the Count, he would have offered too small a profit for the accountant to risk handling.

The traveling bank was passing through the capital and its tellers weren't terribly happy to be taking Alenan currency. "This is the last time I'm going to accept it until that country gets itself fixed." The Count left his assistants thumbing through the bills on the dining table to move onto the relative privacy of the hotel suite's balcony. To keep from falling into the nodding side of his addiction, the Count kept on his feet, slowly pacing the scroll railing. "You noticed none of the royalists traded in anything but the crown coin. They haven't lost more than pocket change. You might as well start getting your customers used to it."

"They're more likely to switch to the Sierran dollar," Enzo told him.

"Not with this coming out." The Count motioned for one of his guards to give him a tablet from inside and then flicked through the screens until he found a page that caused him to frown. On his next pass by the lounge chairs, he handed it to Enzo. "That virus looks like it came from Sierra: Sierra software, Sierra virus protection, and a visit to the plants by a Sierran technician last year."

Enzo read the technician was missing.

"Theory online is Sierra was trying to force Alena into renewables. They'd make a fortune in contracts. Now, instead, there is talk Sierra might invade."

Eye-rolling disbelief played across Enzo's face. "You're too old to believe in such fantasies."

The Count looked over his thin, aging body. He looked older than his fifty years, and he knew his preference for thick buttoned sweaters paired with slip-on shoes didn't help. "I'm young enough to think there are monsters under my bed."

"Well, you should know, you invited them. But you don't actually believe the lies you're repeating about Sierra?"

"Not in the least. Remember, I am the bank."

The Count's smugness just didn't play well on him, but Enzo had never been able to take the man seriously. The increase in his fortune had barely changed him. He did dangerous business in a luxury hotel with six guards now, but Enzo still regarded him as a meek suburban bookkeeper. "Come on then, what do you know?"

The Count looked like he might play hard to get, but he had so few confidantes, and he'd been holding onto it for ages. "The right hand of Sierra gives money to the rebels to buy weapons, which the left hand is selling."

Enzo laughed. "And all the money is still with you, you skinny bastard." Enzo could imagine the reclaiming of Alena was not going to be as straightforward as King Remius imagined. "I suppose the militias are armed for urban warfare?"

"President Pavlović and General Marič just got bent over the knee of the clergy and repeatedly buggered by the royal house." The Count was still smiling with secret knowledge. "Who knows what they are up to?"

"I'm guessing you do. Now tell me your secrets."

"Tell me yours first. Where is that redheaded fiend of yours? I'm not going to believe any longer you don't know."

"Why do you care? She only ever freaked you out."

The Count rolled it around his face. "Yes and no. *Meh.* Let's say I miss her creepy stare."

"No." It was not the sort of thing anyone would miss. "Sell me something else."

"You're walking around with a great deal of money and no protection. I keep telling you to take one of my guards until she returns."

"No, that doesn't fit either." Enzo knew the man too well. "This is about money, but not mine. What did she do? Who does she owe?"

The Count turned his head and pressed his mouth together tight before admitting, "Bad, bad people, my young friend, very bad."

He walked away saying, "And I'm afraid this is a secret monster the bank has to keep under the bed."

<center>~~~~~</center>

Pressured by Sierra, members of the World Security League wanted to send turbines and technicians to repair Alena's coal power plants, but quietly Laudin suggested Erentrude would reduce production and raise the price of lithium. The political secretary assured the world's most powerful countries that Alena would soon be connected to Erentrude's power grid, making the turbines superfluous to the country's needs.

While the King and his advisors crippled Alena into submission, Sable continued to stay in her rooms to prevent pulling the General away from the effort. Remy couldn't guess what she was doing in her mind to repair, and in many places to simply recognize, the territory, but he found her at all hours cross-legged or kneeling on the floor, focused inward and not always serene. He would press her to talk, but she would only speak ambiguously, saying, "Such strange memories." And once, when he caught her still half in a daze, she offered, "We never should have trusted Orrick," but that was old history from the War of the Nobles four hundred years ago.

The first month of winter had been too hectic with managing the revolution for dinner in the hall, but as events settled, the advisors and company resumed their places.

The General was accounting for all the knives near Sable when Remy's visiting cousin remarked, "You must find your freedom from the convent exhilarating." Francis meant to continue with an invitation to travel, but Sable looked aghast. Her lips parted in gaping disbelief before she could think to hide behind the blankest stare.

Struck with a reality most of those present were well aware, Sable felt too self-conscious to speak the lies the evening required.

While Sable struggled to reappear as congenial, Catherine diverted the table's attention with, "Francis, I believe you have just returned from the far north? The winter this year looks set to be cold."

And Francis, unaware of how she had offended, was glad to take hold of any hand to help her out of the frigid water. Well versed in the innocuous dialogue of the weather, she replied, "The fields are completely frozen over. Soon we will see those wonderful images of skaters on the lakes."

But Sable wasn't recovering. Her exchanges remained tense and unnaturally forced with a smile meant to appear warm, but the result only served to chill the receiver.

When the taxing evening was over, Sable stopped in front of the door to her rooms, telling Remy, "I will join you tomorrow."

But he replied, "Come speak with me now, and if you still like, you can leave."

In his rooms, she kept space between them, choosing a chair at the edge of the seating arrangement.

He said simply, "Tell me what you are thinking."

270

"Free of the cloister, yet I cannot be trusted to walk alone."

Remy was thoughtful, considering how to appease without sacrificing any precaution or safeguards. "If there were some time without incident," he offered with hope, "perhaps then," and he left the idea open.

"I am not so much aggrieved by the conditions of it as the need for it." She was remembering something painful, which she winced to repel. "I should be glad that I have any mind left to lose. I am angry and hold the Cloitare responsible. Perhaps, as you say, with time." But her expression was slowly turning ever more murderous.

Remy recalled the images Catherine had shared many months previous of Sable walking the halls, checking the antique weapons to find them all—each and every last deadly one of them—securely fastened to their racks and now bolted into the wall. For the first time clearly, Remy realized Sable was truly not sorry for anything, and if she was, it was only that she had not gone far enough. He told himself house arrest was a blessing because if she was anyone else, she would be in jail; but then it occurred to him, no, in reality, she wouldn't.

There had been no reason for Catherine to share with him every assignment entrusted to the Guard Dog, and because it had not greatly concerned him, he had not retained each detail that was.

"You really don't want to do this to yourself," Catherine had warned, but he had insisted. A quarter of the way through the file, he retrospectively agreed and set it aside. He had been awake beside Sable with a chest full of power when he finally went back to it. Flicking through the pages on the screen, he would pause to look at

271

the small movements that played across Sable's face while she slept, distressing dreams he would softly talk away. At first he assumed the nightmare images that haunted her were from the Cloitare, but the further he read, the more he wondered. He knew Catherine was incapable of feeling remorse, and she had used the Guard Dog with punishing callousness for remaining anonymous. Sable would have been seventeen when she first made contact with Catherine, and the spy chief had used the five years of their involvement to test the limits of the Guard Dog's usefulness.

Sable had come to Catherine with rumors from the streets, and the spy chief had returned the favor by taunting the unknown informant to do better. The first year had seen Catherine simultaneously ridiculing Sable while throwing scraps of praise, encouraging her to form an ever widening and eclectic chain of contacts until Sable was turning over confidential reports from Alena's senate. But Catherine wasn't satisfied. Remy read the exchanges as his chief of intelligence provoked ever greater acts of fealty, deriding the agent she called pup for their hesitance to kill. Within two years, Catherine was alternately calling her agent a guard dog or a lap dog, depending on how aggressively they responded to her calls to protect the realm from its enemies. Only in the last years had Catherine finally curbed her criticism as Sable provided secrets from Sierra's military and wordlessly murdered according to her handler's demands.

Remy had scanned the report from the beginning to the end again, seeing clearly how Catherine had pushed Sable to acquire more skills to be recognized as valuable, and all the while Catherine was learning how to motivate and manipulate her agent. Yet from the start, Sable had jeered right back, full of certainty she was capable of anything the spymaster could imagine, but unless Catherine gave a specific threat against his life or the realm, the Guard Dog would dismissively refuse to act. And there was proof on every page that Sable's smug arrogance was justified. It was the reoccurring detail that most troubled Remy at present: somehow Sable was able to go damn well anywhere she pleased. It was obvious any restriction of her movements now was only because she permitted.

It might have sounded like it came out of nowhere when Remy asked, "What happens when there is someplace you are determined to go but I do not agree?"

Sable thought of the several ways the conversation could go and felt sick to tell the truth. "If I can't persuade you, then I won't go."

"If you are sincere, this is perfectly fair, but you look even more miserable than before."

"It is many things, Remy, but it is certainly not fair." Dispelling the long night of discontent, Sable rose to press her body into his, deliberately misleading him when she said, "I can be more persuasive than you realize."

REBELLION

The Erentrude embassy reopened in Sierra with an extraordinary number of diplomats. Laudin thought Girard was destroying the credibility of the ambassador. For every agent she had working out of the embassy, she had a fifty more that had never left the streets.

Between Alena and Sierra, Catherine had no veteran agents to spare for non-critical surveillance. When the deputy chief of intelligence brought her the report with video of what had transpired that morning inside Erentrude, she insisted on speaking to the agent who had witnessed it.

Since the pilot's unexplained disappearance, Catherine had been following the entire suspicious lot from the prison, everyone from the major now posted on the border to the guards scrubbing floors at the foothill military base, but of particular interest to her was Lieutenant Fallon. Of all those present when the aviator vanished, only Fallon had any history with Sable.

Catherine put the inexperienced agent in front of a laptop with the video he'd taken paused on the screen. Starting on a frame of two men carrying a large rug, she said, "Walk me through it," and then sat down beside him.

"This is one of the off-base apartments popular with the army stationed here," Agent Mitchell told Girard. "There was no sign of reconnaissance. These two just showed up at the lieutenant's apartment." They were dressed in blue mechanic's overalls with floppy summer hats and knitted winter gloves. The time stamp playing on the video marked it as just minutes after sunrise, so the mirror sunglasses were an especially absurd element of their disguise. Beyond an open stairwell on the apartment's second level, the video started with them dropping the rug outside Fallon's door.

Interference crackled in the long distance recording as they spoke, "I'll call him." Catherine watched his breath steam the cold air.

"Are you fucking serious?" The larger of the two parodied the expected conversation, "Hello, soldier? Uh ... can you come outside?"

They looked at the second apartment behind them and then back down the stairs across the frost covered lawn to the full parking lot where Agent Mitchell was concealed behind a darkened back window. After several lost moments where it became obvious they had not planned very thoroughly, one struck out with inspiration to knock on the door.

When the door opened, they stood for so long unspoken, Fallon had to ask, "Yeah? So what's this about?"

"Your carpet," was offered and then silence.

Catherine could imagine Fallon was taking in the picture before him and finding it off. Finally, she heard him say, "Not mine. You've got the wrong place."

"Can you check it to make sure?"

"Dude, that's not my rug."

"But we're supposed to give it to you."

"Says who?"

The question hung in the air until the larger one figured out to say, "It's here on the tag." Catherine watched him bend to make out something cryptic on the hidden side of the rug. "Says … *Mom*. I think it's from your mom."

Fallon emerged shirtless in shorts to inspect it. He rubbed at his face to wake up and then leaned over the rug to read a tag that was evidently not there. Aware the other man was circling to get behind him with his hand behind his back, Fallon challenged, "What the fuck is this?" He knew the whole scene was wrong, but it was so illogical to his morning mind, he watched in dismay as a sedation gun was jabbed at him.

"Fuck off, man." Fallon leapt aside so the injector failed and discharged compressed air.

Without further hesitation, the larger one grabbed Fallon behind the neck and tried to pull him to the ground.

The agent spoke to Catherine, "They're going to dance around in a circle like that for a while."

Fallon and his aggressive visitor each had a hand locked on the back of the other's neck while their free hands battled to twist the other under control. Tripping every attempt to sweep the legs out from under their opponent, the rug was being shuffled around the landing.

"Dose him for real." The one fighting was getting angry.

They slammed into the neighbor's door while the person holding the sedation gun lunged wildly in and out of the fight, discharging the gas canister with a hiss as evidence he had not struck flesh.

"Fucking inject him with it," was the insistent demand.

"No, fucking don't," Fallon returned, still trying to wrap his arm around the other's.

The two circled the upper landing, bodies bent at the waist as they forced each other down.

The neighbor's door opened and then angrily among them was another half-awake soldier in boxer shorts, questioning, "What the hell?"

In a shriek of terror, the uncertain attacker pressed the sedation gun to the man's neck. The high pressure discharge of sedatives was silent, but it engaged the secondary immobilizer so that Girard and Mitchell heard the electric arc of volts. Mitchell tightened his eyes, wincing as the soldier stiffened and bounced off the wall before dropping outside his door; and over it all, the attacker repeatedly screamed, "I don't want to do this!"

"Well, do it anyways," the other one growled, as he started to lose his grip and the battle.

"Five seconds, five seconds." He applied the gun to Fallon, hysterically counting over the popping static, "One, oh god, two, blessed three, he's falling!"

Releasing Fallon to the ground, the one who had been fighting rose to tell the other off. "You're a fucking halfwit when not at a computer."

277

Catherine and the agent watched the two arrange and then rearrange the bodies to get space to unroll the rug. Dragging Fallon to the carpet's edge, they struggled to start the roll with the Lieutenant's weight. "Turn, fucker, turn," and below that was the sound of a distressed moan.

"They get there eventually," the agent sat back, grimacing at the rough handling while the two tucked and pushed at the carpet until they stopped it against a wall.

The second soldier was trying to draw his legs to his chest when the angry one hit him again with a second dose and an extra current for good measure.

"Yep," the agent affirmed what she already knew, "they're just going to leave him there on the landing."

"Their tactics are fascinating," Catherine mused.

With great and unexpected trouble, they tried to hoist the roll onto their shoulders, gripping at the ends, then dropping and trying again to shift the weight at Fallon's hidden knees and arms. They made it no further than their hips before giving up and moving off. Held under their arms, they fought each other for balance down the stairs, bending the soldier crooked with every step.

The camera moved away from their progression across the lawn to film the moving truck's license plate and other identifying numbers. The two reappeared to heave Fallon in the back with one disappearing behind the rolling door while the other drove away.

"I thought they would move him to a safe house," the agent said with apologetic regret. "I had no idea they would take him to an airfield."

The video showed the truck beneath a battered cargo plane with Ellis Dee, the General's missing pilot, standing impatiently at the open back. "I was still waiting for command to tell me what to do when they took off."

They had used a fraudulent copy of Fallon's bankcard and military ID to rent the truck, but the taunt that annoyed Catherine the most was the false flight plan they'd filed, mapping a route into Alena with intentions to land at Eudokia Field.

It was noon before Girard called the General. He had already learned about the abduction, but he had problems far more serious to contend with.

FIVE HOURS EARLIER

Sable was gaining control over her dreams again. She put her subconscious mind on its knees and then held it silent while she guided the disconnected fragments back to their former alignments. The practice this time was proving more difficult than when she was a child. Just recognizing the act of dreaming while it occurred could elude her, but once she identified the violent madness as sleep, she could subdue the deceived mind, convince it there was nothing to be battled, and then once it was settled, she would focus on the shattered landscape, methodically fitting the jagged edges against their matching parts.

In the silence of the dream, someone called out to her for help. For a moment, it was clear, but then the electric spark against the skin took her back. She woke someplace between fighting and screaming. The pulse in her hand from Remy's neck made her stop.

She was abruptly shocked into stillness hearing him say, "You're safe. You're with me."

She watched him lying beside her, no concern for his own welfare despite knowing he had an assassin's grip on his throat. Lightly now, she brushed her fingers over the veins to coax back the color, tired herself of hearing the words *I'm sorry*.

But he was not worried. Pulling her close, he pressed her against his body and felt her exhale, and with it came the power. She inhaled and again, with a tremor in her throat, she gave him strength he felt in his chest.

"Are you doing what I think?" He felt at risk for finally asking.

But she pulled herself deeper, giving stronger and replied, "Yes."

"How?"

He knew that she smiled. "We are bound."

For a while it was enough, he understood, but then as she moved apart, putting her mind into the distance, looking for what had so alarmed, Remy began to think again. "Explain to me how."

She started to move away. "I don't like it, but I am," she hated to say it, "Cloitare."

He was baffled. "And this means?" He pushed back to see her and found her eyes open but faraway and searching with great intensity.

She was looking at a burning landscape, metal—rent and twisted—spread across a frozen lake. White crystals showered down like snowflakes, but they didn't melt in the flames. Instead, they settled thick on the Clementyne crest, falling across the bull until the red-jeweled eyes ceased to shine.

"There are things I know, and today I know something is wrong." She came back from the vision afraid. She said, "Take me with you." When he looked sad to have to refuse, she didn't hesitate to change her voice, to plead and persuade, "Please, Remy, *take me with you to the flats.*"

~~~~~

Salt Mountain was not where the General expected to be flying in the morning, and everything about Sable's edgy demeanor had him alert. When they landed in the foothill military installation to avoid the violent drafts of the mountains, the King's close guards wanted to move them all into waiting vehicles, but Sable stopped to stare.

Between the blades of the helicopter and the car's open doors, she studied the elevations with unfocused eyes, looking but not seeing the landscape like anyone else. As though she wanted him to see also, she pushed back the General's arm, resisting the direction to enter the car, and guided his attention to the mountains. She was in the peaks, moving through tunnels populated with men. She thought she could account for them with what she knew. They would be moles, hacking at the rocks for chunks of lithium, but, she tapped her head, "Nothing is clear," and the General thought he heard her complain, "The shattered eye is blind."

Berringer spoke softly aside to the King's security leader, "Captain Olson, contact all the posts in Salt Mountain. I want confirmation everything is secure."

On the road winding up, Sable was still traveling apart, farther afield, searching for the threat, for the trail of what was going wrong. She thought of the train wreck, the sudden break in the rails, and how everything could turn so disastrously fast. She moved her mind through the five cars, down the road, up the rock cliffs, and then, lost for the continued sense of danger, she pushed against the drivers, but still she could not find the source of her foreboding.

Back into the peaks, she opened her mind, silent, waiting for something to surface. She was in the distance when another electric surge against the skin made her gasp, grab her wrist, and change the focus of her concentration. "I'm fine; it was nothing," she assured Remy, but for the briefest shocking moment, there had been a call for help and she remembered. She had heard it first within a dream, but in the panic of waking, she had lost it. Someone had reached out to her through a bond, but as she listened again to find them, the voice in pain was gone.

Sable felt a stab of terror for what it could mean. She went looking first for Nika and knew from the bliss of her mind that she was either flying or burning something down. Sable wanted to linger, but her presence cast a shadow of fear over Nika's calm. She left Nika to find Enzo, determined to check every connection until she found the fault.

They entered the bowl of the mountains with Sable unaware. When the vehicles stopped before the pumping station, she was touching on Enzo. He was satisfied with a recent victory that made Sable think he'd beaten someone in a game and she would learn next if Max had been the loser.

While Sable traveled, the King's plain-suited guards left the surrounding cars to enter the concrete and steel structure. The pumping house was a modern industry in a stone empire of old forts. A long, rectangular box with doors on either end, it was pressed against the edge of the field before the rock began to rise. Pipes filled with brine passed through the long wall facing the wide open flat where the King would often stand.

"I don't like this," the General admitted. "We are provoking our enemies with what we're doing and having you out here is reckless."

Remy acknowledged the concern with a nod. Outside the car was a familiar routine. Uniformed soldiers from the last two vehicles had spread to the corners of the building and then beyond into the pipes. Half were scanning the peaks with binoculars while the team's commander radioed the stone post high on the ridge, "Taurus one here, everything secure?"

"We got stormy skies with rising temperatures and a high chance of boredom," was the jocular report.

All the actions were standard procedure: the signal from the commander that cued Captain Olson to usher the King from the car and the team waiting to take their positions around him. Knowing she was prone to wander off in her mind, Remy pulled at Sable's hand to make her follow. They walked the long side of the station before the pipes with the General looking across the white flat to the smudge of mountains too far away to see the farthest posts.

It was the very thing Berringer did not want to hear from the soldier on the corner: "Movement at bearing two one zero. Distance two hundred meters." There was a shift at the corners as sights moved to the called location.

If precautions were not in place, the General knew the mountains offered a potential location for snipers, but the elevations were barren rock, and the old forts that circled the peaks were scanned with thermal imaging. It would be near impossible for any gunman to set up without being spotted coming across the open terrain. But the General knew that if he were fully determined, he and most of the special services around him had a chance of getting through.

He stopped and told Captain Olson, "Return them to the car."

No warning preceded it. Less than one hundred meters from the vehicles, there was an explosion on the flat that shot a white plume of smoke and salt through the air. Like sleet, fine crystals rained down on the cars.

Remy pulled Sable to him. With her face pressed against his chest, she felt the family pin in his jacket puncture the flesh on her cheek and knew the sharp gems of the bull's eyes would be redder with her blood.

The call spread from Berringer who was moving fast to the corner, "We've got mortars. Look for the spotters. Light up two one zero."

Army machine gun fire made Captain Olson shout to be heard, "Into car one," but as the team pushed forward, from the center of their formation, he felt Sable spin to toss the guard on her right and then come around to kick him off the King.

Any life at the called location was finished with propelled grenades, but Sable wasn't letting the King go forward. The team was momentarily baffled by the unexpected resistance whirling in their

285

midst but promptly issued stern commands to move as directed while stepping in again to regain control.

But Sable put her back to the King, ignoring his exasperated warning, "This is not the time," and knocked away the second attempt to pull them for the cars.

Forcefully backed into the pipes, toward the wall, Remy abandoned the appeal for reason and was instead wrapping around her to pick her up when he felt the air pressure rise and a sonic shock numb his nerves. He threw Sable behind him, taking her down under him to the ground.

In fast succession, three more mortars fell across the front cars. Glass, tires, and metal ripped hot shrapnel through the pipes. Separated from the team, Sable felt it hit the King, repeated punches that drove them both into the salt.

The guards came up bloody, shards cutting across their exposed heads, hands, and legs, and fragments were wedged in their vests.

Remy straightened, pulling Sable with him to put her flush against the wall.

"You've been hit. I felt it." She ran her hands through his jacket to his back and felt the blood.

"Find me the mortars." The General watched from the corner as Olson cut into the King's jacket. Having already radioed the foothill base for armored support, he turned now to muffle the order, "Send in choppers."

"No." The King was calm. "The risks are too high. Look at the skies, Lucas. There will be downdrafts where they fly."

The army commander told Berringer, "We need to secure the ridge."

Taking binoculars from the closest man, the General pointed them forward, "Lead your team."

With Olson ripping through the King's jacket to stop his bleeding, Remy kept Sable before him against the wall. Surrounded by military veterans, she was the only one confused. "Why can't the posts take out the mortars?"

"They will be hidden and they could be anywhere." Remy remembered a night of mixed mortars and artillery from his youth. "They might be over the ridge or six kilometers away, and because they fire straight up, they can be behind an outcrop of rock, a house, or anything that gives cover. But without forward observers to tell them where they hit, they'll be firing blind."

Sable felt Remy stiffen under the pressure being held against his ribs. She cast her voice to the General, "Do you know about the tunnels?"

More than three voices repeated, *"Tunnels?"*

She answered Remy, "In the mountains is a system of tunnels for the moles to mine lithium." She pointed behind her, toward Alena. "Mostly south and east, that direction, starting maybe one kilometer past where the first spotter was killed."

The General was searching the mountains with binoculars. He had a balance not even Sable could disturb. In communication with the men climbing the rocky incline, the General warned, "Be aware there may be tunnel openings," then to Sable, "Have you seen them? What do they look like?"

"I've never been in one, but I've been told there are multiple points of access from the houses in the hills and also concealed in the rocks."

The General radioed impassively, "Movement at your zero nine zero. Distance two five zero." In response, the wind carried the sound of automatic fire down the hill and bounced it off the rocks.

"They are not showing up on thermal," came across the radio.

With the shots still echoing, a single explosion threw salt and smoke from a meter-wide crater before the side door opposite the General. The soldier on the corner dropped his gun and cursed the pain that bloodied his hand. Then three more volleys crashed across the entrance and roof.

As Remy pressed Sable to the wall, she felt the first dip in his strength, a heavy relaxing against her that wasn't intended.

"We've got another spotter," the General warned. "Find him."

Sable went into the distance.

"Movement at three three zero," the soldier on the corner called, and heard it repeated until the forward observer was found, but the radios were alive confirming, "It's all blue on thermal. They are not showing."

Mixed with gunfire and grenades, another three mortars fell in the center of the roof. Metal sheets crashed inward across the pumps while the team commander reported, "The enemy is not showing up on infrared."

Sable hardly heard it. She was at the limits of her perception for what should have been unknown. What she found among the rocks was not angry; it did not hate them. It was excited, focused energy, but much more anxious than the soldiers of the King's Army. "Four men, maybe your mortars," her eyes were searching blindly forward, making Remy look at his chest, but she pointed over her shoulder, "just over two kilometers that way."

"Lucas, look for mortars at one eight zero, distance two k."

They silently considered it before Berringer radioed, "Commander, look for mortars at bearing one eight zero, one five zero from your position."

For several minutes, gunfire echoed through the peaks. The General thought the King was looking hazy, so to keep him engaged, he repeated what was heard across the radio, "They've encountered two teams coming over with RPGs."

Mortars fell again through the hole in the roof bringing two pumps to a metal rending stop. Weaker now, Remy crushed Sable's body so that when it was over, Olson had to help him stand upright.

"We are right in the middle of it," the Captain complained, but he knew the open flats would get them killed.

"Sable, are you going to let them try for the last two cars?" The General was hoping her sense was reliable.

Now they heard over the radio, "We sighted the mortars where you said, but they disappeared, and nothing on thermals."

289

"They're in the tunnels." Sable could see them clearly, but all around, the mountains loomed threatening in every direction. She had not looked, did not believe there was time, and in the distance, she still felt pressing danger. Without searching, she did not want to be the one to make the decision to go forward.

Hands gripping Remy's jacket, she pressed into him, her cheek against his heart.

Remy felt her exhale, felt her power in his chest, a yielding of her own energy that bolstered his strength. With his mind once again clear, he knew that to stay would mean his death, and to go could kill even more, and while neither was amusing, the King could not help but smile to know his master strategist looked to his prescient wife who looked to him to solve it.

"Lucas, Captain Olson is going to take Sable and me in the remaining car. After I'm stitched back together, I'll expect you to have answers for me."

~~~~~~

Girard arrived at the military base while surgeons dug shrapnel out of the King. She had taken over the conference room with the bagged belongings taken off the dead and captured attackers laid across the table. Only one phone from the forward observers was still intact. As had already been done by the General's team, she sent again the last number to be called then stopped the call in the cell she held in her other hand. It had been marked as belonging to the suspected rebel commander.

290

Catherine had scrolled through most of the phone by the time the General arrived. For all the bloody guards she'd passed, the General looked untouched. The soldiers were calling him Stone Bear, "Standing there with mortars falling all around like he was made of stone." Not much had changed, except in their day, he'd been called a Snow Bear and had been made of ice.

She had a laptop arranged before an empty seat with the video she'd seen of Fallon's abduction paused on the screen. Before he sat, Berringer handed her a tablet with a wholly different image on display. Catherine walked with it to the far end of the room, speeding through the video as soldiers silently pursued the morning's attackers through unknown tunnels ending with their capture in a garage stacked with mining tools and weapons. The helmet camera recorded the eight men's long wait on their knees for transport vehicles to arrive. Hands zip-tied behind their backs, they repeated a single statement to every question asked: "I am a free man with Free Alena."

The General had been long paused on the image of Ellis Dee at the airfield while waiting for Girard to finish the fast play of events. She turned saying, "Better leadership and they would have escaped." Motioning to the laptop, "I didn't expect that."

"When I was first informed, I was led to believe it was done by professionals."

"Don't write them off yet. Lower the player."

Behind the video were scanned images of Fallon's forged military ID with a photo of a nondescript face and then receipt of payment for the moving truck going through his bank.

"Hell of a morning," Berringer said.

Catherine turned a bagged pistol over asking, "Do you mind?" When he indicated he didn't, she began breaking it down, looking for new parts, repairs, or engravings.

"The pistols and rifles were made here in Erentrude, but they date from the time of separation. They could just as easily have been issued to a conscript as belong to someone's grandfather," Berringer dismissed them as unhelpful. Not on the table were the high explosives. "All the manufacturing stamps that couldn't be filed off the mortars and RPGs are Sierran, but they sell them throughout the world. Tracking them back to the merchant." The General threw his hands up at the impossible task. "But *that*," he pushed a grey camouflaged suit across the table, "You should recognize that."

The thermal blocking suits that had allowed spotters to creep unseen past the army posts' infrared cameras were a technology designed by Sierra. Nearly a decade ago, Catherine had obtained the plans by abducting a scientist's child, and Remy had threatened her with exile if she ever did it again. Maybe it was shame, but Erentrude had never put the design to use, so the suits on the table could have only originated in Sierra.

Catherine picked up the suspected commander's phone again. Running through the photos, she found one taken in a mirror. "Is this him?" The man was nearly their age, but he'd squeezed himself back twenty years into what Catherine guessed was his old conscript uniform. He didn't look comfortable.

She said, "We know this is the work of President Pavlović, but to prove it, we need to start by getting this man's supplier." She ran her finger over the posing figure, thinking how she might persuade Berringer to let her get the answers they required. "Once we get the supplier, we have a chance of following it back to Sierra." Catherine's voice was soft, deliberately soothing. "Just permit me a little room to link Pavlović to this and we've won. He'll be too busy with his own survival to spare a thought for what we're doing in Alena."

Berringer didn't want to look at her. "Catherine, tell me what you want."

"I want to use the Guard Dog."

The General did not expect to laugh. "Oh, Catherine," he chuckled into his fist, "I thought you just wanted to torture him."

"Listen, Lucas," she brought her hand down hard on the table to show she was serious, "I would send the Dog to get information I knew I couldn't acquire with a thousand velvet lies, and she'd always bring it back. Besides having the information now, while we can use it, I want to know how she does it."

Berringer was troubled by all the allusions to the occult he had already seen, and now the soldiers were saying the Queen map-hacked. "Gaming cheats to see the enemy," the commander had explained.

To Catherine, the General said, "What I'm hearing is you want to do this before Remy wakes up."

"Let's just show him to her and then see what you think."

~~~~~~

~~~~~~~~

Lieutenant Fallon sat in his shorts on the edge of a chair with his hands bound behind his bare back and a blanket thrown over his shoulders. The three people in the room had put on balaclavas before dumping him from the rug and then shocked him into a twisted wreck when he fought to escape. He'd stretched the burning tingle from his muscles to find himself on an unpolished wood floor, taped at the wrists and ankles, staring at an unfamiliar word carved by knife in the elaborate base molding. Above it in ink, there was more graffiti, all of it squiggled with crescent moons, little rivers, and strangely placed apostrophes. He'd rolled his eyes and groaned, knowing it was Sierran.

He'd been lifted by the largest of his abductors to sit in a chair with threadbare upholstery, and then the man withdrew to rejoin his companions in the corner of the room, arguing over a piece of paper and whether to show it to him. The whole loopy exchange was convincing him they were just one clown short of a circus.

"Fuck, I don't know why none of us has a picture of her, but this will do." The girl had an accent from someplace farther east than Sierra.

Fallon rolled his neck, taking in the high ceilings plastered in decorative details. The wide, intricate crown molding spoke of a past that had been confident with its wealth, but the wallpaper was sloughing off the walls and the paint beneath was peeling. The sheets tacked over the windows spoke of lasting poverty.

The girl in black was insistent. "It looks like her."

294

But the thin one who had first dosed and volted him disagreed. "It doesn't even look human. Did you draw her hair with my marker?"

"Well, it *is* red," the large one nearly laughed.

"It's just going to confuse him," was the point of the thin one's argument while the girl asked him to do better.

Fallon said, "You might as well let me see and decide for myself."

The girl pushed through and held the drawing to his face. "It's a girl," he observed, "with a fountain of blood spewing from her head."

"Those are braids. Red braids," she defended.

"Have you seen her?" the big one asked.

"You hauled me here to ask that? You could have asked that at my door." But they weren't amused. "No, I've not seen this creature." But he knew he had. The Cloitare had brought her to the plane in Eudokia.

~~~~~~

The eight captured men were scattered in offices throughout the base with soldiers standing guard. In front of the open door of one office, General Berringer watched a man shift against the constraints that held his hands to his waist and then adjust the chain that led to shackles at his ankles. As though the new clothing chaffed, he pulled

295

at the shirt to get the Clementyne bull away from his heart. He could not sit still, but if he mistook it for anxiety, it could not be helped. The slick wooden chair had its front legs cut shorter than the back and he continually slid forward, making him appear to squirm in his seat.

Catherine found Sable in a medical room near the surgery with the King's close guards. They were all quiet and waiting. Everywhere was evidence they had been in the cabinets of bandages and had treated each other. Only Sable was unharmed, but she still wore the blood of the King and his men.

The sight of her made Berringer nervous, but she merely glanced at the captive before taking his phone from the General. For nearly an hour, she paced through the hall with it, scrolling through every call made and received, the messages, texts, and applications.

"You don't need me to talk to him," Sable finally told Girard. "Everything you need to know is on his phone," but she didn't give it back.

Wanting to fully see him, Sable took the few steps that would place her beside the General.

"You were quite sure of yourself to bring your real phone," Sable told his lowered head. "Not that it would have made much difference, but you didn't encrypt it, you didn't even lock it." She shook her head rather sadly. "What were you before you decided to become a rebel?"

"I am a free man with Free Alena," he raised his chin but spoke directly ahead to the wall.

296

"You are *not* a free man," Sable corrected. "You're a prisoner and you're also a fucking idiot."

The voice startled Catherine as much as the words, but Berringer was unmoved. It was the same street accent that had once called him a motherfucker and threatened to brawl.

"Your name, Mark Ansel, your address, your bank details, your mother and father—god help them, you are a bad son for dragging them into this—and your pretty married lover, among others indiscretions, are all over this phone. But what would make you a dead man rather than an imprisoned one are these contacts you stored." The phone clicked out sounds as Sable brought up the first thing to annoy her. "I am so tempted to call Radimir." The prisoner's head shot to the side then back down. "No, you weren't so stupid as to write his name." Sable passed the phone to Catherine to look at the number. "You remember scary Radimir? I can't speak for you, but those pictures I sent of his work made me rather pale." To the General, Sable explained, "Radimir is the first link in the supply of weapons. He delivers for General Marič." She looked back to the man wriggling in his chair. "And I bet Radimir knows all about your family. Doesn't his fondness for the blade alarm you?" Paging through more screens, she pulled Catherine next to her to say, "But none of this proves anything if it were not for this peculiar number." Passing it to Catherine, she said triumphantly, *The Count.* To the slack-jawed face the rebel gave her, Sable pressed her lips into a kiss. "As I said, you don't need me to talk with him. Two slaps and he'll squall a hurricane of information. Here, I'll even start it."

The General stepped before Sable to block her move through the door, but she was smiling in angry jest, never thinking she could get away with it. He motioned they would be going to the conference room down the hall.

Berringer didn't know who Radimir or the Count were, but he knew all about General Marič.

~~~~~~

Enzo pushed Nika's silly picture away. "The army picked up a redhead in Eudokia. Where is she?"

"Listen, dude," Fallon tried to reason, "I don't know anything about your redhead. I'm just a low rank soldier at a desk."

"But you were in Eudokia."

"Never heard of the place."

"Mission Retrieve?" Enzo cocked his masked head. "Heard of that, Lieutenant Fallon?"

Fallon's face rose with surprise before furrowing into confusion that such obviously inexperienced, to the point of embarrassing, people could possibly know about Mission Retrieve, but still he maintained, "No, I'm not the sort to get sent on missions."

Clinching his hand around something Fallon couldn't see, Max accused, "It's in your file."

"Stop lying," Nika advised.

"Dudes, seriously," Fallon put on his best face of sincerity, "I don't know anything about a redhead or what you're talking about."

The Lieutenant jerked away as Max lunged at him, and he stayed tightly flexed as Max stepped back out to bounce between his two feet, flexing his hand, preparing to do fuck knew what. Having seen the boy in action with a sedation gun, Fallon trusted him least of all. He leaned to the side to see what he was being threatened with but couldn't make it out. Talking to the jumpy balaclava, Fallon tried to get him steady, "Just calm down, dude. I'm obviously not going anywhere. No need to get twitchy."

Enzo looked around to see what Max was doing, wondering what he had at his side, then the ceiling seemed to crash down on him with Max's unexpected war scream. Gargling high-pitched notes in the back of his throat, he made Fallon's eyes go big and Nika scream in sympathetic terror. Enzo saw Max's arm swinging down with black enamel sticks gripped in his fist, but not one graceless thing about it looked anything like Marlow.

Before the points could touch, Fallon pushed back in the chair, half stood and then fell forward to drive his shoulder into Max's gut, shouting, "Not that, dude."

Nika was running in place still screaming when Max hit the ground with Fallon on top, all three of them now yelling at the other to stop.

The noise was too much. Enzo didn't understand why any of it was happening.

The taped and constrained soldier was pushing his joints against Max, insisting, "Calm the fuck down," while trying to pin his attacker with his weight. But Max was crawling backward, kicking himself free and wildly slashing long scratches into Fallon's bare skin.

Enzo went in to separate them. He grabbed the soldier by the arms, trying to swing him around, but missed the next stab of the sticks. They slid down Fallon's chest leaving bloody welts in his flesh before Enzo could snatch them away.

"God-*fucking*-damnit." Fallon was incensed. Hot stinging streaks covered the top of his body.

But Max was baffled he had not really hurt him. "How the fuck does she use these things?"

Staring at the blood on his chest, Fallon snapped, "Tell me she doesn't make a habit of this shit." Then setting his jaw to growl at himself, he didn't need to look up to know he had their concentrated attention.

~~~~~

The roles were shifting again. The Queen Mother was once more the Guard Dog who had not shared with her handler all she knew. "I didn't want you destroying their lives," she said.

Berringer was cross and flummoxed, "The moles in the tunnels?"

300

"Or the Count?" Catherine demanded.

"Neither. And for one, I am truly sorry," she told the General. But it was to Catherine she needed to explain. "The Count is the bank. Perhaps I should have mentioned him, but he was never a threat to Remy and he still isn't."

"Is that what's required for you to share what you know?"

Sable looked at the General blankly, saying flatly, as though it were obvious, "Yes."

Catherine already knew this. "The bank, how does it work?"

Berringer watched the two women at the table talking over the rebel commander's phone and wondered how they had ever worked together. Catherine demanded complete control and absolute loyalty, and Sable gave what she wanted.

"This is the program that let the commander contact the bank." The phone clattered with the sound of shivering teeth.

Catherine was obviously insulted. *"Chatter?"*

"Yes," Sable would have been amused if Remy were with them.

"A network free phone system," Catherine told the General.

"Voice over IP. Done correctly, it's nearly impossible to trace." Sable didn't lift her head. "Here is Mark Ansel's account and this account belongs to the Count. Ansel gave this PIN to verify he had money with the Count. But don't send it again. You can tell by the suffix it's a throwaway, not meant to be used more than once." Sable gave the phone to Catherine to inspect. "If you're big and

301

important, like President Pavlović or General Marič, a permanent PIN will take you directly to the Count. If you have cash to deposit, he will go to you, or if you're transferring funds, he will provide an account number. The rebel commander was not considered important, so he was waiting to get a message back." Sable leaned into Catherine and opened a file in the program. "If he were depositing cash and were trusted, he'd get back a location to meet. But Ansel was receiving money from one of the Count's customers."

"Are you following this?" Berringer asked Girard.

When she agreed, Sable spoke to the General. "This is what would have happened: President Pavlović sent his PIN to the Count who learned he wanted to make payment to the rebel commander. The Count gives Pavlović a transfer number which would show payment to ... oh, some aid fund for food or medicine in a developing country, but it would actually belong to the Count. Pavlović gives the temporary PIN to the rebel commander and he confirms the money is present and then gives the Count the account number to pay it to for weapons. Now the money goes to General Marič who sends Radimir to make the drop."

Catherine knew Berringer was slowly putting it into place. She told Sable, "Tell him about General Marič's grand plan."

"I imagine little has changed in the last year?" Sable asked the spy chief.

"Nothing to transform the big picture."

"President Pavlović and General Marič obviously don't have the relationship you and Remy share," Sable told Berringer. "But the

302

malice General Marič has for Pavlović is not known to the wider public. We could practically go straight to him to sell out Pavlović for this attack."

"It's President Pavlović that wants Remy dead, not General Marič," Catherine said.

When Berringer showed skepticism, Sable continued. "If they were working together, the rebels could have gone straight to Marič for weapons, but they had to pay. Now, if General Marič had wanted the King dead, with what we saw today, we can assume he would have sent his own snipers. But Marič wants the King alive, and he wants him mad. There are a lot of things Marič could have sold the rebels, and we're alive because he didn't. He's been looking for a way to slow lithium production for years, counting on the cascade effect it will have on Erentrude's wealth, and here these moronic rebels come giving him the perfect solution."

"Did you know Marič's been supporting the royalist for some time in Alena?" Catherine asked.

"He wants the King in Alena," Sable assured. "And he'd be more excited to think we could tie the weapons back to President Pavlović."

"If we only expose this as Pavlović's work, we'll be facing a military dictatorship in his place." Catherine smiled at the General's obvious doubt.

The General was hearing wild conspiracy theories straight out of Girard's fantastic PIT. "And how do you know all this?"

Sable glanced for Catherine's consent before answering. "Radimir recorded General Marič discussing it." She looked again at Catherine. "And you've sort of used the Count before, you just didn't know it. The payment for that recording is still locked in trust with the Count. I had to drop that whole exchange to go change out the soil report, so adding to the mayhem of the train wreck, Radimir never got paid."

~~~~~~

"You, get the fuck over there," Enzo shouted Max into a corner. Propping Fallon against a wall, he took wet towels from Nika and dabbed at the soldier's blood. "I'm real sorry about that. He was never properly socialized."

"He attacked without warning."

"Yeah, he had a bad role model. So, who is this *she* you referred to?"

Fallon shook his head in tired exasperation, "Dude, seriously? Do you think I am just going to sit here and fall apart because your lunatic friend tried to stab me?"

"He's all but admitted they have her." Nika was done. She pulled out her phone and took a picture of Fallon looking irate. She passed the phone to Max and demanded, "Send it."

Enzo was still trying. "Were you guys really at the hospital to get the King's cousin?"

"You got it," Fallon winked.

"*Heh*, that's bullshit. You were there for the Bound Bride." Enzo thought he had him.

But rather than sinking with admission, Fallon furrowed his brows with the deepest confusion, saying, "Wow, to know so much, you people really don't have a fucking clue what's going on."

~~~~~

The General was still trying to get his head around the idea that Sable, as the Guard Dog, had sent Catherine video of General Marič actually putting his grand plan into words when they were interrupted by a soldier at the door of the conference room. In his hand was the General's common phone, a nuisance with its public number, Berringer left it with others to answer.

The General glanced at the phone's screen and became very still. "Leave this with me for now," he told the soldier. Face held rigid, he handed it to Catherine who burst loud with spontaneous laughter before passing it back.

Sable didn't like the way the General was studying her. "What?" She pointed at the phone wanting to know what had happened.

"I'll show you." Catherine was full of suppressed glee.

She pulled her laptop from the center of the table where it had been left and again started the video of Fallon's abduction.

305

At first, Sable forgot she had the defenses of a nun. Recognizing something familiar in the postures, she squinted to focus the image, thinking she might know the people on the screen. Then they spoke and she went wide-eyed paralyzed. When Fallon emerged and the sedation gun hissed compressed air, Sable pushed back from the table. For just a moment, she found the mask to become impenetrable Cloitare, but next they stunned the neighbor, and she raised her hand to cover her eyes, but still their frantic voices reached her. Exhaling in disbelief, she peeked through her fingers to confirm it really was as bad as it appeared. "Oh, please stop," she pushed the laptop to Catherine, begging, "Can we just skip to the part where you prove I know these ridiculous people?"

Catherine forwarded the video to pause on Nika in an ugly beast of a plane, which Sable refused to recognize, so Berringer handed her the phone with Fallon looking cross and the message demanding, "Release the redhead."

~~~~~~~

Marlow's Chatter account had been inactive for over a year, but now it connected to Enzo's and rang through to his cell. He was silent because he didn't believe he would actually hear her, but she said, "It's nice to know I was missed."

"You have no idea. Where are you?"

"Well," she sighed, "explaining that would be rather convoluted. Suffice it to say, I am safe. I love what you did, but now I really need you to release Lieutenant Fallon."

"Not a chance. Not until it's proved to me you're not being coerced, and that means you stand with us at your back. And I have to say, being on speakerphone doesn't do anything to convince me."

"No, I don't imagine it would." She did not exactly laugh. "Do this for me," the pause was long, "play this very safe. I will try to protect you from my end, but for now, assume you are playing in a burning house. Stay well underground and I will get back with you soon."

Sable was done cooperating. She laid the rebel commander's phone on the table and told the King's two advisors, "When Remy wakes up, I am going to get Fallon. And while I'm gone, I'm getting proof from the Count that President Pavlović tried to kill us and General Marič supplied the weapons."

Berringer was torn between vexed disbelief and certain fear it was true. He warned her, "Remy will never allow it."

She wasn't happy, but she meant it, "You are going to find that he does."

THE GUARD DOG

Through the long afternoon and into the night, every time the King awoke, Sable would press her lips to his head and murmur words encouraging him to fall back asleep until Berringer became convinced she was whispering magic. He'd left her at first to interrogate the prisoners, but each hour he returned to find Sable leaning against the King's ear, the more unsettled he became. Late in the evening, the General returned and wouldn't leave.

The base in the foothills had never seemed menacing, but the clouded night was falling darker than any he could remember and the dim light in the room could not hold it back. Sable could barely be seen where she sat beside the King. The General took a seat beside her.

"You want to tell me how you knew to keep Remy out of the front cars today?"

When he had given up hope she would answer, she said, "I am Cloitare."

"Sable, I have no idea what that means."

"I can see things you can't. The things you might feel as wrong in your gut, I can see plainly." After a moment she added, "Well, I used to see plainly."

When Remy began to move into consciousness again, Sable meant to rise and talk him back under, but the General held her arm and told her to stay. It had been done so benignly, she mistook it for compassion. Thinking the General perhaps worried she was tired, she ignored it and shifted again to get to her feet, but he held her now firmly, and when she met his expression questioning, it became clear he meant to prevent her from reaching the King. Between them it was understood he didn't trust her. Sable relaxed not to fight.

It sounded like she was praying.

"And who do you pray to, Sable?"

The General thought she said, "Aidan," but there was also something else. She kept up the rhythmic cadence, intoning words too low to be clear. He leaned closer to hear what she said and then closer as she spoke lower until he felt her hand on his neck and the words rush up to take him, *"Before the creator's light was my eternal night, it rises again to hold you."* His head fell weak onto her shoulder.

Supporting him by his throat, she turned in her chair to lay her other hand against his chest and push him back, whispering, *"The darkness takes you down, quiet to the ground, you rest."*

There was a nightmarish sense he was aware but couldn't move, like a dream where he thought he was awake when he wasn't.

She kept whispering, *"Let the blackness lay over you and when you awake, the night conceal the memory."*

It felt like just moments and he was back, struggling in the dark, trying to pull himself conscious, fighting against a sleep that was terrifyingly heavy yet left him on the edge of waking. He heard her moving around the room and knew she pressed herself to Remy, telling him to stay asleep. He was sure he could surface. He tried to speak, to shake it off, but this brought her back. In the frightening place between dreaming and waking, he willed himself to be still.

309

And she stood before him, studying him, looking to see if he would move, waiting until the nightmare was about to explode in his mind as a scream.

Next she pulled the phone from his hip, which all his instincts tried to block, but his form was thick and lifeless, unable to respond. Her voice was amused, "You're a hard one to put under." Then her hands were on his throat and chest again. The last words he heard were *"Return to the night."*

When he woke in the morning, he felt a similar hand against the back of his neck. He startled to his feet taking in the scene around him. Remy was sitting on the edge of the bed looking wrecked, and also in the room were Sable's four sisters. Two were humming and Amele reached for him again, her alluring voice asking him to sit back down, but the General was having none of it. He knocked Amele's arm away and shouted them out, "Every last cursed one of you out," until it was just he and the King.

He pulled a chair to sit under the vacant face of Remy and started to talk him back to life. "You and I have been places, my friend, but no place like last night. It's over. The sun is rising. I need you back out here with me." Remy's eyes focused. He might have yawned, but the threat of pain stopped him.

Lucas kept talking to him. When Remy appeared as alert as his injuries would permit, Berringer asked, "Where is Sable?"

"I've asked her to bring back Lieutenant Fallon."

"On her own? You sent her without guards or protection?"

"I'm sure I wouldn't do that." But he was too tired and confused to know.

Before the General could speak again, the door to the room was pushed hurriedly open by a red-haired rogue he had never seen. He ordered her down, immediately moving to drop her, but she spun from his reach.

Still staring absently ahead at the wall, Remy said, "Lucas, relax, that's Sable."

She backed away from the gun he had drawn, pressing her hands against the air to pacify and give space.

The scars in her palms, the wide bracelet on her wrist, then the sticks in her hair had him trying to place her as Sable.

"Are we cool?" It wasn't Sable's voice. She tried again, changing the way she held her face, looking more like a nun and saying with careful, refined inflection, "I am going to put on my robe, then everything will be fine." She reached warily to pull the black fabric from the end of the bed, hiding first her braided hair under the headdress and then concealing the jeans and boots beneath the clergy's long garments. When she lifted her head, she was Cloitare.

Berringer holstered his sidearm. "You were busy while I slept." He wanted to accuse her of something that would make him sound crazy.

"You were tired. I had hoped you would sleep longer." She motioned to Amele who had come to stand in the door that they were leaving.

311

But Berringer pushed Amele back and shut her out. Blocking Sable's exit, he said, "Remy, I don't think you know what is happening."

Very calmly, still gazing directly ahead, he returned, "Sable is going to get Lieutenant Fallon."

"And you're sending her alone?"

"I am perfectly safe." Her voice was slow and full of breath.

The King met Berringer's eyes, convinced with what he was saying, "She is perfectly safe and capable, Lucas."

"Remy," Berringer commanded his attention with his military voice. "You would not send her. And never without guards. You would not do that."

The whole time Sable was sliding her steps over to the King, countering with a smooth insistence, *"I am perfectly safe and capable in the world that was my own."*

"You're right." Remy drew his brows together in confusion. "I would not do that."

Berringer noticed Sable was looking between the two of them, vacillating between still beguiling the King or coming down on him like a hammer to knock him back into the night. While she incessantly coaxed, he tried to ride over her. "Tell me now you're not letting her go."

But she was persuasive. *"The night knows no worries. Tell the General to stand aside."*

Remy was starting to hurt. He felt where his ribs had been separated. He felt the tears through his back radiating fire into his chest, and this talk was ripping at his lungs. He squinted against the threat he might cough, the muscles contracting and promising more pain. Sable and Lucas were now scuffling to reach him, which further hurt his head. He heard Sable rumble the angry words, *"Obscuring darkness!"* and push through to place her hands against his face while Berringer stumbled to a knee.

"I'm so sorry, this is too much." She kissed his cheek. "Please forgive me. You need to lie down."

He felt her exhale, giving him not power but heat and comfort. She was trying to lead him into the softness of the bed. "You will be careful," he told her.

"You can't send her alone." Lucas's voice was outraged.

"No, of course not, you'll go with her." Remy felt Sable harden in his hands.

While Berringer gripped the railings of the bed but was still unable to pull himself up, Sable became more insistent, *"Go to sleep."*

"Sable," he held her hard to keep from falling where she pushed, and she knew Remy was talking through, "promise me you won't hurt anyone."

"It is all going to be fine." She was entrancing. *"The night is long; you want to embrace it."*

But despite her enchanting assurances, he was still coming up. "Promise me you won't kill anyone."

313

She again began to form the deflection that would mollify, but he was hurt and she had to be gentle. *"The darkness protects,"* she began when Remy pushed further through, clearly seeing, "This is a bad idea."

Before she lost him completely, she made the concession, "I promise. I promise to hurt no one. Now stop fighting." And he did. One hand on his chest, one wrapped around his neck, she lowered him into peace. "I will do what you say, but you must *go back into the night."*

~~~~~~

Through the hours of darkness, Catherine had watched Sable turn into the elusive Guard Dog. It started with a call to her sisters to gather supplies that had been collecting in the sisters' room, concealed from the General's inspection. Sable talked Amele through the cabinets and wardrobes, requesting phones, SIM cards, electronics, tools, clothes, hair dye and sticks, then boldly, as the Queen, she arranged to have the sisters brought to her by helicopter. Catherine had not helped, but she certainly did not interfere because Sable had agreed to deliver her contacts for Catherine to use as spies.

When the sun began to rise, Catherine was still observing from the edge of activity. She saw the five nuns sweeping fast through the long corridor of the base's main building with the General in pursuit. Berringer had stopped to hold the wall, looking for several moments like he might retch, and this delay left him a good length behind. He tried to jog to catch up, but again had to stop and gain his balance, huffing from his gut like he was trying to expel toxic fumes from his lungs.

Outside, Sable paused to look over the airfield. She was shaking her head, displeased with what was on display: jets, transports, helicopters, all modern military aircraft she didn't know how to fly.

Catherine followed loosely behind the General while Sable questioned a soldier on the field. The nuns were off again, going where they had been pointed to a small passenger plane beside the storage hangars so far out it was barely visible from where they stood.

Berringer quickened to a steady jog. When Sable heard her name shouted, she took a shoulder bag from Amele and started to run while the four sisters turned to confront the General.

The feint and dodge across the tarmac with the nuns was the most absurd thing Catherine had ever seen. She couldn't understand why Berringer was set on avoiding getting close when he could easily swipe aside every sister in the group. Before they could surround him, he sprinted wide into the grass, forcing them to lift their robes and give chase if they hoped to delay him.

Catherine wasn't important to the sisters, so she jogged straight in line with Sable who was pulling open the hangar door to grab batteries off the floor. Looking back to see the General cut ahead, Sable knew she had no time for steps or ladders. She tossed her bag and the batteries high onto the wing.

The General was impressively faster than the sisters and they soon billowed behind, calling words into the wind. Sable was under the plane hurriedly unblocking the wheels when he got his feet back on the pavement.

Not yet upon them, Catherine heard Berringer yell, "You're not leaving," but Sable was already climbing through the blades to swing herself onto the wing. The General had no alternative except to jump and grab a handful of her robes, then quickly, before she had a chance to shed it, he sharply snapped the material to yank her down.

She was slipping, one foot sliding along the blade, spinning it around, her fingers losing grip on the smooth metal casing. She abandoned the intended escape to pivot and jump to the ground.

The General was ready. He had seen Sable in the Basilica repel the mothers with her rage. She came up purring about the darkness, but he was already shouting her down. His fear and anger were real, afraid she was about to put him face first on the tarmac when she got her hand around his throat.

"The night returns," and his peripheral vision went dark before he knocked her off.

The scene was utterly surreal. Catherine found herself stepping away to distance herself from any part of it. Sable appeared to be thrashing in too much fabric, but her voice was sultry calm, and the General was casually blocking and restraining while loudly raging, demanding silence from the nun who was also queen.

Unable to maneuver in the confinement, Sable was trying to get separation, so the General kept her close. Because she was not out

316

to kill him but subdue him, Berringer's greatest concern was the hypnotic somnolence of her voice. He released his grip just enough for her to spin but held the belt so the slipknot dropped from her waist.

"*Darkness is all around,*" her words were compelling, turning the morning into night. She reached back to get her hands against his pulse.

The General could hardly see her, but he knew how she would try to evade an attempt to catch her wrists. She flipped with the expected pressure and when she did, he wrapped the belt around her throat and pulled her back.

"*Black—*" was all she managed and all he saw before he tightened the band to stop her speaking.

To keep her from landing the heel of her boot in his leg, he kept them spinning in the dark, but still he could feel her stretching to get behind at his face, looking for any purchase to stop the choke. He forced her forward, but she used the space to wrap her hands through his and cartwheel to face him, ready to thrust a knee in his groin.

Blocking her kick, forcing her around, he heard Catherine's worried voice warning, "That may be a bit excessive," and then, "*That* definitely is."

But all around another wail was rising, threatening malice he couldn't see. He jerked the belt taut and ordered, "Tell them to stop."

The force of Sable nodding *yes* tugged against his hands, but when he gave her a chance to speak, the word she formed again was

317

"*Black*—." He stopped her short, yanking tight, but the sisters finished for her, saying, *"Blackness falls."*

It fell hard, driving him down with its own strangling force. He pulled them both to their knees.

Catherine felt it, too. She meant to shove a sister aside, saying, "Whatever is happening, it ends now," but the aggression finished in a slur. Drunken weakness collapsed her into the nun. Grappling down the length of the clergy's raiment, Catherine thought the pitch black in front of her eyes was merely Cloitare robes.

But Berringer knew he was blind. Vertigo made him reel, but he could also feel Sable clawing at her neck, so the General extended a final warning, "One more chance to call them off."

She stopped fighting and was instead waving up currents of air, signaling the sisters to halt their rumbling speech.

When they were silent, he could barely find his voice. Heaving for the air that Sable also wanted, he asked, "Do we have to keep doing this?"

Sable shook her head *no*, emphatically *no*, so he would understand what he couldn't see.

The slight release left her gasping for air while prying at the belt to let the blood flow evenly through her veins.

For the moment, she was quiet, so the General curbed his rage. "This has been interesting, Sable, but now I would like to see."

When sound broke from her mouth, he cinched the belt, not willing to risk where her words would send him. Sable snapped her fingers in one direction so Amele answered from the position, "Your vision will return soon."

"Soon, Ok. Well, until it does, you and I, Sable, are going to remain here and you're going to tell your sisters to shove off."

Sable swayed with the vigorous assertion they should disappear. He barely heard the movement of their feet across the asphalt, and when he looked to where they should be walking, he saw nothing in the dark.

Moments later, Catherine, confused, trying to stand but staggering and close to sick, slurred the question, "Oh, Sable, what did you just do?"

Berringer asked Girard, "Can you make out the sisters?"

"I think they're waiting just beyond where I can see."

"Send them into the main building, Sable." Light was gathering in a dim circle before him so he could perceive the outline of her pointing to where he said. Shadows laid heavy at the perimeter, preventing him from confirming where the sisters went, but Sable's physical defeat was apparent. Still feeling the belt ready around her neck, Sable gave up and sat back on her feet.

The General didn't dare relax. "I'm not under the illusion anymore I can stop you going where you want," he began. "It's pretty clear the sisters got your pilot friend out of my prison and you've just been humoring us by staying in your rooms. The question is what are we going to do about your plans for today? Will you walk with me back to the base?" Sable was motionless, giving nothing. The farthest buildings were shimmering at the edges. Berringer asked again,

319

"Sable, will you give up this idea of flying out of here?" When she still gave no indication she might answer, he said, "You can nod an agreement," but she shook her head *no*.

"I'm glad that's your answer because I wasn't going to believe anything else. And I'm not going to have you back in there confounding Remy with your whispering whatever-the-hell that was you did with the darkness, and damn it, Sable, you do realize it's wrong?" Sable sunk a little lower. Berringer looked across the field taking in the morning light as it reached the corners of his vision. He thought briefly about snapping Sable's neck while he had the chance. His fists were tight with the intended action, but he released the idea as an impulse that would destroy them all.

"It wasn't right how you got there, but we're going to do as Remy said and go get Lieutenant Fallon."

Sable became tense, leveling her shoulders, showing an obstinate straight-backed refusal to have him along.

"You intend to keep that promise to Remy? You think you can bring back proof of Sierra's involvement and not hurt anyone? You, Mad Sable, with sharp sticks in your hair?"

To keep from falling, Catherine placed a hand on Sable's shoulder and leaned into her furious face. "Take the offer. It's solid and you need him," and before Berringer could correct her and say it wasn't an offer, she added, "It's the only option open to you now."

Catherine watched the mental struggle play across Sable's face. Coming to terms with having been beaten, Sable grabbed the belt and ogled at Catherine.

320

"She wants to speak."

When he released the tension, he was surprised by her vehemence, "Seriously, General, *what the fuck?* You have no right to still be standing."

"Technically," Catherine's lightheadedness added to her amusement, "neither of you were left standing. Just imagine if you worked together."

~~~~~~~

Catherine had hoped the two could work in concert, but before they could get in the air, several more conflicts wrapped them together. They fought like two siblings over Berringer's phone until Sable broke it apart and ground the SIM card under her foot while the General tried to prevent her. Then she set her destruction on the military transponder, opening the shoulder bag of tools and electronics to rip it out of the dash despite the General's protests. She hurled it from the side door over the wing, insisting she would not allow them to be tracked.

Their anonymity secured, Sable disrobed to leave, putting the Cloitare garments in a seat, but the General stood in the aisle with his hand out and his sights on the sticks in her hair.

After he'd snapped them in half and sent them out the door in the same path as the transponder, he ran his eyes over her jewelry looking for alterations. There was a wide bracelet on her right wrist she wouldn't risk taking off for the scar, but on her left, in the center of a collection of bangles, the General saw filed edges and sharpened rims, and superfluous to the knit sweater was a braided belt dangling down her side from a loop at the hip. He held his hand out again, but she waited with a face of incomprehension until he confirmed it, "Give me the parts to the swinging blade."

Fuming yet silent, she surrendered the separate pieces of the improvised weapon, but while she did, Berringer thought her gaze stayed a little too long on his sidearm. "Sable, understand now that would be a mistake."

Having already trespassed all royal rights, he said, "To hell with it," and patted her down for hidden weapons. Flung out of the plane to where Catherine stood, a sheathed knife joined the broken collection of what each considered unacceptable.

Finally, they looked to be in some sort of vexed agreement to take off. The last Catherine heard was Sable on a fresh phone from the bag saying, "Things have changed; I have company. Take the Pigeon someplace safe and I will find you."

~~~~~~

The plane had two sets of controls and the General kept wanting to lift the yoke not to hear the pines brush the underside of the fuselage. Sable had taken them north above the clouds and then flown east over Alena and the old forests dusted in snow, through the cellular blackout, forever east until he had changed out three batteries and watched with trepidation as she descended into the tops of the trees to avoid radar. He'd been asking for hours where they were going and now he asked with dread, "Are you taking us into Sierra?"

"They are not stupid," was how she agreed. "They are not very skilled on the ground, as we witnessed in the video, but they're damn clever behind the scenes. They knew better than to strike a bear and then try to hide in Alena with your troops controlling all the routes of transport."

The sun was setting when she handed control over to him, telling him, "Keep us low." She swung in her seat to set a laptop on her knees. Fingerless gloves skittered over the keys. She instructed him to fly south and then showed him what she had tracked to a field at the edge of the woods. "My beloved Pigeon."

"Fallon?"

She laughed. "No, a plane."

"GPS." He wasn't impressed. "I thought you would find them with more magic."

"And here it is just boring software and a chip."

"You know I have to tell Remy why he can't trust you?"

Sable felt it like a punch. The thought Remy would shun her again made her slump, and Berringer regretted saying it so early. She said, "No doubt it's for the best." Then trying for greater detachment, "The mothers have their own plans and I am the heart of it. Just like Remy wants to expand, so too does the Cloitare." But she was too worried to be removed. "The clergy have been waiting more than just the four hundred years of this agreement for a chance to control the throne." The General knew she was staring at him. "When I said they

323

were in my head, you thought I was mad and now you think you understand, but your distrust isn't enough." She hated it was true. "You should have shot me that night before I ran away."

Her desolate sadness filled the cabin. She swung back into her seat and he felt the controls push away from his hands until the trees brushed at the hull again.

"And it's all too late now. If I died tonight," she pushed the plane deeper into the limbs so they scrapped against the metal, "the mothers would twist it as the fault of the King and the public would hang him." The General heard her breath deepen and looked to see her fighting back a strong emotion. "I have considered, as a way to avoid any confusion, gathering a crowd before the Basilica and running a sword through my chest," and to accentuate it, the plane's blades ripped through the branches.

Uncertain what she intended, the General pulled up on the yoke before him.

"But the outcome would be the same." She shrugged and pushed the yoke harder down. "My every action can so easily be turned against Remy."

Shredded greenery and snow shot past the side windows. He strained harder for elevation. "Sable, let me have the controls."

"I should never have accepted the title of mother." She moaned to have been so foolish. "If I ever try to publicly explain what side I'm on, they will drop me so fast to floor," Sable shoved at the column to hear the trees screech again, "you'd know by the mangled wreck they make of me that I have been gentle with you."

324

"I appreciate it. Now relax. Back off the controls." Then hoping to divert her attention, "Show me the tracking program on this laptop again."

But instead, she increased the power and pressed the rudder to direct them south east, laying heavy force into the yoke to take the plane into the trees while the General fought to make it climb. "I hope you never know the emptiness of having no control whatsoever over your own life."

Trying to reason with Crazy Sable while pulling against her tenacious downward thrust, he said, "I sympathize. It must be hard."

"Harder than wrestling the controls out of your hands so we can land." She pushed the rudder east along the line of the woods, leaning her weight into the yoke to keep the nose from tipping over. "One of us has to let go first, and with the force we're applying, you'll throw us into a stall and I'll slam us into the ground. This was a strange time to start an exercise in trust, General." Clear of the trees, Sable switched down the landing gear.

Ahead on a logging road was the cargo plane Berringer had seen in Fallon's abduction. Sable worked the pedals to align the plane while they both kept excessive pressure on the controls.

"Damn it, Sable." The General hooked his arm through the yoke to keep it up. With his free hand, he reduced the power and dropped the flaps.

"Don't let go now." Sable's mood flipped to manic exhilaration. To counter the General, she put boots on the yoke, using the strength of her legs to force the nose toward the ground.

325

The road was coming fast, and Sable wasn't relenting. The General wrapped both arms through the controls just to bring the plane level.

"Righteous hell, this is great," she was laughing insanely while Berringer cursed, "You're a goddamn monster."

Their speed was dropping, bringing the plane to the ground with the blades about to tear through the road. Sable said, "This is dangerous. I think you should pull up."

The General put a foot against the front panel to pull harder, bringing the nose over the horizon. "Give me some slack."

The back wheels touched the road. "Oh, you want me to let go?"

"No!"

But she did. Throwing her hands in the air to signal an uncontested surrender, she dropped her feet and let the nose shoot into the darkening sky. Gravity held her hard against the seat so she couldn't help them if she wanted.

Tearing down the road on the back tires, looking for all to see like they were doing a wheelie, the plane stalled. Sable was still laughing when the front wheel settled on the road. "Text-book landing, General, a perfectly timed stall. Catherine was right, I'm teaming up with you more often."

~~~~~

Enzo had many ideas of how the exchange might start, but Marlow stalking the road with General Bear in a hell of a row was not expected. Steam in the bitter evening air showed they were arguing over each other with neither listening. When they made it a quarter of the way to the Pigeon from where they'd landed, the General wrenched Marlow roughly to face him.

From the place they watched in the woods, Enzo cringed, telling Max, "She's going to bust him upside the head."

Fallon scoffed, so Max snarled, "What the fuck do you know about it?"

But the Bear told Marlow off, berating her with such booming emphasis, Max could nearly make out the sharpest words, and Marlow just took it, gloved hands never leaving her sides. Enzo frowned, "He must have something pretty damning over her."

Fallon did the face again, the wide-eyed *you people are clueless* befuddlement that made Max want to hit him and not stop.

Looking both recalcitrant and chastened, Marlow set off for the Pigeon once more. The General kept tight beside her while scanning the woods they had flown out of, then back across the road to the field of sawn trunks scattered amid piles of snow-covered brush and rejected logs. Well beyond the clear cut and past the fields with replacement saplings, the setting sun obliterated the outline of the nearest town.

Nika crouched under the wing of the carrier plane and Marlow smiled wide to see her, but the General held his arm across her chest

327

to stop her going forward. He was looking into the woods where Enzo and Max thought they were hidden with Fallon.

Enzo watched the two bantering back and forth until Marlow started to dodge past, then, like thunder without warning, the General commanded, "Lieutenant Fallon, stand up!"

"That man has you trained." Max tried to kick the back of Fallon's knees down, and the wooded area rustled with wild movement.

Marlow hung her head.

"Come here, son," Berringer called.

But from the woods, "The girl first."

Then Marlow, "Whoa, whoa, everyone just chill. And *no*," she pointed at Nika who she feared had a gun behind her back, "before you do anything crazy, just wait." She turned to face the General, speaking for several moments until he grabbed her by the throat and gave her a shake.

Nika was out from under the wing running into it, hearing Marlow insist, "I didn't. I swear, I didn't." But then she did: she cast her voice to Nika and demanded, "*Down.*" Nika tripped into the dirty snow, pistol scuttling ahead, and Marlow rumbled, "*Stay down*," then voice higher to reach the woods, "We're cool. Everything is fine."

"It's not looking very cool from where I'm standing," Enzo called. "Both girls get in the plane."

The General's hand had come to rest on Marlow's shoulder while she insisted, "I didn't. You're just jumpy. It can't be helped if what I say persuades. It did because it's reasonable." She gently ducked his grip and walked for Nika, saying for everyone's benefit, "We're not going to touch the gun."

Marlow gathered up Nika, pulling her straight, holding her close, kissing her cheek, saying, "I love you. This was very brave."

Standing in the road embracing her friend, the General again reconsidered what he thought of Sable. Always changing Sable. Dear enough for three people to risk their lives.

He was taking the gun from the road when he heard, "I never thanked you for that coffee," but before he could answer, Sable spun the pilot around and walked her toward the side of the road, cautioning, "Let's not antagonize him or he'll offer you another."

At the edge of the woods, she called, "It's way too cold for you guys to be out there. Fallon is going to go with the General, and we're going to talk in the Pigeon."

The trees crashed with movement and Enzo's voice reached her before they emerged, "You're leaving with us."

"No," the denial caught in her throat, "but I will explain so you understand why."

~~~~~

The Pigeon, with its exposed ribs and grated metal floor, was freezing, but Sable was glad; none of them would find it odd she kept her gloves on. She ran her exposed fingertips over the surfaces,

329

turning on a set of lights, then the electric heater that would only keep them a degree away from dying. She knocked at the empty space in a desk where her memory drives should have been, then opened a cabinet and ran her hand under sweaters to find a set of sticks. She pulled her hair up, sliding the sticks through her braids, remembering. Remembering more than what had happened in the Pigeon alone, remembering everything over the years that made her fiercely love the three people with her. And all this too was shattered. Denied. Sable was bitter, teetering on saying, *To hell with it* and powering into the sky to leave the General cursing himself for not knowing better.

She dropped onto a bench seat at the back, holding her head against the screaming that always shouted, *But Remy*. There was always Remy, and her every action kept taking them closer to the ball of destruction in the future that was blood and guts and Cloitare, and within it was her conviction the clergy would kill him. She had seen it: Remy missing, gone from the distance, the bond severed, the peace shattered, and the General demanding, *Why?* Why she had done something or why she hadn't. Back when she could see, it would often change.

Enzo thought she rubbed her hands together because she was cold, but she was trying to wipe away the scars, return to a time before her mind had been broken, when she could see clearly, could step lightly to avoid certain chaos.

She said, "I have had the most shockingly bad year."

Nika sat down beside her and tried to hug her, but Marlow stiffened and slid down the bench. "I used to wonder why people cried. Now I've learned all about it and it really should be avoided. Seriously." She held her hand up to stop Nika. "Tears are too awful and being here, with what you've all done, I'm about to lose it."

Lighting a cigarette, Enzo placed it in her shaking hand while she said, "I need something stronger."

"I've got a bag of sunshine." He started cutting out synthetic anodyne on the glass screen of a tablet. "But I thought we would be celebrating."

Marlow did a line and then passed it to Nika, half smiling as she said, "I'm wrecking all the best parties these days."

~~~~~

The Pigeon was quiet, the tablet was clear, and the four could almost think it was warm. The metal seats felt like plush cushions, and where Enzo leaned against the hull, it was deceptively soft. Nika had laid her head in Marlow's lap, and Max had no idea he rested flat on metal grates.

"We might as well get down to it." Sable kicked at Max with her boot. "Shall I assume you cracked my encryption?"

"Oh boy, did I." But he didn't open his eyes.

"What in holy motherly mindfucks?" Enzo leaned forward. "Are you working for the royals?"

331

Marlow inhaled slowly and sighed. "In a way, I suppose I am, but really," she tried to show him pity because she was about to overturn his life, "it is so much more than that."

Nika wanted to pat Marlow's leg and say it was fine, it didn't matter, but her hand fell to the floor. She could feel Marlow twirling her hair and figured she already knew they didn't care, so Nika kept drifting away.

Enzo looked at the two wasted souls and said, "Well, you might as well tell me."

"It's better this way." Pulling the fresh phone from her pocket, Marlow handed it to Enzo with a photo on the screen.

"Queen Sable," Enzo observed. "The motherliest fucker of all."

Marlow laughed. She tried to speak but had to wait. Finally, she pulled the smile on her mouth down to look more serious, admitting, "I miss it here." She petted Nika's head until she had her muscles under control, and then started again, "Look at the picture," and when he looked up, "No, Enzo, really look at the face."

He saw nothing, then maybe something. He looked at Marlow. She had changed the way she held her eyes, and when he looked again, also her mouth. He remembered how she looked when they first met, and now she looked much the same. Her face had no emotion. He asked, "Are you her double?"

"No." She waited. "Look at the photo then look at me." He raised his head to the Cloitare Stare.

332

"Fuck no! Fuck. You. No." Enzo shoved the phone away, sliding it down the length of the bench.

Running her hand through Nika's hair, she let him exhaust the first pitch of hysteria and fall back into the drug. "Cut us out some speed because I'm about to make things worse."

Enzo dug in Max's pocket then started chopping out different lines. He wouldn't look at her. He wasn't sure he believed it. The things he knew about her, what she'd done. He was glad he was high, but speed, he agreed, they needed speed. It would clear his mind.

Enzo snorted, winced and cursed "Blow me" for the burn, and then passed to … "Do I call you Sable?"

She raised her head sniffing. "As you like."

Now he stared at her, couldn't stop looking. It was every bit Marlow drawing up another line over Nika's wrecked head. "This is really whacked out weird. Are you really?" He stretched down the bench to retrieve the phone and look again. "You were scary enough before." He looked out the front of the plane. "We abducted a soldier."

Sable laughed, scattering powder. "Yes, you did." Then she saw he was nervous and set the tablet aside while pocketing the bag of speed. "You're under my protection, for what it's worth."

"Well, if fucker hadn't had his hand around your throat, I'd say it was worth a lot."

"Yeah," she tried to excuse him, "he's had a bad couple of days, and I've got a really cloying voice." She smirked without explaining. "That aside, I need a favor."

333

Enzo looked around the plane, smiling, nodding, feeling superbly ironic, "Sure, the Queen needs a favor."

She was absently making a twist with Nika's hair. "I need you to set up a meeting with the Count. Tell him to expect Marlow."

"You need money?" He looked set to offer.

"No. But you should know the trade in lithium for your batteries is about to dry up."

"Man, you weren't kidding about wrecking parties."

"The army learned about the tunnels." Sable frowned over the lopsided bun she'd made on Nika's head. "There was a situation. I had to tell the General. I'm not exactly certain who I betrayed in doing it, but it sure felt like I had been marked for hell. Divided loyalties." She shook her head sadly, thinking Remy was never going to speak to her again after learning what she'd done to get here. "My loyalties are all over the place. If you'd like a taste of it, the King's intelligence chief wants to recruit you."

Enzo was glad for all the drugs. "You got any more wrecking balls you plan to swing through here?"

"No, I think that was the last." Sable pulled the sticks from her hair and fastened them through the mess she had made of Nika's. She patted them in place so that Enzo knew she meant to leave them. Pulling the great mass of red braids up, she harmlessly tied it with more braids. "While I'm sure the chief would love to be regaled again and again with your comedic theatrics on the ground, what she really desires is access to your contacts, which brings us back to the Count. Set up a meeting."

~~~~~~~

There was a question Berringer had wanted to ask repeatedly over the past year. The question rose to shake its fist at the sky every time he had to deal with Sable. He had sent Fallon to the military plane to bring back Sable's bag of electronics while he blocked the Pigeon's front wheels with felled logs from the field. Just in case, he told himself, because he was long past thinking there was anything for which she was not capable.

With another cell from the bag, he left Fallon to explore its contents while he walked out into the high trunks of the clearing.

"Why?" he asked his father. "Why did you train her?" He was deliberately vague knowing the phone wasn't secure or encrypted.

The laughter was expected. "How did my little monkey give herself away?"

"The first time by flipping all over the room with a sword."

This was not met by amusement but a lengthy pause. "The *first* time, you say. Maybe we don't speak about the same creature."

"Your pet has turned into a monster, and she's a hell of a thing for me to keep caged."

"The only *she* I have trained to flip you could not keep caged if you tried."

"I learned that today. Why did you train her?" In the silence waiting for his father's reply, Berringer watched Fallon unpack the bag. The waxing moon against the snow made it easy to see the inventory being ordered on the road: phones, circuit boards, multi-tools, USB drives, and more circuits and cables which meant nothing to him. All he really recognized was that Sable's friends had dressed Fallon thickly in layers for the cold, which showed a level of decency he could respect despite what they'd done.

His father's question was simple and direct. "What has happened?"

"She's off the rails." Berringer didn't know if he was just bemoaning his fate, trying to find someone to blame or someone to help. "She played a game of low-flying suicide with me tonight while talking about running a sword through her chest, but so much has happened, I sometimes forget she went on a killing spree with an axe."

"Where are you?"

Berringer looked around, and now he laughed. "Sierra. She brought me to Sierra."

"Bring her to me."

"I have to get her back."

"I don't care if you have to accept the mantle of traitor yourself." His father was severe. "You will bring her to me."

~~~~~~

Flicking ash and passing a cigarette back into the plane, Sable left her friends behind. To the General, she gave a wry smile of recognition to the logs under the wheels, and then she laid her hand on Fallon's shoulder as he knelt in the road repacking the bag. "You Ok, Wi Fry?"

He was prepared to be formal, but something changed with her touch. He was honest. "I got ganked by noobs camping my base, so I'm never going to live this down."

"Do what all the pros do: blame it on lag. In this case, it was the latency of the early morning mind."

"Yeah, *heh*, that's good. Lag. My ping was too high for PvP."

The General understood no part of their amusement.

She turned from Fallon to tell him, "We're waiting for a message back from the Count. He'll send a time and place to meet to my phone. It could come in hours, a day, or at most three. I expect the meeting will be in Erentrude."

She was waiting for his response, staring him straight in the eyes while her pupils zoomed in and out, making him wonder what drug was driving. Just looking at her made him tired. More tired than he had ever been. He was beginning to feel the frustration of having no control, doing the bidding of his father over the will of his king for the benefit of a lunatic queen. He was too tired to fight and hoped she was as well. He motioned to the military plane, indicating they were leaving, but not registering agreement or contradiction to what she had said.

When she made no attempt to go near the cabin, but instead sank into one of the passenger seats with the bag of electronics, he would have thanked any nonexistent god of her choosing—including

Aidan—that he didn't have to argue or explain why she was never getting near the controls again.

Wanting a body in the seat to prevent any midair excitement, he had the Lieutenant sit as copilot. The fullness of the moon in the cloudless sky outshone the light from the instrument panel, ensuring the General could fly by sight, and in the brightness, he saw Fallon's grinning relief to be free. Fallon was pointing out objects and dials he recognized from a flight simulation game, and the General didn't correct him when he was wrong.

Back over the woods flying north, the General turned east for the sea instead of west for Erentrude, and shortly after, Sable came to kneel between the seats.

"General?" Her expression was big with a question. "The coast? *Really*?" She regarded him as mad.

He exhaled long and shook his head to show he wasn't happy about it either.

"*Uh ...*" At a loss, she tried to throw her eyes at Fallon. "I'm wondering how well you've thought this through."

He understood the appeal of returning nothing.

She said with hidden meaning, "I've only ever been out to this area alone."

"Same with me."

"Then," she was grasping, trying not to mention the third person, "*uh* ... maybe this is a problem."

"Not if you turn the night black."

338

Sable retreated. In moment, she called, "Wi Fry, will you come back here and look at a glitch in this program?"

ORSON FERIDON

Venerable, elderly, and old were just a few of the descriptions that always shocked Orson Feridon when they were applied to him.

"I have an elderly gentleman here who needs to be put at the front of the queue." The agent had delivered him to the ticket collector, and Orson had felt brief irritation that he was going to have to wait on some old geezer to get his ass in gear before he could get on the last ferry.

He'd been a senior for twenty years and still couldn't get accustomed to it. It did have its advantages though, like tonight, they weren't going to leave an old man stuck in the capital with snow on the ground. He liked it better when he had been ushered to the front because of who he was, but he had not come to Sierra some forty years ago to be recognized.

And after four decades, it required no special thought to appear Sierran born and bred. His wool suit had been tailor-made two generations ago to fit a man slightly larger than himself. It was worn at the joints but still strong, a testament to its quality, just like the elegant hand-stitched leather shoes that had been resoled at least a dozen times. When he was still sought with aggressive urgency, the only thing that could have given him away was the canvas brace on his right hand. He still needed it to support his mutilated bones, damage that had healed while he hid, too leery to seek help, unwilling to risk any report of the unique injury that played on the news. The recording was old black and white, slow stuttering shots of him tearing apart an office he'd been locked in for his own protection while rioters broke into the cells to hang him. The image would resurface every couple of years, and, as time moved on, the captions had changed. Last he'd seen, he was being used on the network to attack psychology: *Self love is for pussies.* At the lowest, he'd played in an ad for calcium: *Orson Multi-Minerals: Repairs the damage no matter how you got it.* Then the video would play of him taking a broken chair leg and bashing his bones until the compliance shackle slid from his hand.

Even with the brace, he had the appearance of a country cousin to the King. He looked like two thirds of Sierra, the whole family near bankrupt but raised on tales of when their ancestors had been rich. There was a promise they would rise again, and until then, everybody had been instructed to keep their wits together and not allow appearances to slip. He played his aged and prejudiced part while the young, so far removed from the threats of war, wore secondhand clothes donated in Erentrude.

When coal ran the world, Sierra was a capitalist haven full of industry, a manufacturing powerhouse with jobs for millions. Then, in the span of two centuries, they became so wealthy they stopped producing, becoming instead consumers of the inexpensive technology of their neighbors. The global move to renewable energy left Sierra behind, but not their previously resource-poor neighbor, backward and religious Erentrude. Now it all came down to storage, which was the lithium found in the bowl of Salt Mountain. It seemed to happen overnight, every weapon Sierra had ever sold the Clementyne Dynasty was pointed back at its maker.

The wheel of change was still spinning Erentrude up and taking Sierra under. Orson had been born in the kingdom's ascension, a privileged child that had made his way to the side of the king. More than anything, he wanted to go back, but the Cloitare had put an end to that. He'd been labeled the greatest betrayer, the killer of a king. And his revenge, he had been told, was threatening suicide, talking about running a blade he would have taught her to use through her own chest when it was meant for something else.

Orson had been in the capital when he got the call. "Off the rails," his son said. It was next to impossible for the master strategist to imagine the impassive girl he had trained would ever learn any emotion that might lead to despair.

He had recognized her cool isolation in the midst of the same crowded last ferry he was on now. She had been looking straight ahead at the viewing window that mirrored the lights from inside, laying a hard, penetrating gaze on the passengers at her back. It was one of the few times he remembered his age and he'd deliberately used it to get what he wanted, tottering off balance until he was offered the seat at her side. He had already seen her pale eyes with the small speck of black before sitting down, and she must have thought she was safe to stare at him through the reflection of the glass.

He had told her without insult, "What you're doing is considered rude."

"I apologize." But still, it had taken her a long moment to look away.

"If you hope to blend in," he had offered, "you need to control that Stare." And when she didn't blink to even acknowledge he had spoken, he added, "It's called the Cloitare Stare, and it's the sort of thing that would give away the Bound Bride."

This had brought her attention back, but she wouldn't return his smile.

The nuns had said she was cloistered in meditation, but Orson, better than anyone, knew the Cloitare were full of lies. He believed nothing they said, for when the clergy were speaking, they were lying. When the Cloitare felt the need to make a defense, truth was never a part of it. He had assumed the Bound Bride was dead and the mothers were preparing a substitute, hoping enough time could pass for them to slide her in without notice. Of all the fortunes he never thought to be blessed with was a runaway nun, much less the Mawan, Destroyer of Time.

"The hair is good," he had told her, "but your clothes are too new." He had yawned and relaxed, filling out his seat and taking over the whole of the shared armrest until he'd pushed into the space where she clasped her hands in her lap. When he felt the skin on her arm, he made a face of disapproval, showing he had recognized another problem. "One of the difficulties in maintaining that Stare is you've dropped your heart rate so low you feel cold. All of this on its own is enough to betray you. But what happens if you suddenly need to defend yourself? You're going to pass out."

Her stillness had been profound.

"And now just imagine if I were actually looking at you and not through the obscurity of this window, I would see I had startled the last remaining circle of your pupils completely away. You are hiding in a nun's defense when it is the very thing that will get you recognized."

She had decided to hear no more.

"I need to know but one thing about you to know a thousand," he had said. "I can see by your steady intake of breath that you are not going to be smart and ask me to teach you. Instead, you are going to try to convince me I've had a bad dream."

While he had laughed, she held her lungs full, wavering, considering how to proceed.

"Well?" He had looked straight over to her. "Let's see what you've got. Persuade me!"

Finally, he had made her smile. In the next moment, she had turned to lean her forehead, for all appearances affectionately, against his and the rumbling tingle of her voice had reverberated through the bones in his face while her hand slipped across his lap to his chest.

A quick clip across her throat had started her coughing. He had buried her head in his lap to slap her back and held her down with a twisted wrist. For the benefit of those near them, he had spoken in Sierran, "Damn lollies, I am alvays varning you about svalloving candy."

She was his favorite pet because the last thing he expected was for her to recover and be laughing against his thigh. With the flush of blood through her veins, she had begun to feel warm and he had let

344

her up. Recomposed in her seat, she had decided to return his smile. "So, now I am a little smarter," she had said. "But before I ask you to teach me, you should know," she had looked at the brace on his hand and then to his eyes, "I have been looking for you."

It was over a year since he had last seen her and tonight his son was bringing her back.

He didn't know how the Cloitare had found her, but that she would be found he had known. It was getting late and he had trained her too well. She had been so secret and elusive the clergy couldn't find her, but he had his eye on the endgame and was determined she was going back to the convent, had even been prepared to betray her himself. Then an unexpected reprieve, the story dominating the news was the Bound Bride was returning to the palace convent to be presented to the King.

Orson had watched with the rest of Erria as she led a procession of nuns across the courtyard. He had held his breath, wishing she could hear him silently reinforcing, "Swallow your pride, pet." But his worry was unfounded. She had knelt without hesitation, subservient to the King. Next followed the glorious stretch of time when her obstinance was an advantage; she had stayed low until she brought the clergy down with her. And he had smiled to know the last move would be his.

~~~~~~

~~~~~~

It was a scene he never expected to see: his son, the greatest joy in his life, walking the path home with his favorite pet. They could almost, but not entirely, muffle the sound of their footsteps across the shell and gravel walk. Orson knew it disturbed them both, but if they stepped into the needles from the pines that lined the path, they would encounter the twigs he'd lain to crack under human weight. Another time they might have tried, but they had come with a guest. Sable's hand on the back of his neck assured Orson the man was aware of next to nothing.

Orson had come to stand at the base of the porch when he heard the plane come in to land. To protect it from the winds that could tear across the island, the plane sat in a shelter that he and Sable had cleared from the woods when she returned with the knowledge of how to fly.

Of the five tenets he had taught her, the fifth was to know the way of all professions.

The fourth was to have no preferred weapon, to be familiar with them all. Even so, while splitting wood, she had shown her preference for the axe. It had not surprised him. Like the Cloitare, the axe was not subtle. It was not a weapon of warning with which to knock back the foolish. The axe did not tease and was in no way coy. When in motion, it allowed no room for quick change, and when it struck, it was heavy with a single intention. The redheaded scamp coming down his walk was a thin ruse for a dark purpose.

He was curious why she was disguised, but not entirely, as Marlow again. In the bright night, each step she took between the shadows of the trees on the snow confirmed his suspicion that she concealed no deceptive weapons, neither sticks in her hair, nor belt around her waist, and considering the exasperation of his son, he doubted any of the bracelets on her wrists were sharpened.

When they cleared the trees, Orson walked out to embrace his son. He said his name as was given at birth, Theodore, then held him strong with love and pride, and Theo returned it with equal affection. It had been nearly a decade since he had last been home, and the separation was a loss for them both.

Still holding Theo by the arms, Orson looked at Sable. She bowed low, taking the man in her grasp down as well. Tense muscles tightened under his hands making Orson wonder what disturbed his son more: that it was confirmed beyond all doubt now he had trained her, or that she was a queen and showing respect to the worst sort of traitor.

~~~~~~

The discomfort of his son continued. Theo watched as his mother assisted Sable in drugging the young lieutenant under his command completely unconscious, and while Sable whispered for Fallon's compliance in swallowing the pills, it became clear to Theo that his mother also knew about the Cloitare's murmuring secret.

347

His father pulled him away from the distressing scene, taking him back into the original vaulted chamber of the log and stone hunting lodge. Passing the drinks cabinet, Orson grabbed up two tumblers and a new bottle of Sierran voški and kept herding his son forward, farther from the duplicity and into the circle of the sitting room. On the edge of the cracked leather couch, Theo dropped his head into his hands to rub away the tension of his thoughts while his father sat on the carpet with his legs crossed, pulling from his jacket pocket a folding knife. Orson cut the lead seal from the neck of the bottle, then, returning the blade to his pocket, he poured with his braced hand before pushing the drink across the low table to his son.

"You look tired," he said.

Theo lifted his head to take the tumbler. The smell of the place, the old leather, the chopped wood, the smoke, and then finally the drink, had Theo on the verge of relaxing, but his nerves were shot, his heart was angry, and his mind had been overturned. "Ever since *that*," he pointed to where they left Sable, "that …, I don't know what to call her, but ever since she was returned, there has not been a moment's peace. And the last two days have destroyed my understanding of what is real."

"It was not long after I learned about their ways I was called a traitor and had killed my dearest friend."

After so many years and strong denials, it was clear: "They made you do it."

"I have always maintained my innocence, because I am. The Cloitare killed him, but they used my hand."

348

Theo looked to the sound of Sable speaking with his mother. His face was hard with the memory of every lost opportunity to kill her.

Orson said, "Know your enemy, Theodore. It will always remain the first and most important lesson in strategy." But his son was tired, his expression for murder did not change. He was not yet the master he could be. Orson asked, "Who is your enemy?"

Theo felt like a child in his father's eyes, but before he said anything to confirm it, he gave the question long, considerate thought. "My enemy is the enemy of the King."

His father smiled and waited. It was the way he taught, and it could be infuriating, especially for the son, but Theo knew if he didn't resist, if he calmly accepted there was more to learn, he would be rewarded with a significant insight. He broke it down silently in his mind: *My enemy is the enemy of the King. The King's enemy is the Cloitare. The Cloitare desire ...? Control. My enemy will gain control by removing the King.*

Sable's motives did not fit the description. Theo's face became resigned, looking more tired than before. He said for his father's gratification, "Sable is not my enemy."

Orson lifted his glass, saying before he drank, "You must ensure it remains that way."

Theo returned his tumbler to the table. "It is time you told me what you know about my enemy, how they became your enemy, and why."

~~~~~~

"When the Clementyne Dynasty asked the Cloitare for help in winning the War of the Nobles, at the very moment of their agreement, every future king became an enemy of the clergy, an adversary to be subjugated while the mothers concentrated power. The crown is not their only foe. The Cloitare are the enemy of the people, though neither may realize it. But mostly, the Cloitare have been the enemy of the future," the master strategist wished he had seen it all as clearly when he was his son's age. "The only concession I will allow them is it is not entirely their fault. They have spent the last four hundred years in a deliberate misunderstanding, the obfuscation of Master Aidan."

Theo gently corrected his father, "Well, Aidan can at least account for the last twenty-odd years."

"He can account for them all." Orson was harsh with unspoken accusations.

"The man is how old?"

"The *man* ..." Orson huffed a breath out while thinking. "The man must be nearing his late fifties by now."

Theo puzzled over what meaning laid behind the inflection, and when he could make no sense of it, he said wearily, "In the best of times, I have no patience for riddles, and you know that. Tell me what you mean plainly."

"I wish I could. What I know is what Sable will share, that the man, his body and flesh, is younger than me, but Master Aidan is very old. And I do not doubt he is a master."

350

"Master of what?" Theo had never been sure.

"Sable, tell my son of what Aidan is a master."

Sable may not have been his enemy, but the General had studied her as though she were. His father's request met her as she entered the room and kept her pushed against its edge, walking the outer perimeter in slow avoidance. By her own admission, she would only divulge information when it was a threat to Remy, and the General could see her loyalties were under pressure.

Orson smiled apologetically to his son for the silence at his back. "Is it a secret again? Or are we just not telling Theo?"

As though her palms were dirty, Sable stopped to scrub her bare hands against the sides of her jeans. She gave her answer to the fire at the far end of the room. "Master of the mind. Master of travel. Master of creation. Master Architect of the Cloitare."

While she deadpanned the achievements, Orson kept an appreciative grin on his son. "Aidan would be the most dangerous of them all if he were not so damned attached to the things he made." Halting her progression again, Orson asked Sable another question, "But he's not very good at destroying his creations, is he?"

The long stretch of silence proved she wasn't going to respond. She began walking again for the hearth when his father answered Theo himself, "He's not. But no architect can build on land that has not been cleared." His father was now clearly antagonizing her. "Can they, pet?"

She stopped closer to the fire to cast a defensive glance back. Her posture was full of warning.

351

Orson laughed at her and said, "We'll come back to it. While you're there, cut my lovely wife some kindling." When he returned his attention to his son, it was clear his entertainment with riling his pet was over. "Sable is not the first rebellious nun I've encountered. There was another that came to me while I held much the same position as you with the king. But Callias Clement was no Remius. He was fully grey when he took the throne, and he didn't have a clue what to do with it. The man had never been taught how to manage the army or the people, and he certainly didn't know how to control the Cloitare. Decades before being crowned, he had a second youth with me while trying to avoid taking another wife that could give him children. I was a little older than Sable and he was about the same age as you when the Cloitare told him they'd annulled his marriage."

This was not what history had written, and Theo was surprised. "He hadn't asked for it?"

"Hell, no. He didn't know they had done it till they dropped the documents in his lap with his father's blessing. We spent a year looking for his wife, Carina, or ex-wife, or whatever she was by that point. The mothers had locked her up in a convent in Alena, and I was the fool charged with breaking her out, which is a whole other story. After that, we spent another four years with her dodging both his father and the clergy." Orson raised his eyes with the memory. "Not only them but the teenaged bride with the wide childbearing hips." He measured his hands to either side of his crossed knees. "Hell of a good time we were having until they caught up with us."

"They have a way of quashing all the fun." Sable was kneeling at the hearth.

"That they do," Orson agreed.

In sensitivity to Berringer's fear of her with weapons, Sable used the hatchet with small, controlled strikes, splitting a quartered log into thin fire-ready strips against a large circular stump on the stones.

"Callias was a good man, but a bit of a puss. He had no fight in him. Would do near anything to avoid conflict. All he wanted was to keep Carina and me near. He did the marriage thing and then dutifully hammered away at his new wife until she was pregnant. When she began to show, the King sent Callias off to represent Erentrude in the Continental War. The palace essentially didn't see him, Carina, or me for another thirteen years, except once a year, Callias and I would go home for his son's birthday."

Theo gave the sardonic appearance of appreciating Callias's virility, "And sired three more children."

"Wide childbearing king-accommodating hips." Orson chuckled to himself.

The story was about to take a sad turn and Orson was not eager to continue. He watched Sable place another log on the stump and gently split it, slicing it down until she had a pile of sticks. She originally had a habit of rolling the handle of every weapon over her hand with a flourish. It had been an unnecessary action when the purpose of picking up a blade is to cut. Her vaunting display was best left for entertainers, and he'd had to repeatedly knock the weapons

353

out of her hands to show her the weakness. Lesson learned, she became methodical and precise with a sure flexible hand until the blade was committed to a strike, then she and the edge became fixed. Now she was closed, her movements furtive and suppressed.

He continued watching her for the cause so he could correct it. He was frowning for many reasons when he resumed speaking. "Callias was sixty-five when he was made king and sixty-five when I killed him." Sable left the blade against the block, waiting for the worst of the story she already knew to be over. "The wayward sister I spoke of earlier had come to the palace convent from Alena and was known to me from the escapade in freeing Carina. The Cloitare had sent Sister Agatha specifically because we had a history. The mothers just couldn't imagine after reeducation she would dare again to help me." Orson swirled the voški in the tumbler and looked at no one. "Callias hadn't been king for more than a month when Agatha brought me parchments from the convent's library detailing the nature of the prophecy the nuns were awaiting from the Clementyne and Cloitare agreement."

Turning her face to the fire, Sable left a curtain of braids hiding her features. Theo looked between her and his father, reading subtle signs of guilt and condemnation.

Orson shook his head to dispel his thoughts. "It's not her fault." He drank the voški while his expression changed to strong determination to explain to his son another part of the story Sable had long known. "The Cloitare have been waiting these last four hundred years on a great destroyer, the Mawan, Destroyer of Time." Orson

354

pointed at Sable. "The public knows her by three comparatively fluffy-bunny names, but the nuns don't use those titles behind the double doors."

"Catherine's been swearing for seven years you had another title."

Both men watched her motionless form and knew from experience she had no intention of responding. Orson spoke to her willful silence, "Sable is quite familiar with what the Cloitare expect from the Mawan, so to her I did not need to explain what Agatha told me, but I am hoping she will clarify it for you."

When time had stretched to an uncomfortable length, the General opened his mouth to put a question to Sable, but his father signaled for him to wait. In the quiet stillness, Theo could hear water running through pipes under the house, his mother's brisk movements in the kitchen, utensils clattering together under the faucet. The washing stopped and turned into the whisk of a broom against the floor and then the slosh of a mop against the tiles as his mother nervously cleaned.

Finally, Sable relented, saying, "It is quite self-explanatory." She stood and put her back to the fire. "The Cloitare believe time refers to an era, and they most obviously do not want me to destroy the age of religion."

"And Aidan?" Orson asked. "What does he wish destroyed?"

She gave her answer to the General. "His understanding is different. He is a master of time. I do not say this to insult your intelligence, but you cannot begin to conceive of what this means.

355

Your experience is limited, far more limited than mine, and I scarcely comprehend it. I have fleeting glimpses of clarity, seeing time as finite and then again as infinite, as matter and then energy, as both, and even knowing this vacillation should be impossible, I believe between the two there exists something else, a space which Master Aidan is familiar." Sable's passionate explanation halted abruptly. She spoke now to both men. "If any could guess the will of Master Aidan, it would be me, and I would not dare, so let that give you pause before either of you try. But the desire of the clergy is base and obvious." She told the General, "They have interpreted the revelations to mean the destruction of the realm so that the new age will belong exclusively to them. With a mother as queen, they will have consolidated their influence." Then suddenly angry, she said, "The opportunity should never have been presented," and in her fierce expression, the General was certain she was denouncing him.

The visual exchange between the two was strained and Orson didn't want them at odds. He pulled his son's attention back, telling him, "That is what Agatha showed me in the parchments, the coming of the Mawan and the expectation of absolute power. At the time, I had no idea what the Cloitare could do with their voice. I took the nun and the information to Callias, but that man," Orson grimaced, holding his mouth tight against speaking his real thoughts. "You would think after thirteen years of being sent to every godforsaken war in the world to represent Erentrude, he wouldn't fall apart to hear someone might want him dead. But that is exactly what he did. He shushed us both with wild, terrified eyes, like someone might hear when the rooms were empty except for us. When I tried to show him the parchments, he fled behind the desk, telling me, 'There's not a thing we can do about it. Best that we forget it.' But I rather liked the young heir, Remy's father, and I saw no reason to pass this legacy onto him. Callias was royal, but I had a bad way of pushing him around, arguing with him to win. I wanted to make the parchments public, go to the media, and confront the Cloitare, but on this he was adamantly opposed. He had us in a whispering quarrel when the damnedest thing happened. We noticed Sister Agatha staggering drunk around the room. She had a hand to her head and was bent at the waist reaching out for something to get her steady. Callias became hysterical, whimpering that she'd been poisoned." Orson shook his head at the logic and then furrowed his brow to say, "But she *was* sick. And she was terrified."

Before she could turn back to the fire, the General saw a pained expression of empathy on Sable's face.

"Then everything went to hell. Callias was behind the desk fainting to the floor," Orson threw one hand in the air, "Agatha was hyperventilating," he threw up the other, "I'm thinking they're both entirely too delicate when the door opens and into the chaos come two rumbling mothers. God damnedest thing I have ever felt. I was weightless and didn't know I was falling until I cracked my head on the arm of a chair. Even once I was down, I wasn't certain which way was up because I couldn't feel the floor. I was certain I was floating and was trying to get into a stable free fall, but there was no equilibrium to be found. And everything was white. Even when I thought I had closed my eyes, there was this stabbing blindness from too much light. Glaring, snow blind, white.

357

"The light was cold, like ice against my neck, that's when I realized someone also had their hand against my chest. It felt like the mother was sending freezing water through my veins. Her voice was brittle, crackling hard, telling me I was going to be enlightened by her instructions and inspired to obey. She assured me what she was saying was true: we were in the ice-covered wastes of the poles and were never coming out. We had been there for weeks on a sheet of barren ice. Look around, she urged me, and see nothing but the wild, frozen desert, it would dispel any doubt. She told me to feel my split lips and the dead flesh of my frostbitten fingers. If I listened, she told me, I could hear Callias crying, begging me for help. And she was right; Callias was weeping.

"She assured me what she was saying made perfect sense, his suffering was unnatural, as we were both going to die of exposure. I was cruel not to do as he asked and end his life. It was my duty to follow his order, her order, and accept direction. She convinced me it was better Callias should succumb to my skills than the weather. It was what he was begging me for, and he was certainly begging. I could hear him pleading for mercy. She told me to see his abject form prostrate before me, and through the harsh white of the storm, he was there. He was imploring both God and me to save him.

"He was distraught and the desperation was wrenching when I agreed, assuring Callias I would kill him. He begged stronger and I struggled against weakness to crawl beside him. He was sobbing and the mother told me to hear his command to act swiftly. I would strangle him in my arm. It would be mercifully fast and painless, a simple constriction of the blood and he would be gone. But then there

358

was a knife pressed into the frost damaged flesh of my hands. Heat from the handle began to return life to my fingers and my mind. The mother urged me to end his pain quickly, but I was confused and getting angry. I would never use a blade on someone I loved. I had been fully prepared to kill him, but not hurt him.

"I was saying, 'Wait, wait, everybody hold. This is not right.' Then blustering fury as the storm unleashed driving spikes of ice on the wind. I felt the force of the gale knock me back. I could hear whispering on the wind and wanted to demand whoever was there to come forward, but my voice and my body were gone; ethereal and without form, there was nothing to respond. Then Callias started shrieking about wolves, something with fangs and claws, some animal tearing him apart, and all the while there was whispering, two voices whispering through a piercing wind, snarling beasts yapping, Agatha was screaming, the light was everywhere, stabbing, freezing my eyes blind. I had the knife and was cutting back the dogs. I began to feel the heat of their blood on my hands, warmth that spread to my mind, making me wonder why the nuns were on the ice, backing across the empty waste of the poles. Agatha was screaming hysterical denial while hiding the parchment back in her robes, sobbing for another chance, swearing all forms of eternal allegiance until the guards burst through the door.

"It was still so very bright and I was squinting to see, but you can imagine what I saw. The cuts on Callias's body were deep and precise and certainly mine. The mothers were silenced, the storm was over, and the sickness had seized me. I knew I had acted out of madness, but I was desperate to prove to myself I was not responsible, that I had been controlled, somehow hypnotized by their voice, but this was also insane. If it had not been for the last words of Agatha, I might have killed myself, but before the guards could haul me away, while the mothers tried to silence the raving sister, Agatha, desperate to escape what they had in store, tried to appease again by weeping, 'I vow my voice to the destroyer.' Her *voice*, not her life—the warrior's greatest gift—but her voice."

~~~~~~

The sound of the fire dominated the room as each person remained silent in their own thoughts. The General's outrage was divided. In his mind played the video of Sister Agatha before the King's Security Council, too deranged to give evidence of what she had witnessed, wailing from the ruins the same as he had heard ripped from Sable's tortured body. Also playing in his mind with clarity, as though it too had been recorded, was his father's skilled hand killing Callias while the murmuring of the Cloitare controlled the blade. But the sharpest image came from his memory, one of Sable whispering to the King.

The memory brought him to his feet, stalked him across the floor to escape his own hostility, and then turned him to accuse her. "And you used the same cursed voice to manipulate Remy."

Sable faced the room with a weariness greater than a sleepless night could explain. "I did not convince him of anything false. I *am* safe and competent in this world. And I did not do it lightly. I will pay

360

the dearest price for it." She explained to Orson the presence of the drugged soldier in his house.

"Ah, pet, you've made my son distrust you." Orson patted the rug. "Come sit beside me and let's see what we can do to fix this." To his son, he explained, "Sable plays a very poor game of strategy. There is not a pawn on the board she will not sacrifice the queen to save."

"Which is the same as surrendering the King."

"Do you hear?" Orson's wry question was aimed at Sable. "Perhaps you will accept this as true now you have the conclusion of two strategists on the matter." He watched her sink fluidly to the carpet at his side, facing him with such obvious fatigue, his criticism was gentle. "Did you ever win a single game relying on defensive tactics over strategy?"

He knew the answer and she would not argue her protection of the pawns.

Orson dispassionately continued, "You reveal yourself so my son is not the least surprised to hear what the Cloitare can do with their voice. In making known your greatest strength, you choose the life of your friends over the life of the King." When Sable turned to deny it, he asked, "The first tenet?"

Do not get caught. Sable closed her eyes.

"Is the King aware of what you've done?"

Stubborn silence kept her head bowed.

To his son, Orson said, "I doubt we have time for us to sit here all night while I outwait her, so you answer: Does the King know?"

"I intend to tell him."

"You will not." The directive was firm, but Theo's expression showed the matter was not settled. "Whether she is deserving of it or not, he must trust her."

Theo choked on his first response out of respect for his father. Pacing back across the wood floor to the rug, he looked down on them both. "Explain to me why."

"It was never meant to come to this," Orson addressed Sable, "but, for whatever reason, it has." Then to his son, "There is a war coming and she needs to be by his side."

"The war will get no closer to the King than it already has."

Orson was dismissive. "Your wars with Alena and other sovereign states scarcely threaten the King's life. There is a much deadlier war coming."

"And I will be the one to defend the King." He could no longer hide his ire.

"Before it's over, I am sure you will." Orson studied his son. "You're under the misunderstanding I trained Sable to protect the King. Master Aidan trained her for that. I, the master strategist, trained the Mawan to eliminate the threat before any defense of the King need be made."

The General stepped back from the admission. He felt the couch touch his legs and dropped as the realization weakened his knees. He looked at Sable kneeling in deference to his father, both hiding scars deeper than the skin, mutually driven by more than just a grudge against the clergy, each dangerous enough alone but here they were united, a whispering assassin under the direction of an experienced strategist with the common goal of destroying the Cloitare. It was well beyond mad, and he felt responsible for them both. He remembered Sable pooling blood on Remy's carpet, dead certain she was right, looking to him for approval, and he understood now it had not been her insanity alone that night swinging the axe.

~~~~~~

With his son's path corrected, Orson spoke to Sable, "Now, pet, show me what it is you hide from me."

Theo's eyes were still fastened wide in alarm on him when Sable's expression joined them. In the next instant, she hid her panic by staring into her lap.

Orson chuckled at them both before pouring more voški into his tumbler with his braced hand and holding his other open for Sable's secret.

"You'll feel a damn lot better if you take that." He pushed Theo's still untouched drink toward him.

His son took the glass and sank back into the leather while Orson flexed his fingers and looked surprised to have an empty hand. They both watched Sable check her appearance, reviewing her clothes, looking for something of importance.

363

Orson laughed. "Have you been away from me that long? You think maybe I speak of something in your pocket?"

She abandoned the effort to find an object to offer and instead became very still, hardly breathing, waiting, feeling trapped.

With pity, he ended it. "Give me your hand."

The hopeful tension he might get it wrong dropped from her shoulders. She closed her eyes and forced herself to comply.

He expected to push back the bangles to find some mark of suicide on her wrist, but instead he was stopped short by the X cut indelicately into her palm. He was staggered. It took all his will not to show it, and the only reason she didn't feel his horror was she was too busy willing herself to be calm to spare him a thought. He said, "Your other," and confirmed there were two.

He had seen it before. Sister Agatha had been marked a traitor for helping him. She had readily surrendered her hands to remain Cloitare, telling him the ritual for being cast out was far worse. But Orson could not imagine Sable would freely kneel to receive any Cloitare judgment.

"Did you accept the salt willingly?"

"No."

"Did Master Aidan do this?"

"No." She frowned at the idea.

Orson was sharp with anger, "Then why did you allow this to happen? Was my training for nothing? Have I wasted my time on you?"

364

"Father—"

"Theo, be quiet."

Orson was surprised to see her face soften with pity, as though she were preparing to comfort him.

"I was in the train wreck last year in Alena, that is how Master Aidan found me. I was too hurt to escape." She did not want to continue, but he was showing no tolerance for the delay. Taking her hands from his, she unfastened the wide bracelet, but before letting it slip, she grimaced one more look of sympathy and then extended her bare wrist.

He studied the scar for meaning, knowing it was an electrical burn, thinking perhaps she had been wearing a metal bangle when hit by lightning, but then she said simply, "Compliance shackle."

No punch to the gut could have winded him like that. He quickly clasped her wrist to cover the damage, as though he could deny it had happened. He remembered, and he knew for her to have scars, her memories would be worse.

"I couldn't fight them with it on."

Of all the things for her to say, as though he needed to be told. Orson pulled her head onto his shoulder to keep her from saying anything else, to give him time to regain composure.

When he could speak, he whispered with hatred, "Aidan?" and his fingers relaxed to grip her wrist like a sword.

She tightened in defense, drawing back. "No. He would never. He was unaware."

"Unaware." Orson did not believe this.

"He was," she insisted. "From my first memories, twice a year Master Aidan would go someplace distant where I could not feel him, as though he ceased to exist. Before he left, he locked me in a cell." Sable tried to make it sound acceptable. "Both to protect the mothers from me and me from the mothers. They were meant to stay away," she bit the words with malice, "but they did not." She prepared to put the bracelet back on, but Orson would not release her hand.

"For what did they find you at fault?"

Sable struggled to speak through her sudden rage. "Mother Vesna claimed I was an imposter."

Worried by the mania that pinched at her eyes, the General slid his glass to the end of the table and leaned forward.

But she was familiar with his every restraining action and turned on him further enraged, "I never accepted any title until I did so for Remy," then back to Orson, "so it's rather fucking rich they put a blade to my hands for their convictions."

"And now that you have accepted the title of Queen Mother, what does Vesna say?"

Sable stopped breathing. When she resumed, she was removed and cool. "Vesna is dead."

Orson smiled and looked pleased. "Despite the shackle, you managed to strike."

Exhausted by the fast range of emotions, she dropped her head with guilt. "No. I went back."

366

Before he could speak the harsh look on his face, Theo began to explain, "She went back to save—"

But Orson cut him short, "I can't figure out if you want to kill her or defend her."

"I did go back to save them," Sable told the General, "but I took the axe for Vesna. There was no place in the whole of the world she could have hidden from me that night." She turned again to Orson. "Vesna gave me plenty enough reasons to want to kill her before the shaming began, but once it started," Sable rolled a growl in her throat with the memory, "she really put herself into it. She'd already done a slow carve on my hands, but because I wouldn't offer them to the salt, she laid on the controller for the dozenth time until the shackle left me weak enough for the mothers to pry open my bloody fists. Vesna took pleasure in doing it first, but every last mother in the convent filled my hands with salt."

Sable was quiet, swallowing fury. Trying to diminish the effects of her words, she assured, "After a few handfuls, I couldn't feel it anymore. It no longer hurt. It was the nerve of it that infuriated me. And hearing *Neither to give nor receive* a hundred times is incredibly trying." Sadness tempered her anger. "I couldn't believe Mother Isabelle would do it. She was my only hope to stop the ceremony. I kept watching her approach in the line, hand full of salt, thinking she would bring her voice of reason to the affair, that she would intercede as she had always done, but she wouldn't look at me, and when I realized she was going to bow to Vesna's will, I couldn't speak to even ask. Of all the mothers I didn't want to find me at fault,

367

it was Isabelle, so I fought harder to get off my knees, trying to push back from the altar, but there were far too many mothers pressed against me. For all the energy exerted, I managed only to get my hands into fists, and for a moment, I thought it was the pain of splitting open the cuts, the salt, and fresh blood that made me scream, but it was Vesna. Every time I could get my hands closed, I did, and every time Vesna laid on the controller with greater frenzy. Isabelle didn't wait for the mothers to open my hands; she dumped the salt over the struggle, and when I had enough strength to look for her, she was hiding deep behind the initiates in the corner.

"After the mothers, the sisters circled through and we went through the whole cycle again: me refusing to accept guilt and Vesna going happy with the controller; me screaming and then someone dumping another handful of salt in my hands. I had my head on the altar trying to collect my wits when there was a break in the rhythm. I knew a sister was before me and I thought she planned to emulate the mothers and wait until she had my attention. The audacity," Sable spoke through her teeth, "the pure nerve, it filled me with greater hate than I had managed for any of the mothers. I lifted my face expecting to see a future mother, someone ingratiating themselves to be accepted, but instead it was a nun on the verge of tears, and I heard the salt she held drop to the floor."

Sable looked to the General and said with poignancy, "Amele." She struggled with her voice to tell Orson, "I didn't know her. She had trained in her youth somewhere else, but she said to me, 'I came as your sister to welcome you home, not to hurt you.' Vesna demanded she act in accordance with the clergy's judgment and the bowl of salt was pressed at her, but she refused to take any. Then down the line of waiting sisters, salt started dropping to the floor in succession. Amele turned to beseech the remaining sisters to follow her lead, asking, 'If she denies guilt, *who* are we finding at fault?' and more salt dropped. I had the briefest glimpse of deliverance, but then Vesna demanded, '*Quiet*,' and the mothers descended on Amele. I was terrified for her. I said, 'Sister, just take the salt and give it to me,' but she returned, 'I believe you are innocent,' and over us both the mothers were rumbling, '*Obey*.' They had her surrounded, trying to force her to take the salt, bending her hand up to pour it into her palm, but she kept fighting to throw it off. I was begging, 'Please, just take it and give it to me,' but she was crying, 'I cannot hurt you,' and then to the watching sisters, 'This is sacrilege,' and all the while the mothers were commanding, but Amele wouldn't yield. It was chaos that seemed unending until she threw them off and sank to the other side of the altar to grab the knife, meaning to lay it into her own hands in solidarity with me. I was horrified and said without thinking, 'For the love of night, not yourself, stab Vesna.' She rose fully dedicated to following my instructions, but the floors shook with the combined voices of the mothers dropping her to the ground, and with her they took all of the nearby sisters. I was swearing I had controlled her, but the mothers had heard and knew I hadn't. She was damned. She was damned the moment she dropped the salt to offer me salvation, and I returned it by pitching her into the flames. They hauled her out of the assembly hall and then pressed the salt on the sisters down the line that had dropped it. Three more refused to take part, refused even though they knew the punishment would be severe. They too were being dragged from the hall. I warned Vesna, 'If you hurt them, I swear upon the darkest night, I will kill you,' but she was unconcerned, telling the row of sisters to continue.

"I thought the only way I could help them was to throw as much confusion into the remaining ritual as possible. I hoped to lose the four sisters amongst something worse, to so riotously upend the ceremony, everyone would be forgiven. Every sister that was near, I tried to drop, scare, or influence into violence. You can imagine how Vesna reacted. There was pandemonium at the end: the youngest sisters who were farthest away were crying; the child initiates were fainting; the floors were covered in salt; the blade was repeatedly lost then found in the commotion, rising in a fist to be taken down by a rumbling command; the mothers were trying to instill calm over Vesna's love of the shackle; and through it all, I was either screaming or rolling threats. It was already mayhem when Master Aidan became aware.

"He truly had not suspected this would happen," she told Orson. To the General she said, "You have only just begun to see the Cloitare, but to understand them, you must understand Aidan. He is a master of the mind, the only master the Cloitare knows. He is the original thought, the mind that first allowed travel. At the time of this ritual, my mind was very nearly as perfect as his, but I lacked the experience to be even a fraction as powerful. It didn't matter. For Aidan, I was a tool.

"He moved in and from my mouth came blinding white authority to stop. But his command was following my dark terror and

Vesna had already acted again to end it. Aidan was wrapped in my pain, lost in my scream, and couldn't prevail over my voice. Vesna knew she would lose if she didn't keep him trapped, and she was set on expelling me from the Cloitare. She was gathering and focusing the minds of the mothers, keeping Aidan submerged with the shackle, but she couldn't shatter a mind she couldn't reach, so she had to let me surface, which brought Aidan into the room. He demanded silence, but she struck hard with the full force of the mothers and then put us back under with the shackle. When she again relented, I returned to find everything slow, the water of my mind freezing over. She struck again before Aidan could speak. She was striking to chip away my voice, and because of the shackle, Aidan could neither get through nor out. The wide open waters of my mind were turning to ice, so to save me, Aidan tried to drown me, taking me deep into the dark, but Vesna had the control to stop it. The two were tearing me in different directions and I kept returning to a more shattered landscape until the only thing I could recognize was Aidan.

"I was trying to hide behind him, or within him, and out of desperation, he showed me something, something at the margin where the black meets the light, a way to escape." Sable furrowed her brow in the same lost way the General had seen a number of times before, when she was confused about how she had arrived at some unexpected place. "He reminded me how to travel past the distance through time to something else." She was squinting to focus far away. "It was a different type of night and I can almost remember the way back." She searched harder, saying, "It was a trick of memory in the dark," but then, unable to find it, she frowned and returned her sight to the room.

"The four sisters were safe while Aidan remained, but once he had me united with Remy, he returned to the unreachable silence where I cannot find him. I call for him to help, but the distance is empty and there is no direction to throw my plea."

Orson still held her hand and ran his thumb across the scar. "Why are you calling him?"

Sable laughed without humor. "Your son has not told you I am mad?"

She'd previously had two facial expressions: laughing irreverence and a cold calm that always threatened to fall into the Stare. He'd seen more emotions cross her face in the last hour than in all the years he'd trained her. He asked sincerely, "Are you?"

Eventually she dropped his gaze, but the silence continued. She knew the answer, and part of her wanted to toss it off breezily for the General to confirm, but she was too tired for levity, too tired to have committed to such a serious conversation as well. "When I went to get the sisters out of the cells, I took the axe off the wall in a mind of fixed purpose. It was to kill Vesna." She looked deeper into her lap. "But I got a little carried away."

Theo sat back at the understatement.

"I killed three mothers before Vesna, and then I killed another four when they challenged my authority."

Orson covered her wrist so it would not affect his judgment. "These mothers could have prevented you from freeing the sisters?"

372

At first he knew her silence was not obstinance, she was thinking, but then having the answer, she did not want to share, so he waited. She finally sank with the admission, "I did not give them the opportunity to try. The first two mothers followed me to the cellar, harassing me down the stairs, telling me I had no right to interfere or enter the cells. When they barred access to the entrance, I gave them no warning to stand clear. I swung the axe and cleaved from jugular to heart, and then freed the blade to swing again and stop the second's command to be still." Sable lifted her head without remorse. "Then I saw what they'd done to Amele. After Aidan left, she had no protection. She looked like she'd been beaten, but for all the times I had ever been mentally knocked to the floor, and save for the ritual with the blade, I had never known the nuns to be physically abusive. I asked the sisters, 'Did they hit you?' and Ava told me, 'They made us hit each other.' She looked at Amele and told me, 'We thought she was Vesna.'" Mania twitched the corners of Sable's eyes.

"When the sisters shrank back to see Vesna and four more mothers enter the cellar, I could not have granted the mothers mercy if they begged. While they took in the scene of the two dead nuns, I readied the axe again so there would be no doubt of what I intended. I put the axe into a swinging arc and the mothers quickly united. With one voice, they demanded me *'Down,'* and the sisters behind me fell, but so too did the momentum in the blade, dropping into the nearest mother. I explained, 'Things work a little different in a mind that's been shattered,' and with the blade stuck in the mother's shoulder and chest, I pulled her forward to the ground and used my foot against the

373

handle to hammer the blade through her ribs, clarifying further, 'Many things just slip straight through the broken spaces.'

"Not understanding how I was unaffected, the mothers started backing for the steps. They were rumbling cold, bringing light, trying to slow and chill my advancement, but I was growling back dark heat. They tried again united, ordering me *'Down,'* and when I smiled at the attempt, they broke and ran for the stairs."

Lowering her eyes, Sable slowly rolled and wet her lips like she was tasting the memory to come. She said, "I'm afraid you will find me inexcusably cruel. I willfully ignored the third tenet so I could enjoy Vesna's fear."

The General tried to remember the tenets of the Wind. Uncertain he had them in the correct order, he asked, "The third?"

She gave the answer with respect to Orson, "The purpose of picking up a blade is to cut the enemy."

Orson nodded once.

"I used the blade less to cut than to grab Vesna from behind, propelling it around and then pulling it back to catch her in the guts with the lower corner of the edge. Once I had her hooked, I stepped in to wrap my left hand around her waist, gripping the top wedge, and then together with the handle, I yanked the axe head deep into her core." Sable acknowledged, "I was cruel," and after a moment, "but I wasn't done. I knew the wound I gave her was mortal, but the death would be protracted, and there was time for her tell me the Cloitare's plans."

The General was unaware he had been pressing back into the couch until her words pulled him forward with interest.

"She was panicking, trying to stem the blood, and hysterically berating, 'You were never more than an anodyne dream and now look what you've done.' I swung her to face the sisters, reminding her, 'I warned you not to hurt them.' Then I gathered the blackest night, drawing it over us to hide in the deepest shadows. *'Quiet,'* I told her until we lost the other mothers in a mind without light, and then, when it was only she and I, and it was too dark to see, I spoke to her as the ghost she had slain. 'I swore on my knees at the altar where you held me that I would kill you. It was an oath you made me make in my own blood. And now I have returned to give you the promised blade.' In her ear, I whispered, 'Your life is void.' She was shaking in dismay, simpering fear because the truth of it was clear. But I wanted her smothering in despair, so I pulled regret into the dark, strangling her with the remorse of failed ambitions, torturing with, 'There were still so many things you wanted to do, so many intentions left undone.' The loss of the years left her whimpering. I told her, 'Look at the blood that cups in your hands,' and when she did, I asked, 'Was I worth it?' But I didn't wait for her to answer. I buried her in desolation, letting her believe she was alone, waiting for the terror to escape her mouth as a long, petrified cry."

Sable could not keep the malign brutality from showing as pleasure on her face. "Vesna thought she had known fear," a moan rolled in her throat, "but then I joined her."

375

Reliving the mental hysterics as Vesna writhed to get away, Sable lowered her head and covered her mouth to conceal her enjoyment. She tried to control her pulse, wanting to make it sedate, unaffected, telling herself, *Slow. Slow. Calm the fuck down.*

But when she pulled herself upright, Orson could see she was crazed. He strained to hear her continue. Leaning into a hoarse whisper that seized his imagination, her voice drew him in to force the impression on his mind. "I took her to where I began, to the black, and on the edge, I held her, showing her the drop, and then threatening to loosen my grip, to pitch her into the void, I tipped us forward without balance."

Orson felt himself teetering on the precipice and groaned to shake off the image.

Sable wrapped her hand around his neck to pull them closer, her voice lower, "I wanted her to see and tell me if I was still an imposter."

Changing the way he held her wrist, he motioned with his braced hand for his son not to come farther forward.

"I've never known, I've always doubted, and there was never a skeptic I could show that could endure it. But Vesna, if I took her deep and lost her or dropped her, her suffering would be too brief." Sable's hushed voice reverberated across the bones in his face: *"I showed her the black abyss that cuts through my mind."*

Orson gasped. Reeling away from the chasm, he lost his equilibrium so that his head dropped onto her shoulder, but still he vehemently gestured for Theo to wait.

Nothing more than a subtle murmur, she laid her cheek against his to tell him, "I didn't know if I could hold her in the fall."

Afraid she planned to step straight off the cliff, Orson pushed back, assuring, "Sable, I don't need to see the depths."

She clutched harder, following his retreat, "Do you want to know what she saw?"

"Tell me but don't show me."

Her breath shuddered against his neck, laboring to change, her voice adding volume but no more releasing him than her grip. "Vesna only knew the weightless floating of the light. She had never fallen heavy through the night, feeling the pressure of air parting, wind wailing, wanting to scream through the descent but too choked by heat and drenched with dread to find her breath. 'You had so many plans,' I told her. 'Feel them shear off your mind, slipping away into waste.' And like rocks off a breaking ledge, they crumbled, dropping faster than she could save them. Clinging to me, but reaching for what was being lost, I made her choose when I released her to plummet."

Orson swayed. Digging his fingers into her shoulder for support, he began to bend her hand into her arm.

"On the rushing air, I heard her pleas to be saved. Once again entwined, I warned her, 'If you do not free yourself of this deadly moment, when we hit, you will break, you will shatter as I did.' Then I showed her the ragged bottom."

Through the punch of panic, Orson blocked Theo's reach for the hand Sable had around his throat.

She kept whispering, "'If you hope to survive, we must move into the future.' Then wrapping her tight so a shriek of fear was pushed from her lungs, I dropped us with careless speed through the dark."

Already falling, he lost stability and plunged even faster. The contents of his stomach rose to his mouth. He didn't think he could be heard over the blasting gale, but then—piercing sound—Sable's sharp cry cut through the blind dive.

Recognizing the control Orson threatened against her wrist, her voice broke with the sound of concession under duress. She bent with his direction, words rising not to be muffled against his chest. *Slow. Slow. We are not falling,*" she pleaded to be heard. "The light of the fire reveals this is true."

Out of the dark and back in his home, Orson had no sooner relented than Sable straightened to start again. "Mother Vesna maintained a single ambition." Still locked around his neck, she stared into his eyes. "Can you see it?"

Swallowing against sickness, "Sable, I am not Master Aidan."

"You are always so close to being a conscious witness." She pressed again, but he remained closed. "The future has no place for kings. Do you see the palace?" She pulled once more at Orson's attention, whispering, "It is dark. What light shines flickers from flames. But not disaster. Look, it is wax. They've ripped out the electrics. Look, Master Orson," she demanded, yanking firm to pull him in. "See through me. Do you see the queen?" Sable pressed the image into his mind. "A mother in robes with a veiled crown for a headdress. See through the veil. Her features are mine and Remy's. The children beside her all girls, all robed, all hers. There are no kings in the future. Only Queen Mothers. And I am the Mother of them All."

~~~~~~

The future Sable showed him felt grim. The image of the Queen Mother surrounded by her robed children all staring with dead eyes was unnervingly sinister. Orson shivered off the touch of cold and turned to his son. "If the Cloitare come to rule, they will take the country back to the impoverished past."

The General told Sable, "We must keep your children away from the clergy."

"Perhaps it would have been that simple," but she twisted her mouth to show it was unlikely. "I think, though, by the time that daughter was old enough to be taken as a novice, Remy would have been killed, you as well, or in no better a position to help than your father. And I ..." She looked away. "I saw my future. I was overwhelmed to the point of mindless, having bowed to accept the title Mother of All." She told Orson, "Before Vesna slipped through my hold, I asked her how they could possibly hope to make me accept the title and Vesna said, 'A mother will do anything for her child.'" Sable's expression turned severe. She became ruthless. "Well that future is over. I have changed it. I had myself sterilized. There will be no children."

The General rocked as though the room had been moved.

Orson could only ask, "Sable?" wondering what she had done.

"The clergy do not yet know. Neither does Remy. But the future has been irrevocably altered." Now she was at a loss. "When the mothers find out …" Sable left the idea hanging with trepidation. "What are they going to do? They will change the meaning of the prophecy to fit their ambitions, but how? I took the lead, but I don't know where I have taken us. None of this was supposed to have happened," she reminded Orson.

The General had heard none of her concerns. He was still reeling. He declared as fact, "It can be reversed."

"From the incinerator?" she scoffed. She was once more harsh with finality, "I wasn't fucking around. The option is gone. Removed. No need to consider it further."

Disbelief made him look her over. "When?" He hoped she was lying. "How?" But he knew she was nuts. "What did you do?"

"You'll remember that Remy did not speak to me for over six weeks. In the first weeks, I left Ava in my room after dinner and went to a clinic in Alena. Your people that follow me are not very aware; one nun looks much the same as another to them. I was back by the next evening." She shrugged as though it was nothing. "No one thought I had left my rooms." When he still appeared to be in doubt, she became impatient. "You need to accept that it will become known I am sterile. The public does not need to know why. Catherine will turn it to some advantage and a surrogate will be found to have the King's heirs. Understand," she stressed, "anyone can have the King's children, but only I could have Queen Mothers. The whole future the clergy imagined is now ashes."

"So too are the plans we made." Orson turned her hand to study the palm. He told his son, "It was always a possibility Sable would be captured, and for such events we prepared." From the beginning, he had been particularly careful with this topic, concerned Sable would see through his excuses to discover what he taught was not a contingency plan but as fixed as his commitment to return her to the Cloitare. "She was meant to forget her pride, act humble, and gain the mothers' trust." To Sable he said, "You have given yourself away."

Silently she agreed. She picked up the bracelet again to cover her wrist, but Orson still would not release her hand. She was apologetic. "I lost all perspective."

"No, pet, I am not finding you at fault. What happened is beyond such criticisms. But the battlefield in no way resembles anything we devised, and from behind your own lines, you just indiscriminately set the field alight." He smiled at his son still in shock. "Sable is the worst strategist with the poorest judgment I have ever taught, but on this she was correct. She took the lead to stop the enemy from leading." With affection, he squeezed her hand. "I could not have asked you to do it, but—"

Sable called him short with blunt familiarity, "Yes, you could have and you would have. We are agreed on the goal." She said flatly, "Win by any means."

Orson lowered his head with respect. "The second tenet is uncompromising."

"And now?" Sable asked sincerely. "I held my resolve through the worst of it but was still tricked into saying yes in the end. There was no plan for outside the convent. None of this was meant to happen. And maybe you've noticed, but I have no idea what I'm doing."

He recited to Sable: "Suppress the enemy's abilities, foil his plans, and then command him directly."

"Yes, but *how?*"

Orson stared at her while he considered. His features appeared harsh and critical, but Sable was unconcerned by his expression of concentration. She loved when he focused his wits on the fight. She pushed against his mind to feel the ordered timing of a deadly battle as he played each move in advance, predicting his opponent's reactions, guiding them to their fall. Sable could feel the certainty of his moves but could not guess the actions.

After much time had passed in silent deliberation, Orson finally spoke. "For as long as possible, you must keep secret from the mothers what you have done, how you have destroyed their plans. This will prevent them from formulating new ones while you set them on a new path." Taking both her hands, he said firmly, "You must go back into the convent and lead them directly."

Sable tried to pull away.

"With Master Aidan gone, you are the head of the Cloitare, the sole and uncontested oracle. You can determine the Cloitare's future.

Your position should be stronger than any, but you are weak because you will not use it."

"Remy won't allow it," Sable gave as an excuse.

"Nonsense. You are in Sierra," he offered as proof. "You will convince him."

The General growled disapproval.

Orson ignored him to ask Sable, "In the future shown to you, as your young daughter trained in the convent, who were the Council of Regents?"

Sable frowned unaware.

"You must learn this to control them."

Knowing he was right, Sable sagged forward at the prospect before her. "United, the mothers are now stronger than me. I accepted the title of Queen Mother and allowed them passage through my mind. It was foolish to think I could deceive them. I thought I could elude them, leave them lost in the broken spaces, but instead," Sable winced at the memory while trying to find the words. Her accent changed to the street, "Those bitches went cold and froze a path to travel. Their commands no longer slip through the cracks. I lost the one small advantage they'd given me."

"And what did you gain?"

"A grander title and easier access to the one mind."

"Learn to use them. You must accomplish far more than was initially required. You need to win over the young, divide the mothers, and set out a definitive, clear, and accessible new objective to occupy the clergy. You have much to reclaim." Thoughtfully he traced the X on her palm with his thumb. "More than reclaiming lost territory, you have moral authority to reclaim." Sable clinched her hands into fists. "Mother Vesna gave you a valuable gift." She yanked free her left hand but Orson held tight to her right. "A gift you can bestow upon the most loyal and faithful of your followers." And while Sable began to turn her head *no*, Orson finished, "You will divide the Cloitare with the mark."

"*No, no, no, no, no,*" she repeated in a whisper until it was little more than a mumble of breath while she twisted in Orson's grip.

"You will start with Amele and the three other sisters," Orson explained calmly as though he were not grappling now to still both of Sable's hands. "Cut wide so their hands scar like yours, but do not wait for them to heal. While they are fresh, take the four sisters into the cloister so that every nun understands the new division."

"Ok, father, let her go."

Orson took no notice of his son. "Play an active role in the ceremonies, and the young will be eager to wear the sign of your most-trusted followers."

Wrists held against Orson's brace and laced with his good hand, Sable was becoming frantic. *"Why?* Why would I do this?"

"It will utterly fracture the Cloitare. The few mothers whose pride will allow them to be cut will wear the scars as an admission of wrong-doing and the young will wear them proudly as a sign of devotion to you."

Sable thought back to the soldier on the train, falling apart when he pulled the blade from her hip. She had been familiar with the reaction, had even expected his emotion; she could sympathize, but, at the time, she could not empathize, had no understanding of what caused his distress. Trembling against Orson's direction, Sable felt certain Vesna had succeeded in expelling her from the Cloitare. She shook her head, saying, "I can't do this."

"Yes, you can. I have taught you well how to use a blade."

"No. It's a profane desecration of the flesh."

"Yes, *exactly*, and tonight you will stop hiding your scars of innocence."

"Not Amele." Sable was sinking. "Not Ava, Chloé, or Evie. Name anyone else, but not those four."

"What about me?"

"Oh fucking hell no." She was dizzy with revulsion because Orson was already shouting behind him into the lodge, "Marie, bring me a boning knife and salt."

Dropping her head onto their hands, Sable cursed and pleaded, "Blackest night, please don't do this to me."

"You're going to do it to me." Orson was cheerful. "You will see it is very simple. I will consider it a gift, a way for you to honor me for all I have done for you."

"Ok, hold the madness." Pressing across the table, Theo signaled an end. "This has gone far enough."

"This, my son, is between the Destroyer and me, so you can just sit back and finish your damn drink."

"No, father, this is now between you and the Queen's guard."

Orson laughed roundly. "So now you're her guard? You can't protect both her and the King this evening. If you want your king to live, Sable has to take control of the Cloitare. I've just told her how. Now did you hear a weakness in my strategy?"

The General looked at Sable still pressed as if in prayer to their combined hands. "I haven't heard the final plan, where all this," his gesture whipped across the two of them, "cutting of palms leads."

"And you won't. Tell him why, pet."

"If the mothers thought you knew, they'd tear through your head to find it." Sable lifted her attention to him. "I drank a bottle of anodyne so they wouldn't discover any more of my secrets, but they had already learned that Orson Feridon trained me and they could guess why. They know he still lives on the island where he buried the last two mothers who approached him because I revealed it, yet I never opened my mouth to speak. I can't go anywhere without a pocket full of pills to drown them in nightmares should they come into my mind again, and at some point, to advance their objective, they must. You can't know the final plan because you don't know how to hide."

At his mother's unsuspecting entrance with knife and salt, Theo rose to turn her away, but Orson called, "Bring it here, Marie."

Sable became instantly dire, warning, "I will drop every last one of you to the floor."

386

Orson single-mindedly matched her, "If the Mawan will not honor me, then I will take my own life in disgrace."

Marie demanded in wild alarm of both Theo and Sable, "What is happening?"

"Give me the knife, Mother."

Skirting the outside of the room as Sable had done, Marie kept the knife close to her chest to avoid her son's approach, saying, "Your father does not threaten." To Sable, who was locked in a combative stare with her husband, she urged, "Whatever he wants, do it."

Cloitare cold, Sable agreed, "I will mark the sisters. I agree to your strategy."

"You will honor me first with proof of your commitment."

The struggle had flipped so that Orson now tried to free his hands from Sable, requesting, "The knife, Marie," but Theo was also insisting, "Give it to me.'"

Sable's face was inscrutably neutral making Marie rage with the order, "Honor him as he says!"

"Mother, I have this under control, just give me the knife."

While Theo spoke, Sable stopped fighting Orson and instead put emotionless eyes on Marie, signaling her to retreat with her son to the fire.

In the manner of a nun, Sable bent low to show respect while her hand went to his jacket pocket. She paused with grief to find the knife where she expected. As she rose to the task, Orson said, "I wish you did not insult me with the Stare."

387

Head still bent, Sable explained, "It's either your blood or my tears. You can't have both."

"You have learned how to cry?"

"I have."

It was unexpected. He watched his son overtaking his wife, promising, "I will fix this," and lifted Sable's face to ask, "Who taught you? The mothers?" He was relieved to see her expression turn sardonic with denial. "Remy?"

"Yes."

Orson's smile broke into a private laugh. "I would never have wished the curse of love on you, but now that you've got it, I might as well train your demon to fight."

Theo had claimed the kitchen knife from his mother, but when he turned to deal with his father, Orson's manner was dedicated to instruction.

"If you wait until the King is under threat to take control of the Cloitare, it will be too late. You cannot waver. With unrelenting resolve, and without mercy, you must act fast and strike hard."

Resting his hand over his pocket to keep Sable's fingers on the knife, he said, "If you show mercy to the sisters, to Amele or any one of them, you are choosing their lives over the life of the King. Above all else, you must decide firmly where your loyalty lies. Be resolute that every action reflects it."

Before allowing her to release the knife and sit back, he waited for Sable to assent, "I swear it; I will mark them."

"Master Aidan has trained you to defend the King, but you cannot afford to fall into defensive habits. To defend is to allow the enemy to lead. Your every action becomes a counter. You must *never* allow the enemy to lead. You will lose."

Sable could see it clearly. "I will return to the Cloitare and direct its path."

"Attack strongly and calmly. Feign fear, anger, or boredom to lure your enemy into position, but on no account relinquish your serenity or balance."

Sable blinked away the Stare.

"Advance steadily, never retreating, never allowing the clergy to rest or recover. When they fight back, deflect it with an attack so they cannot strike again. If they falter, attack stronger. Do not relent. You must completely cut them down."

~~~~~~

The night wore on as Orson fleshed out the strategy and reinforced tactics Theo hoped were merely analogous with the blade. Theo had guided his mother out of the room with assurances he would prevent the lesson from descending into bloodshed, then slowly he paced between the fire and entrance hall to stay alert, listening to his father guide Sable into war with the Cloitare.

Theo could find no fault with his father's plan, other than he was familiar with the people involved. He did not care to imagine

Sable cutting Amele's hands. He did not want to hear Remy refuse Sable's request to return to the Cloitare because he did not want to think what it meant when Remy agreed. Laudin was going to pop like an overcharged battery when Sable extended her authority into Sierra, and Girard's PIT was about to get taught a lesson in conspiracy theories.

He was jumpy from hearing his father repeatedly put illusory blades in Sable's hands, instructing, "Strike before they have a chance to look around." Reminding, "One cut serves as both attack and defense." And tersely correcting, "*Chase*. Chase them into disarray and then cut them down." But overshadowing every ill feeling was the complicity of the evening of which Remy could never learn.

Theo watched the time stretch into the small hours after midnight while his father chided Sable for not knowing how to keep the Cloitare preoccupied. "Modernize the temples," he offered. "And the convent. Hell, update the Basilica with electricity," Orson laughed. "Increase the number of recruits. Round up every delinquent, angry, unstable, attention deficit, and otherwise troubled child to keep the mothers continuously busy with unacceptable initiates. Maintain constant disorder with no hope of recovery. If they look even slightly complacent, announce you are allowing men back into the clergy. Chase them. Relentlessly chase the mothers with change.

"And more appearances. Speak weekly at the Basilica. Randomly revise the meanings of the prophets, your role as Queen Mother, the function of the Cloitare. Be unpredictable. Upset every routine. All of these changes will draw out the proposed Council of

390

Regents. Those with the highest authority will be forced forward to resist your alterations. Identify the mothers with the largest influence and then attack the greatest threats. Divide them. Concede to the wishes of the weakest; steadfastly refuse the strongest. Completely shift their balance of power. Cut away every advantage and leave every hindrance."

From the beginning and through every lesson, his father kept pulling Sable's marred hands before her eyes, prompting, "Mother Vesna gave you a valuable gift which you will share," forcing her to focus on the scars and then making her affirm, "It is a gift."

Theo could not tell if it was rage or if she was about to sob on the words, but the statement remained incomprehensible until the emotion was concealed behind an impassive Cloitare Stare. Hours later, his father told her, "You have hidden long enough," and Sable reemerged to speak with stiff compliance.

When she hesitated, Orson would tap, glance, or rest his hand on his pocket until Theo finally realized the importance. It was late and he was desperately tired. He berated himself for not seeing it sooner. He idly came to sit on the edge of the chair to their side, trying to appear casual, as though he were merely observing. For his trouble, he was reminded you could not beat a master strategist who from one thing knew a thousand, who could see the real intent of every action and defeat it before it started. And for his trouble, he was also reminded you could not trick a Cloitare who could see plainly what others felt as a subconscious doubt. He had barely moved his hand for his father's pocket when he was effortlessly blocked and then lightly slapped across the cheek with his own hand, and before his father had even begun to laugh, Sable had already moved under their conflict to snatch the blade away from his attempted confiscation.

Deferentially offering it back to the master to threaten her with, she assured the General, "It's fine. The knife won't be used. I've got this." Then to Orson, "I swear, I've got it." She lifted her palm in front of her face and smiled. "It's a gift. A goddamn lovely fucking why-didn't-someone-give-it-to-me-sooner gift. It's so splendid, everyone gets two."

CORROBORATION

The King had only just come from surgery when Girard released the details of the attack at the lithium mine to her Propaganda and Information Team.

"President Pavlović tried to assassinate the Queen Mother," was the story emerging from the PIT. "If King Remius hadn't shielded her with his own body, Sable would be dead."

"Your PIT monster has rather overexcited the herd," Laudin told Girard.

Since Sable and the General flew off to retrieve Lieutenant Fallon, Girard had barely lifted her head from the assortment of tablets and laptops on her desk, and she glowered now to be informed of the obvious.

The day following the attack, while the King recovered under sedatives unaware, the religious had taken to the streets, surrounding not only the Basilica in Jenevuede, but the Erentrude embassy in Sierra, President Pavlović's house, and the King's palace. Not wanting the foothill military base encircled as well, the PIT reported the King was at the Royal Jenevuede Hospital in the capital, and to support the idea, Girard and Laudin demanded of the colonel who was acting in command while General Berringer was absent to place troops at the site.

The Cloitare mothers steadfastly refused to speak and calm the congregants, flatly informing both Laudin and Girard they were lying when they said Sable was beside the King; but still this was the excuse given to those who gathered appealing for proof the Queen Mother was unharmed and the Chosen King alive. Knowing it was going to settle very little, Girard released a much-edited version from the surveillance cameras outside the pump house showing the moment Remy turned Sable, covering her to the ground, and then Remy sheltering her against the pump house wall until their escape in the remaining car. A palace spokesperson read a statement from the Queen Mother calling for patience until the King was stable enough for her to leave his side.

A full day after they left, with the sun again lighting the horizon, Berringer called.

Sable had installed encryption on the phone but warned it didn't match Catherine's, so the General was still speaking vague, "The three of us will be back around sunset."

Catherine, like Sable, was going on her third day awake, and the General didn't feel as though his first night under Sable's nightmarish influence had been restful either, so when Catherine asked, "Can you make it sooner?" the General was less than pleasant with his reply, "Not unless we're throwing the laws of physics to the wall as well."

Catherine kept her eyes on the live news video while typing instructions to a Sierran station chief. She asked the General, "Will you be bringing back the proof I need?"

While it was still dark, the phone texting the Count's location had been pushed on him by Sable, and he had endured her demands that they leave his father's house immediately to make contact at the hotel in Jenevuede. The General had been eager to depart before the sun rose and the winds came to the island, but it was to get Sable back to Remy. Only taking control of Lieutenant Fallon again had silenced her, and the General knew if he left himself open at all, Catherine would be the next to start. He would only offer to her question, "That's uncertain."

The long pause before he spoke told Catherine he was being stubborn. She said, "Let me talk to her," and in the second extended gap of silence, she expected to be denied, but then Sable was saying, "Good morning, kitty."

Catherine shuddered to be reminded. She asked directly, "The proof?"

"Waiting to be picked up, but our man here is a bear to reason with."

"Is he aware of what's going on?"

"Well," Sable scanned the tablet in her hand, "he's flying and I am only just seeing it."

"Show him and make it clear the proof is damn well required at this point."

~~~~~

Leaving Fallon sleeping in the back of the plane, Sable came to sit sideways in the copilot's seat. Hands out in treaty, she faced the General. "I promise, I won't touch anything." She bent her head to the

395

tablet in her lap, aware he could not relax with her so near the controls. "Before we hit Alena's blackout, there have been some developments of which you should be aware." Holding the tablet with a picture to him, she said, "This is the salt flat taken near one of your posts on the ridge. Looks like about two thousand people to me." Swiping her hand across the screen, "These are pictures from the International News Channel of the Palace … the Basilica … President Pavlović's house … The embassy looks much the same. Here are shots from around Alena."

The General lingered longer on the last photos.

"Your troops are mostly being pressed on by royalists with support. Look at this one." She smiled. "They brought the tank crew food when there is no food to spare." But then she turned serious. "Of course you know how Catherine would flip all of this on its head without a moment's notice and with just one little agitator."

Looking out the plane's window, Sable wanted to push the yoke ever so slightly down until the tops of the old pine forest could be heard consistently against the hull. Instead, she returned her attention to the tablet, explaining the break in information while she searched. "I'm showing this to you as I find it." She scowled and started a video. "This is headlined *Sierra Sword Rattling*. That can't be good."

The reporter spoke amidst a crowd at the edge of the Basilica: "Relations between the two countries have hit an all-time low with the attempted assassination of the religious leader of the Cloitare, the Queen Mother Sable. The attack left King Remius Clement of

396

Erentrude seriously injured with shrapnel. This powerful video shows him covering the Queen Mother with his body while mortars hail down around them. Sierran President Pavlović condemns the violent action, but also the allegations he insists originate in Erentrude of his involvement. 'I vehemently deny these accusations of complicity. The source of the rumors will know the full weight of our authority when it is discovered.' But rumors continue to spread that Sierran technology was used in the attempt.

"President Pavlović was forced to deploy the military to regain control of the senate, which was overrun in the early hours of last night by Cloitare adherents. In a similar standoff, radical Cloitare followers have Pavlović's house surrounded. Troops under the command of General Marič used teargas to clear the streets, but the protesters quickly reassembled in growing numbers. Clashes with the military have been limited to throwing bottles and rocks, but social networks from Erentrude have been encouraging their Sierran neighbors to show President Pavlović the "Mother's wrath," alluding to a speech made months earlier by the Queen Mother. Meanwhile, the Cloitare clergy remain silent."

At the end of the report, the General and Sable exchanged worried expressions. Sable laid the tablet in her lap. "You are your father's son, so I assume your strategy will be to deliver a crushing blow from which the enemy cannot recover." Careful to keep her tone from sounding persuasive, she continued, "The Count is in Jenevuede. The proof to destroy Pavlović and Marič is with the Count. And I have the voice to acquire the truth."

The General stared quietly ahead at the western horizon, slowly considering what adding one more infraction to the list of offenses already committed would amount to. Quite a lot if Sable stabbed someone. She truly was not stable, and, he said aloud, "You haven't slept in two nights."

"I can fix that."

Not: *I will go to sleep;* but: *I can fix that.*

Fix, the word kept repeating in his mind until he laughed to himself. He thought he might very well learn his father's ways given enough aggravation and time. To Sable, he said, "I appreciate the small gesture of respect in not lying to me. Now show me how you intend to *fix* it."

She hesitated before pulling the small bag of powder from her pocket and laying it on the tablet's glass screen. "Amphetamines," she explained.

"Sable," he shook his head, "why don't you just go to sleep?"

"You really don't want to be hurtling over these trees in this fragile metal tube with what passes for dreams in my head." She was halfheartedly smirking to take the bite out of it, but the General had heard too much over the night to find it amusing. Ignoring his pity, she challenged the disapproval, "Are you going to tell me you went through the whole of the Five-Day Surge without stimulants? At a time when every army in the world was jacking up their soldiers to get them through the battle?"

Instead of acknowledging the question, he looked her over and asked, "Are you carrying any weapons?"

398

"No." When he looked doubtful, she explained, "I considered grabbing something from the Pigeon or your father, but really, what would be the point? You'd just take it away from me, and getting choked is not so much fun as you might think."

"I'm not a violent man, Sable, and I certainly do not want to defend against women."

"I know that. I am sorry. I should not have made light of it."

The General was not interested in her practiced posture of humility. "If we go get the proof," he hardly believed he was considering it, began turning his head to deny it was possible.

"I'm aware of your concern." She was blunt, "You think I'm going to flip ballistic. But surely you've noticed the focus of my fury is always wearing a Cloitare robe. I did not lie to Remy. I *am* safe and capable in this world. And I know the Count. He does not have any nuns in his employ to give either of us a surprise."

The General heaved air. "If I see anything I don't like …" He looked hard at Sable. "If I say we're leaving …"

Sable bowed her head. "I will follow."

Jaw set forward, he warned, "You could earn a lot of trust with me on this, Sable, and you need to because you are well into the double negatives, but if you so much as—"

"I understand," she stopped him. "You have seen the very worst of me and can't imagine why your father trained me, or how Catherine ever entrusted a single assignment of importance to me. I was once so explicitly, so precisely competent, it is devastating to know what people think of me now. I want desperately to prove myself reliable again, and I realize you are only offering one chance."

"Ok, we understand each other." But he still watched her with ready tension. "Now," gesturing toward the bag of powder on the tablet, "cut us out some lines before Fallon wakes up and tell me what to expect from the Count."

~~~~~~

"Wi Fry, you're confused," Sable's voice had resonated gently, melodically through the cabin. "Accept as true you have not left the plane. You were deep in the darkness of sleep and unaware when we returned to my friends. I wanted once more to speak with them. We stayed all through the night while you dreamed in the dark. The visions before your eyes were the illusions of sleep and like dreams they will vanish with the light of day. Believe me, Wi, everything is fine."

By the time she was done spinning him a new memory, the General had to remind himself none of it had happened, but still it lingered. In the glare of the setting sun, the previous night seemed unreal, and maintaining lucid details of the event became challenging, not unlike landing in the capital airport without a transponder. Every frustrated radio exchange with the control tower brought the General slightly closer to changing his mind.

"You could have just turned it off, Sable."

"And you could have turned it right back on."
400

His troops on the ground kept them from being met by aviation security. Among the plain-clothed soldiers at the Jenevuede Airport were the six Berringer had started training to counter Sable's flipping monkey moves. He figured they might as well get accustomed to her in at least one disguise, and if everything went to hell, get a taste of what they were in for.

Introducing them, he deferred to Sable, "Queen Mother, the head of your new security detail, Captain Nathan Adams."

She hid her discontent. She had already made it known she did not think the heavy retinue he was arranging was required, telling him, "You, me, and Wi are truly more than sufficient for the Count."

He had asked, "Are you planning on leading or following, Sable?"

To ensure the meeting went forward, she had dipped her head, reinforcing her compliance with a flat "Following."

But now, seeing five armored vehicles and seventeen guards, she smiled tight to suggest, "Perhaps we could tone this down."

"I am not completely new to this." To demonstrate, the General removed his military jacket and accepted a long, dark coat from the trunk of an open car.

Sable watched as he changed his shoes, pulled a black knit hat over his distinctly short hair and then rubbed his hand over the stubble on his face. He appeared not unlike a hired thug.

While the General gave instructions to the four team leaders, she looked over the assembled soldiers. Catherine would not approve. Even dressed as civilians, they looked too much the same, and not just their clothes, which looked like they shopped from the same catalogue of business casual. It wasn't even they were nearly all the same age, though it was impossible for her to tell whether it was late twenties or early thirties. What made them indistinguishable was their demeanor, their disturbingly identical carriage of squared shoulders, raised chins, relaxed hands. Both male and female, the bodies were all uniformly toned, muscled, and settled with perfect confidence; and the eyes, every pair steady, serenely certain in their numbers that nothing could go wrong. Everything about them screamed trained professional, military, dangerous, united.

Sable felt an anxious fear she would not have known on her own. More than ever, she wanted to be free to go and do what she did best alone. She could have effortlessly bantered her way down the hotel hall lined with the Count's guards. Known to them, and while not exactly trusted, it would not have roused the slightest suspicion for her to be seeking entrance to the Count's suite. She would have taken the accountant aside and whispered for the proof he would then have happily provided. But instead of *softly-softly*, they were by all appearances going in heavy.

Seated in the back of a sedan with the General, she gave him such a withering look of contempt when all the vehicles entered the hotel's underground parking garage together, he again knew the humor of his father. And he understood the amusement further as she cringed, sinking toward the floor, at the boisterous exit of the soldiers from the cars. Every door that slammed, every shout across the bonnets, and then the loud handling of bags from the trunks, shrank her smaller until she could not stop from sneering, "A little louder and they'll be heard on the sixth floor."

"I wouldn't have thought so myself," but he calmly radioed, "A little louder, please."

In response to his request, two trunks clapped closed, echoing around the concrete structure. The voice of Captain Adams rose distinct above the din of several conversations, "We were halfway down the one-way street when the cop stopped us to ask, 'Didn't you see the signs?' and Lilly says, 'Signs? Hell man, do I look like a prophet?'"

"Cop should have told her she sure drives like one."

They were revelers. Sable sat back to look out the windows and watch the show play across the concrete stage. Parked against the opposite wall, Lilly shouted through the doorman shuttling more dignified guests through the rowdy gathering, "Says the man who flipped on dead man's curve. I don't remember you having a problem with my driving when I winched you out." Lilly fiddled with the hair combs that held her brown hair in a twist. "Tell us, Wilson, why couldn't you read the signs?"

"Too hard to see when it's plastered to the front of his grill."

"No, that wasn't it." Wilson let the porter take his bag, settling it at the top of a growing heap of designer luggage on the trolley. "The problem started with two little iridescent eyes staring dumb into the headlights and my girlfriend banging out hysterical in the passenger seat. But I was undone by the damn power steering. I'm not

403

used to it. I turned her little car like it had eight wheels, and I'm suddenly driving on two in a whole new direction."

Sable could well imagine how much the valets had been paid to be so content with them taking over the entire waiting bay, even going forward with the doormen to keep the circular hub clear. Positioned outside the glass doors, she recognized another armored car that had already been present securing the garage for their arrival, and with it, four more soldiers added to the commotion. As though he didn't know, Sable counted it for the General, "Twenty-four. The Count has six guards maximum. Are we seriously going up there four to one?"

"Not at all." Though the image would have made him laugh if her lack of understanding were simply ignorance and not preference. "I don't like to think about the places Catherine has sent you solo, but I don't mind telling you those days are over." He gestured across the garage, "The military moves big and cumbersome because no one's left without help. There is safety in a team. When we come back down here, we're going to know these cars are still secure because four soldiers will have been guarding both them and the garage access. And your image isn't going to be played all over the media because Lieutenant Parker, in that car over there, is hacked into the security cameras. Our backs are going to be covered by four soldiers watching over the ground floor and there will be another three in the stairwell. Six are on the floor with the Count in two rooms and three are riding up in the elevator with us. Also your total is wrong. It's twenty-six. I've got two on the roof."

The tally made Sable slightly giddy. "And to think, I was going to do this alone."

"And in that thought you were also alone."

~~~~~~

The numbers in the garage were thinning as the soldiers took their positions. Convinced the meeting was going forward, Sable settled, becoming calm, tamping down the most recent line of speed, looking inward to move out into the distance.

No longer animated, the General felt the cool company of a nun beside him. When he told her it was time to move, she followed with eyes that didn't see. Exiting another vehicle, Fallon fell in beside him, whispering, "I hate when they do that."

Berringer quietly returned, "Where's your attention, Lieutenant?"

Corrected, Fallon slid to the other side of Sable. As much as the remaining team looked like they belonged to the same trading firm on holiday, the three of them appeared to have come straight out of the Alenan winter. He and the General looked like unshaven criminals and Sable a soft-footed pickpocket, and they were entering the marble vaulted domes of the Palms. With two hundred years committed to the discrete indulgences of the rich, Fallon wondered how they would make it past security.

But moving into the lobby, Sable raised her face to acknowledge a suited man at reception. With just a nod to the lift operator, the suit's cue was received by the surrounding staff, and the three poor Alenans walked under scrutiny, but unimpeded, into the elevator.

Sable was gone again, eyes searching vacant into the distance, but the General and Fallon watched the suit pick up a phone.

In the center of the lavish dome, a riotous exchange of levity resounded across the polished stones. Calling out, "Hold the doors," three from the group broke apart to enter the antique brass cage.

Looking like they were protecting the little woman from the careless backslapping, shoulder-shaking, and laughing-everywhere elbows of the men, the criminals pushed her to the back against the paneled wall.

The lift operator confirmed, "Everyone's going to the sixth floor."

Before the scroll doors were level with the floor, the sound of uncontrolled hilarity filled the box. Sighting the three new arrivals, the hall erupted with cheer. From the elevator, two men surged forward into a party spilling out of adjoining suites into the hall, but the last was met by a woman and embraced, keeping the lift blocked. Before the operator could coax them out, Fallon stopped him, saying, "It's fine. We're in no hurry."

The General studied the scene at the end of the hall. Two harassed guards were positioned outside the Count's door and the party had them under pressure to join in drinking.

"One shot so we know you're alive." Lilly stood before them extending two glasses in her left hand.

"That's very kind of you, but again, ma'am, we can't accept."

"They're being polite because you're offering them pink sick. Give them a proper drink." Captain Adams joined her with two more glasses.

"Of course, you're right," she agreed and exchanged glasses with Adams while the General moved forward, taking the embracing couple, Fallon, and Sable into the hall. "This is far superior and you simply can't refuse." She held the amber liquid to the guards.

"No, ma'am, but thank you. Now, for the last time, if you could just step back." He looked to where he hoped she would go and caught Marlow's commiserating *sucks-to-be-you* grin. He returned an eye-rolling expression of *No shit*, but then he lingered, almost frowned—Sable could feel it—a warning before his focus went to the carpet, though he wanted to stray to the door, then a barely perceptible jerk to throw it off and he settled into—Sable pushed for it—collaborating regret.

During the quick exchange, the Count's second guard had been speaking into the radio channel of his phone.

The General made a show of apprehension as he guided Sable through the rolling unpredictability of the group.

Eyes blind to the hall, Sable moved into the distance, reaching for the closed room. The metal doors clanged closed behind them while she battled through the raucous multitude, mind free of body, suppressing the desire to mourn the wreckage. *Slow, slow*, she told herself, *quiet like the night.* Heart beating fainter, looking farther, through the wall, searching for impressions, an image, something revealing in form when she found it crowded, the room was waiting, held in angry anticipation, impending violence, too many weapons, and then a sick fetish for pain. She recognized the man.

"Oh, go ahead. I promise we won't tell your boss," Lilly ensured the shots were still on offer.

"Ma'am, you need to return to your room."

From the hall, a new voice emerged, "Well, John, if you're not gonna take them, I will."

"Marlow," the guard responded, "if you'll leave your men out here, I'll see you through." The drinks hesitantly stayed forward in his face, making him impatient. "Ma'am, please, let the lady pass."

Behind them, the party was becoming muted, listening, with only a few now bantering.

"Actually," Sable smiled and looked over her shoulder. She dropped her voice to confide, "Someone was smoking sunshine in the first room. I'm gonna go see if I can score a hit." She stepped back, turning.

"They're waiting for you, Marlow."

Shrugging guilty mischief, "You know I can't resist the scent."

"Marlow," he leaned to call past the older man backing away, covering her retreat, aware the younger of her companions was standing still, watching him. "Marlow, you're already late. There isn't time."

"Ask him to wait." She waved her hand dismissively over her head, mouthing silently, *Invite me,* to the soldiers while throwing her eyes into their room.

"Get the lady a drink," enlivened the group, followed by, "What are you having?" and "Show her the selection."

Laughing, she followed the invitations into the room and then spun, backing away to give the General space to enter before grabbing his shoulder to pull him down to her height, telling him quietly, "Radimir's in there. The Count sold me out to General Marič's weapons dealer."

THE COUNT

In the beginning, the Count had a more civilized idea of how his new life among the deviously wealthy might play. In the eloquent dialogue of an anodyne high, it ran like an old black and white movie where people dressed elegantly, spoke charmingly, and nothing more serious than a passionate slap might occur. He had even briefly changed his button-up knits for a sleek smoking jacket to act his part, but the garment hadn't helped him in the slightest when the first client beat him senseless with the butt of a gun.

He didn't know what begot what, but he quickly learned that people with money to hide were powerful, and powerful people were violent. It was reliable math: as the amount of money being conveyed increased, so too did the level of paranoia; the psychotic behavior of his clients increasing with every figure added to the sum.

It seemed every person he worked with anymore was either a sociopath or a psychopath, and his most powerful client, General Marič, had the most demented maniac of them all as a henchman. Radimir, Marič's enforcer, a short bully with a round baby face full of fat. Crazy angry Radimir, sitting in the Count's hotel suite with his pudgy fingers curled around a combat knife, kissing the blade like a teenage soldier that had never known a woman.

When Marlow came to him to vouch a payment in trust for the lunatic, she'd gotten him supremely high and somehow made it seem perfectly sane to work with a bank outside his control. Even knowing it had to remain hidden from General Marič, he'd agreed. Then Marlow disappeared. The Count took the news with stomach-turning disbelief. Radimir began to pursue him through Erria for the guarantee he'd made, erupting in fury in hotel lobbies, on the street, in restaurants, his tiny eyes disappearing in rage before his tongue would push through the gap of three missing teeth on the side of his mouth. And then the bellowing, "Vhat you take me for? Some pretty little girl you vant to fuck?" Radimir, never caring how much of a scene he made, assured the person he was threatening would smooth it over with any observers, screaming like a child, "I vant my money!" Pounding at all hours on the Count's hotel door with his leering retinue of killers, waking up entire floors with the demand, "Let me in you drug vasted thief!" And once admitted, he'd pace the floor describing how he was going to "slice ewery last one of you from mouth to ass."

For months, the Count had counseled patience, ensuring Radimir that he too wanted nothing more than to get the money out of trust, but he couldn't until Marlow signed off on her end. Finally, convinced he was about to die, he paid the man himself. He still cursed his pride. Trying to maintain some image of dignity and not appear as terrified as he was, he claimed Marlow had signed, but then found himself in the center of his four guards and Radimir's four, pointing pistols at each other over his head while Radimir slapped him from one end of the couch to the other for not turning Marlow over when she surfaced. And the hits were like nothing he had seen in any old movie, except they brought him close to tears, confessing he had paid the man himself. Radimir had left with the promise he would have both Marlow and the money he felt she still owed him.

Having anticipated his revenge for over a year, the lunatic went into spitting conniptions to hear she was making him wait longer to party with a crowd of traders in the hall.

"Go get her." Radimir was standing red-faced, pointing the blade toward the door, and when the Count shrugged wondering how, he screamed, "Drag the bitch in here by her hair."

Marlow was unsettling. She left the Count vacillating between warm endearment and cold chills, but Radimir was truly terrifying, and if he wanted her by the hair, the accountant at least needed to make a show of trying before she broke his arm. He motioned for one of his guards to follow, thinking, *No, that will be your arm.*

The door to his suite opened onto mayhem. Already on petrified edge, the sound from the hall made him quail. A drinking anthem was being bellowed but was interrupted with rowdy cheers when they saw him. It roared into, "Drinks for two more people," while a group of women pushed up to meet him.

He leaned forward to ask John, "Where is she?" and was pointed to the farthest room away.

A brown-haired woman with her hair in a twist asked, "The redhead?" Before he could answer, she called down the hall, "The redhead still in there?" and from outside the room, a man returned, "We've got all kinds of redheads in here. Come down and take your pick."

John told him, "You can't be out here right now."

But the Count was certain, "I can't be in there either," then indicated forward, "We have to get down there."

John blocked one woman's attempt to link the Count's arm, but not the other. The faster brunette told the Count, "Allow me to escort you to a drink," while the second guard ordered, "Ma'am, stand back," but they were too drunk to mind.

The anthem was being chanted again and three unknown women had encircled them. Huddled together, John and another guard shuffled him down the teeming hall while hands kept jostling him with goodwill. Worse were the backslaps that disappeared before they could be blocked, and then the shoulder shakes, gripped and shaken, the accumulating group rocked as the revelers tried to draw the newcomers into the spirit of the celebration.

At the end of the hall, there was a sudden surge and shove through the door that the Count hoped would alert the last guard on his door that events had turned bad. His cry for help was drowned by the wild screaming happiness the three of them being twisted to the ground seemed to elicit.

Face in the carpet, the Count watched John on the floor beside him yield to the pressure that bent his arm behind his back while his mouth was pressed into the wool pile; and then, muffled on his other side, he barely heard the ripping of tape silence the acquiescing groan of his second guard. Searched and found with nothing more interesting than his room card, the Count lay motionless with his hands secured behind his back and the weight of a man against his spine.

Hoots and hollers moved half the drinking cheerfully back into the hall, and while he watched them pretend to banter exchanges with someone in the room, a single red braid dropped before his eyes.

A cool hand found his throat and a velvet purr whispered, *"Remember the night."* Giggling, *"Remember how funny it was?"* Marlow pressed her catching breath against his ear so only he could hear, *"Do you remember? It was so funny,"* until he was chuckling with her. *"It was the funniest night,"* she was choking to hold back how hilarious it had been.

And he had begun to laugh loud, "So very funny!" His amusement carried higher over the noise of the room and into the hall. But it was really not so funny to think his last door guard was relaxing while John was being dragged away with limbs bound, mouth taped, and head bagged blind.

<center>~~~~~~~</center>

The cage to the elevator was open and the lift operator was asking another time, "Anyone coming down?"

Lieutenant Fallon looked back into the suite at General Berringer, and Sable lifted her head from the Count to implore with frustration again, *"Please."*

Fallon told the operator, "No, sorry, change of plans."

Seeing the General coming, Sable pressed low over the Count to speak slowly, drawing out the commands, *"Hush. Be still. Quiet*

414

like the night," so when Berringer hauled him up from under the soldier on his back, he was silent and stumbling weak. The General walked him into the crowded bathroom and dropped him on the toilet.

"How many people are in your room?"

"Husssh, quiet." The Count was swaying drunk under Sable's influence and his balance was not improved with his wrists zip-tied behind his back. He looked at his two guards lying on the tiled floor and told the soldier over them, "Be ssstill."

Sable flipped on the vent and set the basin taps to full to cover the sound of her voice in the hard, resonating space. Cupping the Count's neck, she pressed her cheek to his and whispered until he slurred, "I *do* trust you. I always have." After Sable murmured some more, he admitted, "Well, there's Radimir. He's making out with a knife, pervert. He's got five men: one to carry every part of your severed body. Radimir said he'd carry your bloody red head himself. That was after he choked you with your goddamn braids." He tried to mimic the maniac's accent. "And I've got six," but then he sighed, "Well, you've got two, but I've got another four." He wagged his finger hoping Sable could see it over his shoulder. She pressed into him once again until he said, "No, no, not with that bastard in there. I sent all my tellers away."

In the lull, the General asked, "Weapons?" and watched Sable's fingers tighten around the Count's neck until he swore, "Never. They were never meant for you." But she was muttering through his every protest until he confessed, "Shotguns. My men brought them in bags. But everyone else has handguns." Moments

415

later, he whined, "Oh, I don't know what type. Black things." And then, "Clips? Maybe. I really try not to look."

From the hall, a cry went up, "Two more shots for our new friends!"

Captain Adams discreetly informed the General, "The team from the stairwell is on the floor with us, and two from the lobby are outside watching the windows. Transport is on its way."

Placing his hand on her shoulder to draw her up, the General spoke meaningfully but quietly to Sable, "You're doing good with my trust, but you have to stay here. Understand?"

She returned even quieter, "You're going after Radimir?" And when he inclined his head, she pulled him lower to speak secret, "Catherine is not going to want him dead, or imprisoned." Feeling him tighten, she explained, "She knows who he is, where he is, and what he does, but most importantly, he is prepared to sell out General Marič. If we don't utterly destroy Marič with proof from the Count, Radimir is invaluable. Give me the chance to finish recruiting him."

Expelling aggravation from his chest, the General rose to tell her, "Stay in here. Listen to this man as if he were me."

Once she lowered her head and made a sound of agreement, Berringer told Captain Adams, "It's on you. You're in charge of her. Remember what I said."

~~~~~~

I'm a mercenary, Alowa silently reminded himself in his own language. *Not a yes-man bodyguard*. Watching the little white man throw a foot-stomping hissy fit, Alowa berated himself, *What pink-titted demon possessed me to forget?*

"Vhere? Vhere? Vhere the fuck are they?" Radimir was nose to nose with the Count's last guard.

Alowa felt sorry for him. He'd been left sitting in a chair at the edge of the room; otherwise, Radimir would have had to knock him down to splutter rage in his face. Outnumbered six to one, he never should have stayed behind when the last two went to retrieve their employer. And it was too late now. He offered to find the missing parties, but Radimir returned the suggestion by putting a pistol to the man's head with one hand and a knife to his throat with the other. "I'm not going to have my dick vanked no more. Call him."

Alowa was not concerned when the guard reached into his jacket for his phone. The man was not going to go for a weapon with the odds as they were.

"Vhat? Vhat?" the little man was exploding red when the guard held the phone over his head, then tried pointing it toward the windows, and finally gave up only to frown over it.

"Service is out of range," he read off the screen.

Radimir knocked it from the man's hand with such force it bounced off the shoulder of an unsuspecting guard on the couch and landed back at their feet. Cursing in Sierran, Radimir stuffed the knife in his belt to pull out his own phone and check. Striking the guard

417

across the cheek with the flat of the gun, he informed the bloody man, "They are blocking our signal, you fuckvit."

The whole lot of them, nothing more than primitive knee-bending Errians. Alowa regretted ever coming to the continent. He'd told them to postpone the meeting. He'd told them the crew in the hall were not what they seemed. But nobody believed the redhead would turn. He'd asked them, "Where you think she be the last year if not in jail?" Of course she was rolling on the Count. He never thought he was racist, but the longer he stayed in Erria, the more he said it: *Knee benders.*

"Go see vhat is happening in the hall. I vant to know if that last cunt is still on the door."

"Lo, he not be there," not with the authorities having just cut cell service, but Alowa went anyway.

Cracking the door to peer out, he was greeted with, "Whoa! Big man! Come join us."

"Ah," foot braced behind the door, he shoved the pushy woman back by the head, "maybe not so good idea," and slammed it closed. Returning to Radimir, he said, "They know we know now."

"Vhy?" Radimir slapped the Count's guard with the flat of the gun on every question, "Vhy? Vhy? Vhy?"

"I tell you, she no good after police have her so long." Alowa freed the battered guard from Radimir's grip by yanking him off the chair and tossing him behind.

"You stupid galoot." Radimir pulled out his knife again. "You vant some of it?"

418

"Calm down, little man, they no come for you. They come for the Count. But you make big deal of this, they kill you."

"Oh, that's fucking sublime." Placing his weapon filled hands on either side of his head, Radimir reeled with the idea. "I'll inwite them in for a game of cards."

"Maybe no. They no think they the guest of this party." Alowa spoke over Radimir's head to the other guards in the room, "We walk to the el-e-va-tor." The accent made each syllable pronounced. "We leave this place free if we be calm," he told Radimir.

"That's vhat makes you a stupid galoot. The blubbering bank has already told them I came to kill her."

"So? You give them no ..." he was looking for the word *proof* but went with, "no blood, they let you go. She see you, be afraid, you get her later."

"And vhat does the dumb galoot suggest ve do vith all these guns?"

"Lo, these things?" Alowa wiped his gun on his jacket and dropped it on the couch. "These little things be the Count's."

~~~~~~

When the door to the Count's suite opened, the hotel phone was ringing for Radimir. The General could hear it through the handset he held to his ear and also shrilling down the hall to where he stood in the farthest suite. He passed the phone to Lieutenant Fallon

419

and leaned into the corridor to watch a giant bend his head under the wooden frame.

"*Lo ... lo shre han,*" the dark man was struck back to his native tongue, remarking with slow wonder at how the hall had changed. Gone were the revelers and in their place were black-masked professionals bearing short barreled rifles with large thermal scopes. By three, they were stacked for cover in the open doors. "We be very calm," he assured with gentle composure, leading a trail of men with their hands splayed wide and empty before their chests.

"You are in the presence of the King's Army," a gunman identified the squad.

"Lo. Lo, we be very happy to leave the King's Army."

"You will all be going down then?" The unmasked General stepped between the soldiers and held his finger over the button to call the lift.

"We be very happy to leave."

"Slow and steady," the General cautioned. "We have no issue with any of you, but I'm going to ask you to clasp your hands behind your heads so no one gets jumpy."

Putting his hands on top of his head, Alowa stepped slowly down the hall. "We be very calm. No one get," he smiled quizzically, "*jom-pee.*"

"Come on." The General motioned them forward. "Slow. Keep space between you," he individually directed the five men until they were separated through the hall. Hand open flat, "Ok, that's far enough. I want to thank you for remaining polite and cooperative."

420

But at the end of the hall, lingering half concealed behind the frame of the door, were two more men. "Come forward," he called.

"Fuck you. I'll come forvard when they get in the elewator."

"We be calm," the voice rose to fill the space.

"Yeah, ve be fucking calm, but I'd rather see vhat they do vith a galoot like you before I sving my balls out there."

"If you will just come forward, we will get you out of here," the General said.

Cracking his neck, "When the elewator comes, ve'll see."

"Sir, you obviously think you're more important than I do, so let me tell you plainly, I am not interested in you or what you've done. I want you out of here. But the lift is not coming until you step out of that room." The General looked nearly bored with the passing of time.

"Come, man, be calm and we leave."

"Vhat'd the money molester say about me?"

"I am not here to share information with you, sir. My sole reason for living right now is to get you out of my sight. If you would please step into the hall so I can see you're not a threat to us, I will get you on your way."

After a longer wait, Radimir tightened his mouth into an exaggerated scowl, turned his head side to side and declared, "I think I vould like it better if you came down here and conwinced me."

"Lo, be calm. He be calm," the big man assured.

"Sir, if what you need is an escort, I will happily hold your hand."

"I talk with him," the giant began to turn.

The General gently stopped the move, saying, "I'm afraid I need you to stay where you are, and again, I appreciate your calm leadership through this."

Shouting over the exchange was Radimir, "Yeah, I think I vant you to come hold my hand. I am wery afraid."

The man's sardonic assertion was undermined by the gut punching scream of male hysterics that startled the delicate balance of the hall.

"*Lo shre han.*" The big man looked over the soldiers into the room from which it came.

The guards at his back began falling back for the suite, and immediately the side rooms emptied of soldiers. Rifles pointed at their heads, Alowa heard the sharp commands, "Get down. Down on your knees."

Certain he wanted no part in it, Radimir slammed closed the door.

Captain Adams wondered of what exactly he had been left in charge.

She had said it so very kindly to the Count, "I understand, Radimir is scary, but now you have to learn that I am far scarier."

Holding his head with compassion, she laid her cheek against his, and then, one hand slipping to his throat, she struggled to control him.

He jerked them both right, tried to shake her off by slamming back into the toilet's cistern, then down and left, he banged his head against a cabinet.

Adams came forward, but not knowing what was happening, he hesitated. The Count stood upright, wild-eyed, arching back to get away from her, but she followed with her voice. Adams heard, "*falling through the dark*," and suddenly dizzy, he braced his hand against the wall while watching the Count drop shrieking to the floor.

Covering the Count's mouth with her hand, she kept him screaming. In the curve of the Count's convulsed body, she knelt with her mouth pressed to his ear. Adams wanted to address her, but her name could not be spoken in the room. As the General had done, he placed a hand on her shoulder to gently pull her back.

She glared up at him with hard penetrating eyes, staring a cold warning until he looked away. He had forgotten by her dress she was Cloitare. Looking down the length of the mirrored cabinet, Adams sought advice from the other soldier guarding the Count's two guards, but he only shrugged, unaware of what to do. Adams turned his

423

appeal into the room where Fallon and another soldier stood over three more bound captives, and while both returned alarmed expressions, they also had no suggestion of what he might do.

The room had noisily cleared of soldiers when the Count broke the calm. Now, hoping to prevent further disruption, Adams came down on one knee beside Sable and tried again. Speaking softly, he began, "I am a little concerned—" but was stopped short as her hand laid flat against his chest.

She raised her head from the Count to draw out the word "*Hush*," and then, hand sliding to his neck, "*Be still*." She rumbled a slow breath through her throat before dropping her full attention back to the quaking puddle on the floor.

Adam's reactions were thick and slow when General Berringer snapped his rank, "Captain," and then, "Damn it, son," the General pulled him through the bathroom door to take his place at her side.

She turned on him the same eyes, but rather than shrink away, he demanded, "What in hell's great waste basket of plans are you doing?"

Adams was certain he could read her lips answer, "Recruiting."

~~~~~

"I'm going to tell you the same as I told Adams when I made him head of the Queen's security. Do *not,*" Berringer stressed it to Lilly, "let her get her hands around your throat or near your chest. This is not a suggestion, Captain. You block her or knock her off if it comes to it."

Lilly did not look eager for the promotion, or the certain demotion that would come of it.

"Don't worry, kid, I've got your back. And like I explained in training, you're not going to hurt her. The Queen Mother has evasive moves you've never seen before."

While the remaining teams filled the second room with both the Count's and Radimir's guards, Lilly studied the room in which she had unexpectedly found herself responsible.

In the bathroom, the Count was heaving sick into the toilet, and on the tiles, his two guards gagged until the tape had to be removed from their mouths; the two lieutenants in the crowded space weren't fairing much better. At the suite's dining table was Sable, staring blind ahead as though none of it concerned her, and kneeling in the center of the plush seating arrangement was the giant, head bagged, wrists and ankles secured. Then there was Fallon, sitting on the couch beside the giant. Having been so recently abducted, he still had the gall to be looking on her with headshaking sad-mouthed sympathy.

Like Adams, Lilly wondered of what exactly she had been left in charge.

425

Outside the suite into which Radimir and his last guard had retreated, a team of six prepared to enter. The General stood in the long hall wanting to be at the front of the action, but he well remembered what he thought of senior officers disrupting a practiced team to play hero, or, as this generation would accuse, *to get a chub*.

He had told them what he wanted from the operation and then left it to the team leader to see it through, making only one refusal: "Nothing stopping you from using your thermal scopes, but how about we not ignite smoke grenades in the Palms? Instead, how about we just turn out the lights? Maybe use your NVGs?"

"But General," Adams had mockingly whined, "it's not as much fun." Glad to be free of the Queen, and not entirely certain why, the team leader was as jacked up happy as if he had snorted a line of speed.

On the unblocked military frequency, Adams received confirmation that a soldier was standing by the circuit panel, ready to throw the breakers to the sixth floor. "The suits aren't happy about it though."

"They should be grateful they won't have to rip out all the carpet." Hand on the shoulder of the soldier in front of him, he said, "Alright, it's a green light rave. Let's bang."

All of the sixth floor went dark.

Dim light from a battery-powered bulb escaped the open door of the closest room and made the hallway bright through the unit's NVGs. Wilson swiped the Count's room card across the reader and then pushed the door into the weak resistance of a barricade. In consideration to the Palms and its guests, the plan was to enter without shock grenades, but the barrier changed that. The man behind him held a stun grenade above his head for the team to see and then showed it to Wilson before tossing it through the meager opening. In the instant following the blaze of light and deafening explosion, the fourth man shoved into the door, skidding back the obstruction.

The delicate antique furniture of the Palms gave away easily, leaving tables and chairs overturned in a pile just within the entrance. As the fourth man fell back into the stack, Wilson waited until the second stun grenade was thrown before leading the swarm into the room. Looking left and then following the barrel of his rifle right, he quickly moved forward in a circle looking for threats. By the time he had secured the corner behind the door, the whole six-man team was in the room.

Room clear of targets, their focus settled on the sliding doors to the left of the sitting room, cracked enough for Wilson's thermal scope to pick out a hotspot beside the bed. A heavy blanket had been pulled half off the mattress to form a mound at the corner, and concealed within the heap, Wilson's scope showed several bright patches that he recognized as a face and two hands on a shotgun.

Adams saw it too. Through the green-tinted image of the night goggles, he followed the long glowing lines of lasers from the team's rifles as they converged on the spot. This was the green light rave, an unfair game of blind laser tag, but as General Berringer would readily admit, "If you're in a fair fight, I've done something wrong."

427

The dots were crowded on the man's head, and Adams knew in a moment the man would feel the heat of the lasers in his eyes. He would give the fugitives the chance the General wanted.

"You, beside the bed with the shotgun, drop the weapon." Then more demanding, he was shouting from low in his throat, "Drop the weapon. Drop it now."

To escape their line of vision, the guard tried to move right, but his intended cover entangled him. In the dark, he fumbled one foot forward with the gun.

On the first round released from Adams' rifle, Wilson and a second soldier each put three more bullets through his head. The thermal scopes showed the splatter as white on the wall.

From inside the room came the shout, "Vait! Vait! I vant to talk."

~~~~~~

On the table, a battery-powered bulb gave faint light to the room. Another like it illuminated the bathroom where the Count had curled himself tight on his side.

Sable had closed her eyes to relax in the shadowy quiet of the room. At first, the sound of inhaling matched her breath so she heard it as her own, but then it became louder, drawing heavy and deep. She looked to Alowa dragging hard against the black bag, pulling the fabric against his nostrils and turning his head in her direction.

428

"I smell you, Marlow."

At the closed door, Lilly said, "Quiet, prisoner."

But he pulled stronger for the scent. "You smell like bad weather. You smell like the sky before rain." As he spoke, Lilly moved to silence him. "You smell like lightning. Like the gods when they cry."

"I had no idea." Sable came to her feet and walked forward to position herself between Lilly and the seating arrangement where Alowa knelt.

"You make that man scream?" he asked.

Lilly looked to the side of Sable and motioned Fallon off the couch and onto the giant.

Stepping back, Sable pointed her finger at William and shook her head *no*.

"I know you make him scream. I smell," bag huffing, "the fear. These people afraid of you."

"Are you?"

"You wear the grief of the gods as perfume. What you think?"

Sable sat across from Fallon and silently suggested he sit again as well. She kept to the far edge of the opposite couch, keeping as much space as possible between her and the giant that was causing so much trouble. "Alowa, I never quite understood what you were doing with Radimir. He's a crying tantrum in a suit."

"I tell myself this also. I am no bodyguard. War is better. Cleaner." He shrugged his shoulders. "There was a girl. I think I love her. I stay. I no love her. I stay. Here I be."

"There is a chair behind you." Sable held her arm out to stop Lilly from going forward.

"You no make me bend the knee? Lo, maybe you make me bend another way."

Sable smirked and then warned Lilly against taking offense. As he struggled with his weight and size to get to his bound feet, a rapid burst of rifle fire could be heard from down the hall. Sable could not keep Fallon from rising, and had she wanted to keep Lilly from pushing through, she would have had to grapple her to the floor. When Alowa felt the chair at his legs and managed to sit without being struck back to the carpet by the soldiers, Sable said, "I'm sorry about the hood. I wish I could take it off, but I don't have a lot of sway around here."

"I think about this also. I think maybe you no speak the truth. I think you have power. I ask myself, 'Why that little girl with the King's Army?' I think I know who you are."

"Quiet," Sable snapped. She looked from Fallon on one side of the man to Lilly on the other. "If you ever want to be free again, it would be wise to guess wrong."

His laughter was big and booming. "That man in the hall, I know who he is too. He is General Bear. He have no plan to let anyone free. And he be a great knee bender if he let Radimir live."

"If Radimir dies, it will have been his own choice."
430

"Lo, you defend him, he defend you. No one be free. What you want from me, Ommawa?"

Even trussed up as he was, there was something distinctly noble about Alowa. Sable studied his large build and the small line of color that could be seen on his neck beneath the bag. She had not been able to place her fondness for him before, but she recognized it now. He reminded her of Aidan. "What is this word: Ommawa?"

"Mother." His bagged head cocked to the side, "Mother of nations when we in peace. When no peace," the bag straightened with his back, "mother of war."

Closing her eyes, Sable exhaled with all the hate she reserved for prisons. "You are not being very wise, Alowa, and you are a long way from home."

"I think this also, but I think maybe you make me your guest."

~~~~~~

Moving quickly forward, the soldiers split to either side of the sliding doors.

"Vait, don't shoot. I vant to talk."

Not to give away the team's location, Adams retreated down the wall to reply, "You are in the presence of the King's Army. If you want to live, lie flat on the floor."

"Vait, ve make a deal."

At the toppled barricade, the General stood beside Adams. Both men faced the sliding doors while the General listened to Radimir bargain, "I am a wery important man. Who is your superior?"

Like a goddamn prophet, the General was thinking, *I can see the future*. If not Catherine, then Sable would convince Remy to release Radimir back to General Marič. It mattered little which, one of them would see the man go free to benefit Girard and the Ministry of Intelligence. Catherine played a dangerous game of espionage while he had to provide security, and not ten minutes earlier, the prized Sierran was intent on dismembering a woman.

"Your superiors vill vant to talk to me."

And from what the General had been told of the weapons dealer, he did not think Radimir would be less inclined to kill that woman should he learn who she was.

"I vant to make a deal."

Adams was waiting to see if the General would negotiate, but when the General finally spoke, it was directed at the Captain. Without a trace of emotion to reveal his thoughts, Adams was told, "Secure that room."

"If you want to live," the Captain shouted, "you need to lie flat on the floor now." Adams then took his place in line with the team.

The flash and bang of the grenade was followed by the doors sliding back and the team moving forward. The terms for survival had been given before they entered. The short burst of gunfire meant Radimir had not complied. The outcome gave the General no pleasure, but it did drop the tension from his muscles, leaving him deeply relaxed and, when he thought about the future, satisfied.

~~~~~

The first room on the sixth floor had an uneasy level of resentful compliance stiffening both conversations. The lights had returned, the cellular block was lifted, and the room held only one target of interest. At the long side of the dining table, the Count sat between Sable and Fallon. He was cold and harshly sober, fully aware of his complicity, and feeling sick for a dose. The nausea shuddered through him at every encouraging sentiment uttered by Marlow.

"Let me help you," she said gently while opening his laptop and sympathetically arranging it so he could continue to hold his trembling arms against his rolling guts.

Feigning calm, he muttered, "Thank you," but all the while something primal inside him was wailing fear. The terror crawled up his chest and tightened his throat until it choked him silent, leaving him feeling small, like an animal whose only hope for survival was not to be seen.

Observing the three were Lilly and the General, watching but discussing Lilly's reluctance to embrace the new assignment. Given a choice, she would rather be in the hall overseeing the conveyance of Radimir's guards into transport for detention. There was no illusion in the Palms anymore that the group of revelers was anything other than soldiers from the King's Army. Their sharp commands could be heard

433

through the closed door of the suite, and louder as Lilly opened the door to the expected knock.

Taking the dark roll of fabric from Wilson, she closed the door to inspect it. Tucked inside were syringes and alcohol swabs, a lighter, spoon, and cotton, and then both medical-grade liquid anodyne and a bottle of powder she'd been told was sunshine from the streets.

Walking to the end of the table, she held it flat against the polished wood and looked severely upon the Count. His face was damp with sweat, and when he spied the bundle on the table, he shivered.

The Count had never shown his gear to anyone—had never shot up in front of anyone either—but he was well past what a smoke or a snort could fix; he needed to pierce a vein. Barely audible, feeling like he was cringing, he said, "Please, I will take that."

But Lilly was hard with disapproval. After several moments of glowering disgust, she opened the roll to prepare the dose herself.

The black plunger had hardly drawn from the glass vial when Lilly pulled it out. The Count was afraid. He found his voice. "Young lady, five milligrams is not going to cut it. If you would, please, allow me." And held out his shaking hand.

"I'm not interested in getting you high, sir. This is enough to keep you from hurting."

"I assure you, it's not." And then, with as much grace as he could manage, he explained, "I am a thirty-year junkie with the

434

tolerance to prove it. Anything less than twenty and I will vomit in this nice man's lap."

Sable nodded to back him up while Fallon scooted away. The Count had tears in his eyes that had nothing to do with grief, but the sick of withdrawal that ached in his muscles and bones.

Lilly was staring at Sable, wondering how to address her before giving up entirely and asking with subdued politeness, "Will you please leave the table while this man takes care of his business?"

The Count sneered, "Why? Do you think it's going to insult her delicate senses?"

"No," Sable explained as she got to her feet, "she thinks you might stab me with it."

The Count erupted on Lilly, "I am retching sick over here and you think I'm going to share?"

Standing beside the General, Sable spoke on the Count's behalf. "He really will need at least twenty milligrams to be of use. And that's not nearly enough to make him feel normal. If you had any pity, you would allow him thirty-five."

The General's jaw was tight with what he was hearing, not wanting to imagine how Sable was so familiar, but he spoke evenly, "Captain, give the man a total of twenty milligrams."

"Bless you, Marlow. Bless your little red betraying head. I'll defend you as the most charitable backstabber I have ever known." Tying off at the table, the Count went for a vein in his arm. Fallon looked to the ceiling, but Lilly coldly stayed on every move. When

435

the Count removed the tourniquet and withdrew the needle, he was derisive, "Not even a head roll from that miser's portion."

The small measure was enough to make him want to speed through the exchange to get rid of them so he could get more. He watched his precious kit leave the table with Lilly and could hardly take his eyes from it when she stopped on the other side of Marlow. But the proximity of something so dear to something so harrowing jolted him. He tried to place the memory of a nightmare, what it was with the sighting of Marlow that made his chest tighten. He wondered if he had actually gone through the convulsed bawling withdrawal on the tiles he remembered, the dark drop into madness with Marlow holding his head, at once tender and yet the intention seemed murderous, as though she intended to solicitously drown him in shadows.

He was thinking it with no intent of speaking aloud, "There is something about you that is dark and malignant."

He felt the memory spasm through him when she returned to lower her head to his ear and whisper a confirming, *"Dark as the night."*

To be free of them, of the heavy gloom that had settled in the room, in his veins, pounding despair through his blood, he would give them what they wanted so he could have what he needed. He explained to Lieutenant Fallon, "The bank's security is layered. Location verification runs through my cell." The Count called the electronic bank, "Only certain locations between cell towers are permissible, such as here in the center of Jenevuede, and only from this cell's identity module. The bank texts back a random question to answer through the laptop. The second security layer is biometric authentication by voiceprint ID linked to this computer, and the final is finger vein identification."

Fallon took the cell to read the question aloud, *"How do you feel?* Seriously? The bank asks that?"

"One of many hundreds prearranged by myself; no second guesses. Any error and I will be notified, and if I don't respond, the account will be locked. So, young man, if you are thinking of installing a keylogger on this machine, or any other devious rootkit, allow me to save you time; unless you can do something with biometrics no one else can, your chances of successfully hacking my accounts are zero."

Sable concurred, "And repeatedly failing is so disheartening."

"I wondered what you knew of it, Marlow. It caused me great inconvenience." While he spoke, the Count typed an account number into the laptop's login screen. "After the third reset, I was forced to fly to one of those tiny island nations so loved by us tax evaders but in the middle of a near-empty ocean. Setting it right again cost me several days." Unable to look at her, he told Fallon, "Now be quiet." He depressed the microphone and answered the question to the waiting load screen, "I feel more like I did when I came in here than I do now."

"Huh," Fallon nodded. "I don't know what you just said, but I think you summed it up for all of us."

Since he was young, the Count had a knack for seeing through systems, whether it was manipulating the curve of his university's grading structure or any country's tax laws, it was all about understanding the weakness to exploit the intended defense. If he wrote code, he would have been a hacker, but instead he shifted money from country to country under inventive corporate accounts, hiding his clients behind nominee directors that never knew what they were signing, or what businesses were linked to their names. He began unraveling President Pavlović's deposits, following the money from bank to bank. From the first deposit, originating with Pavlović's Sierran account, to the sham children's charity on Alowa's home continent, then over to two more corporations and back to the rebel commander, Mark Ansel, it all ended in General Marič's account, a private offshore foundation with Marič as treasurer. Fallon saved the whole meandering transaction to an external drive.

"You have killed me as surely as if you shot me in the head, Marlow."

"I'm sorry it has happened like this," she was sincere. "I've not done you any favors, but I have also not yet killed you." She rubbed her hands against the rough denim of her jeans, feeling guilty for the cooperation she had not quite finished extorting. She took the laptop and accessed the bank holding Radimir's money in trust. Sliding it back to the Count, she showed him the funds had been released to him. "You have been bought and paid for. You belong to Intelligence Chief Girard now." To escape the reality of having just enslaved someone to another, she dropped into the Stare, becoming a nun with a heart too slow for remorse. "You will find Girard takes moves against her agents very personal. In addition, she has paid too much to let you die. When she's done with this fiasco, none of these events will have been about you. It will have been a strike against General Marič, a killing of Radimir for actions against the crown."

The Palace

Sable sat alone in her rooms looking into the distance, into the past, searching for the place that everything went so wrong. The path started splintering after returning to the palace. She had exited the cars in her robes, red braided hair hidden beneath the headdress, looking like a nun. Catherine was waiting, insisting there was no time for Sable to dye her hair black again; the situation in the capital had become unmanageable. Confidant the soldiers would not fire on their own countrymen, Cloitare adherents had pushed into the hospital. The silence of the clergy could be endured no longer. Desperate to confirm the promised future still lived, no amount of mace or force would keep them out. They had surged down the halls demanding information, racing up the stairs to disperse through the floors, looking for the room under guard, filling the hospital until they confirmed the King was not present. Their patience at an end, it had turned into a riot.

Ushering Sable through the back of the palace, Catherine pressed a tablet into her hands with words on the screen designed to placate the people. While Sable read, Catherine quickly described the scenes of turmoil, "They set an ambulance on fire, looted the pharmacy, and now they're hurling medical equipment out the broken windows of the top floor." Those below in the throng still pushing through the doors were lucky to escape with just broken bones. But with bodies crushed against the walls at the entrance, and the medical staff scattered or hiding, the injured could not be treated in the pandemonium. "The crazies at our gates are being placated with every treat we can offer from the kitchen's pantries, but you've got some red-handed zealots in the plaza who just battered down the back door of the Basilica." Directing Sable out the front of the palace as though she had been inside all the while, Catherine rolled her eyes at herself for putting the Queen before the public in her Cloitare robes.

To the few news cameras permitted through the gates, Sable spoke from the top of the stairs.

"My children, the King is recovering at home with your Queen Mother. Your devotion through this darkest time has given me strength." Then finding the prepared words offensive in their restraint, Sable cast them aside to speak for herself, "The King I love with absolute devotion has been harmed. We all share the same anger. It is what makes us a family. But as your mother, I am telling you to stay calm. Remain peaceful. Understand your mother's watchful eye has already seen those responsible. You will witness great changes in the coming days, and you will know, as will they, that the King's justice recognizes no borders."

She had spoken without seeing him first. Here Sable looked closely at the past, seeing tiny hairline fractures begin to emerge.

But the first real crack dividing the future that might have been from the future that was unfolding revealed itself outside the King's rooms. The General had stopped her, pulling her back by the arm in the moment before she would enter. He wanted to speak the thoughts that had been troubling him. "Sable, we cannot hold these secrets. We cannot hold them and say we faithfully serve the King. It makes us both liars and deceivers." His face was set with resolute

441

conviction. "And, while it may not be the worst, it bothers me the most: it is completely inappropriate for you and I to be sharing the same secret."

Sable spoke softly to settle the distress. "We leave words unspoken to save the King's life." As the General began to shake his head in strong denial, Sable explained, "Let us remove ourselves to get a bit of perspective. We will make it about another person, Catherine, for instance. If there were something Remy might learn of Catherine that would cause him to lose all trust in her, yet this secret did not harm him, would it not be wiser to stay silent and allow him the full benefit of her skills? Her protection of the King knows no limit. Should he be denied this for the sin of omission?" While the General's expression showed he was considering it, Sable continued, "If Remy learned all the secrets kept by his advisors, he would have no advisors left. And then he would be in greater peril than any secret could have caused."

"You may be right, but the man has a right to choose. It is his life. I would not want anyone concealing from me information that could get me killed, especially not for the sake of trying to save my life. Not only do I have a right to know, I would likely have a better idea of how to deal with it. To do anything less makes a man seem incompetent."

In both their arguments, Sable could hear the truth. One was the rationale of the soldier, the other of the spy, and in neither did Sable completely trust. Knowing her own desire was to remain quiet, Sable asked, "What are you suggesting?"

442

"We tell the King everything."

Sable stopped breathing. Finally needing air, she expelled, *"Everything?"* And when the General nodded curtly, her words came hushed with disbelief, "You would reveal your father?"

"I can do it knowing Remy will see it fairly."

"Will he?" Sable was afraid to even consider it. "You know him better than I." She stared at the floor, "I could never reveal Master Orson. Perhaps you should ask him if he wants to be revealed."

"No. When we explain what the Cloitare did to him, Remy will understand and he *will* be fair."

Sable rolled a sound of understanding in her throat. "As explanation, you mean for me to tell Remy that I influenced him with my voice."

She looked condemned, so the General said gently, "He will forgive you."

"Perhaps." Sable felt fear seize her heart. The sleepless nights were shaking through her nerves; the drug to combat it had tipped over into angst. Feeling her face flush with sorrow, she forced herself to speak so as not to cry. "When he learns, he will not trust me. He will guard against any threat of persuasion and return uncompromising denials to my every request. Do you imagine he will allow me to go behind the double doors?" Sable frowned the answer *no*. "If I don't lead the clergy, or directly control the Cloitare, when the mothers kill him, which of us will regret this conversation more?"

443

The General wanted to clear away all the misconceptions that had been deliberately created in Sable's mind. "You are following my father's advice, and though I love him and it pains me to say this, you fail to understand his desire for revenge is more important than whether it gets you killed."

Sable found a cold smile to offer. "That is precisely why I can trust his strategy. We have agreed to win by any means."

The General pulled back. "You said there was no plan for outside the convent." His eyes narrowed on her. "You meant and you still mean for them to kill you."

Raising her brows, Sable turned her head slightly, giving possibility to the statement.

Angrily, the General's voice rose without tolerance, "This is not what Remy would want. He would tear down the doors to save you, and he'd destroy them all if he found you dead."

She lifted her expression as though her mind had sparked with illumination at his words, and then instantly regretted it.

Livid with the realization, his voice boomed, "And that is *exactly* what you two are counting on."

"Not *exactly*, there's a bit more required of the outcome than just getting myself killed so Remy reacts."

"Tell me."

Too weary to fight, she admitted, "It will end with the King as head of the Cloitare."

The General was momentarily silenced then somber with approval, "That's good. That's very good."

"I know."

"But you intend to die. And *that*, Sable," the General spun around to escape it and then turned to face her again even angrier, "is madness. Pure lunacy. That is not a plan. That is a tragedy. You have been taken advantage of because you do not understand strategy."

"But I know your father does."

"You intend to go forward with it? I am asking you to believe me, such a plan is unfit."

"I trust Master Orson and I swore to him I would follow his strategy."

"I was there, I heard. But I also heard him tell you to decide where your loyalties lie. And then, above all other considerations, ensure your every action reflected it. You cannot say your loyalties lie with Remy and still follow my father's plan. You are either loyal to Remy or my father." He could see Sable was becoming confused. While she held her face in consternation, he pressed, "Decide." And when she stepped away from the ultimatum, turning her face to avoid the conflict, he ordered her like an insubordinate soldier, "*Now*, Sable. Choose."

Startled by the strength of the command, she lost her cool, angrily answering, "Remy. Of course, it's Remy. You already knew that."

"Then we tell him everything. And I, the strategist to this king, *our* King, will devise a plan that Remy will approve, and it is not going to involve your death."

~~~~~~

The fractures in time became far more serious when Sable followed the event line through the King's door. Catherine had left her speaking to the public to have Remy woken, but as yet the damage had not been done.

Sable pushed through the distance into the past to feel him pulling up with the softest, warmest memory of her on his skin, in his arms, weighing heavy against his chest. It was the drug, Remy told himself, but it was also Sable. She had once pulled him into the same heat and comfort, smothering him in a desperate embrace that had been euphoric, consuming, and black, and now each time he awoke, he felt it again.

Through the long hours she was gone, he had asked every time he surfaced, "Where is Sable?" Once he clearly understood he had sent her to retrieve an abducted soldier, he became alert enough to demand she be contacted and brought back. He had refused further medication to get his head wrapped around the explanation that she could not be reached. But then, feeling the rips in his flesh with every breath, he accepted small doses, a faint reminder of Sable's touch. It kept him waiting, even when he slipped into sleep, he was expectant, waking in panic, mad with himself and everyone else that she was

446

gone, out in the world, no one knew where, facing risks he repeatedly imagined as fatally violent, involving guns, hostages, blood, and always Sable uncontrolled and deadly mad.

Making it no further than the sitting room, Remy agreed with Branson that going farther was unwise, but they both knew impossible was the accurate word. Even before he heard them, he knew she was near. He listened to the rise and fall of Lucas's voice through the door and recognized Sable as the cause of the General's frustration.

To Catherine, who was dismayed to irritation that the two were arguing in the hall, he instructed, "No, let them continue." So much of what he could remember seemed surreal. Lucas's voice brought some of it back, a hazy recollection of agreements and discord.

Then Sable had entered dressed as a nun but with a face full of grief to see him. Her voice broke saying, "Remy," and she'd come forward to sink beside him to the floor. Pressing her head to his leg, she was on the verge of crying. "It would kill me to lose you."

He waved the room empty of people. Pulling her face up to console her, he asked, "Sable, where have you been?" And then tears spilled down her cheeks. "Sable, forgive me. I don't know what came over me to send you."

She begged, "Oh, hush, please don't say that."

"No, Sable, I should never have sent you out there. I could not be angrier with myself."

Then over each other, Sable pleaded, "Please don't, it's not your fault," while he insisted, "I sent you to I don't know where."

447

"Remy, please, please believe me. I will tell you more when you are well."

He had asked suspiciously, "Tell me what?" and then forcefully, "Tell me now," while she tripped over poorly formed deferrals.

Finally, he grabbed her attention, demanding, "*Sable*, tell me now." And she had. One confession led to another.

He would question what he was hearing and she would sob out increasingly disturbing answers, admitting she had used her voice to manipulate him, confirming the faint memories that played like dreams in his mind of her fighting Lucas, both of them struggling to take control of him. And more outrages as she explained she had done it to protect her friends, same with all the liberties she had taken to free her friend from Berringer's prison. Then, when he thought nothing more shocking could be revealed, she left him stunned inarticulate to tell him she had sterilized herself.

At her confession, great yawning gaps broke wide upon the path, preventing any retreat. The future was diverging, going horribly wrong.

He had asked, "Is there anything else?" And when she looked confused that there could be more, he became harsher. "Do you intend to continue hiding from me that you trained with the same master strategist as Lucas?"

Eyes closed, head pressed low beside his knee, she was not going to answer.

He asked, "What were you two quarrelling about?"

448

"He insists the only way forward is to tell you everything."

~~~~~~

The General was not expecting to be called back to the King's rooms, but the moment he saw Sable kneeling on the floor, crying into Remy's leg, he knew exactly what the night held in store. He had started it—he could hardly fault her that—but he had expected the King to be healed, or, at the very least, a night's rest for everyone.

Gravely pointing him into a chair, Remy's expression was fierce. "As you have suggested, tell me everything."

The General began at the most logical place. "My name is Theodore Feridon. I am the son of Orson Feridon."

"The *son*," Remy repeated. He took a moment to fully appreciate it before saying, "I should have seen your skill was not simply that of a student."

"You knew?"

Remy nodded.

The trust ripped at the General's heart. "And you left me responsible for your safety?"

Remy's tone was severe, but the words gave the General relief, "There is no one I have greater faith in than you."

The General knew he had no right to ask, "Will you tell me how you knew?"

"There are only so many masters of strategy with an emphasis on the tactics of war, and while they are not exactly boastful, they certainly are not hidden, and none of them could claim you as a student. The moment Catherine learned you had sworn secrecy to train, she took it as a personal project to find your teacher. She's been convinced for more than a decade you could only have been trained by Feridon. But you have been giving yourself away little by little over the years, certain in your defense of Feridon that the Cloitare killed my grandfather." Remy put his hand on Sable's lowered head, "But Sable gave you both away entirely with a look. You did not expect Catherine to miss it, did you?"

Running his fingers over the fabric of the headdress, Remy felt the braids. He said, "Take this off," and when she did, he stared at the change. In the delirium of drugs and persuasion, he had seen it before. Unsettled by the memories the red hair evoked, he spoke very pointedly, "Lucas," and it was evident that his name was to remain the same, "tell me the rest of it."

~~~~~~~

Laudin joined them in his bed clothes, but Catherine had come from her office. They sat beside each other on the couch, eyes wide in readiness, hearts racing when Remy's furious eyes laid on them, and grateful when they fell back to Sable on her knees or the spent and regretful looking general.

450

The King's voice was affected by the rigid control he had over his temper and pain. "Sable has admitted to me numerous acts of willful betrayal, and my chief of defense has just told me his name is Theodore Feridon, son of Orson Feridon, who is also the strategic master of my wife." In the pause, Remy reprimanded, "Catherine, I am aware part of your reaction is shock, but this is not the time to be smiling."

"Right." And she appeared to be eating her lips.

Waiting in unblinking disapproval until she gave the impression of being solemn, he finally said, "We are all going to start again. We came together over two decades ago to plan for the future, the very future we are now facing. These will be our most defining years and I will not go forward," his voice started to rise, "with deceit or disloyalty shadowing our moves. This is the time, Catherine, Jacob, to lay out your every indiscretion, because there will be no immunity in the future."

Laudin had heard the call to come clean plainly enough, but his thoughts were stuck on something else. Half glancing at Berringer, his mind repeated, *Son of Feridon. Son of Orson Feridon? No.*

But the King didn't notice Laudin as his unwavering attention was on Catherine.

"One little thing," Catherine could almost trivialize it, "I tried to kill Sable." Shaking her head at the paradox, "Sent the order to the Guard Dog."

Catherine would have received the brunt of Remy's condemnation had Sable not closed her eyes, wishing it had not been admitted.

"And you knew this." He said this as a statement to Sable. When she inclined her head in agreement, he had to wait until his escalating annoyance allowed him to speak. "You did not tell me. Why?"

"It was not my secret to reveal."

"And how many secrets, Sable, do you still protect for others?"

Sable turned up imploring eyes, wanting to explain that no confidences she kept could harm him, but Remy looked from her big black eyes to Lucas's and then to Catherine's.

All of their pupils were huge. Remy demanded of Sable, "What are you on?"

She answered timidly, "Speed."

When the outraged glare met Berringer, he admitted, "Amphetamines."

Then Catherine, "Whatever Sable had in her pocket."

Remy pressed his temples to overcome his irritation and looked hard at Laudin.

"I had a coffee," he said.

"I expected. I am looking to see what you have to confess."

"Oh, yes, of course." His focus swept over the red-haired Sable, then onto the son of Orson Feridon, and finally to murderous

Catherine. He was flummoxed for an answer. "Well, after all that, I am feeling very much like a middle-aged bore. The most I can plead guilty to is a bit of porn on my office computer."

~~~~~~

The whole horrible night of confessions had left the future irreversibly altered, the path divided with Remy on one side and Sable on the other. He would not allow her to cross over. Sable pushed at the future hoping to see a bridge, any sort of reprieve, but the future had not yet settled from the explosive changes wrought over the three nights her hair had been red. Infinite possibilities like dust from rubble obscured the prospective landscape.

The call Laudin made to the Sierran president had hardly cleared from the air.

"Arrest General Marič and resign," Laudin instructed after Catherine sent President Pavlović the damning proof gathered from the Count. "Do this and we will not make public the details showing how you funded the attack against the Queen Mother. You may keep your secret accounts and embezzled money, but you cannot remain in power." Laudin had enjoyed the angry breath of acceptance he heard across the phone. "As I know you wish to show gratitude for our leniency, when you depart to spend more time with your family, you will wish the children of Alena great speed in rejoining the motherland, and you will take special care to praise the people of Erentrude who will suffer with their brothers and sisters of Alena while power from the electric grid is shared between our lands. I am sure you will also wish to admire the enormous amount of food and medicine King Remius has made unconditionally available to Alena."

The Sierran senate had Marič answering for missing weapons, and with no statutes on violations of international codes of conduct, the Inspector General's office was ripping apart every operation he had engaged in since holding the rank of major. His future seemed set to be dismal when Pavlović announced his resignation and the senate called for early elections.

But almost immediately, Marič enlisted the help of a public relations firm that went to battle with the PIT. Catherine's Propaganda and Information Team derided suggestions Marič was, as the soon to be published book was titled, *A True Son and Hero of Sierra*.

"As a colonel, Marič ordered the taking of civilian hostages." The PIT released video, increasing the volume of the residents' terrified screams as they were herded by the military into a school gymnasium.

But the PR firm returned, "He made a bold move that saved the lives of Sierran forces," and their video showed the soldiers returning home into the arms of waiting family.

The PIT argued, "He only got out because he killed practically everyone that came to reason with him."

The PR firm glossed it as, "Marič won't leave one Sierran behind."

"WTF are you talking about? The SOB knowingly called down artillery on civilians' homes."

"He blew the shit out of those insurgents! Motherfucking hero of our troops." The PR firm played solely to national pride with no regard to coherent argument.

To protect the Count for future use, Catherine could not afford to link Marič to the attack at the lithium mine in the same way as she had Pavlović. And Pavlović, afraid of facing charges of corruption, was shielding the Count as though their futures were the same. Instead, she released the video of Marič scheming to get Alena under the control of Erentrude and the King on Sierra's border.

The warmongering allied Sierra's liberals with the religious and sent them both onto the streets to call for Marič's arrest. Catherine could do nothing to prevent the nationalists from turning the gatherings bloody. The fighting escalated into riots that left hundreds dead, thousands injured, and several neighborhoods in the capital burning.

Laudin pressured the World Security League to get involved, but by the time they called an emergency session, Marič had already responded by instituting martial law.

The Attorney General lost quick interest in General Marič's crimes, and Sierra's senators were kept at home under guard of the army; it was for their own protection, the public was assured.

As Girard had predicted, if Pavlović went down and Marič was not utterly crushed alongside him, a military dictatorship would arise under Marič's command.

With Radimir dead, Catherine followed Sable's early suggestion to turn Alowa and use him in Radimir's place. Catherine had warned, "Marič will kill him, you know?"

But Sable had responded without concern, "A body in a prison or a body in a grave, it makes little difference. The risks are worth taking if he succeeds."

He had departed from the military prison leaving Catherine puzzled, cryptically telling his new handler, "Give my thanks to Ommawa. I be her happy guest."

When questioned who Ommawa was, he said, "You ask someone great in the Cloitare; they know who Ommawa be."

It was left as praise to a god not found on the Errian continent.

Unaware of the exchange, Sable followed him in the distance, and little by little her horror grew to realize Alowa intended to honor his word to Catherine and not use the opportunity to escape home.

"Oh, you noble fool." Sable closed her eyes on the disastrous attempt to free him.

She wished for the mastery of Aidan, the knowledge and experience to influence from afar. The most she could do was linger on him, a dark doubt in his mind.

Darker than ever, she was miserable with fatigue, unable to sleep for the screaming dreams, and everyday more wretched in the certainty she had lost Remy.

At night he kept her near, but not with affection.

Sable remembered returning the first time from the salt flat, how Remy had pulled her back into his bed and she had given him all the fierce energy that had been building in her chest, releasing to him the intensity that made her unpredictable and chaotic; then free of the frenzy, and deliriously tired, she looked across the bed for her clothes, preparing to leave.

"Where are you going?" he wanted to know. And when she told him back to her rooms, he said, "Stay."

"I will in the future." She smiled assurance.

"And why not tonight?"

Leaning over the edge of the bed, she grabbed her skirt. "It would be better to wait."

Arm wrapped around her waist, he pulled her back. "Sable, I want you to stay."

"Soon," she placated. Kissing his neck, she then tensed to be released.

He rose up over her, "Explain to me why," and watched as she searched her exhausted mind for an answer.

"You will not rest with me here." Her smile was coy.

But she was too new to the game and the playful insinuation did not suit her. He knew she was being evasive. He said simply, "Explain."

She repeated without guile, "You really will not rest with me here." Then after he waited without moving, she added, "I don't sleep well."

457

The realization fell across his face. "You have nightmares."

"When I regain control of my mind, I will join you."

"Stay," he said, and she smiled a denial, about to pacify and slip away when he said flatly, "Sable, I am not asking."

It took a moment for the words to fully reach her. Her smile faltered into pale features while her breath stopped and her body tightened.

"Do not react like this. You are my wife. You belong beside me. If you are troubled, I want to know."

Coming down to kiss her, she turned away from his lips to press into his neck, confiding what felt like the greatest humiliation for a Cloitare, "I don't want you to know the disquiet of my mind. Please let me go."

But his reply was, "Go to sleep." And when she finally did, he learned the full extent of the damage that had been done.

She had concealed her hand beneath the sheets to remove the bracelet and then kept her hands hidden. For hours, she'd jerk awake, eyes wide, heart racing, until the night moved on. She went deeper only to wake grabbing her wrist, fighting to possess it; she dug screaming at the scar to remove a shackle that was no longer there.

Wrestling her hand free, he talked her out of the frenzy of the dream and back to him. Then he finally saw her wrist. It was bloody. He saw teeth marks. He wanted to wrap it in bandages, but she had tried and it only made things worse; she'd wake up panicking to rip it off.

Pulling her head against his chest, he thought of the weeks he had ignored her and spoke with frustrated remorse, "If I had known."

With absolute devotion, he had kept her near, but since the night of the confessions, it was his sense of duty that demanded she stay. It was unbearable. In his brusque manner, he made it clear that protecting her from herself was an obligation he was bound to perform.

With no desire for her, his chest was not filled with power and he would fall asleep soon after her. When the first gasp of terror yanked her from the memories that lived in sleep, she would slip away, crushed with shame. The broken landscape that had improved was back to pieces, but the desolation had spread; in the dreams, she was losing so much more than her mind.

The weeks of rejection had turned the terrain more harrowing than ever. Traveling deep into the distance, she wrapped the nightmare around herself to sit in Alowa's thoughts. Dropping further into the terror, she tried to weigh him down, turn him around, by dragging heavy at his purpose, filling him with dread, but on he went, across the borders, to his death, his oath was given.

With a stifled growl of aggravation, Sable stood. She would go to Catherine. She would use her voice to convince the spy chief to call Alowa back. Then feeling futility rising recklessly over despair, Sable said, "To hell with it."

It was all over anyway. It mattered little what she did, she would never be trusted or loved again. One more betrayal would make no difference. Hopelessness made her say, "To hell with it all."

Before opening the door to leave the private halls, she added, "And to hell with subtle." She would have Catherine order Alowa to go home.

The soldiers outside the door requested, "Queen Mother, if you would, please wait for General Berringer."

But Sable pushed through saying, "You know what? To hell with you, too."

Moving purposefully through the main hall, she spun on the single guard that dared pursue. One hand moving fast to his throat, she commanded, "*Down*," and then mentally again, *To hell with it*, she turned to sweep her leg through his while her second hand found his throat, and she growled, "*Blackness falls*," before dropping him hard to the stone floor.

Hearing the remaining guard communicating, "General, you need to hurry," Sable snarled, "You motherfucker."

She was turning around to smash his radio when she saw gliding around the corner of the western wing the Cloitare, five mothers with Mother Maisa intent on speaking.

Maisa reached out to put herself in Sable's mind, first just a tentative foot upon the path to travel, testing for stability, then with force they all arrived.

"Oh, you are fucking not." Sable reached into her pocket for the pills to knock them back.

The action alarmed, escalating one threat into another. The mothers had come with a purpose and they would not be stopped. Rolling vibrations shook the air.

Sable's eyes widened in alarm. Pills in hand, her anger flipped to fear and she muttered, "No, no, no, please, not now," and turned to run. Struggling to open the foil, the rumbling current overtook her. She watched the guard on his radio buckle with her to the floor.

Behind her, the softest shifting of the mother's robes mixed with the thrumming of their voices, bringing them close, sending Sable out into the distance to call for Aidan, but her plea for help fell haphazardly through the empty space, spiraling in the dark until she dropped into Amele. She reached out blindly to stop the descent, grappling for a hold, shrieking through Amele's awareness as she tumbled, but the droning hum in her muscles shook her bones and yanked her back to the stone floor of the palace hall.

Crawling to escape, Sable remembered *To hell with subtle* and put the whole packet of six hazardous tablets in her mouth to chew through the thin metal. Choking on the crumbling powder, bleeding from the foil, she struggled to swallow.

"I've seen what you've done." Maisa slid her hand around Sable's waist to lay it flat against the coughing tension at her abdomen. Sinking down beside her, she gently raked Sable's hair away from her face to whisper, "Now let me show you the future you have made."

Coughing blood into her mouth, rasping in pain from the cuts along her throat, Sable kept forcing down the pills while Maisa wrapped her other hand around Sable's neck to murmur the bleakest revelations.

"Your nights are long and yours alone." But in the vision there was no darkness, just bright burning lights to ward off the solitude. *"Your love is barren."* Maisa clutched at the empty space a child might have lived until Sable cried out in grief. *"Your heart is dead, frozen cold, it's made of ice."*

On hands and knees, Sable tried to grab Maisa's wrist, but the mothers' voices were trembling weakness, and she collapsed instead without support.

"You have wasted his affection. He does not want you. With your darkness, you have destroyed all he felt. You have devoured every form of providence so that your destiny is void." Sweetly kissing her check, Maisa told her, "You are a monster only a mother could love."

The General entered the main hall prepared for Sable's madness with all the anger to bark her down already held in his lungs. The ferocity doubled when he saw her on the floor, held in a mother's embrace, her fingers pulling at the breaks in the stones, trying to drag herself free.

Soft footfalls padded fast into the hall, bringing Amele and the sisters.

Rolling his own thunder, the General was stalking the floor, roaring, "Stand clear. Get away from the Queen," while a second storm was blustering threats with Amele's voice rising from the squall, *"Quiet, mothers. Quiet like the night."*

The murmuring mothers were silenced and Sable quaked with the exertion of getting her hands under herself to push up. In the

462

gathering of his second breath, the General heard Maisa's biting kind invitation, "Only we will have you now. *Return home with us.*"

The General was still coming, bellowing at Maisa, "Move away. Keep your hands off the Queen," but Maisa pulled Sable up with her, turning them both away from the descending fury, into the protecting shelter of the mothers.

The clamor in the hall was shrieking into chaos as the circle of mothers moved off for the western wing, making Amele call out for them to stop while the sisters underscored the demand in such piercing resonance, the General had to shout louder to be heard, but the mothers moved steadfastly on.

The General was nearly on them when Sable cleared her throat and found her voice.

Wailing lament from the hidden center of the mothers' defense, Sable made them cringe. Then the volume escalated with unrestrained grievance and the mothers cowered back to give her space. Wiping blood across her mouth, she looked around for an escape before her attention rested on the door leading back to the King. She moved forward with a sob of gratitude, but then abruptly the visions returned and she stopped as Maisa told her, "He has no solace to offer. You are only a mother to the Cloitare."

Her eyes were gone, replaced by rising terror, so the General changed his focus, reaching out to pacify, "Calm down, Sable. Come to me."

But a mad denial bent Sable at the waist, screaming wordless anguish.

Wincing, the General stepped back and then back again, but Sable's voice was still gaining strength. He felt sorrow turn baleful and put his hands to his ears, then, stooping to avoid it, he twisted away to deflect the sound. Face drawn together with dismay that she could get louder and louder still, he groaned and staggered to find equilibrium until she shattered the balance completely and he slipped with the tipping of the floor.

He heard her incant something malign and terrible, *"Back into the night, reverse the Creator's light, I return to the dark,"* and off the edge into the black, she dropped every person in the room.

A straight plunge through the abyss and into the void, he followed her cry to go home. She alone stood in the upheaval, mouth directed at the unseen sky, pulling down decimating havoc with the damning verdict, *"I call your creation profane, your act abominable. In the darkness, I undo and destroy."*

The General heard her wail turn inarticulate and saw cities begin to crumble in his mind. Buildings sheared off into rubble revealing a skyline set alight. Razed and ruined, the world was collapsing into ash, but the extermination knew no end as Sable called up devastation from her lungs. The ground, smoldering with wreckage, opened like a sinking hole, eating away the edges, showering dust and flames into the widening chasm until there was nothing left to lose. The isolation was vast, the emptiness complete, yet the brutality continued as Sable fought her way toward mindless obliteration.

Afraid and pained, the General kept his hands clamped over his ears, but squinting into the darkness, he could make out light pushing in from the edges. He saw Amele laid low at Sable's feet, arms wrapped around her head to shield against the violence, pleading loud to be heard, begging, "Mercy, Mawan. Mercy."

He felt the first pulse of peace break the despair. He saw Aidan forming from light.

But Sable struck out at the brightness, wrapping it up, pulling it under, accusing, "How dare you make me to feel? I return to you in multitude what you have shared."

The General felt her grief lash against his body, piercing his ears with an unintelligible howl that stabbed his heart and suffocated all reason. He felt the darkness running hot through his veins, chasing down every particle of light. He tried to flee but his muscles trembled and caved beneath his weight. His eyes leaked tears or blood or both while black vertigo and nausea curled him into a ball.

The General could not escape the reckoning coming from Sable's mouth. He could not hide from it, or fight it, or deny it. Heavy and delirious with dread, he dropped with her voice into the desolate void.

MAWAN

Remy felt it like a stab, the deepest loss. He twisted with the pain, flinching from the chest. Her name came from his mouth with alarm, "Sable."

He left his rooms to find her. Forcing the door to her rooms open with too much strength, he called her name, but she did not answer. The room felt empty, as though it had been vacant for years.

He entered the main hall to see bodies sprawled feeble across the floor and knew at once she had done it. Dropping to his knee beside Lucas, Remy pulled at the hands locked over the General's ears and groaned to see them streaked with blood.

Using Berringer's phone to call for help, he looked over the destruction she had wrought to give an account of the number injured. The mothers were piled together, Maisa clutching her damaged heart, the rest swaying to lift their heads, sniffing back blood that spilled far enough to color their lips.

The guards and the sisters lay motionless, faces bloodier than the mothers. Curled on her side, Amele opened her eyes onto him, red spilling across her cheek like tears. Remy asked her, "Where is she?"

The answer was a whisper on Amele's lips, "Into the blackest night, the Mawan travels."

~~~~~~

CPSIA information can be obtained
at www.ICGtesting.com
Printed in the USA
LVHW081700240619
622190LV00019B/1539/P